A Death in the Family

Tish Owen

I'd like to thank all of my readers: because of you, this second book is possible; all of the characters which inhabit the pages of my book, wherever they come from, I'm certainly glad they've landed in my head; my wonderful daughter, Tanya Gattis, and my equally wonderful son, Franklin Gattis, just for being themselves, and my husband Patrick Owen, for not complaining I spend more time with my imaginary playmates than I do with him; Anne Donnelly, Gretchen Blackwell, Scott, Richard, Liz Parrott, and so many more, who have been friends to the end and kept pushing me to get this done; Cat, Debbie and Lou who covered for me when I was supposed to be working; Sydney, Lili, Kaiser, Keller and Acel because you are all so cute; my mother Loraine who, at 100 years old, has left me to my own devices; a special nod to Lori Torpey who owned the real Neon Candle back in the day, oh yes those were the days my friend; my cousin Stephanie Fearman, the nurse who helped me figure out how to kill people (oh calm down, it's not as bad as it sounds); her mother Kathy Simpson who helped me with the Atlanta geography; and to everyone who read the first one and to everyone who said, 'I can't wait to read the next one,' and to everyone who buys it, thank you thank you thank you!

Being a writer is fantastic, terrible, awesome, awful, scary, thrilling, depressing, uplifting, joyous, miserable, crazy, frighteningly sane and sometimes you have to pull an all-nighter; in short, it's just like life except you do it in front of other people who find out all about how your mind works. You know, like reality television or high school.

This book is dedicated to my daughter, Tanya Elizabeth Gattis, you are the most amazing human, thank you for choosing me, I love you.

1

After the Lovin'...

You know how it is the instant you've finished having amazing sex and you both collapse on the bed in a boneless heap? You heart rate is somewhere north of 10,000 Brazilian beats per minute, you're trying to get your breathing back to normal so you can tell him how great it was and you're sweating like a linebacker on a hot Sunday afternoon. Ahhhh. Pretty fantastic, right?

Have you ever had the phone ring right at that moment? It certainly harshes your mellow, to say the least. You have a couple of choices; you ignore the implement of disharmony, but then you'd wonder who the hell it was calling you and how they had such monumentally bad timing. Besides, the sound of an unanswered phone drives me crazy. Or you answer it and try not to sound like you're post-coital. Well this is exactly what happened to me one beautiful, spring day.

"Hello," I said, not quite breathlessly as I sat up in bed.

"Hey, what're you doing? Are you okay? You sound funny, where you at?" My older sister Moira inquired.

She went from chatty to concerned in 2.5 seconds. I should have let it ring. *Shoulda, shoulda, shoulda,* I thought as I hit myself in the forehead with the cell phone.

"Behind the 'at' Moira, I'm fine and I'm in the city," I answered, still trying to get my pulse rate down.

I could hear Derek sniggering behind me. Let's see how funny he thought it was when he didn't get seconds. I poked my tongue out at him.

"Oh, well I wanted to come into the city, but you're already there." She sounded disappointed.

"For?" I prodded. I swear sometimes trying to get information out of my sister is like pulling hen's teeth.

"Oh, you know that shop I like, the one with the tarot cards and the rocks?" she said with such innocence I could see the cartoon butterflies flittering about her head.

"Hmmm … The Neon Candle?" I knew the place. It always smelled of vanilla and the tea was good.

"Right, right. Well, Lori's hosting a séance tonight and I wanted to go, but I wanted company." There was a pleading note to her voice.

Great, just what I needed, a séance to talk to dead people. Yippee! I didn't like where I knew this was going.

"Moira, I'm workin' up here, I don't know when I'll be done, so really I just don't know if I can make it." I tried to sound final.

"From the sound of your voice I know exactly what you're workin' on. You can't fool me; I'm a nurse you know," she said loud enough for Derek to hear.

The big jerk laughed out loud. I hit him with a pillow. He just lay there with the pillow covering his face – his really pretty, totally delicious face.

"Come on, go with me pleeeease, pretty please," Moira wheedled.

"You are a blackmailer, sister mine, you ask me in your little sweet tone of voice and I always say yes, and how come that works for you?" So much for my note of finality.

"It's 'cause you're easy. Ask the guy next to you. So you'll come with, right?" Moira quipped.

I sighed in resignation. "Wow, nice, that'll win you friends! Ugh, okay, what time?"

"Yay!" Moira squeaked like a rubber ducky. "7:30, the festivities begin at 8:00. You wanna have dinner before? You can bring Derek."

Derek had lifted the pillow partially off his lovely face. I sighed and rolled my eyes and looked at him. He tossed the pillow to one side, smiled and the dimples appeared on both sides of his mouth. Derek was my guilty pleasure, no strings attached boy toy. Actually, he was a completely grown man, totally, completely grown.

"Dinner with Moira?" I mouthed.

He nodded and dropped the pillow back on his face.

"Sure, where?" I asked.

"Hmmm, how about the Mexican place in the Gulch? I hear it's good," she suggested.

How convenient, since we were in the Gulch, a most swanky area in Nashville, at Derek's condo. If I walked to the window, I could look down and see 12th Avenue South. We were high enough up I wouldn't even have to put on clothes. Of course, my sister wouldn't know my whereabouts since I hadn't told her much about Derek. Few people in my world even knew his name, which was exactly how I wanted to keep it. He was private.

"Sure, meet you there about 6:00." I answered.

"Awesome, and really thanks for goin' with me, you know I appreciate it and I'll owe you one," Moira said with a giggle.

I snorted. "Whatever. See you later, love you, bye."

"See you later, love you, bye." She hung up laughing.

I put the phone down and fell back on the bed next to Derek. I snuggled in close to him and he slipped his arm behind my head.

"You sure you wanna do this? After all, none of my very large, very weird family has met you yet. Usually meetin' the family signifies a large step in a relationship, so if you feel strange about it, you can back out with no hard feelings on my part." I was suddenly feeling nervous and realized I was talking rapidly with lots of hand gestures.

He grinned and his dimples deepened. His beautiful mocha skin gleamed with sweat. The sight of him almost made me break out in a sweat myself.

"You said 'strange' and 'hard' in the same sentence," he said in a Beavis and Butt-Head voice.

"Why the hell do I fool with you? Remind me again." I laughed and elbowed him in the ribs.

It must not have hurt too badly because he kissed me long and lingering. "Cause you love men in uniform, I'm cute, there are no stings and I'm a hell of a lay." He grinned and his eyes twinkled. "And I like Mexican food." He pulled me closer to him and began kissing me under my ear. "But if you insist, I can show you the real reason why."

"You are naked, and ugly, you know little about strings and you like any food anyone will put on a plate. I haven't seen you turn down nothin'," I teased him.

"Well usually you're right, I'll eat anything that won't eat me first except, I have to say, chitlins," he said and continued to kiss me down my neck to my collar bone.

The word 'chitlins' spoiled the mood he was trying to set. Ugh, I couldn't eat anything which smelled like chitlins when they cooked. I felt the same about sauerkraut and oysters. Oysters don't stink but they look like snot.

"Yep." I nodded my agreement.

"So, what's up with you?" Derek asked me in a quiet voice, still moving his lips up and down my neck.

"Whaddaya mean?" I tried to sound casual but my heart skipped a beat.

He stopped nuzzling my neck and turned my face to his. "Darlin', you are one of the most enthusiastic and inventive lovers I've ever known, but lately, something's changed. You're still enthused, but somehow, you're not really with me like you used to be. You know, like your body is here but your brain is someplace else." He paused, as if reluctant to say more. "Is there somethin' you need to be tellin' me?"

I turned my head and blew out a breath at the ceiling. Wow, there was no explaining it to him. Not in a way which wouldn't leave him doubting my sanity. The man had been paying attention; why I couldn't date a less sensitive, more Neanderthal-like guy, I don't know. Damn, damn, damn.

Truth to tell, sometimes I felt Chick, my dead best friend in the world and possible soul-mate, was in the room and watching Derek and me have sex. Not in a weird, kinky voyeur way. He was just there. Crazy, I know. Even if he was in the room, he wouldn't disapprove; he would want me to go on with my life. He would want me to be happy. He would want me to get laid. But my life had a sad quality to it since Chick died, or rather, was murdered. Some days I felt he was the love of my life and without him I would never marry or have children or grow old with someone. The thought made my heart hurt.

Everywhere I turned there were reminders of him. Everyone I knew had known him, except for Derek. There were pictures of Chick with members of my family all over my house. My brother, Connell, was beside himself and practically sick with grief. He had become even more of a brooder since Chick's death, and he was a world class brooder before. My entire family was in mourning. I felt like everyone was tip-toeing around me, being careful not to talk too much about Chick in my presence. If all that drama wasn't bad enough, we'd been waiting to go to trial for Chick's murderers for a freakin' year. God, I missed Chick so much.

I couldn't tell Derek any of those things. I willed the tears to stay in my tear ducts and not run down my face. It's simply bad form to cry over one man when you're naked and in bed with another man; my momma raised me to have good manners. Okay, that had never been one of the rules she drilled into my head, but I was pretty sure I was right.

I took a deep breath. "I thought we were fun and games, Derek, no strings, no ties, just good company and great sex," I said, still staring at the ceiling.

He turned my face and touched his nose to mine. "Tess, we are, but I thought we were friends too and friends care what's goin' on with each other. Something's changed, and it worries me."

I finally looked at him and sure enough, he looked worried. Shit. I tried to gather my thoughts; I didn't want my words to come out wrong. I didn't want to hurt Derek's feelings, he was a good guy.

"Derek, my mood or whatever – it is has absolutely nothing to do with you, I promise. I swear it on a Bible, if you like. You're a great guy and I love spendin' time with you. I admit I've got things weighin' on my mind and if I've caused you to worry, I apologize. Since Chick was murdered, life's been sad and I'm workin' a lot to keep my mind occupied. Really, it's not you. I know people always say that, but honestly, it's true." I crossed my heart with my finger and smiled at him.

"So, you want to keep doing this?" He sounded relieved.

I decided I would show him how just much I wanted to keep doing it. My heart may not have been in it, but my body sure as hell was.

2

Wasted Away in Margaritaville

The shower in Derek's condo is lovely, completely glassed in with one of those rain shower heads which make you feel like you've gotten caught in a summer downpour. Everything from the floor to the counters was a swirly dark green marble – real marble, not the resin stuff – and the mirrors were kind of Art Deco style. I loved the place; I thought I could live in it, if only there was a fridge. A girl's gotta have a place to store her beer.

The entire bedroom is one big open loft except for the bath and closet. The place also costs more than I make in five years. Derek is a trust fund baby, it was set up for him by his maiden aunt, and the funds were released to him when he had turned twenty-five. His younger sister, Yvonne, got an identical amount. I don't actually know how much money they received, since it's tacky to ask, but he bought the condo, a Harley, a little black

Corvette and a red pick-up truck. I believe there's a bit left over as well, since he never seems to worry about funds. Maybe he just isn't a worrier.

The bathroom was steamy and I was lost in thought until Derek opened the shower door and climbed in with me. If you're going to have a boy toy, then having one who's insatiable is the key to success. Derek was very thoughtful and helped me soap up and in turn I helped him scrub those hard to reach areas. All and all, it was a very satisfying shower and as a bonus we were both clean too.

After our shower, I dried my hair while he shaved. It was a weirdly homey moment, standing there in front of the mirrors together and I found myself liking it far too much. I could feel something akin to panic crawl up my throat from the pit of my stomach. I hadn't signed up for this happy couple thing, only for fun.

I turned off the dryer and went in search of some make-up, clean underwear and any clothing which hadn't ended up in a wad in the corner of the bedroom. I glanced at the clock on Derek's night stand.

"Get a move on, Hook-n-Ladder, it's a quarter till!" I shouted.

"Yes, Great Dark Mistress, I live to obey!"

He came out of the bathroom, zipping up his jeans. He was so yummy. I tore my eyes away from his zipper and finished getting ready. Inside of ten minutes we were out the door. We made it to Mazatlan by five 'til and had to actually wait for Moira to show up.

She came bustling in the front door and spotted us.

"Hello, hello," she said and kissed me. She turned expectantly to Derek.

I took the cue. "Moira, this is my friend Derek Miller. Derek, this is my sister Moira."

They shook hands and Derek said, "I would've known you anywhere, you look so much alike. I feel as though I'm having dinner with the two most beautiful women in the city of Nashville, perhaps in the entire state of Tennessee."

Moira grinned at him. "Wow, does he always talk like that?"

I started to answer her but was interrupted by a familiar, silky voice.

"I see the gang's all here! Sorry I'm late; I had to tip the valet." The voice belonged to my best friend, Marcella Price.

Moira and I are attractive, or so I've been led to believe: red hair, good skin, blue eyes and all. But I do think my nose is too small and my eyes are spaced too widely apart for me to really be beautiful. Mars, on the other hand, is so hands down gorgeous Moira and I might as well stab ourselves in the face with our salad forks and be done with it.

Derek could only stare at Marcella, which is the first impression she makes with most men. She renders them speechless.

"The three most beautiful women in the state of Tennessee," he finally managed to stammer.

Marcella smiled her million dollar beauty queen smile at him, and yes, she was the runner up in the Miss Tennessee pageant a while back. Derek and the guys at the maître d station behind us all swooned.

"Marcella, this is Derek Miller. Derek, this is my best friend Marcella Price," I said.

They shook hands in slow motion while Derek wore a stupid look on his face. God! Mars has that effect on every man she has ever meets. She's so beautiful and charming and well dressed and kind of perfect. I sized her up; her long dark hair hung in exquisite ringlets, her make-up was television commercial perfect, her dark velvety skin was flawless and her light green eyes glittered like emeralds. She was wearing a little white off one shoulder dress with a gold belt, gold sandals which laced up her legs, and a matching gold purse. I felt like a lumberjack compared to her, an ugly, hunched back, goat footed, lumberjack. Some days her perfectness made me want to join a convent in the Himalayas.

"Come on, gang, we've got a table in the corner between the kitchen and the bathroom. See how I take such good care of you. By the way, I'm not unhappy to see you Mars, but how did you get roped into this circus?" I frowned at her.

"Oh, I am delighted to see you too, dearie." Mars kissed me on the lips. "Well, I haven't been to the Candle in ages, Moira didn't want to come to the city by herself and I heard we were going to have dinner with Derek. Who could resist?" She grinned again.

We all sat down and I noticed Derek couldn't take his eyes off Mars. I found myself feeling a bit jealous. Jealous? Me? Such was an unexplored emotion to attach to the situation. Derek wasn't my boyfriend; he was my friend with benefits. I promised myself I'd look into the odd feelings later.

"Hey Derek, wipe your face, you seem to be drooling." I smiled sweetly.

"So, Derek," purred Mars. "Tell us everything about you. Tessely has been very stingy with the details. Of course, now I see you in person, I understand why she kept you under cover."

I had to laugh at her obvious attempt to charm the man. He was saved by the waiter who took drink orders. I certainly needed a Margarita, frozen, salted rim with lemon, not lime. We ordered appetizers too, of course.

When we finished, Mars turned back to Derek and touched him on the arm. "Okay, honey, spill it. Our girl has been seeing you for more than a year, which is a record for her. Have you cast a spell on her?"

Derek smiled and his dimples showed. I loved his dimples, I found myself wanting to lick them.

"Oh no lovely Marcella, much more the other way around I think. Your girl has bewitched me and I can't seem to loose myself from her charms."

Mars grinned back. "Oh, you are a silver-tongued devil for sure. I think I like you."

Thank God the chips and salsa hit the table before the bull-shit got any deeper.

"So, tell me more about this shop you three are gonna visit," Derek queried as he attacked the cheese dip.

Moira jumped right in. "Well it's a metaphysical shop which carries stones, jewelry, incense, books and tarot cards. They have classes and special events too. It's owned by a friend of mine, Lori Torpey, I just love her." She paused just long enough to take a sip of her drink. "Tonight we're going for a séance. I'm really excited, and I can't wait."

Derek raised an eyebrow. "A séance, as in talking to dead people? That kind of séance?"

Moira and Mars both looked at me. I opened my eyes very wide and shook my head a tiny bit. I pointedly went back to my chips and salsa. Just because I didn't need a séance or a Ouija board to talk to dead people did not mean I wanted to share the information with the entire population of Mazatlan, or Derek. I'd kill them both later for getting me into such a mess. Then I could talk to *them* with a damned Ouija board. Derek looked around the table at each of us.

"Why? I mean, what are you hoping to learn or to gain? Is there someone you want to contact?" he asked.

The chip basket was empty and I waved it to catch our waiter's attention. The action also kept me busy; I was happy to let someone else answer his question.

"Well, no one in particular, I'm just fascinated by the occult and these events are always interesting and usually fun too," Moira said.

"It's a night out with these two, whom I love, it's different and I like it too, I get dinner in the city, there will be wine and last but not least, there's you. It's a win-win." Mars smiled.

There was silence and I knew I ought to say something. "I'm just along for the ride. I don't really need a séance."

Mars almost choked on her drink. I glared and she got a grip. I narrowed my eyes and thought 'shut the hell up' at her. She just smiled at me because she thinks she's funny. I growled under my breath and turned it into a 'yummm' when Derek looked at me oddly. I put my head down and sucked on my drink. A fresh basket of chips landed on our table and I was grateful for the distraction.

"So, Derek, you wanna to come with?" Mars asked innocently.

That was it; I only had to decide what method I would employ to kill her because I was definitely going to kill her. I held my breath and tried to stare a hole in her perfect hide.

"Well, sure if y'all don't mind me gumming up your girl's night out. I've never been to a séance or to a metaphysical shop. I lead a very sheltered life, you know." Derek grinned.

Damn a monkey! I couldn't believe it! First the dynamic duo horned in on my date and screwed up my day off. Then they invited my date to a freakin' séance, where dead people would talk and most likely they would talk to me! I needed more alcohol so I signaled the waiter by waving my glass at him. The silence had gotten awkward and I realized I needed to fix the problem.

"Sure, what fun." I tried to sound sincere, which I certainly was not.

Dinner arrived and we concentrated on our meal and some chit chat, 'Where do you work, where are you from, seen any good movies lately', you know, small talk. Who says chit chat sucks? The less we discussed the séance, the better I liked it.

The meal was great and my tank was full. I leaned back and took a contented breath. "Desert?"

We lingered another thirty minutes over fried ice cream. It was delicious and I was full as a tick. The full belly took my mind off the upcoming events and I relaxed.

Moira checked her watch. "Hey, it's just about time to get on the road."

Suddenly I got nervous. "Let me have one more drink."

"Get a roadie; it's almost time for the fun to start," Moira said.

For the record, sadly, we don't have roadies in Tennessee. You can buy a beer and wrap it in a brown paper bag, which is very classy, but you cannot walk the streets with a very fine nine dollar drink in your hand. It's a sad world in which we live.

3

Mama Told Me Not to Come

The Neon Candle was close by and since it was a mild spring night, we decided to walk.

"So," Derek asked. "How does this work exactly?"

Moira was all too happy to fill the man in. "Well, sometimes there's a medium who will contact the dead for you. It's helpful if you bring some item which belonged to the dead person."

She beamed, she was so proud of herself. I wanted to smack her in the head with a stick.

Derek raised a perfect eyebrow. "Such as?"

"Oh, well, an article of clothing or a picture works really well," Moira answered.

"Whew!" Derek wiped his brow in mock relief. "I was afraid you were gonna say a finger or an ear."

"Ha, funny, really funny," I said in annoyance.

Derek moved closer to me as we walked down the sidewalk and slid his arm around me. "What's got your goat? You mad 'cause I'm taggin' along? I can go back home, alone, dejected, sad. Did I say alone?" He batted his lovely grey-green eyes at me.

"You suck, Derek. Who could possibly send you away when you do the puppy dog look? You know it works too which is why you use it. Unfair!" I declared.

Everyone laughed at me and we continued toward our destination. I wasn't mad, not really, just extremely uncomfortable. Derek didn't know how much dead people loved me; the subject had never come up. How do you tell someone you see dead people? Crap!

I could hear the conversation in my head. 'Oh yeah I see dead people all the time, they love talking to me. Could you pass the mustard please?' Double crap!

I continued to walk and tried to ignore Mars, Moira and Derek. They were laughing and Mars and Moira were flirting with Derek. Upon reflection, I found I really didn't care, since neither of them would actually put moves on him. Mars was too loyal and Moira was too married. I mulled over my earlier reaction, I wasn't a jealous person and it worried me. Derek and I weren't in love or even a couple. We were friends with benefits, period. I mentally shook myself and banished the green-eyed monster from my brain.

I liked Derek a lot; in fact, I was in serious lust with him. He was a great lover, handsome, built like a brick shithouse, had a good sense of humor, we were both Mets fans and he didn't make relationship demands on me which counts for a lot in my world. I'm fairly independent, if you overlook the fact I live with my parents and my grandmother in the house where I grew up.

I don't like to be pushed or told what to do. This most likely comes from being the youngest of seven siblings; I haven't checked my theory out with a shrink yet, maybe I should. Derek doesn't push. Plus, he lives in the city and is completely separate from my real life. He's kind of like going on vacation; great fun, an exotic locale, exciting rides. Derek is a fantasy, like Disney World! I could be whomever I wished to be with him. He has no preconceived ideas of me and how I should or shouldn't behave. I didn't like my fantasy life and my real world colliding. Damn.

As we drew near the shop I could see the neon candle burning in the window. It actually is a neon sign in the shape of a candle, complete with a flickering flame. The shop is in an old building but the outside is painted bright, cheerful colors. I glanced down as we entered the front door and read the message on the door mat: 'Peace to all who enter here.' Nice sentiment, I thought. We were greeted like old friends by Lori as soon as we came through the front door. She floated toward us on a cloud of swishing skirts, tinkling jewelry and vanilla.

"Hello Moira! And you've brought Marcella and Tessely, I can't believe it. To what do we owe the honor? And who is this handsome young thing?" Lori squeezed Derek's bicep and batted her huge brown eyes at him.

He grinned, he couldn't help himself. Really, no one can resist Lori. She's somewhere around forty, I think. Rumor has it she was a model at some point. It's not hard to believe, she has the most amazing bone structure, a dazzling smile, tall, curvy, and her long, brown hair cascades down her back. She also knows how to use her feminine charm.

I looked around the place while Lori flirted with my date; good thing I had decided I wasn't jealous. The shop was tastefully decorated with lots of merchandise and glass cases with expensive jewelry. There was a fireplace and a book nook. Comfortable chairs were set round the shop in various corners and most of them, I realized, were occupied. A small, square wooden table was set up in the middle of the shop, and on it were several candles, some stones, a crystal ball and the cursed Ouija board.

I hate Ouija boards. They're made and marketed as toys but they aren't toys. They're a means to contact dead people, usually the kind of dead people who are hanging about the lower planes looking to cause a bit of trouble. You know like the high school drop-out thugs who hang around the parking lot at the school dance hoping to get laid or get in a fight? Same kind of mentality. Troublemakers.

Ouija boards ought to come with a warning label like cigarettes. *WARNING: THE PSYCHIC GENERAL HAS DETERMINED OUIJA BOARDS MAY BE HAZARDOUS TO YOUR MENTAL AND EMOTIONAL WELL-BEING AND MIGHT CAUSE THINGS TO GO BUMP IN THE NIGHT!*

I took a closer look at the board in question and found it wasn't one of the mass produced items. It was handmade from oak; the letters and words were wood burned into the surface and it was finished in a shiny polyurethane seal. It was quite lovely, for a damned Ouija board. I backed away from the thing as if it were a live rattler.

Make no mistake, Ouija boards work just great for contacting folks on the other side. I spent a fair amount of time at sleep-overs as a kid and someone always brought one. Everyone would gather around and attempt to talk to dead people, who never failed to make an appearance. I never needed a fancy piece of cardboard to talk to the deceased, thank you very much.

Lori was making her way around the room, having a moment with each of her guests while offering wine and other refreshments. She was being the perfect hostess. The four of us settled in some empty chairs and I kept eyeing the Ouija board as if it were going to explode. I was positive I was about to be outed. How did I get into this mess? Oh yeah, my darling sister and my best friend. They would pay, I grimly vowed.

Lori took center stage next to the table and smiled at everyone around the room. "Now many of you have been here before, but for those of you who are newcomers, I am Lori Torpey and I own the Candle. Tonight, we're going to use this Ouija board to contact the dearly departed. Be patient, sometimes it takes a moment to get their attention, they're quite busy you know. Diane, could you get the lights please?"

The lights were lowered and, except for candles burning in various places, the shop was fairly dark. Lori was setting the mood.

She took her seat at the table. "Most people think the Ouija board is a toy or a game for children to play with, I assure you this is not the case. Precautions should be taken before you open yourself to the higher realms. Who would like to help me make the first contact of the evening?" Lori asked.

A thin, dark haired, young girl shyly raised her hand. "I'd like to try." Her voice was so quiet I could barely hear her.

Lori motioned the girl to the place opposite her at the table. "What's your name dear?"

"Rosie," the girl answered nervously.

She seemed so young; I had to remind myself she was probably at least eighteen years old or Lori wouldn't have let her participate.

"Is there someone you would like to attempt to contact tonight?" Lori asked in a kind, comforting voice.

Rosie nodded. "I'd love to talk to my cousin, Jim Smithson. He died several years ago and I miss him so much and I just want to know if he's okay." Her voice was sad.

"Then we shall try to contact him. First, we need to put up protections to insure no malevolent entities enter our space and disrupt our evening. Diane, if you will do the honors please." Lori announced.

She gestured dramatically to her right-hand girl, Diane January, who was standing near the front door of the shop. Diane locked the door and flipped the CLOSED sign over. Then she stepped into the center of the store, and closed her eyes as if she were concentrating. She extended her right hand and slowly turned around in a circle; she was creating a circle of protection. I'd seen it done before. Her actions were just fine with me, the more protection the better I always say which is why I usually carry a Beretta and a back-up. When Diane completed the circle, she went to a small table set next to a wall in the shop and stood facing the wall.

"Hail Guardians of the East, I ask your protection tonight from all harm which would come to us from your quarter." She lit the candle and proceeded to the next table.

There were four tables, set at the four walls of the room. Diane made her way clockwise to each table, calling Guardians of the South, West and North. She lit candles as she went. When all four candles were burning, she nodded to Lori who nodded back.

"Thank you, Diane. There now, nothing like a bubble of protection to keep the annoying entities away. We are prepared to contact the dead," Lori intoned in a very theatrical voice.

Oh brother, here we go, I thought as I mentally strapped into my psychic seat belt. Everyone in the room moved their chairs closer so they could see the letters on the board clearly. Seemed no one wanted to miss a syllable.

"Rosie, place your fingertips on your side of the planchette. I'll place my hands on this side and we shall allow spirit to move it as necessary. Lightly now, do not bear down," Lori instructed.

Rosie looked at Lori with big doe eyes filled with apprehension and a bit of fear as well, but she did as she'd been instructed.

"We are attempting to contact the spirit of Jim Smithson. Jim, if you can hear us please answer, Rosie wishes to speak with you," Lori said.

The entire room held its collective breath and most people leaned even closer to the center of action. Nothing happened for a full minute and then the planchette began to move. The girl gasped and jerked her hands away from the triangular object; it stopped moving immediately.

"Now, now, dear, there is nothing to fear. Place your hands back into position and let us see what your cousin has to say, shall we." Lori's voice was comforting but firm.

The girl hesitated for a heartbeat, then she assumed the position and the planchette began to move again.

"Jim Smithson, are you there, is this you Jim Smithson?" Lori asked.

The planchette moved immediately to the word 'Yes' at the top of the board. Again, Rosie gasped but her hands remained steady. She was in the zone and there was no turning back.

"Jim Smithson, do you have a message for Rosie? A personal one so she will know it truly is you?" Lori asked.

Again, the planchette moved to 'Yes' and then began to move through the alphabet.

'H-E-L-L-O D-O-O-D-L-E-B-U-G,' it spelled out.

"Jim! Jim! Jim!" Rosie cried out. "Oh, it's you, it is, it is!" She looked all around the room, excitement shining in her eyes. "He always called me Doodlebug, no one else does. Oh my God! Jim, how are you? Are you okay?"

She was practically vibrating in her seat, tears sliding down her face.

'D-O-N-T C-R-Y D-O-O-D-L-E I-T-S A-L-L G-O-O-D I-M F-I-N-E U N-E-E-D 2 G-O B-A-C-K 2 S-C-H-O-O-L'

"I will." Rosie promised, and then she began to sob, her shoulders shaking. She buried her face in her hands for a moment, and then she placed them back on the planchette.

'T-E-L-L M-Y M-O-M-M-A T-E-L-L E-V-E-R-Y-O-N-E I L-O-V-E E-M N-O-T T-O W-O-R-R-Y I-M F-I-N-E O-K?'

Rosie nodded her head and wiped her eyes with the back of her hand which she quickly put back on the planchette. "Yes, I will Jim, and I miss you so much. I love you; I just wish you were still here with me. I'm so lonely without you. No one else listens to me or understands me like you do ... did."

The planchette spelled: 'I L-O-V-E U I A-M W-I-T-H U O-K?'

Rosie nodded. "It's just hard. So I can talk to you anytime?"

The planchette then it slid up and touched the word 'YES' and then it touched 'GOOD-BYE'.

Nicely done, Jim, I thought to myself. I saw him, a young, handsome, dark haired man who turned away from Rosie and faded from my sight. Rosie was still sniffling loudly. Lori handed her a tissue and patted her consolingly.

"Who would like to go next?" she asked.

Derek leaned over and whispered in my ear, "How real?"

"Why do you ask me?" I whispered back rather too fiercely.

Derek pulled back a little further from me and looked startled as if I had bitten him.

"I thought you knew something about this stuff. So, real or not?"

I held up my hand in a 'talk to it' gesture. "Real," I said grudgingly.

I turned my attention back to the dark-haired woman who was taking a seat across from Lori. As soon as the woman put her hands on the planchette it began to move with purpose and spelled out; 'O-S-U'.

Lori asked, "Do these initials mean anything to you?"

"I went to Ohio State University," the woman said. She looked stricken.

The planchette moved: 'B-I-O-L-O-G-Y 2-N-D S-H-I-F-T M-O-L-L-Y M-C-G-R-E-G-O-R-S B-R-I-T-T-A-N-Y L-I-B-R-A-R-Y'

"Danny?" the woman gasped.

The planchette slid to 'YES'.

Of course, there he was standing next to the dark-haired woman and grinning. He was a good-looking, blonde fella, about twenty or so.

"Danny! This is Danny Gill, we went to school together, he dated my roommate Brittany, we hung out at a bar called Molly McGregor's, and he worked a second shift job and was always falling asleep in the library! I can't believe it! Why in the world are you talking to me? Are you okay?" She was excited and laughing.

The planchette spelled out; 'Y-E-S O-K W-A-N-T-E-D T-O S-A-Y H-I 2 U J-E-A-N-I-E T-E-L-L B-R-I-T-T-A-N-Y I-M O-K'.

Jeanie stopped laughing and grew serious. "Danny, I'm so sorry about what happened, sometimes I still can't believe you're gone. Everyone was so sad. It really is good to hear from you."

She paused for a moment as if she was gathering her thoughts. "Danny was killed in a car crash in our senior year. Everybody loved him, it was just so tragic."

I had to admit it was interesting to watch other people communicate with the dead. Several more people went through the routine and were satisfied with the results. Their dead people came and went but none of them noticed me.

Then it was Moira's turn. I thought she might try and contact Chick, but she didn't specify who she wanted to speak with, just whoever wanted to speak with her. Turned out to be our grandmother; I knew it as soon as the planchette began to move. I smiled.

"Who is this?" Moira asked.

'Y-O-U-R G-R-A-N-D-M-O-T-H-E-R H-E-L-L-O M-O-I-R-A A-N-D T-E-S-S-E-L-Y Y-O-U B-O-T-H L-O-O-K W-E-L-L'

"Grammy, oh my gosh! I miss you so much. We're all so very fine, but miss you. Grammy, I'm a nurse and a wife and a mother." Moira was clearly tickled and a little teary.

I felt myself grinning. My father's mother who died when I was about five was standing close to Moira and smiling. She turned to me and winked. I smiled and winked back at her.

'Y-E-S P-R-E-C-I-O-U-S I K-N-O-W I A-M S-O P-R-O-U-D I W-A-T-C-H A-F-T-E-R A-L-L O-F Y-O-U A-N-D L-O-V-E Y-O-U A-L-L P-L-E-A-S-E S-P-E-N-D M-O-R-E T-I-M-E W-I-T-H C-O-N-N-E-L-L H-I-S P-A-I-N I-S S-O D-E-E-P'

"Yes Ma'am," my sister and I both said simultaneously.

I could feel my grandmother's presence fill the room and it warmed me all over like a hug.

"Grammy, my children say sometimes an old woman comes into their rooms late at night and tucks them in bed. Is that you?" Moira asked.

My grandmother smiled. 'Y-E-S T-H-E-Y A-R-E B-E-A-U-T-F-U-L' then she spelled out, 'C-H-I-C-K I-S D-O-I-N-G F-I-N-E'.

Tears sprang into my eyes so I closed them. I felt her brush by me; the words 'be careful' echoed in my mind and she was gone.

"Bye Grammy," I whispered. I opened my eyes to find Derek staring at me. "Real," I muttered to him.

I got up to get a glass of wine so I was surveying the room when the last person took her turn. She was a blonde in her forties, clearly not happy, as if she really didn't want to play. Her friends were encouraging her so she took her place at the table, resigned to the process.

"Is there someone whom you wish to contact?" Lori asked.

The woman shook her head and placed her hands on the planchette. It immediately began to move. 'J-O-N,' it spelled out.

The woman's eyes widened and she seemed ready to leap up from the table.

Lori asked, "Jon? Is this Jon, do you have a message for someone here?"

The planchette was still.

"Does anyone know a man named Jon without an H?" Lori inquired.

"I do," the woman at the table said sadly. "I know who it is. Jon, what do you want?" Obviously, she was a believer.

The planchette moved to the word 'HELLO', then spelled; 'T-H-E-R-E I-S A P-R-O-B-L-E-M'

"Besides the obvious one, you're dead, you were a shitty husband, a worse father, you failed to contact your children before you shuffled off your mortal coil? Or maybe, you allowed the Whore you married to keep you away from your children for years and especially at the time of your death? Besides all that?"

Wow, I thought, but she ain't bitter.

'U R A B-I-T-C-H', the planchette spelled out.

Not a lot of love there for sure, I thought, but clamped my jaws shut so I wouldn't mutter anything inappropriate as I sometimes have a tendency to do. My brother Dugal claims I have transient Turrets; my mother calls it diarrhea of the mouth. She's such a delicate thing.

The woman laughed derisively. "You're so right. Let's get down to it, what can I do for you, you can't do for yourself? Oh yeah, just about everything because you're dead."

I was still standing and so I was in a perfect position to see the man who materialized at the edge of the room. He didn't notice me but was staring at the woman with her hands on the planchette. I was sure he was Jon without the 'H' or I'd turn in my secret detective decoder ring.

The planchette moved: 'T-H-E-R-E I-S D-A-N-G-E-R'

"Danger?" the woman echoed.

The planchette moved to the word 'YES' and kept hitting the word over and over again as if to drive home the idea he wasn't just kidding around.

"To whom?" the woman asked calmly.

'C-H-I-L-D-R-E-N'

The woman became alarmed. "Our children?"

'YES YES YES YES YES YES YES YES'

The planchette flew across the board so fast it was almost a blur. I broke into a sweat, I knew it was about to become an interesting night.

"From whom?"

'J-O-N-N-I-E'

"The Whore?"

'YES YES YES YES YES,' the planchette hit the word over and over. Nothing like an agitated ghost.

"Please explain how my children are in danger, Jon." She was becoming more and more upset but I couldn't decide if it was because she hated Jon or she believed him.

'M-O-N-E-Y S-H-E W-A-N-T-S T-H-E M-O-N-E-Y D-O N-O-T F-I-G-H-T H-E-R D-O N-O-T S-H-E I-S D-A-N-G-E-R-O-U-S'

"Jon, is she dangerous as in her sense of fashion is nauseating or dangerous as in she'll take a gun and shoot me?" the blonde asked sharply.

'Y-E-S D-O N-O-T F-I-G-H-T H-E-R A-B-O-U-T T-H-E M-O-N-E-Y D-O N-O-T L-E-T T-H-E C-H-I-L-D-R-E-N F-I-G-H-T H-E-R'

"She would actually shoot me? Do you really expect me to believe she's crazy? You can't mean it, that's insane," the woman stated.

'S-H-E I-S I-N-S-A-N-E I A-M M-O-R-E A-F-R-A-I-D F-O-R T-H-E C-H-I-L-D-R-E-N T-H-A-N U'

The woman drew a shaky breath. "She'd hurt my children? Over your money? Good God, they don't want your lousy money, Jon. They'd never be able to launder it clean enough to actually use."

'B-I-T-C-H T-H-E-Y R M-Y C-H-I-L-D-R-E-N 2'

"Hell of a time to remember!" she snapped.

The woman took her hands away from the planchette and covered her face with them. "God Almighty, Jon, what kind of a mess have you made?" She put her hands back on the planchette.

'K-E-E-P T-H-E-M S-A-F-E K-E-E-P T-H-E-M A-W-A-Y F-R-O-M H-E-R Y-O-U M-U-S-T Y-O-U M-U-S-T Y-O-U M-U-S-T'

The planchette was moving so fast across the board I could hardly keep up with what Jon was spelling. I took my eyes from the board for a moment and snuck a look at him. He was leaning forward as if he were willing the woman to believe his claims.

I felt sorry for him despite the fact it was possible he had really screwed things up in life.

"Why should I believe you now when you've never told the truth before in your life?" the blonde whispered.

'S-H-E M-U-R-D-E-R-E-D M-E'

"Oh Jesus." the woman muttered.

Everyone in the room froze; no one moved, all eyes were riveted on the Ouija board. I could see Lori's eyes and they were huge. Then the dead man turned and looked at me.

"Help her, please," he said.

Great, and I thought he hadn't noticed me. I didn't answer him, I just stood there like an idiot clutching my wine glass.

"Murdered you, what am I supposed to do now?" The woman asked with tears in her voice. "Oh God."

'T-H-E T-A-L-L R-E-D H-A-I-R-E-D W-O-M-A-N S-T-A-N-D-I-N-G B-E-H-I-N-D Y-O-U W-I-L-L H-E-L-P'

Everyone in the room turned to look at me while I fought the reaction to turn around and see if by chance there might be someone standing behind me. *DAMN! DAMN! DOUBLE DAMN!* I thought.

The woman turned around to look at me and there were tears running down her face. Yes indeed, she believed the dead guy. I felt like someone had turned a spotlight on me and I wanted to bolt. I stood my ground, but I was sweating hard; I could feel beads of moisture trickling down into my bra.

The woman looked back at the Ouija board. "Jon, how can she help?"

The planchette spelled out: 'S-H-E C-A-N T-A-L-K 2 M-E W-I-T-H-O-U-T T-H-E B-O-A-R-D A-N-D T-H-E T-H-E-A-T-R-I-C-S'

Lori sniffed and said, "Well, a cheeky ghost."

The woman nodded her head, "In death as well as in life. Some things never change, I guess."

She stopped crying and it seemed as if she was getting a grip on her emotions. She turned back to me and asked, "Will you help me?"

I shrugged. "I'm not sure what you need me for, Jon seems to have given you all the information necessary."

I'd been afraid something like this would happen. I spared my sister and my best friend a dark look. They pretended not to notice how pissed I was with them.

"But if Jon is right and his bitch of a wife murdered him, then she needs to be found out, she needs to pay for her crime. He deserves justice. You can … well … I don't really know what you can do. How can you help me? Jon says you can, why? How?" She was definitely puzzled.

Lori said, "The dead seek her out."

Moira said, "She's a private detective."

Mars chimed in, "She's great at both."

Fantastic. If everyone in the room was staring at me before, now their little eyes were practically standing out on stems.

"Guilty on all counts," I said.

I took a big sip of wine, and decided there wasn't enough wine in the place to do me any good. I stole a glance at Derek and he was looking at me as if I had suddenly grown another head. I feared we might have come to the end of a beautiful friendship. I knew I shouldn't have come, or should have refused to let Derek accompany us. But as my old granny used to say, 'shoulda, coulda, woulda don't get the cow milked.' I have no idea how a cow fits into the scenario but there you go. It was done.

"Then you'll help me?" the blonde asked.

"What do you want from me?" I asked.

"I want you to prove the Whore murdered Jon!" she snapped.

Her voice was frigid, she sounded like she was pronouncing a death sentence. I couldn't help but notice she capitalized the 'W' in whore. Nice.

Then the planchette began to move without anyone touching it, my eyes fixed on it and everyone else in the room looked as well.

'NO NO NO NO NO NO NO NO NO NO NO NO NO,' it spelled out.

I looked at Jon and he clenched his fists and shook them at the blonde. He seemed to be in physical pain, which was, of course, impossible, I reminded myself.

"Seems Jon doesn't like your idea. I'm sorry, what's your name?" I asked. I didn't want to keep calling her 'the blonde woman' even if it was only in my head.

"My apologies, I am Georgia Kincaid." She got up and walked over to me. We shook hands. "When the planchette began to move just now, I saw you glance over to your right. May I ask you why? Everyone else was looking at the board."

I really didn't want to answer.

She squeezed my hand tighter, "You can see him, can't you? Can't you?" She stared into my eyes and I saw the desperation in hers.

"Yes," I admitted.

Georgia looked toward where Jon was standing. "Where is he?"

"A little more to your left," I directed her.

"How does he look?" she demanded.

I looked at Jon. "Well he's about 5'10" or so, broad shoulders, nice build, thick, medium, brown hair with blonde highlights which look natural, it's parted on the side and trimmed very tidy. He has a rather prominent Roman nose, dark, brown eyes, olive skin, handsome I'd say, and he looks to be about thirty."

Jon looked at me and was decidedly not happy. I shrugged at him.

"And he's frowning at me," I said.

"He was quite a bit older when he died, so I'm puzzled. Are you sure it's Jon?"

Oh, I was sure.

"Yes." I simply said.

"Then how does he look as he did when he was young and healthy? He died of cancer, a long battle with cancer and he was wasted away or so I was given to understand. At least I thought he died of cancer. I can't even believe I'm having this conversation with you." She paused and looked me in the eye. "I can't believe I'm talking to him! I need to sit down." She moved back to the table and sat down hard.

"Would you like a glass of wine?" I asked.

She nodded, so I poured her a glass of Chardonnay and carried it to the table. Derek brought me a chair; I smiled my thanks at him and sat next to Georgia.

"The dead can appear to the living in whatever form they choose, they aren't limited. Usually they appear in the form they like most, but sometimes in the form we recognize," I explained. I looked at Lori for confirmation, after all this was her show.

"True," Lori nodded. "I would say your former husband was in his top form at thirty, still healthy and happy. It's also a form you would instantly know."

"I'm not surprised he came through tonight. He's been trying to get my attention for some time now; invading my dreams, leaving quarters in my path, turning on music in the house and in the car. I ignored him, I didn't want communication. I was so damn angry." Georgia took a sip of wine and sighed. "Now I can't continue to ignore him if my children are in danger. Plus, I feel I owe it to his children to prove his death was murder and bring the Whore to justice."

She was bitter and pissed off. I glanced over my shoulder and sure enough Jon was still standing there and he looked very upset. He shook his head.

"It would seem clear Jon doesn't agree with you," I said.

"And I give a damn because why? Jon was a bastard in life, neglected his children, was a horrible husband, a liar, a cheater, a gambler and a thief. What he wants doesn't matter a damn to me, he's no longer calling the shots, he's dead. Fuck you, Jon!" She saluted him with her wine glass.

Jon looked at me. "Tell her she's putting the children in danger," he begged.

"He says you're putting the children in danger," I dutifully repeated.

Georgia looked at the Ouija board and then at me, her eyes widened. "You can really hear him?" she whispered.

I drew a deep breath. Here we go, I thought as I bought a ticket to the freak train and climbed aboard. "Yep."

I wondered what Derek thought. Suddenly his opinion was very important to me. I didn't look at him, though.

"You're a detective so you can help me prove the Whore murdered him, and you can hear Jon and he can give you details about what to look for, right?" she asked.

I shrugged. "Sure, I probably can, but first I want you to ask yourself one question: are you doing this for justice or for revenge?"

"Aren't they the same?" Georgia asked.

I smiled a small, tight smile at her. "No, and when you have an answer, call my office and my Juliet will explain my fees. I'll take a look, if I like your answer."

I stood up, retrieved my purse, fished out a card and handed it to her. "And now, Lori, thank you for your hospitality, but I've enjoyed about as much of this party as I can stand."

I looked at Derek and he nodded. I headed for the door before I remembered my manners. "Diane, if you will cut me a door please?"

I looked at the woman who had erected the protective bubble for us. She jumped up, unlocked the door and created a doorway in the protective bubble for me to leave. Which I did.

4

Sisters

I was half a block away before I realized Derek, Moira and Mars were practically running to keep up with me.

"Hey," called Derek. "Wait up."

I stopped in my tracks and waited.

"Hey, are you okay? That was wild, I had no idea you could do something so amazing. What's it like? Is it scary? Is it creepy?" Derek asked sincerely.

I didn't answer but only because I didn't have an answer for him. It had been a long time since I'd explained my ability to anyone.

"Really are you … alright?" He seemed genuinely concerned.

I drew a very deep breath and blew it out. "I'm fine. I see dead people. I can hear them. They love me. It's been going on for almost my entire life. This was exactly what I was afraid would happen tonight."

I didn't look at Derek; I just looked down at the sidewalk. Moira and Mars wisely did not say a word.

"Look, you're upset, let's go to my place and we can sit and talk about this over wine, whaddaya say? Of course, Moira and Mars, you're both invited too. Come on, say yes. I have an unopened bottle of Merlot from Stonehas. It's very tasty," he wheedled.

I still didn't look up. "Okay."

"Come on then, it's not far," he urged.

I knew he said this for the benefit of the girls. He hooked his arm in mine and we took off with Moira and Mars bringing up the rear. It only took a few minutes to reach Derek's building and two minutes later we were in his condo. He played the gracious host and seated us in the living room, got the wine and glasses and joined us.

"Derek, your place is just lovely," Moira said.

"Thanks, I had a decorator help me with it. I don't have great taste but I had an idea of what I wanted and she created it for me." He smiled, genuinely pleased by the compliment. He fiddled with the glasses and the cork as he spoke. "I love the place."

"The view of Nashville is tremendous; I can see the bridges from here," Mars added.

They were all trying to make small talk. All concerned for my tender feelings. God, I hated the feeling of being catered to because I'm in a pissy place.

"You should be here on the 4th of July, the show is outstanding," Derek said as he poured wine for all of us.

"Okay, enough, please. The place is great, his decorator is great, the view is great, let's all cook hot dogs on the 4th and drink beer. That'll be great too." I took a sip of the wine. "Now let's get down to the real nut cuttin' shall we? I see dead people, just like in the movie. I have most of my life, it's not weird or scary. They don't appear with blood and guts or bullet wounds or any of that Hollywood bullshit. They just show up and they talk to me 'cause I can hear them. I knew this would happen tonight which is why I wasn't crazy to go in the first place. Or hell maybe I was crazy. Anyway, I knew it would happen and then you'd think I was a nut case. I may be crazy but I sure as hell ain't crazy about what I saw tonight. Jon was really there, he communicated with me, I saw him and I heard him." I sounded lame and defensive.

Damn, I thought I was going to cry. Why was I so upset? Derek put down his wine glass and moved over to sit next me. He took my hand.

"Tess, I don't think you're crazy. I believe, really I believe. Now the only thing we have to talk about is how you're going to help you prove Jon's widow murdered him."

Okay, I had to admit to being pleasantly surprised. Many people doubt the existence of ghosts or spirits and think those of us who do see and hear them are weird or crazy or liars. Once a fella asked me how it made me feel when people told me they thought what I did was weird. I told him usually my answer was I thought reality television was weird. It got a laugh, but really no one likes to open themselves up to ridicule. I smiled at Derek. I took another sip of wine to give myself time to marshal my thoughts.

"I'm not sure where to start on this. I suppose I'll start with the date and place of death, get a copy of the death certificate, and then pull the will from probate, if it's been probated and if there's a will. Let's see if there's really a large amount of money in the estate and where it ended up. Money provides a motive. I'd like to get his medical records, but with HIPPA it might be hard to do." I shrugged.

"You're right about the difficulty of getting access to his medical records," Moira confirmed.

"What if one of the children asked for an investigation into his death?" asked Mars.

"Nope, that would only signal the widow we're investigating. Jon was adamant she was dangerous and capable of murder. If she's really a nut ball then I'd like to do this on the DL. So we leave the police out of it. We have absolutely no proof anyway so no one's gonna listen to us or investigate but me," I said.

"Okay, what's the next step?" Derek asked.

"If I take this case, it'll mean lots of legwork, talkin' to everyone who might be involved in any way or who might have seen or heard something which will prove Jon was murdered. I'll find out where he died and if it was in a facility, then I'll go there and pray someone will talk to me. If he died at home, I'll find out if he had Hospice or some other group with him at the end. Somebody will know the answer. The organization won't talk to me, but maybe the individual caregivers will open up. I just have to approach them correctly, make them sympathetic to my cause. I also very much want to see the autopsy report if there is one, which I strongly doubt." I sighed and had another sip of the wine, which was very good.

"Wow, you're building this investigation in your head as we sit here. I've never seen this side of you before. It's impressive, and sexy." Derek smiled at me and his dimples deepened.

Mars laughed, "She's not even warmed up yet. You should see her when she gets going, no one can deny her whatever she wants, people will tell her the damndest and most private things. She's like a force of nature."

"Don't try and suck up to me, you got me in this mess. You too," I said, pointing at Moira.

"How could I know the evening would be so dramatic? Honestly, it's usually just cousins and grandmothers and wine. Rarely does murder enter into the picture." Moira threw up her hands. "Who knew?"

I just shook my head. "Given the fact I attract dead people like horseshit attracts flies, how could it not happen? Not the murder part, but the dead guy talking to me part."

"Why are you so sure the dead guy is telling you the truth? Have you considered the fact he might be lying? After all Georgia claims he never told the truth in his life. Maybe this is some sort of a scheme on his part." Derek looked very serious.

"You might be right, maybe he wants all the money to go to the widow and he wants to derail any legal action his children might be thinkin' of takin'." I sighed and collected my thoughts. "But he seemed sincere to me, truly afraid his children are in danger. If I take this case, then we shall see if he was lyin' or not. My gut says not."

"So, you investigate, talk to everyone and get enough evidence to call it murder, then what?" asked Derek.

"Then I call the police in to the investigation, give them all my reports and tell the kids to watch their asses until the police can investigate and maybe indict. It's a long shot Derek. This Jon guy had a long struggle with cancer, he was expected to die, and no one was surprised when he did. My money says there was no autopsy, so how do we prove murder? Without sufficient evidence, no judge in his right mind will sign an order to exhume the body. Unless someone saw the widow slip him something or monkey with his IV, we're hung."

"What if Jon is mistaken?" Moira asked.

I raised an eyebrow. "As in someone else murdered him?"

"More like maybe he did see his wife do something which seemed odd, but was actually normal, and he only thought it was sinister?" Mars asked.

"Hmm. Okay, I'll give you that. He was dyin', probably on morphine I'd guess." I looked at Moira for confirmation and she nodded at me. "He wasn't seein' clearly or thinkin' clearly. He could have been mistaken about what really happened."

Everyone was silent for a moment or two. Then Mars asked, "But you're gonna take the case anyway, right?"

"Only if Georgia Kincaid tells me she wants justice." I turned to Derek. "So you're really not freaked out by all of this?"

He shook his head. "More like fascinated," he said.

"Okay then I'll ask you the same question you asked me earlier in the evening. You want to keep doing this?" I crossed my fingers.

Derek grinned at me. "Oh yeah." He leaned over and kissed me. Then he turned to Mars and Moira. "Look, it's late, so I'd like all of you to stay over and you can drive home in the morning. I've got a guest bedroom and I'm sure I can find you something for you both to sleep in, okay?"

They looked at me for an answer, since they knew I was aggravated with them and didn't want to want to make it worse.

"Sure, a sleepover would be just great," I said.

"I need to call home and tell Bobby I'm staying with you and Mars in a swanky condo in the Gulch. He'll be jealous," Moira said.

She was grinning. I could tell she was a bit excited. After all it wasn't every day she got to escape from the kids and spend the night in a fancy Nashville high-rise.

"Sure, I only have to call the cat and tell her to let herself out," Mars joked.

"Then, it's settled. Let me find some t-shirts for you," Derek enthused.

He finished off his wine and left the three of us alone in the living room. No one spoke till we were sure Derek was out of earshot.

"Sorry Tess," Mars and Moira said at the same time.

They were too, I could tell. Really there was no reason for me to be mad at them; it wasn't their fault, just circumstances. If I'd really wanted to keep Derek in the dark I could've found some way not to go to the Candle, right?

"C'est la vie. Shit happens and all that. Besides Derek seems to be taking it pretty well, he doesn't seem to be freakin' out. He even invited us all to spend the night. So I guess it all turned out alright." I was feeling generous. "Besides I could have declined your gracious invitation and carried him off to bed instead, right?"

Moira laughed. "It was weird, Jon turning up and warning Georgia to leave the estate alone. Like something out of a movie."

More like something out of a Shakespearean play, I thought. "Oh, I don't think so. If you're gonna open the gates to the other side, people are gonna show up. A lot of them did, by the by."

"I gotta ask this, how dangerous can the widow actually be? I mean, it's one thing to kill a half dead man who can't fight back and quite another to try and kill several young, healthy people. Not to mention killin' 'em and gettin' away with it. Do you really think Jon's kids are in danger from her?" Mars asked.

"Don't underestimate her, Mars. If she actually murdered Jon, she'll be desperate to avoid gettin' caught. So I'll withhold judgment on your question until we know more. Besides, if she did murder a half dead man who couldn't fight back then she's a monster and she deserves to be nailed," I answered. "Even if he was the asshole Georgia claims him to be."

Derek walked in with Nashville Fire Department t-shirts and handed one to Mars and one to Moira.

"Wow, the three most beautiful women in the state are spending the night in my house. The guys at the hall will elect me God," he joked.

"Good thing you don't kiss and tell then, 'cause I couldn't stand you if you were any more egotistical." I grinned at him.

"You're right, but I'll bet Joe the doorman will look at me with a new respect." He grinned back.

I laughed. "Your mornin' doorman is 110 years old; he's blind in one eye and can't see out of the other. He won't know if we're three women leavin' your condo in the mornin' or three Afghan hounds."

"Funny, ha ha. Okay ladies, let me show you where you're bunking down tonight." He was chuckling as he led Mars and Moira away.

I headed up to bed. It had been a very long day. I called the house to inform the family I'd be staying in Nashville. I don't have to call, it just seems polite. Besides I knew my mother would be waiting up.

"Hello," Mommy answered the phone.

"Mommy, I'm staying in Nashville at Derek's with Moira and Mars. Just wanted to let you know," I said.

"That's lovely then, tell them all hello from me. Drive safe tomorrow," she said.

"I will, night night."

"Night."

I changed into the nightgown I keep at Derek's house, brushed my teeth and was asleep before my head hit the pillow. I vaguely felt Derek slide in beside me. My dreams all night were of my grandmother warning me to be careful and of Jon, the dead guy, staring at me and pointing his finger in an accusatory manner. I hate it when dead people do that, it makes me cranky.

5

In Loving Memory

Mars, Moira and I took off early the next morning after coffee and bagels with Derek. I was in no great hurry to get home so I tooled along lost in my own thoughts, actually obeying the speed limit. I wondered if Georgia Kincaid was going to follow through and call to retain me. She had seemed determined the night before but sometimes in the cold, grey light of dawn things look quite different.

Since I keep an extra outfit at Derek's, I didn't need to stop at home to change, but headed directly to the office. Jewels, my-right-hand-Girl-Friday-office-manager was on the phone when I opened the door. She put one finger over her lips and kept talking to someone.

I grabbed my adorable gnome mug and filled it with coffee. The mug amuses me, there's a gnome trying to climb out of it and his little ax is at the bottom of the cup. It brightens my day. You can't ask more of a cup. Plus, it holds a huge amount of coffee. Functional as well as adorable, kinda like me. I chuckled at my own brilliant wit.

All I could hear from Jewel's side of the conversation was the occasional, 'yes ma'am, no ma'am' and so forth. I wandered into my office secure in the knowledge Jewels would bring me whatever information she was gathering from the phone call when she was done with it. I fired up the computer and flipped through the emails. Nothing interesting there, unless you think pills for erection at a discount, the fact I was a Balinese princess worth a fortune, or my account with the Swedish National Bank had been flagged was interesting.

Jewels bustled into my office.

"Wow, you musta had a very interesting night last night, Boss. One Ms. Georgia Kincaid would like to retain your services to prove her ex-husband, one Jon Kincaid, was actually murdered by his current widow." She perched on the corner of my desk. "So he showed up at a séance?"

I chuckled. "Oh, he showed up and warned her not to tangle with his widow over the estate. It was kinda like something out of a movie accordin' to Moira. He was tore up from the floor up, I can assure you. He convinced his ex-wife, Georgia his current widow, Jonnie, murdered him and Jonnie would bring harm to his children if they opposed her over the estate. Also, he outed me to Derek in the process."

"Wow, pretty dramatic. Dramatic enough to cause Ms. Kincaid to pay your very reasonable fee to find out the truth. Did Derek freak?"

"No, he took it rather well. Good on the money, I guess. Did she have anything else to say?"

"Uh, funny you should ask, she said to tell you: justice."

I smiled. "Okay, then call her back and tell her to mail a check to cover five days. I'm sure it'll take longer but it's a start.

Make sure she knows this case is going to require a lot of leg work, at least I think it will."

Jewels just stood up and tapped her foot at me.

"Oh," I said, "I told Ms. Kincaid to call me when she decided if she wanted to run an investigation for justice or for vengeance. She hates the widow. I don't think she's too fond of the ex-husband either."

Jewels smiled. "Cool, I'll call her back."

"Tell her what we need, full name, social, DOD, place of death etc., widow's name you know the drill."

"Got it." Jewels waltzed out.

I turned to my computer and tried to concentrate on business but I kept seeing the dead guy in my mind's eye and I felt like he was pushing me to solve the crime even though he bitched at me all night long.

About twenty minutes later Jewels came back in with her pink iPad. "OKAY, boss, I've got the info." She sat down across from me and began to rattle off the particulars. "Jon Clayton Kincaid, 59 years of age, a real estate developer, wife, or rather widow Jonelle 'Jonnie' Mansfield Kincaid, 45. There is a long and rather expensive obituary mostly singing his praises, lots of blah, blah, have a look."

She turned the iPad so I could read it: *Jon Clayton Kincaid, 59, lost his long battle with cancer on January 20th and has gone to his reward where his mother, father and grandparents are waiting for him. Jon was a pillar of the community and a successful businessman who owned Kincaid Properties, Consolidated Properties, HOPE Housing, FAITH Housing and JOY Housing. He is survived by his grieving wife of fifteen years, Jonelle 'Jonnie' Mansfield Kincaid, beloved daughter Anna Nyman, sister Martha Boyd and her husband Steve, brothers Samuel and Martin and their wives Crystal and Marla. Well known for his many business accomplishments, he will be especially remembered for his great love of family, devotion to his church, his passion for philanthropy and community. Jon embodied goodness and had a peaceful loving nature; he will be remembered as a true Southern gentleman. He will be sorely missed. Visitation at St. Stephen's Episcopal Church on the 23rd from 4 PM until 7 PM, the funeral is on the 24th at 2 PM. In lieu of flowers the family asks you make donations in his name to the American Cancer Society.*

Wow! I wondered who wrote it, my money was on the widow. There was no mention of Georgia's children. There was no mention of an interment; usually the obit tells you where the dead guy is going to be buried.

"Jon and Jonnie huh? Man, how horrible. She mailing us a check?" I asked.

"She wanted you to start today so she gave me a credit card." Jewels smiled. She loves it when we get money, bless her greedy little heart.

"Do we have anything urgent right now?" I queried.

"You've written your client reports, I just need to make a few corrections and send them out. We've got a couple of employment background checks, and one bride-to-be wants to know if her intended checks out. She suspects an ex-wife who he isn't claimin'."

"Good, those are things I can do in my sleep. I'll knock 'em out first so I can focus all my attention on Jon Kincaid. I think I'll call the coroner's office in Atlanta first and see what they've got to tell me about him. I bet he never passed through there, since everyone thinks this death was natural causes but it's worth a shot."

"This one's tripped your triggers, huh boss?" She cocked her head and studied me.

"Yeah, Kincaid was so desperate, so very frantic. He's fearful for his children and if he's right and they're in danger then we need to get to the bottom of this fast so no one else dies," I admitted.

Jewels beamed at me and left me alone. I went through the cases on my roster in short order. Easy money, really, and mostly information anyone could get themselves for the price of one of those investigative packages you can buy on the web. But I didn't want to spread such information around. Plus, I know how to really dig for the dirt.

I finished the easy stuff and got to the interesting stuff. Not like I'm fascinated by murder but it is almost always a case study of human nature. Why did the murderer do the murder? With what? Where? How can he or she hope to get away with it? So much more too. The idea of one human killing another fascinates us, otherwise there wouldn't be Court TV, or true crime magazines or murder mystery books or movies or cop shows, right? Not many of my cases involved murder or even wrongful death, mostly just insurance cases, divorces, cheating spouses, employment background checks and other such mundane matters. Rarely did I investigate murder, which was alright with me. I loathe the idea one human being can kill another for whatever reason, except self-defense.

Once upon a time I had a discussion with a gentleman about killing and he said he couldn't take another life under any circumstances.

"Even if the other guy was tryin' to kill you?" I asked.

"Even then," he assured me.

"What if he was tryin' to kill your wife?"

"No, I couldn't justify it."

I had been amazed, blown away by his insistence he could not take a human life.

"What if he was tryin' to kill your children?" I asked.

"No, there are no circumstances which would push me to kill another person." he insisted. "I have been to war."

I didn't believe him. Oh, maybe he believed what he was saying and thought he was somehow above the animal need to survive. At the time, I felt sure if he found himself in a life or death scenario he would choose to live.

I still believed I was right. I'd found myself in just such a situation not too long ago when I tangled with the men who murdered Chick Donnelly, my best friend.

Outside of self-defense, the reasons to do murder are few: revenge, greed, deception, jealousy, anger, to cover up another crime, and crazy. Every murder falls into one of these categories. Think about it and you'll discover I'm right. None of those reasons are good enough to snuff out another human, a true fact all the way back to Cain. Lady Macbeth did murder because she was a greedy bitch and Charlie Manson and his bunch were crazy as loons.

I was getting a bit maudlin. I reached into my drawer and pulled out my secret stash of Lorna Doones, they always brighten my mood and they go great with coffee. I got another cup and settled back into my desk.

I Googled the number of the Atlanta Coroners' office and dialed it from one of my burner cell phones. I surely didn't want 'Maher Investigations' to come up on the caller ID at the Atlanta Coroners' office. The burner phone comes up as 'A.C. Doyle.'

As the phone rang I was thinking furiously on my cover story. Funny how most people won't talk to you if you're honest and tell them you're a private investigator who is looking into a suspicious death. People are just strange. Especially when they find out you have no warrant and no legal backup. The phone rang about six times and just before someone answered it, I knew what to say.

"Atlanta Coroner, Joe Quinn speakin', how can I help?" The strong Southern accent belonged to a very tired and probably overworked man.

"Dr. Quinn, my name is Sandy Byrd and I represent National Mutual One Insurance Company." I tried to sound friendly and chipper.

Of course, there was no such company, but all parts of the name were recognized as insurance company names. If you gonna lie, lie with something familiar, people will accept it easier.

"Uh huh, how can I help ya?" He sounded completely dis-interested in my needs.

"Well sir, I'm trying to tie up the loose ends on a death claim, and wanted a copy of the coroner's report. The name is Jon Clayton Kincaid, Jon without the 'H', age 59, DOD January 20th this year in Atlanta, cause of death natural." I crossed my fingers for luck.

"Well, let me check, you wanna hold on?"

"Sure, and thank you so much."

If you're lying to someone, it's helpful to be polite. I had no allusions Joe Quinn would find a report. My gut said Jon Kincaid went straight to the funeral home since no one had any suspicions. I waited, listening to dead air, pun intended. I hate just listening to nothing, it always makes me wonder if·I'm still on hold. You would think the Atlanta Coroner's office had never heard of Muzak. Luckily, I didn't have to wait long.

"Ma'am, we don't have a report on this fella, so no autopsy. I did find a Death Certificate. Sorry I couldn't help you more." He sounded sincere.

"I appreciate you lookin' for me, I'll get a copy of the Death Certificate myself. You have a good day now." I tried to sound cheerful.

"And you," Joe Quinn answered and hung up.

I did a little more fishing and called every nursing home and therapy center in the greater Atlanta area. There are 47 of them, in case you wondered. During the phone calls Jewels brought me lunch. I looked at my watch and realized it was 1:30 in the afternoon. At which point I decided I was hungry, so I ate as I made more calls. I finally found what I was looking for on my 26th phone call.

"Marietta Rehab and Therapy Center, this is Jennifer, how may I direct your call?"

"Hey Jennifer, how you doin'? I need to speak to someone in medical records please." I did my best to sound incredibly positive and upbeat.

The woman on the other end didn't acknowledge my query but simply placed me on hold. After a few seconds, I heard a ringing sound and then another woman answered.

"Records, this is Marci. How may I help you?" The voice was clipped and businesslike.

"Marci, my name is Jolene Marsdale, how you doing today?" I tried to sound pleasant and charming, since I thought I might be looking at an impossible hurtle to jump so I really poured it on.

"Fine." She didn't sound so fine.

I plunged ahead smiling and being cheerful. "That's good, real good. Well Marci, I work for Great South Insurers and I have a question about a former patient of yours."

"Name," Marci said.

"Jon Clayton Kincaid without the 'H', age 59, DOD January 20th this year, terminal illness." I held my breath for the 26th time.

"I need permission from the family to give you any information, in writing; I'll give you our fax number."

Yahoo! I knew Jon had been a patient in the facility otherwise she would have just said 'no such patient' which was the same answer I'd gotten 25 times before.

"Hang on Marci, this isn't medical information I want, I just need to know which funeral home the body was transported to on the day of death." I crossed my fingers.

"Same answer, in writing, our fax number is 616-555-1212. Did you get that?" She was starting to sound annoyed with me.

"Yes, I did and thanks ever so. You have a nice day now."

"Un huh." Marci broke the connection.

It has been my experience in all medical institutions the medical records department is usually in some dark basement without windows, isolated and completely cut off from the rest of the world. Seemed like a good place for Marci, what with her amazing social skills and all.

Fortunately, I didn't really need Marci's help to find the funeral home; I had gotten that from the obituary. I was just hoping she'd answer my question which might lead to several more questions being asked and answered. The funeral home question was a little icebreaker; I really wanted to know how long Jon had been at the facility before he died, who was with him when he died, did he go from bad to worse in a hurry, those kinds of things. It would've made my life easier if she had answered my questions. But nothing good comes easy, now I was forced to come up with a plan to get information in some other way. Probably the hard way.

The name of the funeral home which received the earthly remains of Jon Kincaid was in the obit I had read earlier. It took me a matter of seconds to find it and see Eternal Hills won the prize. I had my story ready before I dialed the number.

"Eternal Hills, this is Martha, how may I direct your call?"

"Hello," I said in a solemn voice, "I need your help please. My father was entrusted to you when he passed. We had been estranged and I wasn't even informed of his death until days later. I only want to know where he's buried so I can visit his grave, please."

"I'm so sorry for your loss. May I have his name please?" Martha said kindly.

"Jon Clayton Kincaid, I'm his daughter Jillian."

"Give me just a moment and I'll get one of our directors on the phone who will give you as much information as possible. Now you hold on please."

I felt a bit of a heel for fooling her with my sad story, but I figured the facts were true and his children did deserve to know where he was buried. Martha obviously bought my tale so I sat there and listened to the flowery organ music and could practically smell the carnations. Funeral homes always smell of carnations to me.

I waited, secure in the knowledge Martha would bring me the information I wanted. Funeral home folks are incredibly helpful, they're trained to be and also to be kind and comforting. They've seen it all, family estrangements, full out feuds, fights in the front hall, husbands and ex-husbands showing up at the same time. They know how to calm everyone down and defuse the situation. I hoped I'd planted some sympathy seeds which might bear fruit.

"Ms. Kincaid?"

I was so startled out of my reverie I very nearly dropped the phone. "Yes, this is Jillian Kincaid."

"Ms. Kincaid, this is Dorna Moore. I have some information for you about your father. First let me say I'm sorry for your loss."

"Thank you, you're too kind." I tried to sound sad.

"Your father passed away, as you may know on January 20th at the Marietta Rehab and Therapy Center after a long battle with cancer. Dr. Jocelyn Gordon, the on-call doctor for the center, signed the death certificate and his remains were released to us. Mr. Kincaid was cremated within twenty-four hours after his death and there was a memorial the next day. I…"

"Cremated?" I tried to put a little outrage in my voice.

"Ms. Jonelle Kincaid is your step-mother, correct? She told us she had the permission of all the children to cremate and it was your fathers' wish to be cremated. May I assume you did not give permission?" There was a worried tone in her voice.

I knew damn well none of the Kincaid off-springs had been notified.

"No ma'am, none of us were notified," I answered sorrowfully.

"I am so sorry, I know mere words are inadequate, but at this late date it's the best I can offer. This can't be undone. I can only hope to offer you as much of my help as possible." She really did sound sorry.

"I realize this isn't your fault. Families, huh? What can you do? Dorna – may I call you Dorna?"

"Of course."

"Dorna, may I ask you a question?"

"Surely, you may ask me anything and if I know the answer I will tell you." She sounded a bit breathless; this was rather a large faux pas.

"Is it normal procedure to cremate someone in such a short time span after the death?"

"Well, actually, it doesn't usually happen so quickly in most circumstances. But your father had been in terrible health for so long and your step-mother requested us to cremate immediately. She said she couldn't bear the thought of him lying here in the funeral home all alone. She was very convincing. We complied; we saw no reason not to do so. Plus, we had the ability to do it; there was no line, if you know what I mean."

"Thank you, Dorna, you've been a great help to me."

"I only wish I could do more."

I was sure she meant it, she wanted to be nice as pie and hope I, well actually the Kincaid kids, didn't sue her ass off.

"You've been grand, now you have a nice day."

"I'm just so glad I could help in some small way. Bye bye."

I hung up and leaned back in my chair to think. The doctor signed off on Jon, probably without much of an examination. Why would anyone look twice at a guy who had been diagnosed with cancer and who had been dying for months and months? They wouldn't.

Jon was cremated within twenty-four hours of his death, which it made me think I was on the right trail. Twenty-four hours from time of death to the crematorium is a very short time. By law, in most states, all the immediate kin must be notified and sign off on the cremation before the procedure can go forward. Sometimes it takes a few days at the least, but not in Jon's case.

The money trail was the next order of business. I typed in Georgia Public Records, hoping the will had already been probated. If so, then it was available for me to take a look and see what was what.

The phone at Jewels desk rang and she answered it.

"It's Lori Torpey," she said.

"Okay, put her through." Jewels sent the call to me. There was dead air for a second or two and then the connection was made. "Hey Lori, what can I do for you?" I turned away from my computer.

"It is more what I can do for you, dear Tess. Will you take the Kincaid case?" Lori was obviously concerned.

"Ms. Kincaid has paid me for five days' worth of my expertise and has given me the correct answer to my question, so I'll be takin' the case to see what I can find. As a matter of fact, I'm already workin' on it."

I heard Lori draw a deep breath. "Then you must listen and heed my words. I see great danger in this for you and for others as well. You did not ask me to divine for you and usually I consider such to be a breach of ethics but as this occurred in my store I felt obligated to do so."

"I understand how you could feel way, but really Lori please don't worry, I'm takin' this case 'cause I want to and you aren't responsible in any way. Also, I know what I'm doin' or at least I hope I do. I'll be careful, I promise." I really didn't want her to worry about me.

"In my divination, I saw fire and death. I laid cards for you; forgive me for doing so without your permission but I do feel so responsible. The Tower and the Death card both showed in the spread, signifying disaster and an ending to the situation. I cannot warn you strongly enough this matter is dangerous and if you indeed take it on you must guard your back at every moment. Others are at risk as well." She sounded practically breathless.

A little ice crystal of fear formed in the pit of my stomach. "You think the four Kincaid kids might be harmed as well?"

"In my cards, the Queen of Swords was with the Tower and Death, she brings destruction and true death if she can manage it. She crosses three young women and a young man; the Kincaid children. She crosses you as well. She is bitter and cunning and evil, I fear. Do not underestimate her, many have before which has led them to despair."

The hair on the back of my neck rose up. I believed Lori was right and the widow was a bad woman who was desperate to remain unchallenged. At least I would be if I murdered a cancer patient. I had it on good authority prison sucked.

I blew out a breath. "Duly noted Lori, I will be extremely careful. Light a candle for me for protection please."

"Yes, I will, to the Virgin so she may wrap you in her blue mantel and keep you safe. There are others I will petition as well. I will do all I can with the Spirit world. The physical world is for you to deal with, dear one."

"Thank you, Lori, I appreciate your efforts."

"I can only wish the Kincaid woman has not spoken so freely in front of so many. My customers are dear to me, but this is much too juicy and exciting, people will talk. One never knows who knows into whose ears such a tale might fall."

"True, in which case I guess we'll just have to cross our fingers."

"Blessings on you, dear one, we shall speak again at another time,"

"Bless you too, Lori, and thank you."

"Oh, and Tess, I will send you a little incantation to banish spirits. I think you might make use of it."

I smiled. "Thanks Lori, I appreciate that."

I broke the connection and sat pondering the message. I wondered which Tarot card had represented me; I'd have to ask her the next time we talked. On second thought, maybe I didn't want to know.

Lori Torpey was good, as good as any psychic you might see on the TV and if she said a thing was so, then it was so. But I also knew the future was not carved in stone as it had not happened yet and so could be changed. I believed her, but I believed in my Beretta as well.

Flashbacks

I lay in my bed and started at the ceiling. After we buried Chick I took up full time residence in my room for a while. I lay in bed and thought about Chick, his life, his death and the bastards who murdered him. I cried a lot over my loss and his loss and the future which would never happen, but mostly I just stared at the ceiling.

For the first six weeks I mended, I had a broken jaw which was wired together, a concussion, some broken ribs and a nasty inch long bullet wound over my right ear. I was in no small amount of pain. I went to Chick's funeral but afterwards, I retreated to my room. I couldn't go to work and didn't want to go out of the house. I had to visit the doctor regularly so he could tell me I was healing well. I had to be driven to and from the doctor; I was an invalid, physically and emotionally.

My body mended, but my heart didn't. I stayed holed up in my room despite pleas from my family to come back to the world.

For the first time in my life I locked my bedroom door to keep my loved ones out; I knew they'd just walk in and harass me, which was unacceptable. As I had foreseen, every member of my family came to my door and knocked and talked and begged and consoled, they even brought baby Steven to try and lure me out. Low of them, really low. Mars and Jewels came too and talked to me through the closed door. Mars cried and accused me of trying to break her heart. I sent every single one of them packing. I was so miserable I just wanted to be left alone so I could wallow in my misery. I didn't understand how they couldn't understand! The only ones I allowed in were the dogs. They didn't ask anything of me, and it was comfortable to be surrounded by all that warm canine snuggling.

On a Tuesday, six weeks after I had almost died, the doctor removed the hardware from my mouth. It was liberating and I made my mother stop at Tilly's so I could celebrate with solid food. It was strange and awful to be out and sitting in a booth at the restaurant, to have to speak to people. I had my first and only anxiety attack about half way through the meal.

My mother drove me home without a word of complaint. But I could see the tears sliding down her cheeks as she clutched the wheel. It took a mighty effort for her to withhold advice and I appreciated it.

Since I could eat solid food, and remembered how wonderful it tasted, I continued my food celebration for several more weeks while I savored everything I'd been missing. But I had my celebration at home, alone in the middle of the night.

One morning, before daylight, I woke up knowing someone was in my room. Slowly I slid my hand under the pillow and touched the Glock. I opened my eyes and saw Chick was sitting on my bed just staring at me.

"Girl, you got to stop this. You're gonna die in this room and it ain't your time yet," he said sadly.

He frowned at me and I sat up, leaving the gun where it was hidden. The dogs roused a bit, realized there was no danger and snuggled back down.

"I know, you're right, but I can't seem to make myself get up and get dressed. I don't want to see anyone or talk to anyone or do anything. I just want to stay here under the covers forever." I realized I was crying. It was the most I had spoken to anyone in ages and it hurt to talk.

"Baby, I know how you feel, but you're alive and kicking and you got a lot more living to do. TisTis, get up, take a shower. Maybe I can't smell you but I know you're ripe. Go back to the world of the living. If you ever loved me, do it. I can't stand watching this."

I flopped back on my pillow and my tears rolled into my hair. "I love you still and there's a big hole in my heart where you used to be," I sobbed.

"I'm here, always here."

"Not the same, not the same," I sobbed at him.

"Get up, get dressed and go see that Derek feller, he seems like a likely candidate for ya. He's worried about ya jus' so as ya know. He keeps callin' and textin' and you keep not answerin'.'"

I stopped sobbing and hiccupped. "Are you spyin' on him too?"

Chick laughed. "Not spyin', just checkin' up on." Then Chick grew serious. "Connell's in 'bout the same sorry shape as you 'cept he does go to work and he showers. He sure is drinkin' a whole lot of beer, it's puttin' pounds on him and it ain't attractive. Now get the hell up, he needs you and your family needs you and Mars and I need you to live."

"Chick," I whispered. My heart ached.

"Up!" Chick demanded. "You're better'n this, stronger'n this and smarter'n this. I always said you were the best human I ever knew, don't make a liar out of me."

"I love you."

"I love you too and will always love you no matter what. Now do it. Do it 'cause you love me."

I couldn't argue, how could I? "Okay." I swung my legs around and sat staring at him.

All the dogs shifted and Holmes, the King Charles spaniel, growled at being disturbed.

"Come visit me again soon?" I said piteously.

"Yep, if you take up your life and move forward. I won't come here and stare at a crazy, smelly hermit." He wrinkled his nose.

I laughed. "Okay, message received." I felt so tired I just wanted to lie back down but I knew I couldn't. Chick was right, I was alive and it was high time I acted like it.

"That's my girl." He blew me a kiss and was gone.

"Damn ghosts, in, out, waking people up, won't take no for an answer, bossy as hell too," I grumbled.

I fought the urge to fall back into my nice soft bed and instead dragged myself into the shower. The hot water felt wonderful against my skin and I soaped and lathered and rinsed, I washed and conditioned my hair and I even shaved my legs and pits. I admitted I'd been living in a rather crazed state for a while, almost two months according to my grandmother when she had come to my door three days before.

Maybe I was crazy after all if you considered how well armed I was in my little asylum. There was a loaded Glock under my pillow and the Beretta was in plain view on the night stand, there was also a Taser in the night stand drawer and a filleting knife tucked under my mattress.

Up until Chick was murdered, my home had been a sanctuary, a refuge from the outside world. It was where I came when I was sad, lonely, hungry, tired and it had always been the place where I was wrapped in love and safety. Then we were invaded one dark night by men who wanted to kill me. I hadn't harmed these men in any way, hadn't stolen from them, cheated them, wronged them or kicked their dog. I was simply a liability who possibly knew too much and they had come to kill me in my bed in order to insure my silence. They had failed miserably, and as a consequence one of them died and three were on trial for many, many crimes. There was a neighbor on trial too but I tried not to think about her, she just pissed me off. Those thoughts were too dark and would only lead me back down into hell.

The villains had been caught, trials were to come and justice would be done, none of which made me feel any safer. So, every night before I laid me down to sleep, I locked my bedroom door and checked my weapons before I turned out the lights. It had become a ritual; first the Glock, then the Beretta, then the taser and lastly the very sharp knife. Paranoid? Maybe I was, but I would rather be living and paranoid than a dead person.

Something inside me changed the night of the invasion; I didn't realize it until I stood under the streaming water in my shower the morning I decided to live. Oh. I knew I was more cautious, was never far from a weapon and constantly watched my rear view when I was being chauffeured around. But something else changed and I had not been able to put my finger on what it was, just something was different. As the suds rolled off my body I realized what was missing: my trust of others. Not blind trust, but the trust that most people were pretty okay and meant well. I realized I didn't believe it anymore. I stopped rinsing and just leaned against the wall, I needed to grasp the idea before it slid away and ran down the drain. I was fairly cynical, given what I did for a living; I had seen the seedy side of life. Until the disaster with Chick, I hadn't seen cruel and vicious.

I had discovered there were men who would do murder for money and enjoy doing so. I knew a neighbor you had known all your life would sell you out for money.

In the past, I had believed most people were honest, good God-fearing folks who were just trying to make it in the world.

But a blinding revelation came to me in my shower, and I realized there were wolves amongst the sheep.

I also discovered something about myself as I stood there with the water pounding on my back. I found I could kill another human being if I needed to, and I could decide who needed killing. Maybe, just maybe, I was a wolf too.

I hadn't killed anyone during the craziness surrounding Chick's death. Oh, I had done some damage for sure, but no one had died by my hand. What had honestly changed within me was the sure knowledge I could take another life and I wanted to and even hungered to do so. The realization hit me: I had never hesitated, harbored no doubts about what I'd done and hadn't lost one minute of sleep over the damage I had caused. Such a bitter pill to swallow. I had always thought I was one of the white hat wearing good guys.

By the time I finished my shower and soul searching, the sun was up. I gathered my dirty laundry and dropped it down the chute to the basement. I changed my disgusting sheets and sent them to the basement as well. Maybe I should have burned them instead. I picked up dirty dishes and then the dogs and I wandered down the steps. In truth, the mutts bounded down the steps and then danced all around the kitchen as happy as if they had good sense. My father and grandmother were seated at the table and my mother was at the sink. They all looked up at the commotion.

My grandmother smiled at me. "Welcome back," was all she said.

My father smiled too and patted the chair beside him. I sat and he leaned over and kissed me on the cheek.

My mother turned all the way around and stared at me. "Thank God," she whispered.

There were tears in her eyes. How great is that? I made my mother cry by showing up to breakfast.

Mommy came to the table and sat down; she eyed me up and down. "You better take up jogging again pretty quick if those shorts are any example of your expansion."

I had to admit they were a bit tight. I had put on at least ten pounds during myself imposed exile, despite the fact I couldn't eat! How the hell do those hermit guys always look so skinny? Probably because they don't drink beer.

"Thanks for noticing, Mommy. I'll get right on it. Right after breakfast." I grabbed a plate and loaded it with bacon, scrambled eggs and two biscuits, which I liberally slathered with butter. "So, what's the special occasion? Usually it's toast around here."

"Your mother heard the shower running," Daddy said and he worked on his own breakfast.

There are no secrets in this house, I thought. "Thanks Mommy," I muttered.

"Well, it's been weeks since you've eaten a hot meal. Besides, I like biscuits too. Hand me that honey pot." She held her hand out.

No fanfare, no *how are you doing*? Are you feeling better, dear? Nope, just pass me the honey and go on a diet. Welcome back to the land of the living, I thought to myself.

I laughed out loud at the memory, pulled the covers up to my chin and snuggled in for a good night's sleep.

Just before I dropped into the Land of Nod, my phone chirped at me. I groped for it, knowing it was a text. It was from Derek: *hey beautiful have a good nite.* Short, sweet and to the point.

U2, I sent back. I sighed and rolled over, but this time with a smile on my face.

7

River of Dreams

At least sleep was my intention, but it was overruled by the dead guy. I was dreaming something pleasant having to do with beaches and boat drinks when I felt myself coming to consciousness. I sensed there was someone with me and cracked one eyelid open. There he stood, Mr. Jon Clayton Kincaid, right at the foot of my bed.

"Gosh," I said, sitting up. "Can't a girl get any sleep around here?"

Mr. Kincaid had no sense of humor, he only glared at me. "Sleep when you're dead!" he snapped. "For now, wake up and listen to me."

A demanding dead guy. None the less, I wiped sleep from my eyes, sat up in my bed and made myself comfortable.

"What can I do for you, Jon?" I asked as I tucked the covers under my armpits.

"I asked for your help to keep Georgia and my kids away from Jonnie and her craziness, not to open some goddamn investigation! You're putting everyone in danger!" he shouted at me.

He stood glaring at me, he was a world champion glarer. I bet when he was living he could intimidate people with his laser look, but he was dead and dead guys don't scare me.

"Well Jon, here's the deal. You are dead. Georgia is alive and she is payin' me to conduct this investigation. So I'm doin' it, okay?" I smiled in what I thought was a very winning way.

Suddenly he was in my face. "Are you insane? Jonnie murdered me and she'll stop at nothing to get my money. Nothing, do you hear? She intends to keep all of it and maybe share some of it with her daughter, but not one dime will go to my kids. Murderers by definition murder people. So, you listen to me, this is how it's going to work…"

I held up one hand at him. "Pal, you need to understand if you don't stop yellin' at me I'm gonna bounce your ass outta here and into the next life so fast it will make your ectoplasmic head spin."

We spent the next few seconds staring at each other. I heard the dogs at the door, sniffing and whining to get in. Great. They obviously thought since I was awake it was time for a midnight raid on the kitchen. To give them credit though, dogs are pretty sensitive and they also probably knew I had a non-corporeal visitor.

"Be realistic, Jon, if your wife murdered you for money then there's a threat to your children," I said reasonably.

"That's exactly what I've been trying to fucking tell you!" he growled at me.

"Jon, there's no reason for bad language. In my opinion, Jonnie is a bigger threat to your children if we don't investigate and get the law involved and put her in jail. She'll always be wonderin' when the kids are gonna come and make trouble for her. She may just decide to kill them to remove the Sword of Damocles from over her head."

"She just wants the goddamned money; as long as she gets her way she'll leave them alone," he snarled.

I was delighted dead guys don't spit when they talk since he was right in my damn face. I was getting very tired of Mr. Kincaid.

"No guarantees there, Jon. My way is better: we prove murder, take her down, your kids are safe and maybe rich to boot. It would help if you could give me more information about how she killed you."

"Were you born stupid or did someone drop you on your god dammed head? I'm telling you to leave this alone and I, by god, mean for you to do it!"

His face was all snarly and his eyes looked mean. But he was still dead. Believe me, brother, it ain't the dead ones you need to worry about, it's the live ones.

"I warned you, Jon." I paused and took a deep breath and intoned. *"Get thee gone now foul one from this place, For this is not your plane or your space, Your plane of reality is near, But it is not now it is not here, I demand get thee gone from my sight, I command you for it is my right!"*

Jon disappeared like a soap bubble.

"Wow," I whispered. "How cool!"

It was even better than revoking a vampire's permission to be in your house. I shook my head at the thought. Who the hell would be dumb enough to invite a vampire in anyway? Good to know Lori was right when she'd given me the incantation with the assurance you could send dead people back to the other side. I'd have to thank her.

I knew Jon would be back but maybe the next time he'd be politer. I reached for my phone and hit 'record' then I documented the entire encounter and dated it. Tomorrow I'd get Jewels to type it up. Luckily, she didn't think I was nuts, at least not about encounters with dead people. By the time I was finished I knew

I wouldn't get back to sleep for a while so I decided to get a snack. I got up and opened my bedroom door and found four very hopeful canines lying in the hall.

"Okay mutts, let's go see what kind of leftovers there are in the fridge."

I started out of my room and realized the dogs weren't following me. They had all gone into my room and were sniffing and poking around. I'd been correct; they did know I had a visitor.

"He's gone, let's go to the kitchen."

Satisfied the room was empty, they all followed me. We trudged down the stairs and I rooted around in the fridge until I found some lasagna. I shut the door and showed my find to the dogs.

"Look here, Mommies' good homemade lasagna. Sit and I'll heat it up."

They sat and I popped a small bowl into the microwave. I retrieved their bowls, threw some kibble in each one. The microwave dinged, I grabbed the lasagna, dropped a spoonful into each bowl, and mixed it up real good. I know dogs should not be given human food but I believed with my little trick they'd think they were getting the same thing I got and not feel mistreated. Sneaky, right? I feel less guilty then if I don't share.

I procured a beer for myself. I hoped the food and the beer might serve to make me sleepy again. Damn Jon Kincaid anyway, I was having a very lovely dream. He seemed the type of guy who was accustomed to telling everyone what to do and getting his own way all the time. Man, I hate guys like that! His boorish behavior made me doubt all the nice things I'd read in his obituary earlier, not as if I'd believed any of them in the first place. I truly wondered if anyone mourned him. Maybe he just pushed his widow too far one day and she killed him in a fit of pique. I took another sip of beer.

If I truly believed his death happened in such a manner then I might have had second thoughts about the investigation, but he seemed so positive Jonnie represented a grave danger to his children.

I polished off the rest of my delicious midnight snack and headed off to bed. The dogs followed me, of course. I'd let them get into the habit of sleeping with me and I didn't have the heart to tell them no. They all piled into my bed and we snuggled down and fell asleep almost immediately.

Despite his banishment, Jon invaded my dreams. I saw a hospital room with a thin, hairless man curled up in the bed in a semi-fetal position, whom appeared to be sleeping. He had wires and tubes running in and out of him and there were several monitors to record his vital signs and send them out to the nurses' station somewhere down the hall. The machines were whirling and clinking and beeping. There was a respirator tube which went down his throat and was secured by tape. The machine made a very distinct noise as it pumped air into Jon's lungs. It was difficult to believe such an emaciated human being could be alive. Judging from his physical appearance, I would bet he weighed less than 80 pounds.

The windows of the room were dark and it felt as though I was looking at a scene which had taken place in the wee small hours of the night. I could practically feel the cold, sterile air which permeates hospitals and nursing homes.

The door to the room opened silently and a nurse with platinum blond hair walked in. She looked back over her shoulder as if to make sure no one had seen her enter the room. She didn't turn on a light but moved straight to the bed. She looked at all the monitors as if she was trying to read them.

The man in the bed stirred.

"Georgia?" He muttered.

The woman gasped and drew back in surprise. Then she leaned in toward the man. "No, not your precious Georgia but Jonnie, your fucking wife." There was venom in her voice.

I knew the man in the bed was Jon. Even though it was difficult to resolve his appearance in the dream to the shade I had seen, I knew. Jon opened his eyes and tried to focus on his wife.

"What? No … surgeries. No more. Let me go. I'm tired, so tired. I won't agree to any more." The words were spaced far apart and his voice was barely above a whisper. The cadence was odd and then I realized he had to speak in time to the respirator which filled his lungs with air. His eyes slid closed again.

"No, no more surgeries for you. I know I promised you before but this time I mean it. There've been a dozen and with each one I hoped you'd die so I could be rid of you and gain some peace. But you just keep living; I mean what the hell does it take to kill you?" she snarled at him.

"You hate me?" Jon didn't open his eyes this time; his voice was an even softer whisper. "Soon gone, soon now." he gasped.

"To answer your question, yes I hate you. You are a prick, a womanizer, a gambler and a bully. I can't wait any longer for you to die, dear husband, I have plans and I want everything coming to me. Really, Jon, why couldn't you cooperate and just die? I thought the last surgery would take you out, but no you're still here to vex me. I mean, you can't eat, you can't shit, you can't breathe, why are you still here?" The woman leaned close to him and her face was twisted with hate.

Jon didn't move or speak for several seconds. "Soon." he breathed.

"Not soon enough, now the doctors want to try some new experimental stem cell bullshit and want me to okay it. If I don't say yes, it'll look bad, as if I don't want to help prolong your precious life. I can't have the neighbors talking or have dear Anna think I don't want to help you. Poor little thing, she loves you so. God alone knows why. And what if it actually works? I can't take a chance."

"But you begged me to get the surgeries." Each word cost him strength and energy, I could tell.

"I hoped you'd die on the table, but no, just like in everything else, you disappointed me. And oh yes Jon, I know what you asked the nurse. Did you think I wouldn't find out? Do you think these people who work here don't know which side their fucking bread is buttered on? Did you think Little Nurse Big Teats would actually call your lawyer without going through me?" Her voice was by turns seductively silky and then sharp and hateful. The effect was weird and creepy.

Jon opened his eyes but they were unfocused and rheumy, a dying man's eyes. "The will." He seemed to be concentrating on the woman and suddenly his eyes focused. "Why are you dressed like that?"

"I'm thinking of changing professions. I know you want to change the will, but it's not going to happen. I didn't put up with your sorry ass all these years to have to share your assets."

She padded to the IV hanging from a pole by Jon's bed. She pulled a hypodermic needle out of her pocket and removed the protective cap.

"Don't worry Jon, this won't hurt a bit." She emptied the needle into the reservoir and stepped back. "This is a mercy after all you've suffered. You should thank me. I signed a DNR for you, Jon, so you don't have to worry about being brought back." She sounded positively cheerful.

Jon looked at the tube which would bring the fatal dose of medication into his body and reached for the needle in his arm. Jonnie covered his paper-thin hand with her own to keep him from pulling the needle out. He was too weak to resist her and he went limp as if the effort has just about used him up.

"I'm ready. Promise you'll deal with my children fairly." His speech was slurred and slow.

The drug she had added to the IV was taking effect. Jon closed his eyes but the machines continued to whisper and click around him, the respirator kept pumping air into his lungs.

"Oh, don't you worry, Jon, I will certainly take care of your children if they cross me." She smiled a positively wicked smile.

She pocketed the hypodermic and slipped out of the room. Jon wasn't dead when she left but he would never wake either. A few minutes later the machines which filled the room began to whoop and send signals to the nurses' station informing them Jon had left the world. It was still dark outside. I had read an article somewhere which claimed most terminally ill patients died in the middle of the night.

I opened my eyes and lay there in the darkness of my room, feeling the warm comfort of dog bodies around me.

"Holy shit!" I whispered.

On the Road Again

I must have dropped off to sleep at some point after my dream because when the sun hit my window and the dogs began to stir I felt as if I had gotten some ZZZs. How the hell I fell asleep after such a dream, I cannot begin to tell you. I was still creeped out by it even with the sun up. What a piece of work Jonnie Kincaid was, a murdering, crazy piece of work. It never occurred to me to doubt the truth of the dream. It just felt right.

I had to wonder what Jon had ever done to her to piss her off so bad. She was vicious to him. How could anyone speak that way to such a pitiable human being? How could anyone murder him, or anyone, in cold blood? Of course, I didn't know the whole story; Jon could have bedded her sister, stolen family heirlooms, traded her dog for a shotgun, and yes, I do know someone who actually did all those things. I admitted my dislike of Jon Kincaid, I found him to be overbearing, obnoxious and arrogant. Those were his good traits. Of course, none of those traits were reason to kill a man in the middle of the night. I didn't know the whole story, but I was pretty sure I could find out.

I let the dogs out of my room and got through my morning ablutions in record time. I took the stairs two at a time to the kitchen. Mommy, Daddy and YaYa were having breakfast. I grinned at them.

"Mornin'. I'm just gonna grab a piece of toast, got a long day ahead of me." I reached for a slice of toast and Mommy slapped my hand.

"All the more reason you should start the day out right. Sit and eat, you can take five minutes," she said.

As long as I could remember the rule in my home had been breakfast first. None of us had ever been allowed to leave with an empty belly. I guess some things never change, even with only the four of us in the house. I'm not even sure why I thought I could slide by. She was right too; everything would keep for the fifteen minutes it would take me to eat a decent meal.

"You're right," I admitted.

"Of course she is," said YaYa. "Now how do you want your eggs?"

I had my two eggs fried sunny side up, with a rasher of bacon, and two pieces of toast. I would run it off later, I promised myself. Truth to tell once you get out of the habit of exercise, it's damn hard to get back into it. Ever since my self-imposed exile the running had become rather hit or miss. I swore to myself to do better as my waistband cut into my tummy.

"What's the big hurry this morning?" Daddy asked as he passed me the coffee pot. "You look like your chomping at the bit to get out of here."

"And you're dressed real nice too," YaYa added.

Like I never dressed nice! I was dressed to impress today in my black linen pantsuit, red silk blouse, minimal gold jewelry, with a black bag and shoes to match. I thought I looked almost as good as Mars always looked. Which reminded me I needed to call her.

"Well Moira and Mars dragged me to the Neon Candle the other night and I ended up with a client who wants me to investigate the murder of her ex-husband." I mopped up egg yolks with toast.

"Tessely, I don't like for you to investigate such things. It's not safe, as you found out to your sorrow," Mommy said. "You almost got yourself killed the last time you tangled with murderers."

I didn't think this was a fair statement since I'd tried every way in the world to stay alive but thought better of saying so.

"Yeah," agreed YaYa. "Can't ya' find a nice embezzler to capture, or some guys runnin' a Ponzi scheme? Or thugs who are taking advantage of helpless little old ladies like me. Those are always nice." She smiled into her coffee cup.

I grinned and my father did too. I heard him mutter, "Helpless, my ass."

We knew YaYa was giving Mommy a hard time. Mommy didn't seem to know it though.

"Good Lord above, Mother, how can you say such a thing? That's not what I meant." Mommy complained.

"No, what you meant was you would like for me to give up my chosen profession, find something safer which does not involve me carryin' a gun, maybe meet a nice guy and settle down. A bonus would be a few more grandkids for you and Daddy, as if you don't have enough already. You do know the world is over-populated, right?" I buttered my toast a bit too enthusiastically.

I was working hard not to get annoyed. We'd gone round and round on this many times before. This was the downside to living in the same house with family. Sometimes you don't get to eat breakfast in peace.

"And what is wrong with that, may I ask? You love chil-dren. Why not a nice normal job where you would be home at five-o-clock and no one tried to kill you on any given day? Is that so much for a mother to ask?" Now the theatrics; her voice went up a notch.

"No, Mommy, it isn't, but if I took a nice safe job, married a nice safe guy, had a couple of nice, fat babies, I'd bore the hell out of you."

Mommy squinted her eyes at me. I knew she worried about my lifestyle, but I was pretty happy doing what I did.

I grinned at her. "You wouldn't love me if I was borin'."

She just shook her head. "I give up, you're hopeless."

She waved a hand at me in dismissal. Twenty minute later I was out the door and on my way to the office. Sometimes it was a pain in the ass side to living at home when you were my age, but in my mind the perks far outweighed the cons. How in the world could I keep four dogs if I lived somewhere else?

My thoughts rolled over from my breakfast conversation to the dream from the night before. Soon, I was replaying the damn dream in my head as I drove. It was chilling. I had to agree with Jon, his widow was a threat and maybe crazy and maybe evil. I got the impression she was bound and determined to keep every dime of the money left to her and no one was going to get in her way. No one but little ol' me.

I hit the office loaded for bear.

"Morning Glory," I said cheerfully to Jewels.

"Morning Boss, you have three messages, they all look like potential work and one message from Ms. Kincaid. Seems she has more information for you." She waved slips of paper at me.

"Okay, I'll call her first. No, I'll call the others first and we can start work on them. Let's make hay while the sun shines." I grabbed the messages from her and headed into my office.

"Coffee?" Jewels called after me.

"Yes please."

I looked over the messages. A shopkeeper wanted a camera installed in his business because he suspected some sticky employee fingers. An insurance company wanted surveillance run on a workman's comp case. Last but not least, a woman wanted her husband tailed; she believed he had a girlfriend. I marked them all with an affirmative and handed them to Jewels as she brought my coffee.

"Ah, thanks, Jewels. They all look good to me."

"Great, I'll call them and arrange payment. Are you sure you're not taking on more than you can handle at once?"

"That's why I have you." I smiled sweetly.

She smiled back and left me to my own devices. I decided I'd finish the task of finding the last will and testament of Mr. Jon Kincaid. I was really curious about the contents. Georgia had given me all the pertinent information on Jon, so I punched in his social security number, date of birth, even his driver's license number. For a moment, I wondered how she had such info since they had been divorced for several years. Never underestimate the power and determination of a woman scorned. It didn't take long to find what I needed. Bingo! It had gone to probate.

I scanned through the document and it all seemed rather cut and dry; all worldly goods as well as oversight of his businesses went to his beloved wife, some personal effects to his step-daughter, $100,000 to the church. Not all wills state the monetary worth of the deceased but this one did. When I got to the part about the worth and value of said properties, my head nearly popped off!

There was *a lot* of money – roughly $100,000,000.00. One hundred million good reasons to kill someone. Holy Cats! Nowhere in the document was there even a mention of the biological children of Jon Kincaid, they got zilch. The will was dated a decade earlier and had been amended several times to add different figures and properties. The beneficiary had never been changed as far as I could tell, although after my midnight movie it sure seemed Jon had *intended* to make changes. The money trail led back to Jonnie Kincaid without a doubt. Now the question was how the hell I could prove she'd murdered her husband. Somebody somewhere had to talk to me, somebody not dead.

I knocked down my coffee while I packed my PI kit. It consists of a hundred dollars in cash, a camera with a telephoto lens, a night vision lens, a tiny spy cam, my Nikon, a pair of handcuffs, extra ammo clips, a lock pick set, a glass cutting tool, a netbook, a fully charged burner phone, a Taser also fully charged, a miner's light, a pair of binoculars, a canister of mace, a floppy hat, three pair of sunglasses, an extra tee-shirt, a wrinkle-resistant outfit, a clean pair of underwear, toothbrush, toothpaste, and deodorant in case I had to spend the night some place.

I was wearing my Beretta under my left arm in my fancy leather tooled holster which I'd won at the Medicine Springs street fair last year; man, I just love my holster. I retrieved my Walther PPK from my bottom drawer and stowed it in my bag. When I'm on a job I always carry an extra gun, just seems prudent. My little Taurus 738 TCP .380 ACP was in the desk, so I strapped on an ankle holster and tucked it inside. It's pink, you can laugh if you want. My brother Dugal gave it to me on my birthday as a joke, but it will put seven holes in you sure as sun rise. A girl can't be too careful. Besides, no one suspects an ankle holster or a pink gun.

I carried my dirty cup to Jewels. She looked up and saw my kit.

"So, where ya' goin'?" she asked.

"Atlanta. I need to start poking around and it seems like a good place to start. Besides, it is a beautiful day for a drive. I probably won't be home 'til tomorrow."

She opened her desk drawer and pulled out a credit card. "You'll need this."

"I'll guard the company card with my life. I'll also call home and tell them what I'm doin' so they won't bug hell out of you." I smiled.

"And you'll be careful."

"I am always careful." She rolled her eyes at me and turned back to her computer. "See you tomorrow."

"You better." she said to her computer screen.

It really was a beautiful day for a drive, the sun was shining and the road ahead looked clear of traffic. I could make it through Nashville and to Atlanta before either city experienced rush hour if I hurried. I was good at hurrying. My plan was to get through traffic and then hang out until shift change at the rehab center, less people to deal with at that time of day. I punched the Bluetooth.

"Say a command," it intoned at me.

"Home," I said. The beeps of the number being dialed sounded in my ear, the phone rang three times and YaYa answered.

"Maher residence."

"YaYa, it's Tess."

"Un huh, and what are you up on this beautiful morning?"

I grinned. "I am up to making an honest living and I wanted to let y'all know I'm on the road to Atlanta and won't be back until tomorrow. I wanna check out the rehab center where my client's ex-husband died."

"Rehab? Was he a dope fiend?"

I chuckled out loud. "I don't think so, YaYa; it's not that kind of a rehab. It's a center for physical rehabilitation."

"Oh well that's not nearly as interestin' then is it? You gonna tell me everything when you get back? You know I live vicariously through you." She chuckled in an evil manner.

"Sure you do, and I can only tell what my client allows me to tell as you well know so don't go tryin' to worm secrets outta me," I warned her.

"Hmmph. You be careful, girly girl, and keep your nose clean."

"Yes ma'am." I saluted even though she couldn't see me. "I love you and I'll see you tomorrow, tell Mommy please."

"Of course I'll tell her and I love you too. Don't pick up no hitch hikers." She hung up without saying good-bye. She never does.

I punched in Sirius to an 80's station and sang with Pat Benatar as I drove. The road to Atlanta was long but uneventful, exactly as I liked all road trips to be. An hour outside of the city I set my GPS for the Marietta Rehab and Therapy Center, and found it without any false stops or detours. I love GPS; it's one of my very favorite things in the entire world right after sex and chocolate.

I pulled into the parking lot, shut off the Jeep, and surveyed the building. It was a single story non-descript drab yellowish colored brick utilitarian building probably built in the 1960's. It had absolutely nothing to recommend it, architecturally speaking. The landscaping was without imagination and drab as well. I checked out the front entrance and didn't see a guard. A definite plus for me. I intended to do several illegal things in that building and the absence of security gave my spirits a lift. I didn't relish the thought of getting busted in Atlanta. Happily for me, I'd made good time, so I settled in to wait for the mass exodus of most of the employees as they headed for home.

I pulled out my laptop and got a little work done while I waited.

Name Game

The flow of people leaving the building finally dwindled off and stopped. I observed the administrator getting into her car. I knew it was her not from deduction but because the parking place was marked 'administrator.' Convenient, right? As she drove away I put my game face on, climbed out of the car and wandered into the building. There was a command center placed twenty feet inside the front door and I approached with a smile.

"How are you? My name is Carole Jackson and I am supposed to get a tour of this facility this evening," I said cheerfully and with a much thicker Southern accent than usual.

Clothes are the first impression you give another person, so I dress the part for whatever I'm doing. Today I wanted to look like I had money, was accustomed to people doing my bidding, and didn't take no for an answer. I had worn my power suit to inspire awe, to make me look serious and business like. My hair was pulled into a chignon at the back of my neck, which made me look rather severe. My normal straight as stick strawberry blonde hair wouldn't fool anyone with sophistication so it had to be disguised.

The woman behind the desk stared at me with her mouth open and a quizzical look on her round pale doughy face.

"Ah," she ventured. "Ah … do you have an appointment?"

I cocked my head to one side and smiled.

She batted her small brown eyes as me and looked rather like a frog in a hail storm. She wore a name tag decorated in balloons which stated 'Hi My Name is Rose.' Good, I thought, names are useful. You can make a person feel comfortable with you when you call them by name and you can use the comfort you create to get information. Or you can be very commanding by using their name thus making them feel subservient and again getting what you want from him or her. The predilection of American companies who force their workers to wear nametags has made life so much easier for people like me.

Important safety tip: This idea does not necessarily apply to people who work in restaurants because those people have a tendency to wear each other's name tags.

I smiled bigger. "Why yes I do. I made it last week. Y'all come highly recommended and I need a place for my grandmother, she broke a hip and needs to get rehabbed." I waited and allowed the panic to set in.

"Oh Lordy, let me, ah, call, ah, somebody."

She grabbed the phone and punched in a number, then turned and wrapped her hand around the receiver. I supposed she didn't want me to hear her conversation, but as I was standing only two feet from her I wasn't sure how covering the phone helped.

"Nan, where's Ms. Thombs?" She listened for a moment. "There's a lady out here and she says she has an appointment to look at the place." She listened some more. "Well I didn't see her leave, I was in the bathroom." Another pause while Rose's face got redder and redder. "You're supposed to keep up with her damn appointments so how is this my fault?" Rose hissed through clenched teeth. Then she nodded vigorously and hung up the phone. She smiled a rather forced and sickly smile at me. "It seems Ms. Thombs has left for the day. I was wonderin' if you could come back tomorrow."

I drew up in mock outrage.

"Gone home?" I huffed. "How is such incompetence possible? We had an appointment!" I let my voice get louder on each word and Rose began to sweat.

"Please ma'am, could you please come back in the mornin'? I don't think she has any appointments then," Rose pleaded with me.

"I drove a long way to get here and now YOU want me to turn around and go home, then drive all this way again tomorrow? Do you think I have nothing else to do? There must be someone here who can walk me around the place! Why can't you do it?" I put my hands on my hips and waited. I scowled too.

"Well, well, ah, I could. Let me get some help on this desk." She snatched up the phone and called the still invisible Nan. "Nan, could you please come up here and watch the desk while I give this lady a tour?"

She lowered her voice to a whisper. "'Cause she is madder'n a wet hen, that's why. Now you come on."

Rose turned and smiled at me, it was a smile which clearly said she thought I was gonna eat her, bless her heart. Honestly, I don't like being mean, but sometimes you just have no choice if you're going to get things done.

"Someone will be here in just a jiffy to relieve me and I'll show you everything," Rose practically stuttered.

Maybe I'd missed my profession and should have gone on the stage. It seemed I was one hell of an actress. I tapped my foot while I waited to show my annoyance, but I kept my eyes peeled for Nan. I really wanted to know which direction she came from, since I surmised it would be the direction of the offices I wanted to get into. Within a minute Nan appeared looking annoyed, it must be catching. She was tall and thin with a pinched face; she looked like she sucked on lemons as a hobby. Her hair was pulled back in a very tight ponytail, which probably gave her a headache, and she was dressed in colorful scrubs. When did someone decide grown women should wear surgical scrubs with clouds and lollypops on them? I frowned at her and she frowned back.

"It's after seven-o-clock and I was supposed to go home two hours ago ya' know." She emphasized the 'seven-o-clock.' She got no sympathy from me.

"This'll only take a few minutes. If Cindy gets here, let her take over for you, okay?"

Rose didn't wait for an answer but escaped from behind the desk and motioned me down the hall to the left.

"Down this hall are the patient rooms. I'll show you an empty one," she offered.

We stopped at a room and Rose pushed open the door and snapped on a light. The room was about what I had expected: beige paint, beige blinds, a television suspended on the wall, two hospital beds, two chests of drawers, an uninspired picture on the wall behind each bed, a fluorescent light over each bed with a pull cord and two closets. Rose walked over to the bathroom and flipped on the light. The room came equipped with hand rails and shower also with rails.

"Very nice," I commented.

I didn't mean it; the room was depressing as hell. I felt sorry for anyone who ended up there. Why didn't they put the people who worked in the place in beige and paint the rooms with clouds and lollypops? What a world of difference it would create.

We exited the room and continue down the hall. All was quiet since it was past dinner and the patients were all in their rooms doing whatever it was patients did in their rooms.

"This is the dayroom," Rose announced as if she was so proud of the place.

She even swept her hand from side to side just like Vanna White. Again, there was not much to write home about, chairs, tables, decks of cards, a big screen television and a piano. There were windows on two sides so at least there was plenty of sunlight during the day. It was still beige. Rose and I walked through the dayroom and down another hall.

"This is where all the rehab facilities are," Rose opened the first door of many and flipped on the lights. I saw all manner of exercise equipment and rails to help a person to walk. There was even a little set of steps with rails.

"Well this is impressive, Rose," I allowed my manner thaw a bit. "This looks like everything necessary to get a person back on her feet."

"Oh, we have more," she gushed.

She motioned me back into the hallway and we checked out other rooms. There were more exercise machines, a hot tub room, and a large room with walkers on wheels and a track laid out around the room.

"They all love this room, sometimes they race," Rose giggled.

I gave her a little smile, which was hard to do as her words had conjured a rather grim picture in my minds' eye of geriatric patients in robes and slippers shuffling around the room in hot pursuit of one another. Rose positively beamed at me; she was so happy I wasn't mad anymore. I felt a bit guilty playing her.

"So, Rose, how many people are working here?"

"Um, well, let me think, on day shift three nurses, two rehab specialists, ten aides, a doctor, me and Ms. Thombs."

"And at night?"

"Well, of course after dinner all the residents retire to their rooms to sleep or watch TV or some other activity to occupy their time until bed. So we have someone on the desk, one nurse, and one tech." She rolled her eyes up to her brow trying to make the count correct.

"Such a tiny number of personal can maintain care for how many patients?"

"Residents, we call them residents it helps them feel they'll get well and be able to go home one day. We only need a few people on the night shift 'cause everyone is sleepin'. You can get a lot of readin' done here at night, students love the night shift. We usually have 120 residents at any given time." She smiled as if she were being brilliant.

"Well that's a plus. Do you make regular rounds just in case something might happen? Or do you have the residents monitored?"

"We only have a few residents that are monitored and those are the ones whose conditions are very severe and well, quite frankly, there's a good chance they might die durin' the night. We don't have a lot of those kinds of residents, but we have a few. Usually if they drop down to that low a level of wellness, we have them transferred to a different kind of facility."

"So, if I put my grandmother here, she would be given a program of treatment and exercise to help her to recover from a broken hip?" I asked.

"Oh yes," Rose positively gushed. "She'd be evaluated and a complete blueprint of treatment would be created for her. We'll have her getting around on her own in no time flat, just you wait and see."

She motioned for me to head back the way we had come and so I fell into step with her.

When we got back to the reception area I walked past it, nodded to someone who was not the lemon faced Nan and stood at the entrance to the hallway. "Rose, what's down the other hall or wing?"

"Oh, that's the administrative offices, nurse's station, the kitchen, our dining room, storage, you know all the things a place like this needs to function."

"Right." I knew where I needed to go on my little quest and I would the first chance I got.

"Are the residents' rooms under any kind of surveillance? I know my grandmother wouldn't like it one little bit. She's a very private person."

"Only the severely ill, as we discussed. They have monitors that feed information into the nurse's station," Rose assured me.

Jon Kincaid had certainly dropped below the normal infirmity for the place and yet he hadn't been moved. I was sure I knew why; the place was easy to get into and out of if you had shenanigans planned.

I was coming to like Rose more and more since she was so helpful in telling me the things I needed to know. We walked back to the front desk way back to the reception area. A young rather gothic looking girl who was reading what appeared to be a text book looked up. She was pretty even with her dyed black hair cut in a sort of punk and spiky style plus ten times too much make-up. I was positive there were tats under her clothes; she wore the obligatory lollipop festooned scrubs but she also wore a long sleeve shirt under them.

She smiled. "Hope you had a good tour, Nan told me you were here. I'm Cindy."

She didn't look like a Cindy; she needed a cool Goth name, I thought.

"My friends call me 'Sin'."

Okay, so she did have a Goth name.

"Hello Sin, spelled with an 'S' unless I miss my guess." I smiled and she seemed surprised. "The tour was great and I am sold on this place."

I was too, no lie. It had no security, the camera at the reception desk was a crappy one. The camera was a direct feed but wasn't actually recording. There were almost no night time personnel to clutter the placed up, and only one nurse making rounds. It was a B&E wet dream!

"Is there a ladies'?" I asked.

"Oh sure," said Sin.

Both she and Rose pointed down the hall, the very place I wanted to be, excellent. I wandered down the hall and the potty was immediately on my right, so I took a chance and quietly slid further down the hall. There was the administrator's office, what looked like storage closets and a room with light emanating from it. I figured that was the nurse's station and sure enough I was right. An African American woman in the obligatory cutesy scrubs looked up from her romance novel and stared at me. Her hair was slicked back into a very tight bun and even with the lolly-pops and clouds on her shirt she did not look cheerful. This was not the nurse I'd seen in my dream, she was not little or young or cute and sadly she did not have big breasts. Those might have helped what I perceived as her over all bad mood. I stopped at her door and tried to look puzzled. She quickly lowered the book as if she didn't want me to see the title.

"May I help you?" Her voice was chilly.

I put on my embarrassed face. "Oh, I've been touring your fine facility and had to tee-tee, I think I just got turned around when I came out."

I smiled like an idiot. I scanned the room around her, there were telemetry machines lining the back wall. There were two other decks present in the room. One was a very practical and business-like look. The other desk was festooned with pictures and stuffed animals and other knick-knacks. I checked the name tags carefully, trying not to arouse the suspicions of the woman in front of me. The highly decorated desk bore the name plaque of Lillian Perkins. Bingo!

"The front door's that way." She hooked a thumb back up the hallway. She did not smile back. Well you can't charm 'em all I thought.

"Thank you so much," I looked at her name tag, "Gina Reese, you've been very helpful."

I did an about face and walked away but I bet her nose was back in her book before I had gone two steps. I stopped and actually hit the loo. I knew I'd better do it right then since there was no way to know how long I'd have to wait before I got back in the place to do my dirty work. I've found a full bladder is distracting when one is trying to be sneaky. Besides one should not stop for a potty break in the middle of an illegal search.

Back at the reception desk, I said my good-byes and took my leave. I think Rose was relieved when I walked out the door even though she was smiling and waving at me. I got into the Jeep and pulled around the corner so I could watch the parking lot and see when the extremely helpful Rose took her leave.

Waiting is when I always regret giving up cigarettes. The waiting on a stake-out is mind numbing and boring. You can't read or play on your phone; you have to watch the freakin' target. Smoking helped to relieve the tedium. On the plus side, I would no doubt live longer and there was no little red burning ember or smoke to give my position away. Everything has its ups and downs.

Fortunately, I didn't have to wait long. Within five minutes Rose came walking out of the building, climbed into a late model burgundy Honda and took off into the night. I pulled back into the parking lot without bothering to turn my headlights on and parked so I could see straight in to the reception desk. There sat Sin hunched over her book, nothing else moved and the night was settling in and growing darker. I settled in and got comfortable. Sooner or later Sin would abandon her post and I could slip into the building, but it might be a long wait.

It was almost an hour before my Goth girl stood up, stretched and came out the front door. I hunkered down so she wouldn't see me. She looked both ways in a rather furtive motion and took off down the front of the building and disappeared around the corner. She had her hand in her pocket as she walked; she was going for a smoke break. I knew it! I gave her a full 60 seconds to get to her smoking spot, pull out a cigarette, light it and take that first drag. As I counted 'sixty-one elephants', I tucked my pick set, phone, camera and miner's light in my pockets. I jumped out of the Jeep and walked straight in the front door like I owned the damn place.

I have found if you act as though you belong where ever you are and you know exactly what you are doing, usually no one challenges you. I took the hallway to the right, snapped on my gloves and picked the lock to Ms. Thombs office in under thirty seconds. I am good. Once inside, I relocked the door, put the picks in my pocket and put my miner's light on my forehead. I love the thing; it allows me the use of both hands when I'm in a place where I have no business being. Happens a lot more often than you might think. There was a bit of light coming in from the street lights which was good, it made my job even easier. The desk was on my right side. There was a row of filing cabinets on the left. Apparently, this facility had not yet come into the 21th century.

Here I thought I was gonna have to hack into a computer. Going through physical files was only slightly less illegal. I grinned. The cabinets were locked, of course, but again I own a top notch set of picks. I figured I'd find files on deceased patients somewhere in the cabinets, but not knowing the filing system I had to go through each drawer. I kept an ear open for footsteps in the hall, but I wasn't worried. After all, the last time I'd broken into an office I had two murdering goons to put the fear of God in me. This time I only had a nurse and a Goth chick to worry about. No contest.

I found the employee files first and thumbed through it until I found Nurse Perkins. It was only one page so I pulled out my tiny spy camera and snapped a picture. I returned the file to the drawer, and the camera to my pocket. The deceased file was in the last file cabinet, go figure. I flipped through the files and found Jon Kincaid. I carried the file to the desk and pulled out my handy dandy spy camera, I wanted every page of that file. I could carry the pictures back to the office and examine them at my leisure which reduced my chances of getting caught flat-footed. I was snapping and flipping pages when I heard footsteps. I froze.

The footsteps passed me by and I heard an annoyed voice mutter, "Where the fuck is that damn girl?"

Gina had discovered Sin was taking a smoke break. Crap. I snapped faster. I'd just finished my task and replaced the file when I heard voices, loud voices, an argument was happening. I crept to the door and cracked it just a smidge. Sure enough, the ladies were having words at the front desk.

"I don't give a shit how bad your nic fit was, you left the place wide open," Gina said angrily.

"Look Gina, what the hell do you think is gonna happen around here? Nothing. Cause nothing ever happens around here. They're all snug in their beds, dreaming of sugar plums. No one thinks to steal drugs from a nursing home since we mostly have Bengay and Ex-lax, so really what's your drama? You workin' for Homeland Security now?"

"Don't you get smart with me, missy, I'll have you outta here on your tattooed ass before you can say 'scat', you got me? Now park yourself in that seat and make sure no one carries the place off while I make sure no one's dead," Gina snapped.

"Fuck you," Sin snapped back.

I couldn't see any of this but I very clearly heard it because it was loud. I guess the girls weren't worried about waking anyone up.

I heard footsteps coming my way. I closed the door and held my breath. The bathroom door swung open and hit the wall, which was my cue to vamoose. I returned the file to the cabinet, stuck all my spy stuff in my pockets and eased out of the room.

I rounded the corner toward the welcome desk and ran right into Nurse Gina who was coming back up the hall. Damn! She made some seriously speedy rounds! She was no less startled to see me.

"What are you doing still here?" She snapped.

"Oh, I had to come back." I could feel sweat forming on my scalp, I needed to get out and fast. "I got down the road and realized I'd left my cell phone in the bathroom." I pulled the phone out of my pocket and held it up to show her. "Thank goodness I needed to call my sister or I might've gone all the way home before I realized what I'd done. Silly me, Daddy always said I'd forget my head if it wasn't stuck on my shoulders." I smiled.

She narrowed her eyes at me and I could tell she was thinking something was smelly in the state of Georgia but she wasn't sure just what.

"Well, I'm so behind schedule, I need to run, thanks for everything," I said cheerfully.

I walked past her and scooted out the door, but not too fast. I didn't run but I didn't drag my feet either. I knew I was only a phone call away from getting arrested or at least detained. I sincerely hoped the lure of her romance novel over powered Gina's suspicion of me and she and Sin were too pissed at each other to compare notes. I was leaving the city limits of Atlanta before I relaxed and released the breath I'd been holding.

My original thought had been to find a motel and bed down for the night, but after my little adventure, I decided to put as much highway between me and Atlanta as possible. I drove on through the night.

10

We are Family

The next morning dawned bright and much too early. I rolled over and pulled the covers over my head, not desiring to rise or to shine. I'd driven many miles, pumped huge amounts of adrenalin through my system, only had a power bar and a bottle of water for dinner and supper, and too much coffee. My body hated me. There was only one cure: a run.

I dragged myself up and threw on some running clothes. The dogs met me at the bottom of the stairs.

"Fine, come on you lot," I told them. I looked around the corner into the kitchen. "Going for a run, don't drink all the coffee."

They all waved and away I went. An hour later my ass was dragging and I cursed my laziness. It seemed like it was taking me forever to get back into shape. I noticed Chelsea's car in the drive and could hear my three-year-old niece, Alexandra, as I neared the house.

"Me, where pups? Wanna see pups," Alexandra's squeaky little girl voice asked.

The grandchildren all called Mommy and Daddy 'Me and De'. It started with Kevin the oldest grandchild who couldn't say shit with a mouth full and the names just stuck. I opened the kitchen door and the dogs swarmed Alexandra who squealed a high-pitched glass breaking squeal only little girls can achieve. I was laughing as I entered the kitchen.

"Hey Chelsea." I hugged my lovely sister-in-law. She is small and petite with light green eyes, short, curly light brown hair and a heart shaped face with a cute turned up nose. I liked her a lot.

Chelsea grinned at me. "Well, Alex wanted to come see the puppies, and all y'all of course."

"Yeah right. Who'd you come to see, Alex?" I asked.

The three-year-old, who is a tiny version of her mother except for hair color, was sitting in the floor with the dogs slobbering all over her.

"Pups," she exclaimed with a big smile.

I laughed again and headed for the fridge. I needed water. "Is there coffee left?" I asked and swigged some H2O, ah God it was good.

"Yes," said Mommy, "I made a fresh pot as soon as the girls pulled up."

I weighed my breakfast choices; tomatoes, cantaloupe, yogurt. I gathered it all up and carried it to the table.

"Do you want me to fix you something?" Mommy asked.

"No ma'am I do not, I need to drop five more pounds in the worst possible way. Hmm … I think I will boil an egg and maybe have some cheese too."

As I added to my breakfast I asked Chelsea, "So how are the other monsters?"

"Oh, everybody's fine. Bridget's going to take communion next month you know and she's very excited and nervous." Chelsea smiled a sweet proud momma smile at me.

I remembered my own First Communion experience, it was nerve racking as hell. We have a small, rural Catholic church, St. Mary's, in Medicine Springs. The school is tiny, but we do have our very own nuns. The Communion candidates are taught the Catholic Catechism and doctrine and theology to boot. Nuns are perfectionists especially when children have to stand up in church and recite. We had to memorize the correct answers to all the catechism questions, since Father would randomly ask questions of us on the big day. We had to stand in line, march in line, sit in front of the church, not wiggle, or giggle, or pick our noses, or fart, and walk up to the priest with everyone in the church looking at us. The worst part was swallowing the communion host without gagging or spitting it out, it's dry and tasteless. We had to practice choking down the host, with an unconsecrated wafer. It was hard work for a seven-year-old. I remember thinking I was going to faint or throw up. Fortunately, I did neither.

"James is seven, too, right? And Ashley? So are they receiving communion as well?" I asked.

YaYa chuckled. "Ashley and Bridget did a rock, paper, scissors game to see who would go this year. Bridget won and Ashley was a good sport. She'll wait until next year."

I paused in my yogurt frenzy. "Why?"

"The dress," Mommy said.

Oh, *THE DRESS*. I nodded my understanding of the situation. The dress was my mother's dress. She wore it at her First Communion, and all of the girls in the family, her sisters, my sisters and I had worn it for First Communion too. YaYa had created the dress. Funny how it didn't look dated even thought it was made in America damn near sixty years ago, from nylon and rayon with a thousand tiny pleats in the skirt and in the very wide collar. Even the lace on the sleeves and around the collar was still perfect. The sash had been replaced many times over the years and each girl received her very own veil as a keepsake, made by YaYa. Unbelievably the dress didn't show either its age or any wear and tear. Of course, it had been worn a grand total of eleven times and it was wrapped up and put away in the cedar chest after each outing. Hell, it might be around for the next generation.

The boys had a tradition too. They each wore Daddy's First Communion pin on their lapels. They got their own pin as well and Daddy's went back into the jewelry box for the next boy. Truth to tell mostly the boys just wanted the ceremony over and done with so they could get their presents and have a party.

For the girls, it was like prom or a wedding and the dress made the day. The dress was precious and amazing. It made you feel holy and beautiful, like you were marrying Jesus. I grinned at the memory.

"What are you thinking?" Daddy asked.

"Thinkin' 'bout the dress." I laughed and my family joined in. "Well, looks like a shoppin' trip to the city is in order."

Our little country church had a small gift shop where we could probably find the white rosary and prayer book which all Catholic children received for their special day. I felt sure Father Bill Sherman had stocked up. However, I usually went to St. Mary's book store in Nashville and bought a First Communion boy or girl porcelain doll. The dolls were dressed in First Communion finery and they were all beautiful. Thankfully the store carried dolls with red hair. Each doll even had its very own rosary as well.

"Actually, I was gonna ask Mommy and YaYa if they'd like to make a shoppin' trip for shoes, and socks and the lace for the veil. I thought we could make a day of it and have lunch while we're out." Chelsea looked hopeful.

"We'd love to!" Mommy said.

"When?" YaYa asked.

"I was thinkin' about Saturday. Dugal can be home with the kids and there wouldn't be a need to rush. We could take our time, and we haven't had a visit in a good long time. I know that's your Bingo day though, YaYa."

Mommy looked at Daddy.

"Nothing going on here," he said. "Except maybe a little yard work."

"Saturday it is then." Mommy grinned.

She loved shopping more than most humans loved a good steak. I felt sure she would pick shopping over world peace. It would be close, but shopping would win.

"Count me in, Bingo can wait 'til next week, Mae can ride up on the bus to Kentucky without me," YaYa chimed in with enthusiasm.

Her usual Saturday ritual was a bus ride with her friend Mae Green to a bingo place over the state line. They were vicious and competitive players who usually came home flush with cash, not to mention many great stories about how they defeated the other players. It was a big deal for YaYa to give it up even for First Communion; she'd be the talk of the bus trip on Saturday.

Alexandra had grown tired of the dogs and them of her so she climbed up in the chair next to me and eyed my food.

"TisTis, you gonna eat all da lope?" There was hope in her bright blue eyes.

"Moocher." I grinned and handed her a slice.

She took it in her chubby little hands and bit a piece out of the middle. She looked at me and grinned as she chewed.

"Good stuff, huh?" I asked and she nodded.

I polished off the rest of my breakfast with Alex's help as the relatives made plans for the shopping excursion. Well, the female members planned and Daddy ignored them. I had already planned my trip in my head; I'd go to Nashville, buy dolls, have dinner and then wild monkey sex with Derek. It was a twofer. What can I say? I'm a multi-tasker. I had to ask myself if it was irreverent for me to plan for wild monkey sex on a trip to buy First Communion dolls. The answer was no.

"Family, I love you but I gotta go to work, so I'm off to the showers," I announced.

Of course, it's never easy to take leave of my family. There is kissing and hugging which must be done first. Alex stood up in her chair and cupped my face in her sticky little hands.

"You bes caresful TisTis, 'ders bad peoples inna world." She was so solemn.

I felt tear prick my eyes. She remembered I'd been hurt last spring and it broke my heart she worried about me. I put a bear hug on her and kissed on top of her golden red curls.

"Don't you worry, baby girl, I am always careful," I assured her.

She grinned at me and did her famous two-eyed wink where she closes both eyes real tight at the same time. Hilarious.

I lined out my strategy for the day as I showered. First, I'd go over Jon Kincaid's files with a fine tooth comb and not just to see about his condition, I wanted more. Nurses and doctors make notes on medical files, their observations and even opinions are usually in there somewhere. I really wanted any documentation about the relationship between the Widow Kincaid, thoughts about her sincerity, his desire to die, anything which might help me to get to the truth.

Chelsea and Alexandra were still in residence when I left the house, so much hugging and kissing happened before I got out the door. I made the quick trip to the office in record time and arrived in a good mood.

Jewels crushed it when she handed me a message. "Ms. Kincaid called and she sounded really upset and wouldn't say why."

"Crap, this can't be good."

My first thought was my little bit of larceny had been discovered and I'd been identified, which would truly suck. I took the message and headed into my office, shaking off my foreboding. I was being paranoid, there was no way anyone made me. I dialed the number and Georgia picked up on the first ring.

"Tess, thank God you called." Her voice sounded ragged.

"What can I do for you?" I asked as I turned on my computer. I wanted to be ready in case I needed to make notes.

"All three of my children have received phone calls from Jon's stepdaughter, Anna. She told them she'd found some pictures from when they were all children and she wanted to send them along. She also told them she wanted to make sure they were all dealt with fairly. The reason I'm so disturbed is she ended the phone calls by asking each of them to never tell Jonnie about the phone call. Then she said if any of them wanted to get in touch with her they must call her cell phone and never call the house. According to my children she was adamant about and even sounded scared. Tess, she's frightened of her own mother! How much of a danger does she represent to my children?" There was real anguish in Georgia's voice.

"I have no answer, but if we can prove Jonnie was in any way responsible for Jon's death, we can make sure she's neutralized. Then your children will be safe."

"Jon was right, she is crazy." She paused and changed gears on me. "May I ask where you are in your investigation?"

"You're the boss, you have every right in the world." I debated telling her about the death bed dream and decided against. "I went to the rehab center yesterday in Atlanta. I managed to make copies of Jon's medical records and I found out who else worked at the place, kinda got the lay of the land you might say. I haven't had time to actually go over the records yet, I got in late last night as you can imagine."

"I can't believe they gave you access to his records like without her permission, you must have made some fast friends there. I thought there were laws." She sounded amazed.

Oh lady, if only you knew, I thought, but I wasn't telling. She might be the paying client but she had no right to know how I obtained my information, especially if my methods were illegal.

"Oh yes, everyone was just sweeter than pie, great place. I'll go over these records and let you know what I find out. In the meantime, if you could give me contact info for your children, I'd really like to interview them."

"Two of them are willing but one of the twins and my eldest want nothing to do with the investigation, they both say they don't care if he was murdered and Sandra went so far as to say he deserved no less."

"Wow. Let me have the numbers anyway and I'll get Juliet to set up appointments. She can be very persuasive."

"Should I be there?"

I gave it a thought for a nanosecond. "No, I think they might guard their words in order to save your feelings. I want them to speak freely."

"I can understand, but you will give me a report."

"Yes, ma'am."

"I only paid you for a few days, and I'm sure it will take longer. How do we do this?"

"Let me work through what you've already paid for and then we'll figure it out one day at a time, okay with you?"

"Yes. Let me give you the children's numbers."

"I'm going to put you on hold for Juliet, she'll take the info. Try not to worry, we're going to solve this."

"Trying," she said.

I put her on hold.

"Jewels," I called out, "Ms. Kincaid has phone numbers for you. Make appointments with all of them for interviews, please."

"Got it, boss."

Every now and then I thought we ought to get some kind of an intercom thing, but really why? Jewels can hear me just fine if I yell. I opened my kit and extracted my spy camera. I loved the thing; it's about the size of a tube of lipstick and it takes great pictures in low light. Just perfect for the discriminating private investigator. It took a few seconds to plug in and download the files to the computer and then I had all the medical records of the late Jon Kincaid. There were the regular notations, diagnosis and prognosis, outline for care and all the medications, there were a lot of them. There were even notations about his urine and fecal output, ugh. Whose job is it to measure those, I wondered. He had nine surgeries but by the time all was said and done, the lung cancer had spread to his brain and several other organs. From what I could see the surgeries, medications, chemo and radiation didn't even slow the disease down. Cancer is so hateful. No one deserves to die like that, well, okay maybe Hitler. At one point Jon refused any more surgeries, but he was convinced to have one more by his loving wife. That confirmed what I had seen in the dream. I made note of it.

There were also a few notations where doctors and nurses had made comments on the wife;

'Wife very aggressive when talking to patient, aids or nurses.'
'Wife not well-liked by staff members.'
'Wife talks to patient in disparaging manner.'
'Patient's wife is difficult and demeaning; I can hardly stand to attend when she's present.'
'Patient's wife demanded to speak to doctor on duty and threw a glass of water at me.'
'Patient's wife is a bitch!'

Each notation about the Widow Kincaid, and there were dozens of them, were initialed by an employee, and were universally negative. Jonnie didn't win any friends there. But the one notation which interested me the most was: *'Patient insistent I contact his lawyer for him, claimed his wife was keeping certain people from seeing him.'* signed by the initials 'LP.'

I would bet my last bullet this was Nurse Lillian Perkins. Not exactly a smoking gun, but it was one more straw for the camel's back.

By the last days of his life, Jon Kincaid could not take in food or drink and was kept alive by medical means. He was expected to last only a few more days, there was a signed Do Not Resuscitate in the file, notations where the doctor told Jonnie Kincaid to make the final arrangements. Seems she did make arrangements, although not the ones the doctor had suggested. I had to wonder what she might have used since the drug didn't raise any eyebrows on the staff.

No one was surprised when the warning alarms went off in the middle of the night. Jon was checked for vital signs of which there were none. The on-call doctor came in and signed the death certificate, the widow was called and the remains were sent to the funeral home. No one suspected a bloody thing. Why should they? Kincaid had been dying for almost two years before he finally gave it up in the middle of the night. Whatever medication Jonnie used to take the man out had left little trace. What the hell could it have been? I'd ask Moira. It's so handy to have a nurse in the family.

I looked at the signature of the doctor on the death certificate, one Jocelyn Gordon. I flipped back through Kincaid's files and found her name or initials over and over, so she was familiar with him. I wondered if she'd talk to me. Highly doubtful but worth a shot. I picked up the phone and called my sister.

"Hello Tess, what's shakin' with you?" Moira asked.

"I'm workin' on this Kincaid thing and since you got me into to this mess, you owe me."

She sighed. "What do you want?"

"Kincaid died in the middle of the night, his wife slipped something into his IV. The drug took effect almost immediately and he got drowsy and his speech became slurred. Of course, he was in lousy shape anyway, so he didn't have much to fight back with I reckon. No one suspected anything; the on-call doctor did a very cursory examination on Kincaid and signed the death certificate. So what would do that, kill a person fast and not leave him looking all jacked up?"

She laughed, I suspected at my terminology. "Well several things; Potassium Chloride would probably be the best choice. It stops the heart somewhere in between one and five minutes after it is administered. It causes severe heart arrhythmias, the heart spasms out of control and then stops beating. It'd look like a heart attack."

I typed the name into my notes on the case. "Hmmm no trace?"

"Well, potassium levels spike after death, and when muscle tissue is damaged, huge amounts of potassium are released. The heart is just a big muscle after all. But if the numbers were too high it would show in an autopsy on the guy and maybe send up a red flag if the M.E. was really on top of it. I'm assuming it didn't happen?" she asked.

"Right as rain and he went into the oven faster than you could say, 'Bob's your uncle.'"

"How do you know this, if one might ask?" Moira sounded suspicious.

"Well, one might ask and one might be told it came to me in a dream. This Kincaid guy is nothing if not pushy and persistent. I saw the widow inject something into his IV and immediately he got slurry and lost focus."

She was silent for a moment. "So, are you still pissed off at me? I didn't mean to screw things up for you."

"I know, and you're forgiven, I absolve you." I made the sign of the cross with my right hand over the phone. "But only because Derek doesn't think I'm a head case."

"Only because he doesn't know you well yet, it'll come in time."

"Wow thanks, your support means so much to me."

Moira chuckled. "What'll you do next-- hey, wait a minute, how did you get access to Kincaid's medical records?"

"Well I could tell you but then I'd have to kill you."

"Jesus Christ Tess, I swear you're gonna go to prison one of these damn days. You broke in and stole them! Have you taken leave of your senses?" Her voice kept getting higher and higher.

"Give me a break, I needed to get some answers, I'm trying to solve a murder here. Besides I didn't steal anything, I haz a camera."

She was quiet for a few seconds. "Jesus, I think I'm speechless. Okay I have to get back to work, just watch your ass please. You'd look shitty in orange."

"Yep, makes me look sallow and washed out, I shall be careful ma'am. See ya later, love ya, bye."

"See ya later, love ya, bye." She hung up.

I sat there, looking over my notes. Potassium, who knew? I take it every morning! Man, oh man, there are lots of ways to kill people.

11

Material Girl

"Hey Jewels, will you get hold of Rod and see if he can handle the workman's comp and the shop surveillance, please? Give him all the particulars."

"On it."

I could hear Jewels as she explained the two situations to Rod Jordan, my go to guy for camera installments. Rod's services were an easy fix for two cases. I'd bill the clients for the hours he racked up and the camera for the shop. Rod had a commercial truck was worth a million dollars to me, bless him. Almost no one looks twice at a work truck. The vehicle actually belonged to Rod, he slaps magnetic signs on the doors when he was working for the dish company and the company compensates him for mileage. To his credit, he never did work for me when he was on the clock with them. If Croesus was looking for one honest man, he would have to look no further than Rod.

The first two cases were easy but the possible philandering husband tailing job? Not so much. It would have to be done old school, sitting in a car taking pictures, following the guy wherever he went, all the while being careful not to get made. Most people are oblivious of their surroundings, which is why eyewitness accounts are not very reliable. But a person who's guilty is usually more careful and has a tendency to look over his or her shoulder frequently. Therefore, caution was called for; an irate unfaithful spouse could turn on you like a yellow dog. I should know, once upon a time I got a gun shoved in my face by a pissed off husband who tumbled to the fact I was tailing him. Not an experience I'd care to repeat. In my defense, it happened a long time ago before I had become so stealthy.

I pulled up my calendar and looked at the week. If the husband was really cheating, I needed twenty-one days of following him at different times to prove it, my standard window of time. No one can be careful all the time, even the most careful cheater made mistakes. I'd need to rent a car and trade back and forth with Jewels too; tailing someone in the same car day after day is a sure way to get caught. Especially true when you drive a bright red vehicle with 'PI4U' on the plate. But driving a rental car the entire time might look suspicious to a suspicious person so I'd trade up. I'd work surveillance around the Kincaid's interviews. I could sleep next month, I promised myself.

My next order of business was to ring up Mars; I thought she might be afraid I was still mad at her.

"Hey." Mars knew it was me from caller ID and she sounded a little worried.

"You're forgiven."

"Whew, I'm glad to hear it. Did you forgive your big sister too?"

"Yep, we're all good. I had an interestin' call from Lori, she's worried about me workin' this case."

"Oh, so Ms. Kincaid did call you after all?"

"She did. Lori threw cards on the situation and she saw blood and fire and tears in it. Which gives me pause, so I'm packin' an extra gun."

"Hmmm, beside the two you usually carry?"

"Yeah, I'd rather be safe than sorry, don't ya know."

"Good, 'cause if Lori laid cards without asking then I'm happy you're taking her seriously. So … I'm gonna change the subject. I had a showing and I think I might have a contract before the sun goes down!"

"Are they new people?" I wanted to know.

We'd had a lot of people move here over the past few years, claiming they wanted to get to back to nature. Then they bitched about how far away civilization was and weren't satisfied with our little country stores and butcher shops and home owned restaurants. Oh no, they moved in and then set about trying to change things as quickly as possible, determined to bring the city to us in the form of chain drug stores and pizza places. City people, bah.

"Yeah but I think they're gonna fit in fine. They're young, he works in the city and she's pregnant with their first."

"Ah domestic bliss. Speakin' of, how's it going with my brother? Give me credit, I've tried to be good and keep my nose out of it, but what's happenin' with the two of you?" I had to ask.

Mars sighed. "Well, we have spent some time together, but he's in a bad place and he won't lean on me even though we've known each other for a million years. It's frustrating the living hell out of me."

"Yes sir, he is frustratin' and stubborn as a mule on Sunday. You want me to talk to him? I need to pick his brain about something anyway and I could just slide into a conversation about the two of you," I offered.

"GOD NO! He and I haven't even discussed the fact you know something's going on. While we're on the subject, something physical is not going on, we're just hanging out and exploring the possibilities."

"Thank God, the image of the two of you doin' the nasty kinda turns my stomach, if you know what I mean, Miss Overreaction. I was just offerin' to talk to Connell, now I won't even mention your name. As a matter of fact, if he asks me anything I'm gonna pretend like I don't even know you, okay. Oh yeah and I won't tell you anything he says about you."

"Bitch. So seriously, what's next on this case?" She didn't really sound mad.

"Well I've been to the rehab center in Atlanta and it looks like a nursing home to me, terrible security, a skeleton crew at night and crummy locks. Maybe when this is all over I can sell them a system."

"God, you're horrible," Mars laughed.

"Hey, a girl's gotta eat. I got hold of Kincaid's medical records and went through them; I desperately want to talk to one of the nurses who I believe befriended him and the doctor on call for the rehab center. I suspected Kincaid wanted to change his will, then I went through his records and my suspicions were confirmed. I found a smoking gun, or so I like to think, in the form of a notation from a nurse who claimed Kincaid asked her to contact his lawyer. The notation claims Kincaid told the nurse his wife was obstructing him, which is motive. The nurse just used initials but after much snoopin', I believe I know who she is and I think the doctor might tell me she was surprised at the timin' of Kincaid's death." I hoped.

"How in the world do you know about the will changing thing?" Mars asked.

"Let's just say it came to me in a dream." I laughed when Mars sighed at me. "As a matter of fact, I've been losin' lots of sleep to this case on account of a dead guy worryin' the hell out of me. Anyway, I want to find this nurse and see if she'll open up and confirm what I think. I also want to interview each of the Kincaid children as soon as Jewels can run 'em to ground and set up appointments."

"I really wonder how much they can tell you," Mars mused.

"You never know, accordin' to their momma they've spoken to their step-sister and I want to know exactly what the girl had to say. Georgia makes it sound as if the stepsister is afraid of Mommy Dearest so maybe she knows something we don't."

"It's worth a shot at the very least," Mars agreed.

"True that. Hey, I wanna have dinner with you and Connell soon. I just need to visit with him, Chick tells me he's in a bad way. I thought he was a mess too and he's been avoidin' me. Grammy confirmed it for me at the séance. But if you invite me to dinner, then he won't get pissed thinkin' I'm motherin' him. I promise I won't mention anything about the two of you. So, if you're available, you wanna call Connell to make sure he's game?" I wheedled.

"I'll be happy to do it and I'll call you back."

"Oh, I am happy for the contract, even if it is city folk." I was sincere.

"Thank you. Okay, see ya later, love ya. Bye," Mars said.

"See ya later, love ya." I hung up and yelled for Jewels.

"Yes Boss?" She walked into my office. "What can I do for you?"

I pulled up the file on Nurse Lillian Perkins. "Will you call this woman and see if she'll agree to an interview? Also, will you call Dr. Jocelyn Gordon for the same reason? Last but not least, call Mr. Nguyen at the 4 Corners Market and see if Rod can drop in and install a surveillance camera." I handed the doctor's numbers to Jewels.

"Who are we?" she asked.

I looked up at the ceiling and thought about it; I didn't want to spook either woman. "Let's play the insurance card again, 'cause it seems to be workin' for us and if it ain't broke, don't fix it. Work them around the Kincaid kids interviews and get me a schedule as soon as. I'm also gonna need to do some surveillance on the suspicious husband in between, please and thank you."

Jewels saluted and made her exit. I went back to reading the medical file on Jon again, but Jewels interrupted me within five minutes. She leaned on the door jamb.

"I've got the first interview, it's with the nurse. She seemed a bit reluctant like she didn't believe what I was pitchin', but she agreed. It's for tomorrow at 11:00 A.M."

"Another trip to Atlanta," I sighed. "At least according to her address she's on this side of the city. Any word on the Kincaids or the doctor?"

Jewels shook her head. "I've called 'em all and nothin' yet. I left messages. I called Mr. Nguyen and he agreed to have Rod come and make the install."

"Okay, I think I'll take a little trip over to Dixon and see what the alleged unfaithful husband is doin' today. I can spend a couple of hours there, maybe more. Tomorrow I'll be runnin' the roads between here and Atlanta so don't schedule anything else. I wonder where all of the Kincaids are. Why ain't they answerin' their phones?"

"Could be they're workin' and can't talk on the phone at work?" She made it into a question.

"More like they're avoidin' me." I picked up my PI bag and snagged my big stainless steel thermos from the desk drawer. I went into the front office and emptied the coffee pot into my thermos. "Great. Well, they can run but they can't hide." I doctored the coffee with a little extra sugar and cream, hoping it was enough to get me through the day. "Okay, I'm out of here, sorry I took all the coffee."

Jewels just laughed at me and waved bye-bye.

12

Somebody's Watching Me

I took back roads to Dixon and pondered marriage and fidelity and all that jazz. My business is largely made up of people who suspect their spouses of cheating. Sad but true. Most of them are correct, which is also sad but true. Given the statistics on marriage and divorce in America, one has to wonder if it's even worth the effort. I wondered if my own parents had ever strayed and mentally shook myself. What a horrible thought! The more I thought about it, the more I convinced myself they were faithful to one another and if they weren't I didn't want to know. Most people don't want or can't imagine their own parents having sex. Ew! It's even worse to imagine them having sex with someone else. Ick!

Most people would just as soon not know their significant other was cheating, which is the number one reason people get away with the extracurricular activity for so long. Ignorance is bliss. But then signs appear which can't be overlooked, such as hang up calls, your spouse buys you gifts for no reason, or works overtime or leaves for work earlier, loses interest in sex or expresses much more interest in sex or displays new sexual techniques or positions, begins to dress differently, wears a new cologne or aftershave, takes more business trips. There are plenty of other signs too. Suddenly you find yourself wondering what the hell is going on because your spouse has a new circle of friends and there are bullshit sounding excuses as to why you're never invited to meet them. The light dawns, and I get a phone call. An excellent example of these facts is the Carlyle case: the husband started at the gym, began to eat differently and, according to my client, was acting secretive, hanging up the phone when she entered the room and keeping papers locked in his briefcase. She bit the bullet and called my office for help.

That jogged a thought and I hit the Bluetooth. 'Say a command,' the computer voice intoned.

"Office," I said.

"Hey Boss." Jewels sounded busy.

"Hey Jewels, would you contact Ms. Carlyle and get her husband's e-mail address? Get the password if she knows it and if not, I'll play with it until I crack it. I wanna check on who he's been talking to, okay? Oh, and while you're at it, get his cell phone number, a copy of the bill, his social, mother's maiden name, hometown, favorite pet and favorite sport. You know the drill."

"I'm on it Boss, see you later." She disconnected without saying 'bye'; sometimes she reminded me of YaYa who also never says 'good-bye'.

With Carlyle's cell phone bill, I could play around and come up with his password which is usually a mother's maiden name, favorite pet, hometown, favorite sport or something to do with their profession. With a copy of his cell phone bill I'd look for a regularly reoccurring number which occurred outside of regular business hours. Odds were good I'd then have the cheater and not a client of Carlyle's.

Jewels would make calls to all the numbers in question and try and get a name. If the winds were blowing in our favor, she'd get a voicemail and the name would be handed to us on a platter. If not, I'd do a reverse look-up on the numbers. Then it was a matter of catching everybody in the same place at the same time doing naughty things.

However, shadowing the poor bastard was the place to start. I stopped in at the rental car place I use and crossed my fingers. They usually find a nice, non-descript car for me to drive, but I hadn't called ahead and as it turned out, it was a big mistake.

"Hey Bernice," I said to the lady at the front desk. "Tell me something good."

Bernice is a fifty-something African American woman with flawless skin, amazingly complicated cornrows and a friendly attitude. I smiled at her with hope in my heart.

"Hey, Tess honey. I'm afraid I don't have nothin' good today. Alls I got is an orange three cylinder. It's been a real busy day." She winced and so did I.

"Hell Bernice, that's not even a car, it's a pregnant roller skate. It won't go over 40 miles an hour and I'm not sure I can drive with my knees up around my ears."

She laughed but I wasn't kidding; my legs are long. Damn. I sighed. "Well if it's all you've got then it'll have to do even if all the dogs in the world laugh at me as they run past."

Bernice opened her desk drawer and pulled out the key to the non-car. "It's all gassed up and ready to go, how long you gonna need it?" she inquired.

"Just today but I might be back for more before the week is out."

"Not a problem. Maybe next time I can get you a go-cart." She grinned.

I flipped the credit card on the counter and she set about charging me. I was out the door in nothing flat and came face to face with the car. I laughed out loud. It was bright University of Tennessee orange! It was nowhere near inconspicuous and it was humiliating to boot!

I squeezed myself into the contraption and drove to the office park where Mr. Matt Carlyle worked as a tax accountant. It wasn't a huge office park, but it was large enough I thought I could avoid notice, even in an orange car. I drove around until I spotted Carlyle's white Saab. He owned the company and had a staff of twenty, so I reckoned he did alright. I pulled into an empty spot four spaces down and one row back from the Saab and got comfortable. About an hour later Carlyle came out, climbed into his Saab, and took off. I slipped out behind him and kept three or four car lengths between us.

Dixon's not a big town, but it has a healthy population of about 75,000. I was pretty sure I could follow him and stay lost in the crowd, so to speak, if I was very careful.

I followed him downtown and drove around the square twice. I began to wonder if he'd spotted me when we turned by the library again, but then he pulled into a diagonal parking place in front of a restaurant called The Brassiere. He got out of the car and I got a good look at him. He was a big white guy and I was willing to bet he'd played football in high school and maybe college too. Carlyle probably topped 6 foot 4 and he was carrying about 50 pounds extra. He was what folks in my part of the world called beefy. He was dressed in a very nice suit and wearing a tasteful tie and expensive shoes. His thick sandy blonde hair was stylishly cut. In short he was a fella who took extra pains to look presentable.

There was a woman walking up the sidewalk toward my guy. She was close in age to him, mid-thirties and slim, with dark blonde hair cut in a chin length pageboy style, beautifully dressed and wearing expensive heels. She kissed him on the cheek when they met. I decided right then and there she wasn't his lover; they were meeting much too publicly. I took her picture anyway because you never know with people, sometimes it's the danger of being in public together which turns them on. With that in mind, I took several more pictures.

The couple entered the restaurant and I settled down to wait. I intended to give my day to Carlyle and his possible adultery. I slouched down in the seat and pulled my Mets hat over my eyes and was just getting comfortable when the phone rang.

"Tess," I answered.

"Hey Boss, I have an appointment set up with two of the Kincaid children for day after tomorrow, they're both in Nashville. Still waiting to hear from the other two. Where are ya?"

"I'm sitting in front of a restaurant on the square in Dixon watching Carlyle have lunch with an attractive blonde."

"Pay dirt?" she asked.

"Nah, I don't think so, although it would be sweet!" I shook my head in denial. "I'm gonna hang out here and follow him the rest of the day. Put him on the schedule for Thursday and Friday. I want an erratic surveillance on him. I'd like to borrow your car on Thursday if that's alright with you. I'll make sure and clean the gum wrappers out."

Jewels laughed. "All good. So, if I can get the interviews with the other two Kincaid's, shall I amend the schedule?"

"No, not unless they absolutely have scheduling problem and you have to cut into the week we already have planned, but try not to cut into my Saturday if you can help it."

"You got it. Have fun, Boss."

Jewels hung up on me. Smart ass, she knew how much I hated the surveillance part of the job.

Nothing exciting happened during the day except I ate five granola bars, drank six bottles of water and emptied the thermos of coffee. I chewed an entire pack of Big Red chewing gum too.

I hit bathrooms whenever I could and as fast as I could. It really sucks to lose someone because you have to stop and pee.

I followed Carlyle back to work after he and the blonde parted company on the sidewalk. I managed to get her tag number so Jewels could run it, just in case I was wrong in my assumptions. I sat in Carlyle's parking lot and surfed the net, constructed questions for the Kincaid offspring, updated my Face Book and texted back and forth with Mars over nothing except my boredom. I did find out she and Connell were available for dinner on Saturday.

Carlyle went home after work. He made one stop on the way: the Piggly Wiggly, where he bought a gallon of milk. Yawn.

I parked down the street from the Carlyle hacienda and regretted my failure to refill the thermos while I waited to see what might happen. The answer was not a damn thing, unless you count the neighbor who walked his yappy dog past my car and eyeballed me twice. The dog pissed on my tires as a bonus. The lights in the house went out at ten o'clock; I dropped the car back at the rental place and drove home.

I wondered if I could talk the client into springing for a camera in front of the house. I could only take so much mind-numbing boredom. I made a mental note to call Bernice and tell her the tires on the non-car needed a little extra TLC.

13

Rise and Shine

I arose bright and early the next morning, got in a run, showered and hit the road for Atlanta before the sun ever knew it was supposed to be up. The traffic was minimal and I hauled ass.

I was kind of nervous about the interview with Nurse Perkins and when I'm nervous I tend to drive faster. I kept a dialogue going in my head all the way down the highway, how I would introduce myself, broach the subject of the will, her possible answers and how to counter them. Yes, I do talk to myself all the time. It drives my mother crazy.

Five hours later I was in Nurse Perkin's very nice neighborhood. I wondered if she was married or if she made a hell of lot more money at her job than I had previously suspected. Or had she gotten a large infusion of money recently? I made a mental note to check.

I pulled into the driveway, walked up to the door and rang the bell exactly on time for our meeting. A few seconds later the door opened and a thirty something, attractive brunette stood staring at me. She was about 5-foot-2 and maybe a buck-o-five soaking wet, and dressed in casual clothes; jeans, a tee shirt and running shoes. She continued to stare at me. Hard.

"Hello," I said as I extended my hand.

Ms. Perkins rather gingerly reached out and clasped my fingers, still appraising me and not speaking.

I smiled. "I'm Diane Drake from Farmers Liability Insurance."

I flashed a business card and then placed it in her hand. I have several sets of business cards; they come in handy when you're trying to convince a person you're someone you're not. Most people take a business card on face value, which is interesting since you can get almost anything printed for next to nothing these days. Lillian Perkins looked carefully at the embossed card in her hand and then flashed her hazel eyes at me, sizing me up.

"Please come in," she said, turning away to lead me inside.

The house was nice, not over stated, but someone had taken pains to decorate it in subtle colors and arrange furniture and knick-knacks in a pleasing way.

"Your home is lovely."

"Thank you, I try."

We moved down the entry hall and she gestured to a love seat in the living room. "Have a seat. Can I get you anything? I've made coffee."

"Coffee would be wonderful, two sugars and two creams please. May I use your restroom?"

"The powder room is back down the hall toward the front door. I'll meet you here in a moment."

She walked away. She was an incredibly trusting woman. I sure as hell wouldn't have left some yahoo to have the run of my house five seconds after I met her, even if I did think she was with an insurance company. Regardless of her trust issues I hit the bathroom because I did have to pee, but also because it gave me an opportunity to snoop around a bit. You can tell a lot about a person by their bathroom.

Ms. Perkins' bathroom was warm and inviting, with a huge mirror, marble counters and stylish track lighting. No medicine cabinet to peek into, sadly. Only hand towels, extra toilet paper and various cleaners were in the cabinet under the sink. She was very tidy. I could certainly take some cleaning tips from her.

I finished my business and literally met Ms. Perkins at the coffee table where she had two cups of java. We both sat down and she looked at me with narrowed eyes.

"What is it you want?" she asked.

I took a sip of coffee to give myself a chance to frame an answer. "Well, there are just a few questions about Mr. Kincaid I need answered so we can sign off on the policy."

She sipped her own coffee. "Really? I can't imagine what you need to know, everything is in his medical records. It was a pretty clear-cut situation. Quite frankly I'm not even sure I should be talking to you at all, since this is medical information you are wanting. HIPAA laws and all." She frowned at me.

"Lillian – may I call you Lillian?" I asked.

She nodded.

"Lillian, were you surprised Mr. Kincaid died suddenly?"

I could practically see the wheels turning in her head. Her stare became even harder. "Who the hell are you really? You're no insurance rep, I'm positive now." She paused. "As a matter of fact, I want you to leave."

She stood up but I remained seated. I was a little startled by her knee jerk reaction, but I needed to save the situation if I could.

"Lillian, please, just sit down and hear me out. If, when I've finished, you still want me to leave, I won't give you an argument. Just give me a chance, please." I put all the sincerity I owned into my voice.

Lillian hesitated but never broke eye contact with me. Finally, after several seconds she sighed and sat back down. I had to repress my own sigh. I'd won the first round.

"Lillian, I have reason to believe Mr. Kincaid trusted you. I believe he asked you to contact his lawyer for him."

She stared at me and her mouth dropped open. "No one knows … How do you know? I never told anyone. Oh my God!"

I held my hands out in front of me in what I hoped was a placating and calming manner. She looked like a deer in the headlights.

"Lillian, it's okay. A patient asked you for a favor; nurses do a lot more than change out IVs and bedpans, nurses heal the whole patient. He trusted you and you wanted to help him, you're one of the good guys."

"I told her, that's how you know. She sent you here, you're working for her!" she accused.

Lillian's voice edged closer to hysteria and face twisted up. She could only be speaking of one person.

"Her?" I decided to play dumb.

"The wife. Jonnie Kincaid. That's what this conversation is about isn't it? Her! When I told her Mr. Kincaid wanted me to get in touch with his lawyer she practically breathed fire in my face. 'Who the hell do you think you are, bitch, interfering in my life in such a manner? You skanky little whore, I'll have your fucking job for this!' She hissed at me like a snake! I tried to explain Mr. Kincaid and I had been talking and he just asked me. I meant no harm and was only trying to help."

Lillian paused and drew a shaky breath; she took several seconds to regain control. "She's going to sue me on some trumped up bullshit or try and take my license, isn't she? Oh Jesus!" Lillian buried her face in her hands.

"Lillian, it's nothing like you think. Get a grip and listen to me," I demanded and waited for about five beats until she looked up at me. Her eyes were red rimmed and shiny.

"Lillian, this isn't about you at all, please believe me. This is about Mr. and Mrs. Kincaid and what happened the night he died. I'm not here to make trouble for you in any way shape or form, okay? Cross my heart." I bisected my chest with my index finger in a gesture of sincerity.

Lillian looked at me and nodded. One single tear slipped down her cheek. "She hates me so much, I only did my job and tried to make him as comfortable as possible, which wasn't easy given the amount of pain the poor man was in. She'd roll in and start her high and mighty act, orderin' everyone around and talkin' to all of us and him like we were all something she'd scrape off her shoe. She's a hateful, horrible woman."

"I know, she's a true horror show. Lillian, he asked you to call his lawyer and have him come down to the rehab center, am I right?"

Lillian nodded. "Yes, he did."

"Then you saw Ms. Kincaid and told her what had transpired?"

"I saw her in the hall; she was comin' to see her husband. She tried to brush on past me but I called out to her and explained the request. I wasn't tellin' on him, but he was full of meds and I just wondered if it was a fantasy idea of his or not. So I asked. I didn't tell her he thought she was keepin' people from him, believe me, I knew better. I just talked about the lawyer. I wish to God I'd kept my mouth shut. If only I could have that one moment back, I could live the rest of my life as a happy woman." Her voice quavered.

How many people have wished for one moment to make a different choice, I wondered? I knew I had.

"So, she threatened you. Then what?"

"Then she hit me with her shoulder to knock me out of the way even though I wasn't in the way and the hall was plenty wide enough, she just did it for meanness." More tears slid down the woman's face. "What's this really about?"

Now I had to decide if I could trust her and if so, how far. I took a deep breath and exhaled it. "The night Jon Kincaid died, did you see his wife in the center?"

Lillian looked at me hard; I thought she had a clue right then about the true nature of my visit. I waited.

"She was in earlier in the evenin', around eight. She only stayed for about fifteen minutes, which wasn't odd, she never stayed long except when she was gonna talk to our doctor. She cut me a dirty look when she came down the hall and saw me. Then she took off on her broom."

I smiled. "How late where you on duty?"

"Eleven, I took a few minutes to gather my things and clock out. Before I left, though, I slipped into Jon's room to check on him, I just had a naggin' feelin'. He was sleepin', all his vitals looked fine, and so I left. It was the last time I saw him of course." She looked sad.

"Lillian, I'm sorry to bring all this up and upset you. I wouldn't be here if it wasn't important."

She tried to smile and failed miserably.

"You said his vitals looked fine, he seemed to be restin' comfortably?"

Lillian nodded.

"Were you surprised when you come into work the next day to find out he had passed in the night?"

Lillian huffed and nodded her head. "I really was. I mean, he was very ill, but everything said he had some more time left. It sounds silly, I mean he'd been ill for so long and had so many surgeries but it still seemed sudden to me. I didn't get to say good-bye." She stopped talking and her eyes grew big as she stared at me.

"Oh my God," she whispered. "That's why you're really here, you think something else happened. You think she killed him?"

"I … Lillian, I'm just lookin' to put some things in perspective, get all the facts straight, the timeline." I protested. "Nothing else."

"No, you're not. You're lyin'. You're investigatin' a murder." She shook her head vigorously in denial. "I don't know anything, and now you really need to leave." She stood up again. "Please go."

I knew when I was beaten but I had what I come had for; she corroborated the fact Jon asked her to contact his lawyer. I believed it was this event which triggered the attack on him by his wife. I stood up and extended my hand; Lillian ignored it.

"If you tell anyone you were here or I spoke to you, I'll call you a liar. I swear it. I don't want nothin' to do with this." Her voice was steely. "Nothin'."

"Done. I'll leave your name out of my report, not to worry. I never meant to upset you," I said sincerely.

"That woman is evil and she scares the holy, livin' shit out of me. I won't help you if it means bringin' her down on my neck. You have no idea what you're dealin' with. I'm sorry, he was a nice man and … please go away."

I nodded and retrieved my bag. "Thank you," I said.

She hung her head and I saw myself out. I got in the Jeep and sat very still for a minute. Lillian's reaction had shaken me; she was terrified of Jonnie Kincaid. I tried to wrap my brain around that.

Finally, I pulled out my digital recorder and started the Jeep. On the way home, I dictated everything which had transpired. What the hell had I dropped in to?

14

Seeing Double

Morning came way too early for me but I dragged my happy ass out of bed and put in my three miles before the sun was very high in the sky. I had my usual compliment of dogs as well but they seemed to be in a hurry for some reason. I looked at the sky and saw clouds moving in and decided the canines were correct and we should hurry. I kicked it into high gear.

I showered, changed into a business outfit, and rattled down the stairs to the kitchen.

"You got in late last night," my father said from behind his paper. "Everything okay in your world?"

"Good morning all," I addressed the kitchen people as I poured myself a cup of coffee. I sat down at the table. "I made another run to Atlanta yesterday to do an interview."

"That's a long haul," said YaYa as she passed me the plate of toast.

I yawned. "Yep, I hate that drive twice in one day, but as you know I would rather sleep in my own little bed than in a hotel room with a strange pillow."

"Plus the bed bugs," YaYa added.

"Do you actually know anyone who's had a run in with bed bugs?" I had to ask just to hear what she had to say. My granny is always entertaining.

"Well," she pointed her toast at me for emphasis, "Melba Darlin' went to Birmingham for her youngest grandson's high school graduation and she stayed in a hotel on account of her daughter-in-law don't like Melba so much." The daughter-in-law doesn't like Melba on account of Melba drinks, a lot, and she's loud and obnoxious when she does, but I kept my mouth shut. "Anyway, she was ate up with bed bug bites and had to wear long sleeves to the graduation."

YaYa looked at me in triumph.

"Hmmm," I said and nodded my head at YaYa, "I stand corrected. So, one more reason I don't like to stay in hotels."

"They got spray; you can buy it down to the co-op," YaYa offered helpfully.

"Good to know." I had exhausted the topic, I hoped. The idea of little blood-sucking bugs biting me when I slept was less than appealing.

"Did you get the information you needed?" Mommy asked. She was stirring her coffee but her eyes were locked on me.

"I did and I think I did it without tippin' my hand." That was a lie for sure. "I talked to the nurse who attended my dead guy. She confirmed my info, but I gotta say she's scared spitless of the widow, I mean really terrified. It kinda creeped me out. But my money says the conversation is just between the two of us, she won't be sharin' it with anyone. I convinced her I worked for an insurance company." I buttered my own toast lightly.

Mommy looked at me with I can only describe as shock and awe on her face. "But that's a lie!"

"Well, I have over the years worked for many insurance companies, just not one which is payin' me to investigate the death of Jon Kincaid," I said calmly.

I doctored my coffee and did my best to ignore the laser beams coming out of my mother's eyes and boring into my head.

"You watch your back," Daddy said. "I don't much like the feel of this thing and I only know some of it."

"Well, I don't know much more either and I sure don't like the way it feels. I'm packin' heavy and I've got my neck set on a swivel."

"Good girl." Daddy winked at me.

"Whacha gonna do today?" asked YaYa.

"Good question, I'm not sure yet. I hope to have interviews with the dead guy's kids. I got in too late to talk to Jewels, thought I'd call her on the way in to the office."

"Tess, keep us in the loop," Mommy said with a worried look in her eye.

I hate worrying her, really I do, but I can't quit doing what I do. I love it and I'm good at it. Did you know only about thirteen percent of the American work force actually like their jobs? It's true, look it up.

"So are there big plans around here today? Takin' over the world anything along those lines?" I asked hoping to change the subject.

YaYa rose to the bait, bless her heart. "As a matter of fact, your mama and I are goin' over to St. Mary's to take a look at the altar linens and the vestments. Father Bill inherited a lot of old stuff. He's a young, handsome man, and he deserves to have nice new stuff."

Father William Sherman is indeed young and handsome. He's tall and lean at about 6-foot-2, with a head full of wavy light brown hair, and dark grey eyes. When he smiles his face lights up and he radiates kindness. I thought he was somewhere in the neighborhood of thirty-one or thirty-two.

"Plus, he thinks you're just cuter than a speckled pup and compliments you like crazy. I know your scheme. God above, hittin' on a priest," I teased.

"Hmp, I'm just tryin' to do the Lord's work and this is what I have to hear at the breakfast table?" YaYa tried her best to look hurt and I just laughed at her.

"Fine, Mother Teresa, go forth and do good things. Tell Bill hello from me, will ya?" I grinned.

I finished off my coffee and carried my plate to the sink. I filled a roadie with more coffee. I needed to get the hell out of the house. I just really didn't think I could spar anymore with Mommy and she had an adversarial gleam in her eye.

"Try not to worry, I promise I'll be careful," I said and kissed her on my way out the door.

I called Jewels as I walked to the Jeep.

"Hey Boss," Jewels answered.

"Morning Glory. What do you have in store for me today?" I climbed into the Jeep and started her up.

"I have interviews with all of the Kincaid children today. They have different work schedules and so forth but I think you can get 'em all done before supper time."

"Halleluiah! Finally! But I think you're one terribly optimistic girl. They all live in Nashville?"

"Yep, and with not too much drive time in between,"

"Sure, so you say," I said doubtfully.

The greater Nashville Metropolitan area boasts about 1 million people. Those people are spread out over 40 miles from one side of Davidson County to the other. It takes at least 20 minutes to get anywhere from anywhere, and if you think it sounds physically impossible, I challenge you to try it for yourself.

"Okay, give me addresses, please." I reached over and turned on the digital recorder, don't leave home without one. Jewels rattled off the addresses.

"Boss, the wife of the alleged cheater called and wanted to know if you have the proof against her husband yet." She sounded a bit annoyed.

"Damn, I got some pictures, but I haven't had time to get 'em on the computer yet. I'll run the camera by and you can do it. Upload and send the pictures of the woman our boy had lunch with, see if the wife knows her. What time's the first interview?"

"Not 'til 10, you've got plenty of time. I'll see you in a few." She disconnected and I drove.

I ran the camera into the office and jumped back in the Jeep in less than thirty seconds. I had no time to spare if I wanted to get these interviews finished and be home in time for supper. Fortunately, the traffic gods smiled on me and there were no wrecks, radar traps, or loose cattle on my route. The precipitation filled clouds caught up with me about halfway there, however. I slowed down and took my time. We Tennessee drivers are quite famous for the stupid way we drive in the rain. It seems the moisture in the air somehow seeps into our brains and makes us crazier than usual, so I watched the cars around me extra carefully. I made it to the edge of the city limits without incident and pulled over to program the first address into the GPS.

The address was for the twins, Sandra and Sarah. I followed the directions into a nice condo development on the west side of town and found the address. It was actually two addresses, right next door to one another. Interesting, I thought, though I wasn't sure exactly why. After all, who the hell was I to cast aspersions? I lived at home with my parents, grandmother and four dogs.

I observed the place as I walked to the front door. It was well-maintained, painted in appealing colors and landscaped beautifully. It reminded me of a 1930's bungalow. I liked it. I knocked on the door using the brass lion knocker and the door was jerked open immediately. I thought she had been standing there waiting. Some kind of a tiny white dog came tearing around her ankles, raising hell at me. The woman reached down and scooped it up.

"I'm so sorry, so sorry," she exclaimed. "This is Coco Chanel; pardon her, she hates people, other dogs, and cardboard."

She held the dog close to her as it growled at me with what it thought was a highly menacing manner.

"Cardboard?" I couldn't help but ask.

The woman shrugged. "I don't know why but every time I bring a cardboard box into the house she attacks it and rips it to shreds as if it's her sworn enemy."

"The damn dog hates everyone and everything; she oughta be put down. Hi, I'm Sandra," said a voice behind me.

The other twin had walked up behind me while my attention was focused on the dog. I looked over my shoulder at her. Sandra's manner was brusque and sarcastic. I really wondered if she meant what she said about the dog. I looked from one woman to the other and discovered they were identical. They had the same light grey eyes, same oval shaped faces, same long auburn hair worn in very similar styles. It was a bonus they weren't dressed alike. I thanked God for small favors. I could not tell them apart as I studied them. Most of the time with twins you find small differences which help you tell them apart. Not with the Kincaid sisters.

"Good Lord above, Sandy, you are gonna send Coco Chanel into a seizure. She's sensitive, you know."

So Coco's momma was Sarah, I thought as she patted the snarling animal. As long as she carried the dog around I could manage not to hurt it, at least I thought so.

"Coco Chanel, you know Auntie Sandy doesn't mean it, she woves you," Sarah cooed at the critter.

"Gick! I assume you're the PI our mother has coerced into the madness which is our father's life and death? Don't mind Sarah, she always talks to things can't talk back. Sarah, you are actin' deranged, please stop." Sandra stuck out her hand and I automatically shook it. She had a good grip.

Sarah raised one eye brow at her sister and said, "You're just mean-spirited and you're giving Ms. Maher a bad impression of us. Please Ms. Maher, come in and have a seat."

Sarah turned and led the way into the condo. It was comfortable in a shabby chic sort of way, a dozen shelves decorated the walls and on each there were knick knacks; teddy bears, fairies, dragons and, well, just lots of stuff. I thought I spotted what looked to be an entire fairy village. Surprisingly, it didn't look junky at all, just interesting. I figured it would take me half a day to look at everything.

Sarah held onto the growling dog and I was happy, I would have hated to shoot the little shit. The tiny animal kept snarling at me and showing her teeth. I wasn't fooled by the size of her or her tiny teeth, I knew little dogs are the ones who will bite you every time. Why? My theory is little dogs still remember once-upon-a-time they were wolves and it pisses them off they have to walk on leashes and wear sweaters and take baths.

"Can I offer you coffee?" Sarah asked.

"Great, two creams and two sugars please," I responded.

"Count me in," said Sandra.

The entire downstairs of the condo was one large room and I could see into the kitchen from my perch on the couch. Sarah put the white dust mop down in order to make the coffee and the little bitch made a bee-line right back toward me, growling as if she thought she was a pit-bull. She stopped right at me feet, bared her teeth and snarled loudly. I leaned down so I could whisper.

"Listen, you sorry excuse for a fur muff, I don't like you and I have a gun. Go. Away."

The creature stopped growling and cocked her head to one side as if she couldn't believe I wasn't terrified of her. I wasn't, I owned real dogs. Well, except maybe for Clouseau, I'm not so sure French Bulldogs are real dogs.

Sandra laughed. "Go ahead, you'd be doing all of us a favor. Sarah acts like a nut over the fuckin' dog. I think she secretly dresses her in baby doll outfits when no one is lookin'. I keep hopin' she'll run out in front of a car."

I cut a questioning look at her.

"The dog, not my sister." She laughed again. She had a good laugh.

The dog just looked confused, then she walked away from us and trotted up the stairs.

"Who says dogs don't understand English? Maybe I'm a dog whisperer," I quipped.

Sandra laughed again just as Sarah brought coffee to us.

"What's so funny?" she asked.

"Oh, just the idea dogs understand us when we talk to them," Sandra said with a big mean girl sort of smile. She was a snot but she was growing on me.

"Oh of course they do! You have to excuse Sandy, she hates Coco Chanel. I know it's hard to believe anyone could but she does. I keep hopin' they'll make friends but…"

"That ship has sailed," Sandra finished her sister's sentence for her.

I wondered if they did it all the time and really hoped not. "I'd like to record our conversation if y'all don't mind, makes it easier for me to remember things."

They both nodded. I set the recorder on my lap and flipped it on.

"Do you have a pet Sandra?" I asked.

"Goldfish, when one of them dies I can just flush it down the toilet and buy a new one. No muss, no fuss and I never worry if one of them might become neurotic."

"Great stars above, this woman is gonna think you're a barbarian Sandy! Well, anyway, let's get down to business Ms. Maher, what is it…" Sarah began.

Sandra finished, "You want to know?"

They really did finish each other's sentences; I decided the interview was going to be long and possibly weird.

"Please, call me Tess. I'd like for you to describe your relationship with your stepmother." I settled back to listen.

Sarah said, "This isn't easy to say, and I hope you won't think badly of me, but she's…"

"A royal bitch," Sandra finished. "She never liked us, she…"

"Tried to put walls up between us and our father," Sarah continued. "Not such a hard task in the first place, he wasn't very…"

Sandra cut in, "Invested in us. After the divorce, he started a new life, and for the most part…"

"We weren't in it," Sarah said. "We did see him on weekends and holidays, you know, the regular routine."

"Yes, we did," Sandra said in a sarcastic tone. "And she always made it clear we were visitors, not family. She and Anna were his family and we…"

"Were the interlopers." Sarah looked down into her coffee cup and sighed. "We hate her, Tess, I'm ashamed to say it but it's true." She admitted the last part in a whisper.

"Hell, I'm not ashamed; we've always called her the step-monster," Sandra said with a smile.

Sarah nodded her agreement. Nothing like a little honesty, I thought. The whole back and forth thing made my brain swim a bit; I stifled the impulse to shake my head in order to clear it.

"Did you know your father was very well off financially?" I asked.

Both women shook their heads.

"He owned several businesses, all of which did quite well, so the estate is quite large," I said.

"And, of course we aren't in it, are we?" Sandra snapped.

"No, you're not, I'm sorry to say." Which was the truth, I was sorry. It sucked to be shut out in such a manner.

"Your mother believes your stepmother killed your father, possibly because he wanted to change his will. Do you think she's capable of such a heinous act?" I asked.

Sandra laughed, "Bitch eats day old kittens for breakfast."

Sarah nodded. "We believe she's evil and jealous. We knew she wouldn't want us to get anything…"

"From our father, absolutely nothing. It isn't even about the money, she just has to win," Sandra said. "So I do believe she could murder him to insure…"

"She could drive the final wedge between us," Sarah said.

I noticed she had tears in her eyes.

"Good God Sarah, do not cry over that piece of shit. He's not worth one single tear. He sure as hell never cried over you," Sandra said with anger in her voice.

"You don't know, I think he loved us. I just think he was a severely damaged person and didn't know how to show love. No one's beyond redemption, Sandy, you have to believe that." Sarah looked at her twin with so much love in her big gray eyes it took my breath.

"Jesus, Sarah, you are such a bleeding heart."

I was surprised when Sandra reached out and patted her sister on the knee.

"We love each other, which is what really counts. That's what you have to remember. Okay?" Sandra said.

Tears were running down Sarah's face. "I love you."

"I love you," Sandra whispered.

I hated to interrupt such a tender moment but I had a job to do. "I have one more question. I understand your step-sister, Anna, called all of you, could you give me the high points of the conversation?"

Sandra looked pained. "My end of it was short and sweet. I told her to call someone who gave a damn."

"Sandy!" Sarah exclaimed.

"I can't stand the whiney little brat, she's a waste of space and I had nothing to say to her and didn't want to hear anything she had to say to me. End of story." Sandra huffed and leaned back in her seat.

"She and I talked for a few minutes and she said she wanted to make sure all of us, my sisters and Miles, were treated fairly. Of course, at the time I didn't really understand what she meant. Now knowing Daddy had a large fortune, it makes sense. She sounded sad and lonely. I felt sorry for her. Then she said something odd, she said we should only call her on her cell phone and never tell Jonnie she had spoken to us."

"Why do you think she said such an odd thing?" I asked.

"Because her mother is a monster and Anna is a coward," Sandra snapped.

I figured it was time to wrap up the interview. I turned off my recorder. "Ladies, I appreciate you takin' the time to see me today. I hope to talk to your other siblings today and then I'll proceed with the investigation."

"Will you keep us supplied with information or do we need to ask Mom?" asked Sarah.

"I'll have to ask her if I can share info with you. She's the payin' client," I explained.

They both nodded as if they understood but from the identical looks on their identical faces they sure didn't like my answer. Well, I wasn't there to please them.

"Tess, can you come next door with me for a moment before you leave?" Sandra asked. "I'd like to show you something."

"No problem." I held out my hand to Sarah. "I'm sorry you've been upset by our conversation today."

"Please don't worry about me." Sandra gave me a weak smile as she shook my hand.

Coco Chanel barked at us from the top of the stairs as we walked to the door, but stayed put.

Sandra's condo was as different from Sarah as it was possible to be. The place was monochrome colors, all black and white, black leather furniture, shiny white walls, pen and ink drawings on the walls and some black and white photographs, dark wood floors, a white alpaca rug in front of the sofa with two black cubes for a coffee table. It was attractive, but cold.

"Look, let's not beat around the proverbial bush, shall we? I know the bitch murdered my father, not like he didn't deserve it, but I sure as hell don't want to see her get away with it either. I think she's crazy as a shit house rat and I further think all of us, including my mother, are in deep kimchee here."

She moved over to a small table next to the door and pulled out a .38 Smith & Wesson Special from the drawer. I wasn't sure if she wanted to show it to me or shoot me with it.

"I keep this loaded and by the front door as a rule. But until this is all settled, I'll be sleepin' at Sarah's, with the gun. Just know if bitch shows her face, I'll blow it off for her." She returned the gun to the drawer.

"So why share your plans with me? Aren't you worried in the event Jonnie turns up dead, I'll share this conversation with the police?" I had to ask.

"I just wanted you to know we aren't helpless. We Kincaids can protect our own." she said quietly.

"I believe you," I said.

I meant it. There was no doubt in my mind Sandra Kincaid would send her step-mother into the next life without batting an eyelash. Sarah, on the other hand, would be like a lamb to the slaughter. The twins might be mirror images of each other but they were two very different women. I thought Sarah was very fortunate to have Sandra watching out for her.

15

Dr. Feel Good

The next interview took place in a swanky restaurant in mid-town and, yes, it took me twenty minutes to get there. Amerigo had been in business for a couple of decades and the place seemed busy as ever. Not surprising; the food was good, the service fast, and the price was, well, worth the price. I met Miles Kincaid there. I spotted him as soon as I came in; he looked like a male version of his sisters. Where the twins were pretty, Miles was quite handsome. I gave the hostess the high sign and pointed to Miles.

He spotted me too and stood up with his hand extended in greeting.

"Miles Kincaid. Please, sit down, I took the liberty of ordering coffee for you, hope that fits the bill." He had a nice voice, rather soothing.

"I'm Tess Maher, nice to meet you. Coffee would be perfect; I never turn down a cup. I appreciate you taking the time to see me today, Miles."

"No problem, I'm just down the road at Vandy and I'm between classes." He smiled at me.

"Miles, I'd like to record this conversation." When he didn't object, I took out my recorder and placed it on the table. "May I ask what you're studying?"

"As part of the investigation?"

"No, I'm just naturally nosey."

Miles grinned, which made him look even younger than his 21 years. "I'm in pre-med."

"Good for you," I said and meant it; if you're smart you ought to use it. "Do you have a specialty picked out?"

"Oh, I'm just gonna be an old country doctor, a general practitioner. There aren't enough to go around, everybody wants to specialize, which is where the real money is you know."

"I've heard that. So you're not interested in money?"

He shook his head. "I like money just as much as the next guy. I'm lucky I can pay the tuition and not have to take out loans, so when I'm finished I won't have to make a million dollars a year to pay them off. I can be the kind of doctor I want to be."

"So, did you rob banks before college?" Vanderbilt University isn't cheap and I wondered where the money came from for the tuition.

Miles laughed. "Nope, nothing so exciting. My mother socked money away for all of us to go to school, made us all save a portion of birthday and Christmas money and anything we earned too. She's been a fairly smart investor and so it grew. She figured our father wouldn't contribute. She was correct. I was also fortunate enough to get some scholarship money. I work when I can and I think I'll be okay." He paused and looked at me. "Just nosey?"

I smiled back at him, he was quite easy to be comfortable with and I knew down the road he'd have a wonderful bedside manner. The fact he was cute was a bonus. Little ol' ladies were going to love him.

"In my profession, it's always a good idea to know where the money comes from," I said.

"How did you ever get into your profession? It seems a bit odd for a woman and a pretty one to boot."

"Don't flirt with the PI, it won't help you. I'm in this business because I come from a law enforcement family, didn't like the academy and this seemed like a good alternative."

Miles raised an eye brow at me. "I think you didn't like being told what you could and couldn't do to get the bad guys and in this line of work you can skate around corners and not get into trouble if you are careful. I'll bet you are very careful too."

"You sure you wanna be a GP? You sound like a shrink."

Miles chuckled. "I'm just a student of human nature. Being the youngest in my family required I do so for self-preservation. Have you met my sisters?"

"Only Sarah and Sandra so far."

"So you know my formative years were spent tryin' to figure out how to be one step ahead of them, especially Sandy."

"I get it. I'm the youngest in a family of seven children, so I know a little bit about self-preservation."

"Wow, seven? That's a big family!"

I smiled. "It is and most of them have children, which make family dinners quite interesting. There's never a dull moment."

Miles grinned back at me. "Well, so far there are just my sisters and my mom, two nieces and one brother-in-law. But I promise you things are not dull at our dining table either."

I was positive he spoke the truth and wondered if Sarah brought Coco Chanel to the table.

"Miles, do Sandra and Sarah always finish each other's sentences?"

Miles laughed. "And then some. It's unnerving, isn't it? I swear they're telepathic too. Apparently, they didn't talk until they were about four, at least not in a language the rest of the world could understand. They had their own twin gibberish and they seemed to understand each other just fine. For everyone else they pointed at what they needed and made noise until they got what they wanted. Mom says it was weird, I think she was secretly afraid they'd never learn how to speak." He paused. "Sometimes I wonder if it's a good thing they did." He grinned at me.

I snickered. "How did you feel about your dad? For the record, I'm not just being nosey now."

Just as he was about to answer, the server showed up with our coffee and wanted to take our orders. The problem with trying to have a private meeting in a public space, it ain't private. We ordered and our cheerful waitress went on her way.

Miles smiled a sad little smile. "I loved him, Tess, even though he was a hard man to love. He was complicated, you understand? His upbringing wasn't easy, his father drank, and his mother was, well, she was a difficult woman. She spent all of her time trying to figure out how to hold on to enough money to pay the bills and buy food. She was hard, you know – tough as nails. I tried to fit into his world, tried to get on the same level with him, share with him. Nothing I tried worked, everything always had to be on his terms, his way. He never really got the idea other people had their own needs, wants, dreams and ideas. He seemed to think other people were simply players on his stage and they needed to do what he wanted them to do." He sighed. "I'm not sure he saw anyone as an individual person with a life. I think he saw us all as dolls he could move around in whatever way he wanted. When we tried to move our own way, he rejected us."

I was at a loss of for words. It sounded so sad, and so very different from my own relationship with my father. For the millionth time, I thanked God for Daddy.

"Miles, when was the last time you spoke to your father?"

He was silent for a few moments and when he finally spoke he sounded sad and wistful. "Five years ago, come next Christmas."

That's a long time, I thought. "I understand you spoke to your step-sister recently. Will you tell me about the conversation?"

"Anna? Sure, she called me, said she had some pictures of the girls and me when we were kids and she wanted to get them to us. I gave her Mom's address. I saw no reason not to, you know? Then she started to talk strangely, said she wanted to make sure the girls and I were treated fairly but admitted she had no idea how to accomplish her goal. When I asked her what she meant, she seemed surprised, like I should already understand what she was talking about. She went on to explain my father had left quite a large estate. She told me neither I nor my sisters were beneficiaries in any way. I wasn't surprised – well let me restate. I was surprised there was a large estate, not surprised we weren't a part of it. I was hurt none the less, I don't mind admitting it."

I nodded my head at him. "I can certainly understand. What else did the two of you discuss?"

"Anna and I haven't seen each other for years and years. Back when I was a kid, I was pretty jealous of her. She lived with my dad, he seemed to dote on her, and he ignored me when she was around. She got tons of cool presents at Christmas and I got almost nothing from him. I hated her, I'm ashamed to admit it, but it's true. I realized during our conversation I needed to let go of childish emotion. Nothing in our childhood was her fault and the person I needed to be angry at was my father. We talked about our lives and what was going on, just a conversation between two people who used to know each other and had lost touch. It was incredibly surreal." He stopped talking and stared off into the distance.

"I can only imagine," I admitted.

"I felt a lot better about everything when the epiphany of my misplaced anger hit me, but then she said something which really threw me for a loop."

"Which was?" I pushed gently.

"She said if I wanted to talk to her again I should only ever call her on her cell phone, the number she had called me from.

I should never, ever call her at home. I should never, ever let her mother know she and I had spoken. She sounded scared, like a little kid who was worried about getting into trouble with her mom."

Before I could think of an appropriate response, our lunch arrived. When the server left, I looked at Miles.

"Miles, do you really think Anna is afraid of her mother?"

His grey eyes locked onto mine. "Well I sure as hell always was."

16

Devil with the Blue Dress On

My lunch interview with Miles had been pleasant and I left feeling hopeful the next interview would go as well. I was almost positive I could complete all the Kincaid interviews in one day just as Jewels predicted but I wasn't prepared to take any bets.

Jillian Kincaid Marshall lived on the west end of Nashville in the very upscale and toney end of town. The address was for a neat stone bungalow circa 1930. The large house in an expensive part of town made me wonder what the Marshalls did for a living.

I admired the place as I wandered up the walk and rang the bell. Jillian answered within seconds. She was wearing a cobalt blue linen dress which was expensive and well-made, and her gold jewelry was real and understated. The shoes were Gucci. The woman looked as though she was on her way to an important fundraiser at the Junior League, not meeting a PI in her living room. Jillian seemed wary of me when she stepped back and opened the door wider.

"Come in, Ms. Maher." Her tone was less than friendly.

"Please, call me Tess." I walked into the house. It had been lovingly restored and was furnished in a chic 1930's style with art deco pieces as accent. "Your home is lovely."

"Thank you. Please, have a seat," her voice was clipped and cold.

She pointed to a sofa in the living room and I obediently sat down. I was sure without a doubt that this woman didn't want me in her house. Her body language was stiff and when she sat she crossed her legs and folded her arms folded across her middle. I became a tad bit uncomfortable.

Two little girls came running into the room and stopped dead in their tracks, their identical grey eyes fixed on me. They were twins with blond ringlets in a halo around their heads. They looked like little dolls. I smiled at them. I'm pretty good with kids, and they seem to like me. My mother says it because I haven't grown up myself. She could be right.

"Hello," I said softly.

The girls walked to their mother and clutched her skirt with chubby fingers.

"Tranger," one of the girls said and pointed to me.

Wow, isn't it a shame we have to teach children not to talk to people they don't know. Sheesh! As the Wicked Witch of the West once famously said, 'What a world.'

The mother smiled for the first time. "Angeline, Olivia, this is Miss Tess and she's not a stranger, she's GiGi's friend. Can you say hello?"

The little girls peeked out from behind their mom.

"'lo," one whispered and the other looked down at her bare feet.

I smiled again. "I'm very pleased to meet you girls. How old are you?"

They both held up three fingers at me. "Free," they said in unison.

Jillian Marshall patted her daughters on their shoulders. "Sweets, why don't you go play in your room while Miss Tess and I talk, okay?"

The children nodded, took one more look at me, and scurried off hand-in-hand.

"Now Tess, what can I do for you? I know my mother has hired you to look into my father's death. It seems she believes he showed up at a séance in some fortune teller's parlor and talked to her through an Ouija board. You were there as well, and she is convinced he talked to you and told you Jonnie murdered him, blah, blah, blah. So, I'm just supposed to believe you're some sort of a ghost busting detective? Because quite frankly, I don't."

"What do you believe?" I asked being careful to keep my voice calm and even. I knew I needed to step carefully, the woman was pissed and I hoped to dial her back.

"I believe you are a con person who is seeking to take advantage of my mother who has certainly done her share of ludicrous things in my lifetime, mind you. This is just one more thing in a long line of ridiculously bad decisions. I believe you are defrauding her and the whole séance thing was probably a setup since the whole psychic thing is nothing but bullshit. Did I mention my mother is gullible as well? How'm I doing so far?" She stopped in her diatribe long enough to draw a breath. "Look you, my father is dead, there's a lot of old baggage left over with my mother and with all of us. But he's gone and it's done in my mind. I forgave him. Even though all I ever wanted was for him to have a relationship with Olivia and Angeline, but all that's over, water under the bridge. What I would like now is for you to tell my mother you're a fraud and walk away, so we can all move on with our lives." She stared at me hard, her eyes like ice chips.

I attempted to hold my temper, after all most people can go their entire lives and never have contact with the dead, many people don't even believe it's possible. I understand. But it's not every day I'm called a fraud. A nut case maybe, but not a fraud.

I took a deep, calming breath and said, "I'm sorry you feel that way. Actually, I'm a pretty good PI; I do occasionally see dead people and have since I was a small child, not much older than your girls."

"You must take me for as big a fool as my mother is, but I'm not." Jillian's voice practically dripped acid on the hard wood floor.

"In my opinion, you're selling your mother short, I doubt she's anyone's fool, she just wants the truth. I suspect the two of you rarely see eye to eye on any given subject, but that's between you and her. How'm I doin'? I can continue this investigation without any input from you if you desire. Your choice."

She raised one perfectly waxed eyebrow at me. "Who the hell do you think you're talking to?"

"I know I'm talkin' to the daughter of my client, a daughter who doesn't appear to want to cooperate with an investigation into her own father's death, a daughter who looks down on her mother. Keep in mind if I do indeed find enough proof to open a police investigation, you will talk to them whether you like it or not." I stood up. "I won't take any more of your time, Ms. Marshall. I'll see myself out." I turned to go without waiting for Jillian to say anything; I was halfway to the door before she did.

"Wait!"

I turned back to her.

"Give me one reason to participate in this farce," she snapped.

"If your father was murdered, his murderer should be brought to justice."

She stood staring at me. "He left us without a backward glance as if we were nothing but an inconvenience to him. Why the hell should I care what happened to him! I think Sandy's right, he deserved what he got, and it's called karma." She was making a real effort to keep her voice low.

"I get that he was a waste of space as a father, I've talked to your brother and sisters and this seems to be a pretty common opinion. But, if it was murder, then it's still wrong and the murderer needs to be brought to justice no matter how we feel about the victim. It's the right thing."

She stared at me for a full fifteen seconds and when she spoke her voice was so low it was almost a whisper. It was filled with anger and fear and maybe hatred. "You don't understand. If the bitch did murder him and it comes out, it'll be in the papers. Everyone will know, all the neighbors and the people at the club, the other attorneys in Ryan's firm, people at church. I'll be humiliated. Someday I'll have to tell Angeline and Olivia their grandfather was murdered. In the name of God, what kind of a person knows someone who's been murdered? It's a stigma just too horrible to bear."

Her statement hit home and it hurt, I felt like I'd been punched in the gut. I knew someone who was murdered, someone I loved.

"The only answer I have to offer you is justice and truth are more important than what the freakin' neighbors think." I bit the words off as I said them. God, I was pissed at her stupid attitude, after all this was her father we were talking about.

Jillian straightened her back and drew a breath. "I want you to go away. I'll have Ryan file an injunction against your investigation, get your license pulled, and I'll put pressure on my mother to fire you. He's dead, why won't you let him be?"

"Because I was paid to do a job."

"I'll ruin you. If you continue, I will ruin you. Do you understand me? I'll make sure no one ever hires you again. When I'm done with you, you'll be selling shoes at Wal-Mart." She was so cold I felt frost forming in the air between us.

"Bring it, sister, 'cause I promise, better'n you have tried." I turned and walked out the door.

I calmly closed the front door behind me and calmly walked to the Jeep, calmly climbed inside and calmly started the engine. Inside I wanted to scream, to punch something or someone, namely Jillian Kincaid Marshall. What an unbelievable bitch! I pounded on the steering wheel as I drove away, cursing luridly. Lucky for me the phone rang about two minutes later so I was saved from being spotted by some Nashville Metro cop, who would've pulled me over for reckless driving, or just being crazy. I hit the control on my Bluetooth.

"Tess," I snapped.

"Hey Boss what's up?" Jewels asked.

"You have no idea what a BITCH Jillian Marshall is, she is … Goddamn, and Jewels, words fail me, OH MY FREAKIN' GOD! I'm so mad I could push little ducks in the creek!" I shouted.

"Well you'd be wrong, I do have some idea. I just talked to her husband and he made all kinds of charmin' threats against you. He seems to think he's the king of the world and everyone will just give over to him. He's a real asshole, Boss."

I blew out a breath in a huffing sound and just sucked air in an attempt to calm the hell down. "Sorry Jewels, sorry I yelled and sorry he called and sorry he acted like a prick to you. He can blow smoke all he wants, and he might even cause us a little bit of trouble but in the long run he's just spoutin' off, okay?"

"I know but he was just so mean. He made threats, called you a whack job and me an idiot for workin' for you. He pissed me off." She sounded pissed off too, which was very rare for her.

I had to smile. "The hell with him, let the bastard do his worst. Since I've been kidnapped, held hostage, beaten up, shot and chased through the woods by real bad guys, I think I ain't afraid of this Marshall guy."

Jewels laughed. "Right Boss. So what do we do now?"

"I report to Georgia Kincaid, give her the lowdown on her daughter and see if she can give me any guidance in turn. You know, I think I'll wait until tomorrow for that conversation, I'm too pissed off right now."

"Okay, you headed back?"

"Yes ma'am and I think I might get ahead of the rush hour, at least I'm gonna try. I doubt I'll make it in before you head home, so lock it up and I'll see you in the mornin'."

"Roger, be safe."

I hit the button to disconnect and drove as fast as I thought I could without getting nailed by a THP officer. For a moment, I thought about calling Derek and inviting myself to stay over. Then I realized I'd have to explain why I was so pissed off and then I'd have to talk about Chick.

Chick was dead, but he lived in my heart. I loved him, thought about him every day, reached for the phone every time something happened I wanted to share with him, and then was crushed by the realization I couldn't call. It hurt and the pain didn't seem to be getting any better.

I wasn't ready to share any of those feelings with Derek. I wasn't even sure if the relationship we had was the kind of relationship where you shared such intimate details. I wasn't even sure if what we had was a relationship. I guess I hadn't really defined what we were doing, besides the horizontal mambo, which was great, don't get me wrong. I just wasn't sure if it went beyond the physical, and I wasn't sure I wanted an answer to my question. I could have spent the rest of the trip home pondering the nature of things but instead I fought rush hour traffic which I had not managed to get in front of, tried to stay close to the speed limit and did not rubber neck at the three wrecks I passed.

When I realized how long I was going to be on the road, I changed my mind and called Georgia Kincaid. I thought I'd calmed down enough to speak rationally to her. Georgia caught the phone on the third ring.

"Hello," she said.

"Hi Georgia, it's Tess Maher. How are you?"

"Frankly, I have been sitting here waiting for you to call and tell me to go to hell."

"Why would I do such a thing?" I asked but I felt I knew the answer.

"My daughter Jillian called me earlier, probably right after she called her husband. She raised ten kinds of hell with me, called both you and me several kinds of fools and idiots, seems I have no brains and you're a crook."

"Yep, I had pretty much the same discussion with her which is why I'm callin' you. How would you like me to proceed or do you want me to proceed at all?"

Georgia was silent for a moment when she spoke she sounded very thoughtful. "I want you to proceed; I've already told Jillian I wouldn't back down. Of course, she didn't like it, she fancies herself to be everyone's boss. She's the president of the Junior League so she expects to say 'jump' and have you say 'ribbit' on the way up. She's very angry; I imagine you'll get a phone call from her husband, the attorney."

"Already happened, he talked to Juliet, my office manager. She's right insulted." Seemed I'd been on the mark about Jillian being in the League.

"So will you continue?"

"I'll be happy to continue the investigation. I'm not very intimidated by lawyers."

"He's an unpleasant man, a cut-throat litigator and a braggart. As you may surmise I don't care for him in the least. But he's a bad person to have on the opposing side. I feel sure he'll try to ruin you."

"Georgia, I've never backed down from a fight in my life and I sure don't intend to start at this late date. If Jon Kincaid was murdered then he deserves justice even if he wasn't a nice man or a good father or a decent human being. He still deserves justice and I mean for him to have it," I said.

"Good, good, thank you. So now we've settled the question, what's next?" Georgia asked.

"I'd love to talk to the doctor who was on call the night Kincaid died, the odds aren't good with HIPAA, but I'll see what I can do. I've talked to the nurse who was on duty, I won't tell you her name because she asked me not to mention her. I will tell you she's scared spitless of the Widow Kincaid and had nothing good to say about her. She confirmed Jon asked her to call his lawyer because he wanted to change his will."

Georgia gasped.

"What! Oh my God, I can't believe he wanted to make changes. I hardly know what to make of it." She seemed to be astonished at the news. I had nothing but dead air from her for a few moments but I could hear her breathing.

Finally she sighed deeply, "He never seemed to care about the children and I have such hard feelings for him." She paused and I thought she might be crying so I waited for her to compose herself. "If he was going to change his will and include the children then I'm feeling guilty now over those angry feelings I've carried for so long. I confess I started you on this investigation because I truly despise Jonnie, but in the process I also remembered how much I once loved Jon."

"I think instead of guilt you should feel a little bit of kindness toward him since it looks like he intended to do the right thing. Maybe you could even forgive him," I suggested.

Georgia laughed, "Maybe, and frankly that's a very big maybe. Tess, can you tell me why he asked a nurse to call his lawyer?"

"Just guessin' but I'd say he didn't call himself because he was too infirmed, and he asked her to make the call because he trusted her."

"Oh, I see." She sounded sad.

"Georgia, I don't want you to tell anyone he intended to change the will, not even your children. I believe if Jonnie murdered Jon, it was because she knew he intended to make changes. If we want to keep this investigation quiet, you can't tell."

"Oh, of course, I understand. I certainly don't want to bring trouble down on us, or at least any more trouble. Hmmm my other line is ringing. Oh goody, it's my son-in-law." Her voice was flat.

"Well you go and enjoy your phone call, remember not a word about the will."

"I promise and thank you so much, Tess, for not firing me."

I laughed, "You're welcome bye bye."

"Bye."

Strange Days

It was a very long ride home and the only crazy thing I failed to see on the road was a cow being carried away by a tornado. I didn't know it was Drive Like a Crash Test Dummy Day; I must've missed the memo. I was sure happy and relieved to finally pull into my own driveway. I turned off the Jeep's engine and sat with my head resting against the wheel for a few moments just breathing.

"What's up buttercup?" My father said. I grinned without raising my head.

"Just trying to regain my sense of equilibrium, it's been a strange day."

I heard the sound of glass clinking on glass and looked up. Daddy held up two bottles of Fat Tire and offered me one. He always seems to know when I need a shoulder or an ear, an amazing man. He's an extremely sensitive being for a guy born in the middle of the last century, who'd done his turn at war and wore a badge for forty years.

"You wanna talk about it?"

I drew in a deep breath. "Yep, I do."

We walked around the house to the patio together and each claimed a seat on the glider with a view out over the valley. As I sat there I could feel a sense of peace stealing over me. My father is a wise man and he sat and drank his beer in silence, didn't try to push me or hurry me, just let me set my own pace. By such a point in the proceedings my mother would have already asked fifty questions. I firmly believe if I had finished my beer and gone into the house he wouldn't have said a word.

"This case is touching on nerves, Daddy, a lot of different nerves. First, I was outed to Derek, the fireman I see in Nashville, and don't try to act as if you didn't know about him. He's a nice guy, I like him but I wasn't ready to have the 'I see dead people' talk with him. I was pissed at Moira and Mars, a terribly uncomfortable place for me. We've made up, by the way. This Jon Kincaid guy may have been murdered by a real bitch of a woman and no one seems to care he's dead. Well, maybe his son does, but his daughters? Not so much. They're embarrassed by it and they just want it to go away so they can move on with their lives. It sucks. I got called a lot of bad things today by one of the daughters, and growled at by a little wannabe dog, and threatened by a lawyer, and had an amazingly shitty commute home. But the worst thing about today was I realized when Chick was murdered I would have done anything to catch the people responsible and bring them to justice, anything, anything." I tapped my beer bottle on the table for emphasis. "I just think no one feels the same way for Jon Kincaid, it seems they mostly want to jam up the widow or just brush it all under a rug and it makes me kinda sad. He might not have been a very nice man but someone ought to feel bad he's gone. It seems to me the only person who's tore up about his death is the nurse who worked at the rehab center." I took a big sip of my beer.

"Well, different people get different emotions. You loved Chick, we all did, he was a good man who deserved better and we wanted justice for him. I reckon we all thought we'd sleep a little more soundly at night knowin' we'd done our best to make it happen. Maybe this Kincaid fella don't have anybody who feels kindly toward him, maybe he don't deserve to have anyone feel that way about him."

"Daddy, do you believe some people are completely devoid of redeemin' characteristics? There's some who don't deserve to be mourned? Or avenged? I can't believe that." I shook my head. "Murder is murder and the person who takes another life deserves to be brought to justice and the victim deserves vindication. I learned those values from you. Remember when I was a kid and Maudine James shot her husband in his sleep?"

"Yep, I remember. Tucker'd been beating hell out of Maudine for years and years. One night after he went to bed drunk she took his deer rifle and shot him in the head. Hell of a mess she made."

"What'd you tell me?"

"It wasn't self-defense 'cause she wasn't in fear of her life at the time of the shootin'. She may have been afraid he'd hurt her again, and she may even have been a little bit crazy in the moment, but it was murder plain and simple and she had to go to trial for it. Regardless of the fact everybody in town thought she'd waited ten years too long to kill him. Hell, half the town thought she ought to be given some sort of a medal."

I grinned, remembering all the controversy surrounding the events. A lot of folks were mad at Daddy for arresting Maudine, but he did it anyway. I was about ten at the time. "You arrested her and she went to trial even though everyone in town felt sorry for her. He may have been a POS, but even Tucker James deserved justice, you said."

"He did, and Maudine was tried by a jury of her peers."

"Who found her guilty of involuntary manslaughter; she got twelve years, reduced to time served in your jail and five years' probation, oh and community service."

"Right and don't forget a lot of flowers got planted in this town 'cause of her. She still tends flower beds all over the square ya' know,"

I laughed and leaned over to rest my head on his shoulder. "Seems sad to me a person dies and no one misses 'em."

"Yep, it's sad. Not everyone leaves good memories for the ones left behind to hold on to and that's a fact."

"I know," I sighed. "I know."

I dreamed of Chick when I finally fell asleep. He was trying to tell me something but I couldn't make it out. I woke up tangled in the covers, sweaty and frustrated as all hell.

"Chick," I whispered. "Chick Donnelly, you come here right now and tell me straight out what the hell you want."

I sat up and tried to straighten the covers; I finally gave up, got up and shook everything out. I grumpily got back in bed and lay on my back with my arms folded over my chest.

"What the hell, Chick?" I muttered.

It had been quite some time since Chick had showed up in my room and I missed him. I wondered what was going on with him; it was weird to dream him that way. Usually when I dreamt of Chick, it was of the past and the things we did together. In my dreams, he was still alive; it was like watching old home movies. It was good. Never before had I dreamt of him trying to talk to me, and he'd seemed frustrated as if he couldn't reach me. I was a little worried, actually I was disturbed enough I found I couldn't get back to sleep.

Usually when I can't sleep I wander downstairs for a midnight snack, but with the extra pounds I was carrying I decided it was a bad idea. Instead I got up, pulled out my laptop, and opened my notes on the Kincaid case.

"Tess." I jumped a foot.

Chick was standing behind me.

"Jesus H. Christ, you gotta learn to knock, or rattle chains, or clear your throat, something!"

Chick laughed, "Sorry Tess. I was trying to wake you up so I could talk to you 'bout this case you're workin' on; I kept tellin' you to wake up."

"Oh, well, why didn't you just talk to me in my dream?"

"I wanted to talk to you like this face to face, 'cause I was afraid if I talked to you in your dream you might not remember in the mornin'."

I shrugged, "You might be right. Chick, it's good to see you, I've missed you something awful."

Chick grinned at me. "Well, truth to tell, I've been kinda busy over on the other side. Lots to do and learn and plenty of folks to do some catchin' up with too. You know, my folks are there and my Aunt Amanda. They send their regards."

"That's nice; tell 'em I said hey. So, what's up? Not that you need a reason to visit me, of course."

"This case, the murderer is a nut job and dangerous as a copperhead. I just wanted you to know the facts. Jon Kincaid is worried she's gonna hurt his kids. I'm worried she's gonna hurt you."

"She doesn't know about me yet, right?" I felt the slightest bit of alarm.

"Not near as we can tell, but unless she talks to someone about it or writes it down, we can't know. It ain't like we can read minds, ya know."

"Oh, I guess I didn't know. Hey, wait a minute, you said 'we', who's we?"

"Me and Jon."

"Oh Christ. You know Jon's a world class prick, right?"

Chick laughed. "Well he might be but me and him's on the same side in this business. We'll keep an eye on the widder and we'll let ya know if she gets up to somethin'."

"Just for the record, I rather you show up to tell me. I had to banish Jon the last time he was here for being an asshole."

This time Chick threw back his head and laughed and laughed. "Oh, I know all 'bout it, Jon gimme chapter and verse. He seems to think you're quite a handful."

"I'd be willin' to bet those are not the words he used to describe me."

"You might be right." He stopped laughing and looked up as if he was listening to something. "Sorry darlin', I gotta go. The ballgame's fixin' to start."

"Ballgame? You playin' or watchin'?"

"Playin' o' course, you won't believe who with neither. You be careful, we'll be keepin' an eye on things. I just know when she finds out 'bout you, and it's a when not an if, all hell's gonna break loose."

I sighed, "Probably. Chick, thanks for taking care of me."

"You know I love ya, girl."

"I love you too," I said.

He disappeared between one eye blink and another, before he could even tell me who was playing ball.

"I love you, Chick," I whispered sadly.

18

Tell Me Lies

I climbed out of bed the next morning and sat on the side of it, thinking about the visitation from the night before. I decided if dead people were worrying about you, then you might really be in trouble. I pulled on running clothes, gathered up the dogs, and did my three miles.

Running is good for the brain as well as the body. When you hit a certain point in a run, the endorphins kick in and you're filled with a sense of well-being. Plus, the cobwebs get cleared out of your head. I walked back down the driveway in a better frame of mind than when I started and had my day all planned out.

Breakfast was first however. My parents and YaYa were eating and gossiping as usual.

"That Nona Johnson's done hooked herself another man. I heard it from Bev down to the Piggly Wiggly t'other morning when I was in there with Ruth getting snacks for Pinochle. This makes five, ya know." YaYa declared as she held up one hand with five fingers showing. Then she poured cream in to her coffee.

Bev Watts was the checker at the Piggly Wiggly and had been for a hundred years or more; she probably sold groceries to Noah right before the flood. Bev knew everything juicy about everybody and she told anyone who was willing to listen. YaYa was always willing to listen to the good stuff, which the new husband info clearly was.

"Well, maybe she can't be happy unless she has a man," my mother offered. "Some people are like that, you know."

I slid into my place at the table and shoveled eggs and bacon onto my plate. I needed coffee desperately so I poured a cup. I didn't say a word and noticed Daddy was absorbed in the morning paper – or hiding behind it.

"Well if she wouldn't keep killin' 'em off, she wouldn't need to go and find new ones all the time," YaYa chuckled at her own wit. The rumor mill had decided Nona was a serial murderer of little old men with big, fat pensions.

"Now Mama, you know there's no proof of any such thing. Her husbands were all in ill health and nature took its course." Mommy looked at my grandmother with disapproval.

"Maybe she's just good at pickin' sick old men and getting' 'em to marry her," my father offered from behind the newspaper.

"That is an awful thing to say! Nona is as good as gold, always volunteering over at the hospital and the nursing home; she cooks for days on end for the big bake sale over at the Presbyterians and puts in time at the dog hospital too. You're just being mean." Mommy seemed fairly outraged at the idea.

"Just sayin', she gets married and within a few years she's wearin' Widder's Weeds again. I think she's got a good eye is all," Daddy answered.

"Plus all them places you named are good places to find old men," YaYa offered. "Smart is what she is, I say."

I giggled which proved to be my undoing.

"How can you laugh?" Mommy demanded.

"Well, it is funny in a black humor sorta way. I do think she's good to the men she marries, they always look happy, anyway, until they die. So they have a nice few years and she gets a bonus. I say that's a win-win." I buttered my toast.

"You three are horrible!" Mommy snapped.

"But probably right," Daddy said from behind the paper.

I ate, washed my dish and cleared the table all the while listening to the gossip of my little town. I smiled to myself.

"Family, I gotta go to work and earn a little money today, so I am off to the showers," I announced.

"What're you up to today?" asked YaYa.

"Well, I'll devote today to followin' a fellow who might or might not be cheatin' on his wife. I think I'll see what kinda mischief he might be up to on this fine day. It's close, which is good 'cause I am tired of road trips."

"I hope his wife is wrong," Mommy said sadly.

"So do I. They seem to have a nice life, he's a tax accountant, she's a stay at home mom, they have three kids under the age of twelve, a nice house, a vacation place down at the lake, two new cars in the driveway. They go to church, volunteer, were married right out of college, and now this." I closed the door on the dishwasher.

"You'll get to the truth, whatever it might be," Daddy reassured me.

"Okay, I'll see you folks for dinner unless I get a better offer."

I headed up stairs to get ready and spent the next forty-five minutes thinking as I showered and dressed. I had checked the financials on Matt Carlyle, courtesy of his wife, and had found nothing to indicate he was spending money on secret rendezvous with girlfriends. Of course, he was a tax accountant and he'd know how to do things off the books. I had ferreted out some of his clients and made a few phone calls pretending to be interested in hiring the man. Everyone had good things to say about him, there was no evidence he played the ponies, drank to excess, or indulged in any questionable behavior. Yet.

The kitchen was empty when I went back down stairs, so I yelled my good-byes to the family. I heard acknowledgement from humans and dogs as I left. I called Mars as soon as I was in the Jeep.

"Hello girlfriend," she purred.

"Hello girlfriend, what's up with you?" I smiled.

"Wondering where you been. You don't call, you don't write, you don't send flowers," Mars said in a sexy voice.

I laughed. "I apologize; I've been burnin' up the roads on a case which took me to Atlanta twice and Nashville yesterday. It's the case that's your fault, by the by."

"Then all is forgiven. You want to do something soon? Maybe a movie?" she asked.

"Sounds good. It's been long and long since we had a movie night." I sighed. I love movies. "I'll check and see what's playing, I'm pretty sure I'll have time."

"I wanna see that new one with Matt Damon, okay?"

"Sweetie, Matt is always okay with me. I'll call you later and we can make plans."

"Hey, if you'd like to have dinner with your brother and me, Saturday night works for us."

Hmmm, Mars said "us" in reference to her and Connell so did she mean they were an "us"? And if so, how did I feel about it? I wasn't sure and I felt like my doubt made me a bad person.

"Works for me, I love to spend time with the two of you." I couldn't help but feel it would be weird if they were an "us". Damn it.

"You okay? You sound kind of funny."

"I just have a lot on my mind. Work stuff, you know." I tried to sound light and carefree.

"Sure, if you say so. I'll talk to you later." She did not sound convinced.

"See ya later, love ya, bye."

"See ya later, love ya, bye."

She wasn't fooled, she knew me too damn well. I loved both her and my brother. I had very different relationships with each of them, but they were each my best friend. So was I worried about getting left out of the loop if the two of them hooked up? Maybe I was a little bit jealous and maybe a little bit sad because I was relationshipless. Yes, there was Derek, but he was a friend with benefits sort of thing. It was not a share the depths of my psyche sort of thing, tell all my deep dark secrets to sort of thing. My relationships with Mars and Connell and with Chick were deep relationships. I wasn't sure I wanted to add a new person to my secret world. But if my two best friends turned their attention to each other and away from me, then what?

I was being a baby, a spoiled, titty sack baby. I mentally shook myself. Things change and sometimes they evolve as well. Sometimes they mutate, the evil side of me added.

"Morning Glory," I said as I came in the door.

"Morning Boss, you have messages." Jewels handed me a stack of notes from the message book.

"Anything urgent?"

"There's a couple; the mean lawyer called again to say he's issued a restraining order to try and stop the investigation. I'm pretty sure it won't work, but I put a call into Liz just in case."

Liz was our attorney; her office was in Dixon since we didn't use Richard "Buzzy" Aldrin, the local guy. I'm not saying Buzzy's not a good lawyer, he is, but there's a good reason for me to take my business elsewhere. Buzzy hates me and has ever since the sixth grade. There's a thing about a baseball game when I may or may not have broken his nose on the playground in front of the entire sixth grade class and his future wife. Anyway, ancient history, but he still hasn't forgiven me. Some people can carry a grudge, ya know.

"What else?" I asked.

"Stephanie Carlyle called and wants to know when you're gonna get on the stick, her words not mine, and find some dirt on her husband. She is not a happy woman."

"Hmmm, wonder how she'll feel if I find out he's innocent?"

"Boss, I get the feelin' she won't be happy about it. Most women would jump up and down to find out their husband was faithful, but I think this one will be disappointed."

"Well, not our problem. I'm gonna take another run at him today and see what he's up to, maybe I'll have an answer by suppertime. Anything else?"

"Nope."

"So when our lawyer calls back, have the conversation with her and then call me with the news, okay?"

"Without doubt, Boss." Jewels saluted at me.

I gathered my PI kit and headed out to see if I could catch Mr. Carlyle being up to something naughty. I stopped at Jewels' desk.

"Jewels, will you trade cars with me today?" I asked.

"Sure enough." She dug out her keys and pitched them to me; I tossed her mine and hit the road.

Jewels' car is a Chevy Cruise, which I love to drive, so the trip to Dixon was pleasant. I pulled into the office park where Carlyle had his office, spotted his Saab and parked. It was early in the day, but cheating has no time clock. I pulled my visor down, settled my baseball cap over my eyes and opened my net book. I figured I could log onto some WIFI from the parking lot to check on the movie schedule. I knew I was supposed to be watching for Carlyle, but I was parked in such a way I could see everyone who left the office building and stakeouts are boring. I opened a pack of Big Red and settled back.

WIFI popped up, I was so delighted the office park had it. I gathered the facts on the Damon movie in no time flat, checked my Facebook, e-mail and the weather. It took about fifteen minutes and during those minutes no one had come or gone from the building. It was gonna be a long day, I figured.

I figured wrong because as the thought crossed my mind, Carlyle emerged from the front door and headed to his car. He looked like a man in a hurry. I quickly closed down my netbook and started the Jeep. Carlyle pulled out into traffic and I slid out behind him. He took a direct route with no stops to another office building; this one housed medical offices, according to the sign in front. I eased in and found a parking spot with no trouble. Carlyle got out of his vehicle and never even looked in my direction.

I followed him into the building and hung back as he got on the elevator but watched to see what floor he went to; third floor was the winner. I went back out to the Jeep and dug through my PI kit to get my little black business dress. I dug a little more and found the shoes to match. The dress is a simple A-line made from a non-winkle material so I can stuff it in the PI kit bag and it still comes out looking good I bless the human who invented the stuff. The black flats are non-descript. The ensemble looks like something an office girl would wear. Well, any office girl besides Jewels; she wears jeans, heavy metal bands tee-shirts and Converse high tops. We're a little casual at our place.

I grabbed my computer bag and dashed back into the building, found the ladies, and changed into my Girl Friday outfit. I gave myself a last check in the shiny door of the elevator, jumped on board and hit '3'. The third floor housed four offices; a proctologist, a gynecologist, an oncologist, and an oral surgeon. I was pretty sure I could rule out the gynecologist so I started with the proctologist.

I smiled at the receptionist. "Hi, I work for Mr. Matt Carlyle and he forgot to sign some very important papers before he left the office. Could I just slip back and get his John Hancock? I won't be a minute." I held up my computer bag to help sell my story.

She looked at me like I was from Mars. "No one by that name is here today."

I looked puzzled. "Hmmp, well I thought he was coming in today, maybe I mixed things up. Oh my, I just have to find him;

he said he wouldn't be back in the office today! Okay, gotta go, thanks so."

I made my exit and hit the oral surgeon, only to get the same answer, no Matt Carlyle. Strike two.

I breezed into the oncologist office, the receptionist looked up and I smiled.

"Hi, I work for Mr. Carlyle and he forgot to sign some important papers before he left the office. I really need his signature, you know how it is, they forget and you take the heat. Is it okay if I just slip back there and get him to sign? I promise I'll be a quiet as a church mouse."

She just stared at me like I had said something distasteful. "Mr. Carlyle is already in the exam room with Dr. Sanderson. She'd skin me alive if I let you interrupt. You're just gonna have to wait."

She was very frosty with me. I had thought I'd engendered some working girl simpatico with her, but it seemed not. I drew a big disappointed breath and put on my worried face.

"Fine, I understand." I sighed again. "Don't tell him I was here, please, I'll get one of the associates to sign off, which should work. Mr. Carlyle is just so hands on he likes to see everything himself before it leaves the office. Perfectionist, you know. Okay, well, thanks anyway."

She didn't say another word to me just watched me like a hawk as I left. An oncologist-- I knew you didn't go see one of those for a hangnail. Ms. Carlyle stated her husband had been acting 'weird' and I might have the answer to explain his behavior. I needed more, of course, before I could go to Ms. Carlyle. I went out to the parking lot and climbed back into the Jeep so I could do a little research on Dr. Brenda Sanderson. I'd palmed a business card before I left the office.

It took me about ten seconds to bring the net up thanks to the Wi-Fi of the building and I Googled the good doctor. Her website was very nice, professional but not cold. It created the illusion she gave a damn about the health of her patients and maybe she did. Her picture showed her to be quite beautiful with long, auburn hair, a heart-shaped face, and a great figure to boot. The pose was full length, with her body kind of cocked to the side and her arms folded under her breasts. She was smiling, which brought out her dimples, but she still managed to look professional. Looking at her picture made me want to smile. I suppose if you had the big 'C' then you want to be treated by someone who could make you smile.

I always thought cancer made you lose weight but Matt Carlyle looked pretty hefty to me. I had already looked at his website, so I decided to go to Facebook. I scrolled back through his pictures and got a bit of a surprise; Carlyle's photos showed a man who was considerably larger than the man I'd been following.

I opened the case files on him and sure enough his wife had stated he had lost weight, she suspected he had done so on purpose for a mistress. I didn't think so.

I debated what I should do. I didn't have proof Carlyle had cancer, I only suspected it. I didn't want to drop such a bomb on his wife if he was only going for a check-up. But I was fairly sure oncologists did not give check-ups, they gave a diagnosis and a plan for treatment. On the other hand, if cancer was the reason for his weird behavior, then my information might ease her mind. But not really, because if I had to choose between my husband having cancer or my husband cheating on me, I'd choose the bimbo. What a dilemma!

I put my head down on the steering wheel to rest my brain for a moment. When I looked up I saw Carlyle walking to his car. He had a dejected air about him; his pace was slow, his shoulders were slumped, and his head was down. The man was the poster child for bad medical news recipients. I sat staring at him and knew what I had to do; I had to tell his wife what I suspected. I had to do it in person – it was not news you delivered by phone.

I started the Jeep and headed for the Carlyle house. I admit I was depressed as hell. Carlyle seemed to be a pretty straight up guy and cancer is a bitch. I felt sorry for him. I felt sorry for his wife and kids too. I said a little prayer Dr. Sanderson could help him.

It took about fifteen minutes to arrive at the address and I called ahead to let Ms. Carlyle know I was on the way with a report. She was standing on the front porch waiting for me. I hated what I had to do; delivering bad news to a client sucks.

I parked and crossed the yard to her. "Ms. Carlyle, I'm Tess Maher, the PI you hired." I held out my hand but she didn't take it, so I stood there feeling kind of dopey.

"Let's make this fast before anyone notices you're here and wonders who you are. What's the deal, who is she? By the way I got the pictures you sent, good job getting pictures of my sister, really stellar. She can use them on her Christmas cards come December."

She was one unhappy woman and I thought I was going to make her more miserable with my news. I took a deep breath; it certainly seemed to be my week for pissing people off.

"Ms. Carlyle, I think your husband's recent behavior and weight loss might be because he's ill. I followed him to the office of an oncologist today. He was there for an appointment."

She looked stunned. "You're sure he was being seen by him? He wasn't there doing taxes for him?"

"I'm sure. I'm very sorry."

"You're sorry! You have no fucking idea what sorry is!" The woman glared daggers at me and I resisted the impulse to take a step back from her.

"I just knew you'd find another woman and then he'd give me everything to keep it quiet! People don't like philandering accountants, makes them nervous. God. Damn. It. To. Hell!"

Her phone rang and she fished it out of her pocket. "Hello? Oh, I am talking to her right now and you won't believe it, the bastard has been to see an oncologist, that's right a fuckin' cancer doctor. He's sick. Now what the hell do I do? I can't leave him, we're stuck. I have to wait for him to fucking die!"

Her face screwed up and she began to cry loud and long. Over her caterwauling I could hear a man's voice through her phone. Holy Batshit, I had certainly misjudged the situation. Where the hell was my radar?

I decided it was high time to take my leave so without further ado I turned and headed for my car. I'd send her a bill later; I just wanted to get as far away from her as possible as fast as possible. She was volatile and I wanted no part of the explosion I knew was coming. She was still squalling when I pulled out of the driveway.

19

Let's All Go to the Lobby

A mile down the road I called Mars. Her voice cheered me up a little when she answered. "Hello girlfriend, what's up?"

"I looked up the Damon movie – tonight at 6:45 at the Roxy. I need beer and a friendly shoulder, I've had a rather unsettling day and I need to talk about it. You game?"

"For you? Of course. You wanna meet at the Springwater about, what, five o'clock?"

"Good, it gives me time to get to the office and dictate some notes, make phone calls and what not."

"Good, then I'll meet you there. We can eat bad food and talk bad about people who deserve it. See ya later, love ya, bye."

"See ya later, love ya, bye."

I loved the Roxy. It was the original theater in Medicine Springs and like many small-town theaters it had gone through a lot of incarnations. At one point, it had even been a church.

The present incarnation seemed to be working out pretty well. The new owners had taken out every other row of seats and fastened small cube shaped coffee tables in their place. They served a rather extensive food menu, plus coffee, lattes, espressos, beer and wine. The staff takes your order and delivers it to your seat. It's like sitting in your living room and watching the biggest big screen ever. Sheer heaven! Mars and I would be drinking beer and eating popcorn in the very near future. The Roxy also hosts Rocky every Friday night, an old black and white movies night where they served wine, and matinees when you could bring the kids for $2, so they manage to keep the doors open.

Jewels was at her desk when I got back to the office. "Hey Boss, did you get the dirt?"

"Oh yeah I got the dirt." I laughed bitterly as I put my PI bag on the floor and leaned on her desk. "Seems our husband is seeing an oncologist as a patient and the wife is pissed he's not cheating because she wanted to nail him, take him to the cleaners, and run off with her lover. That's the Cliff Notes version."

"Sweet Jesus, howd'we handle this?" Jewels' eyes were wide in shock.

I walked over to pour me some coffee. "Well, we got a retainer. Let's see how many hours I've logged on this and if she owes us, we send her a bill today. If we owe her, we send her a check today. I want this hot potato out of my hands soonest."

I was still stirring my coffee when the phone rang. Jewels answered and I could hear the loud, angry voice of a woman coming through the receiver. I had a feeling I knew who the caller was.

"Yes, ma'am. No, ma'am. I don't know the answer to that, ma'am." Jewels looked at me, shook her head, and continued to talk. "No ma'am, she isn't back yet. Yes ma'am, I'll have her call you as soon as she hits the door." Jewels looked startled and hung up the phone. "Wow, so Ms. Carlyle is hoppin' mad. She wants her money back, you suck as a PI, she's gonna sue you as a matter of fact and she wants you to call her post haste."

"I gathered most of the message from the mad hornet sounds emanating from the phone. Well, she can get in line. Figure her bill out now please. I'll claim two days working this case. Let's get it together and then I'll call her."

"On it, Boss."

I wandered into my office and dictated the notes on the day up to and including the conversation I had with Mrs. Carlyle. I was almost finished when Jewels interrupted my train of thought.

"Boss, Ms. Carlyle paid for two days, so we're square. I'm typing it up.""Okay, I'll give her a call." UGH! I dreaded that call but first started soonest over. I picked up the phone and called Ms. Carlyle. It rang six times.

"Hello." She sounded very pleasant but I doubted she'd continue in the same vein once she realized who she had on the other end of the line.

"Ms. Carlyle, Tess Maher. I've calculated your bill, you paid for two days and I've spent two days on your case. We are even. I'm dictating the notes for you; my office manager will type them up and e-mail them to you before the end of the day. I appreciate your business."

I heard her a big draw breath. "Now you listen here, bitch, you will send me a check for the entire amount I paid you since you failed to do your job and you can stuff your notes up your ass."

I swallowed hard and got a rein on my temper; I don't like being called a female dog. "Well, it's a shame you feel that way, however, there will be no refund and the notes will be sent to you as per our contract. You asked me to find out what your husband was up to and I did. It isn't my fault he wasn't up to what you'd hoped, that's for you to deal with in your own way."

She was silent for a good fifteen seconds. "I guess you'll tell him about everything?"

"Nope, you're the client and you have complete confidentiality. He won't hear anything from me."

"Despite what you overheard and probably surmised?" she asked in a snippy tone.

"Look lady, your business is your business. I don't care who you screw as long as it doesn't involve children or little furry animals. Where you go from here is not my problem, I don't have a dog in this fight."

She hung up on me. Wow! What a pleasant woman.

I finished the dictation and handed it off to Jewels. "Get this done and e-mail it today. I wanna wrap this up so I don't have to fool with that damned woman any more. Include a copy of the contract, highlight the part about refunds, and send her another copy of the invoice."

"I'll make it very clear we don't refund money on services which have been performed," Jewels agreed.

I changed clothes again and Jewels and I spent what was left of the day playing catch up on all the things which have to be done to keep an office running. When I looked at my clock, it was ten 'til five. I tidied up my desk and grabbed my bag.

"Jewels, I'm gonna go meet Mars. I'll see you in the morning."

"Have a good night Boss, I've got it handled." She back hand waved at me while still crouched over her computer.

I covered the distance between the office and the Springwater in short order and actually beat Mars there, which was a miracle. I walked up to the bar. It was early for Springwater and things hadn't gotten rolling yet, so I was the only customer in the place.

"Hey Andy, give me a couple of Gherst House Ambers please."

Andy Fitzgerald, the proprietor of the joint, grinned at me. "Yes ma'am, what else can I get fer ya?"

"I think a SW burger, with mustard, pickles, cheese and tomato. One SW veggie with mustard, mayo and ketchup, drag it through the garden. Fries for me, a salad for my date. Add some vinaigrette and a little cheese on the salad and that oughta do us."

Andy's grin grew. "You ain't got no date, you're meetin' Marcella. That's her order."

While Andy might not be the sharpest knife in the drawer, he remembers how everyone who eats his food likes it prepared. He amazes me; I can barely remember how I like my own food prepared.

I grinned at the former football player. "You got me. Can't pull the wool over your eyes, Andy."

He laughed and the sound of it made me happy. Andy is a good soul. I carried the beers out to one of the picnic benches in the back and waited for Ms. Marcella Price to show up. I had barely consumed half of my beer before she sat down opposite me and grabbed her beer.

"What's up, girl?" she asked and tipped her beer to her lips.

"I just had a rather crazy day and I need beer, Matt Damon, and your company."

Mars laughed. "You don't have to have a crazy day to need those things! So, tell it and I'll tell you mine."

"I was hired to tail a guy cause his wife thought he was cheatin' on her. He's been actin' strange and has lost weight. She figured there was another woman. Anywho … I followed him for two days. Turns out he's been going to an oncologist as a patient and has lost weight probably 'cause he has freakin' cancer. So I went to bring this bad news to the wife and she ripped my face off while having a conversation on the phone with her boyfriend. She's pissed 'cause she can't divorce him since he's sick, now she has to wait on him to die before she's free."

"Wow, I didn't know you had a saint for a client!" Mars grinned at me.

I snickered. "Yep she's a doll and a true humanitarian. She was hopin' he'd buy her silence about the alleged affair since he's a CPA and couldn't afford the scandal. Here's the bonus: she wants a refund of her retainer."

Andy arrived with our dinner.

"Hey Marcella you're lookin' good." He grinned.

She flashed her million dollar smile back at him.

"Hey, you didn't tell me how good I looked! What am I, chopped liver? I'm actually wearing mascara!" I pouted at him but ruined it by laughing.

Andy just walked away whistling.

"So, what's the deal with you and Connell?" I bit into my burger; it was heaven on a bun. Andy could do magical things with dead cow.

"I'm not sure. We have a great time together, we like the same things, have a similar history, a matching quirky sense of humor and…"

"STOP! I'm trying to eat!"

"You asked and I'm tryin' to tell. We work on so many levels but then it hits a wall. We fool around a little. Kissing is wonderful, he makes my toes curl, and then… nothing. He backs away and turns on the TV or goes to the kitchen and fetches beer."

I wasn't sure how to respond. I mean, if it had been anybody besides Connell, I'd have told her to put her shoes on and run home. Men who give mixed signals are not worth giving the time of day, but it *was* Connell.

"I'm sorry, I don't know what to say." I shrugged my shoulders. I felt kind of helpless.

"I keep telling myself it isn't me, but what if it is me? What if he's only being nice, humoring me 'cause he doesn't want to hurt my feelings?" Marcella picked half-heartedly at her salad.

"Oh, Jesus Christ on a freakin' pogo stick, Mars! This is Connell Alexander Maher we're talkin' about. Have you met him? He ain't that nice. If he didn't like you then, he'd avoid you like the plague. Maybe after She Whose Name Must Not Be Spoken, he's gun shy or commitment phobic."

Connell had an ex-wife who really screwed him over and he carried a bad taste in his mouth on account of her. She cheated on him with a used car salesman; I mean, really, who does such a thing?

"Thanks, Dr. Phil, but what the hell am I supposed to do about it? My first impulse is to just stay away from him, but I love spendin' time with him. My second impulse is to meet him at my door naked." She sighed. "I'm frustrated."

"Let's go look at Matt Damon for ninety minutes. He'll make us both feel better," I suggested.

"True that." We finished our food and our beers and went to the movies.

Bad Moon Rising

The movie was great, of course. You just can't go wrong with Damon, he always satisfies. I promised Mars we could all have dinner at Connell's Saturday night if she promised to set it up. It was a good night and made me realize how lucky I was; I had good health, good friends, a family I liked, and a great profession. I listed those things off when I crawled into bed. I believe you should count your blessings on a regular basis.

Next morning, I was up with the sun, made my run, got my shower, and ate a little breakfast with the family all in good time. The sun was shining and all was right in the world. At least, it was until I got to the office.

"Morning Boss, hope you had a pleasant morning," Jewels greeted me.

"Because the rest of my day won't be? Just when I was gonna say thank God it's Friday, too." I wanted to run but knew I couldn't.

"Well, let's just call it challenging, shall we? You have messages. Our lawyer says Marshall can file all the paperwork he wants or has time to fool with, but he can't actually make you cease an investigation. It impinges on your personal freedom and inhibits your right to make a living."

"Good to know. What's the bad news?" I damn well knew by the look on her face there was some.

"Marshall has already filled a restraining order and three injunctions against you to stop the investigation. One, you have no grounds for an investigation. Two, you are causing great personal pain and suffering to Mrs. Marshall by the investigation and damaging his family. Three, Ms. Kincaid has no right to hire you to conduct an investigation, therefore you must cease and desist."

"Hmmm, so I reckon he intends to bury me in paperwork, must not be an environmentalist. Okay, ask Liz to answer each of 'em. Ms. Kincaid can pay her for it. Get an invoice so we can pass it on. I'll double check with Georgia to make sure she wants to foot the bill."

"Already asked and answered. Since we're within our rights to conduct an investigation which we've been hired to do, we aren't breaking any laws so we're clear. Liz said if we received any more paperwork from attorney Marshall, we should just forward it to her and she'd deal with him. She did say you could call her if you wanted. The cost will be minimal; it seems Liz doesn't like Mr. Marshall so she's doing the work for a reduced fee just for the pleasure of annoying him." Jewels grinned at me.

I chuckled. "Bonus. I'd love to hear what Marshall did to put the bee under Liz's bonnet. What else?"

"The aforementioned Ms. Kincaid called you, she wants an update."

"You've saved the best for last. What is it?" I could read her like a book and vice versa of course.

"Jonnie Kincaid called." She handed me the message slip.

I could only stare at it in disbelief. I felt my stomach roll and threaten to release the excellent breakfast I had recently consumed. "Mother of God! What'd she say?"

"She wanted to talk to you and demanded I have you call her ASAP. She was very cool and collected, Boss, like she was ordering a pizza, not like she knew she was the subject of a murder investigation. But if I was a betting woman, I'd wager she knows."

"How the hell can she know? I've been careful. Okay, first I need a gallon of coffee and I'll start with the least obnoxious of the phone calls."

I got coffee and sat down behind my desk. Man, it was barely nine AM and the day had gotten weird. I just knew it wasn't going to get any better either. I dialed Georgia.

"Hello, Tess."

"Georgia, I hope you're having a good day."

"Because you're about to make it a bad day? Too late, I've already spoken to my eldest child six times this morning and her husband twice. I'm now checking caller ID before I answer. They're wearin' me out."

"I'm sure they are, and I'm getting there too. Your son-in-law has filed three injunctions and a restraining order against me. I'm sure there'll be more, he seems the determined type. My lawyer is only too happy to answer each one but it will cost money. So the question is, do you want to proceed?"

"Oh, by all means. I started this to get to the truth about Jon's death, irritating Ryan is a bonus." Georgia laughed. "He's such a sanctimonious little shit."

I agreed except I thought he was a sanctimonious big shit. I tried to frame my next comment carefully since I didn't want to freak Georgia out.

"Georgia, Jonnie called me."

"My God! What does she want?" She sounded startled.

"I don't know yet, I called you first. As soon as I talk to her, I'll give you a report."

"Can she know we're looking into Jon's death? How could she? Oh Jesus, I'll be waiting for your call on tenterhooks. Tess, I suppose I don't need to tell you to be cautious, I do believe she's crazy."

"Try not to worry about me, Georgia, I'll cover my backside. Talk to you soon."

"Bye Tess, and be careful."

I laughed as I broke the connection. I looked at the next message slip and quit laughing.

I took five minutes to breathe and brace myself for the phone call. I punched in the numbers for Jonnie Kincaid and listened to it ring with mounting anxiety.

"Hello." Well, she didn't sound crazy which was a good sign.

"Ms. Kincaid, this is Tess Maher returning your call. How may I help you?"

"Miss Maher, it seems you're digging around in my life and I want you to stop right now."

I decided the best course might be to play dumb; I could do that real well. "I beg pardon?"

"Beg whatever the hell you want but I'm warning you, this bullshit stops right now and right here! Do you understand me?" Her voice got lower and more vicious and nasty with every word. Okay, so I was wrong — she was nuts.

"Ms. Kincaid, I think you must have me mistaken for someone else, I really have no idea what you're talking about…"

"You little ignorant slut, who the hell do you think you're talking to? You stop snooping and asking questions about me and my affairs now or I will crush you LIKE THE FUCKING COCKROACH YOU ARE!" she shouted.

"Pack a lunch. Get in line. Take a number." I hung up, but it wasn't enough to express my anger so I slammed the phone down on the receiver several times. New light-weight phones are just not satisfying to slam.

"DAMN! DAMN! DAMN!" I stood up and walked into the front office. Jewels looked up at me patiently.

"Crazy, definitely crazy! She threatened to crush me like a bug. The conversation started off normal but quickly degenerated into nut ball territory," I explained.

I poured more coffee and found myself wishing for an espresso machine; I was sure regular coffee wouldn't be enough to get me through the day. The phone rang and I was positive I was about to be proven correct.

"Maher Investigations," Jewels answered. "Mr. Marshall, let me check."

I threw back my head in a silent laugh. Perfect, just perfect!

"I'm not sure she's in the building, I know she was ready to leave the office just before you called."

I stirred my coffee and nodded my head at her, she counted to five before she said, "Sir, she is still here, please hold on while I transfer you."

She rolled her eyes and the phone on my desk buzzed. I stepped into my office and lifted the phone.

"Tess Maher."

"Now you look here, I demand you stop and desist with this ludicrous investigation right this minute or I will bury you," the man snarled at me.

I snorted. "Well, I am sufficiently cowed by your ire and will now tuck my tail and run away in fear."

"You will indeed, I'll have your license if you don't and there may even be some criminal charges brought against you." He was rolling now and sounding meaner by the word.

"So I guess you found out you can't bring a stop action against me which will actually make me stop action and now you're gonna try and intimidate me into quitting. Well it won't work, I don't intimidate, I have four older brothers. See, here's the thing; I've taken money to investigate and investigate I will. Do you think you're the first person who's tried to run me off a case? Cause you ain't. Furthermore, from this point on you can direct all calls, inquiries and insults to my attorney, Elizabeth Parrott. Technically I am not supposed to be talking to you since I have retained counsel, you do know how it works right? This is our last conversation." I know I sounded like a snippy smart ass but I just couldn't help myself.

"Maher, what do you want?"

I was a bit taken aback by his question. "What? I wanna do my job. I'd like to do it without irritation from you or others. It isn't necessary but it's nice. I want to get the answers Ms. Kincaid has asked me to get; I want her to be satisfied with my work. And world peace. Yep, I'd really like world peace."

There was a moment of silence then a deep sigh. "How much?"

"Pardon?" A phrase of which I had grown tired.

"To make you go away. How much?" he said.

"Are you trying to bribe me to quit this case?"

"I am asking you how much it will take to make you stop this investigation." He sounded exasperated.

"Wow, you really are a piece of work. Now you've pissed me off for real. First, you accuse me of being a fraud and now you're calling me a whore to boot." I wanted to bite him.

"I did no such thing! I am simply trying to make this god-damned thing go the hell away. My wife is very upset, my children are very upset. I want it to stop." Marshall was spluttering, which I liked.

"You implied I was for sale. I don't appreciate it. Understand, only Georgia can do make this stop and I don't think she will. Your discomfort is unfortunate, as is your wife's and your children's. Perhaps you should wait until they've gone to bed to discuss grown up topics. However, your real discomfort ought to be your father-in-law was possibly murdered. I think your priorities might be kinda out of whack, pal."

"There will be talk," he muttered.

"God forbid, there might be talk! Hide the women and the children and the sheep!" I drew a deep breath to try and calm down, which didn't work. "This is freakin' murder we're talking about, bucko, which is a hell of a lot worse than gossip! So do your bloody worst and try to annoy me to death if you think you can, but you're not gonna stop me!" I was pissed.

"Why can't you just type up a report for Georgia saying you can't find any proof of wrongdoing? Then everyone will be satisfied. You'll get paid and no one gets hurt."

"Can't, I've been paid to do a job. I know it sounds simple and I guess it is, but I told Georgia Kincaid I'd find out the truth and I will. She's depending on me and I intend to come through for her. At the end of the day, all I really have is my integrity."

"You're a fucking crusader, that's what you are. Fine, just stay the hell away from my family or I'll have your god damn legs broken." he snarled.

"Can you say that with a little better enunciation for my recorder please?" I was rewarded for my smartassness with a click in my ear. Good, I was delighted I pissed him off. What a dick.

I stomped back into the front office and scowled at Jewels. "What an asshat! He tried to bribe me to quit the case."

"So I gathered from your side of the conversation. Not like I could help eavesdropping, you were kind of yelling."

"Hells bells, it's not even noon yet and I've been threatened with bodily harm, called names, and offered a bribe! What the hell are we gonna do after lunch?!"

Luckily, after that, things seemed to calm down. I spent the rest of the day getting all my little ducks in a row, finishing paperwork on cases and tax stuff for the accountant. I even cleaned out a couple of drawers. Jewels brought us lunch from Tilly's, which softened the blow of all the boring work I was doing. We had our burgers and fries at my desk and ate in silence. You just don't want to waste any time talking when you're eating one of Tilly's burgers. Really, the burger is so big you can hardly hold it in two hands and it takes all of your concentrations just to eat. Finally, I sopped the last delectable French fry in ketchup, leaned back in my chair, and sighed.

"Man, that was too good," I said.

Jewels nodded her head in agreement. She was still eating.

"Okay," I said as I wiped my mouth. "What other boring junk has to be done today? I need a nap."

Jewels laughed. "No naps for you, I have some clients' letters which need your signature on them and you need to read all your e-mails before you leave this office. There are several which promise lucrative employment."

"Yes ma'am. I need to call Georgia and give her a report too."

Georgia caught the call on the first ring. "Hello Tess, how bad is it?" she asked.

You have to love caller ID. "Well, somehow Jonnie suspects I'm looking into Jon's death. She blew lots of steam at me and threats too. Oh, and your son-in-law tried to bribe me and threatened to break my legs when I refused."

"Good Lord. Now what do we do?"

"Now I just keep pokin' 'til we get the answers, business as usual. This isn't the first time someone has given me a hard time over a case. Try not to worry, okay?"

"Oh Tess, I think it must be 5 o'clock somewhere. Keep me posted."

I chuckled. "Will do."

By four o'clock I was done to death with being responsible and decided to make my escape. I picked up my bag and heeded for the door.

"So are ya' outta here?" Jewels asked.

"Yep, I've had all the fun I can stand for one day."

"Night, Boss."

"Night, have a good weekend."

On the drive home, I considered the conversation I'd had with Marshall. What a bastard! I figured he wasn't done with me, oh no. He'd continue to fire over my bow in hopes he could scare me off the case. I wished him much good luck. Prick.

Jonnie Kincaid perplexed me. How and where had I screwed up in my investigation? The next question was, what the hell was I going to do about it? Besides keep my head down, I didn't have an answer.

The evening passed uneventfully, with no visits from spirits in the dead of night. I was grateful.

21

Eat It

Saturday was spent planting plants which I knew would die in the winter. I did it anyway, with YaYa and Mommy directing my efforts. Daddy pitched in and helped. Don't let anyone tell you digging holes is easy.

Afterwards, I ate lunch, then took a shower and a nap. When I got up I felt refreshed. I threw on some shorts and a t-shirt and headed to Connell's. On the way over I stopped by Bo's Liquors to grab a bottle of wine for dinner. Yes, we do have a liquor store in Medicine Springs. It isn't very large and doesn't have the greatest selection, but it gets us by. I decided on a sweet red from the Grinder's Switch Winery — yep that Grinder's Switch, named for the mythical birthplace of Minnie Pearl. The wine is very good. Mommy taught me to never arrive empty-handed as a guest and even if it was my brother's house, I abided by her rule.

I pulled up to Connell's house where I was greeted by his bob-tailed and rather large tabby cat.

"Hello Tatters," I said as leaned over to rub his pointed, tufted ears.

He purred at me loudly. I was convinced his daddy was a bob-cat; he was just too big and wild-looking for any other parentage. Tatters showed up one dark and stormy night on Connell's back door step, ragged and half-starved and pitiable. Connell took him in and ever since Tatters thought he was an equal partner in the relationship.

The cat wound himself around my ankles. "You comin' in?" I asked him.

He turned his back to me and led the way to the front door. I knocked three times and opened the door; Tatters proceeded me into the house.

"Hey, anybody here?" I yelled.

"Out back!" my brother responded.

I headed toward the deck and found my brother and Mars. Connell was hard at work slaving over the hot grill and Mars was drinking beer.

"More beer in the cooler," Connell said and pointed with his bar-b-cue fork.

"Good, what're we having for dinner?" I put the wine on the table, then snagged a beer. I kissed him on the cheek and perched myself next to Mars. She clinked her beer bottle with mine.

"Steak, potatoes, and roasted corn. Mars is actually gonna eat meat."

I laughed. "Wow, you've gone all out, brother. I'm sure glad I passed up my afternoon snack. Anything I can do to help bring this feast off?"

"Nope, he has the grilling in hand and I have tossed the salad. So now we can just sit back and watch him work." Mars grinned.

"Oh, my favorite thing is to watch someone else work. So, anything good going on around here? Houses bought or sold, felons apprehended, crime sprees, things like that?"

"Actually," said Mars, "I just got a new listing over in Dixon, the price is right and I believe it'll move. It needs to, 'cause baby needs new boots."

"And everyone in town has been unusually law abiding of late. I do have some missing cows out on the west side of the county, but I've discounted the idea of rustlers. I'm betting there's a hole in the fence somewhere and the six cows just wandered off." Connell laughed.

"I don't know, brother, it sounds to me like the beginning of the great Medicine Springs cattle raid. You better watch out," I teased.

"I think if I saw a cow wandering through my yard I'd help him wander on into my freezer," Mars quipped.

Connell laughed again. "And I'd have to arrest you."

Mars held out her hand in the classic cuff 'em pose. Connell smiled and turned the steaks. I kept my mouth shut.

"I've actually checked with my counterparts in a wide radius around us and no one else has any missin' livestock to speak of, so I believe we're safe. I hear you're working on something new, Tess. Whatcha got?" He turned the steaks.

"First, I get to ask how you're doing," I said.

"Finer'n frog hair split three ways." Connell turned the foil wrapped ears of corn over and then attended to the potatoes.

"Okay, not really believing it and neither does Chick. You sure you wanna stick with your story?" I cocked one eye at my brother's back.

"Well, I would say some days are better than others," He admitted. "And you?"

"I would say the same. Some days suck and some days suck more. Okay, now that we've exhausted the subject, I'm working on a new case, which by the way is Mars' fault." Mars tried to look injured but I ignored her. "And I need a favor from you please.

I'd like to know if you have any friends on the force in Hotlanta I could talk to about it."

"About?" Connell asked.

"Murder."

Even though Connell's back was to me, I knew good and well he was rolling his eyes at me. "You wanna give me a little more to go on?"

"I'm working a case. Guy with cancer dies…" I paused and took a breath. "I was at a séance with your sister and my girl Mars, there was a dead guy of course, and he claims his widow murdered him…"

"Tess…" Connell interrupted.

"Hold up, let me finish. I've talked to his kids and his first wife, gotten info from the rehab center where he died, found out there's a shit ton of money in the estate, and I mean a REAL shit ton, discovered he asked one of the nurses to call his lawyer since he wanted to change his will and did not want his wife to know about it. The nurse confirmed it, by the way. I really think this might go somewhere."

"Does the merry widow know you are kicking over rocks?" Connell turned to face me.

"Up until now I'd have said hell no. Since she's crazy and quite possibly a murderer, I sure didn't want her to know anything about yours truly."

"But now?"

"Funny you should ask. I got a phone call from the widow warning me to stay out of her business."

"How'd you screw up?"

"Damn if I know." I shrugged my shoulders. "But I mean to find out."

"Okay, I went to UT with James, he's in Atlanta. I'll give him a call. And now I suggest we eat."

Mars and I sprang into action; we put plates on the table and sorted out napkins, salt shakers, and the butter. I managed to locate three wine glasses in the kitchen. Connell transferred the food from the grill to the table and we were ready. Old habits die hard; we bowed our heads to gives thanks.

"We are grateful and thankful for this food," my brother said.

"And this fine company," I said.

Mars smiled. "Ditto."

We dug in. After the first bite of steak, I asked my brother, "You sure you don't know where those six cows have got off to?"

He just laughed at me. Through the rest of the meal, I quietly observed my brother and my best friend as we talked of nothing consequential. They were easy with one another, but then they always were. Eye contact seemed to linger a nanosecond longer than I was used to seeing. When they touched hands, the touch lingered a bit longer than was necessary too. They weren't all gooey with each other, I guess they'd been friends far too long, but there was more than friendship going on at the table. The evening was pleasant and comfortable and ran late into the night.

I realized I was tired as we cleaned up.

"Alright, I gotta go. I'm wore out from gardening and I think my bed is calling to me. It's been fun and dinner was great since you, my brother, are the king of the grill," I said.

"Why yes I am, and don't you forget it. Glad you came out, little sister." Connell hugged me and kissed me on the top of my head.

"You be careful please," Mars said. She hugged me and we kissed.

As we walked into the living room I grinned at them. "You know I'm careful. I don't take chances, I take my vitamins, don't drink tap water, keep my guns clean, wear sunscreen, and never break the speed limit."

"And you are a liar," Connell and Mars said in unison.

I stuck my tongue out at them. Tatters came sauntering into the living room and wound himself around all of our ankles.

"He wants to walk you to the car," Connell said.

"Hmmmp, he just wants to make sure I'm not taking any leftovers home. He'll probably frisk me."

We all laughed except for Tatters, who cut mean cat eyes at me.

22

Friends in Low Places

_I_ was up early the next morning. The drive to Atlanta was a long one, not something I was looking forward to so very much, and I wanted to get it over and done. Connell's detective friend was supposed to meet with me and I believed the conversation needed to happen in person. It's always much easier to blow someone off over the phone.

I did my morning run and showered before breakfast.

"Morning," I said as I hit the kitchen.

"Morning, honey," said Daddy.

"Morning. What's up for today?" asked YaYa.

"Going back to Atlanta again, I hope. I mean to try and enlist the help of a cop who's an old friend of Connell's. As a matter of fact, I'd better to call brother dearest right now and make sure he's cleared the field for me with his buddy."

I hit the speed dial button on my phone for Connell and he answered on the first ring.

"Good morning, sister. Yes, I have called him, his name is James T. Sherman, and he's in mid-town, so he'll meet you at the Rolling Hill Sandwich Company for a few minutes on his lunch hour. I even have his cell phone for you. Call him when you hit the outskirts and let him know your ETA. I told him he might as well see you since you'll be a pain in his ass and mine until he does," Connell said all this in a very deadpan voice.

I grinned into the phone.

"You are the most bestest brudder in the whole, wide world and you say the nicest things about me and to me. I wove you big brudder." I said in highpitched little girl voice.

"Uh huh. His number is 707-555-1234. Buy him lunch."

"I will. Dinner was great Saturday night, thanks."

"Yep. See ya later, love ya, bye."

"See ya later, love ya, bye." We both hung up. I took a minute to add Sherman's number to my phone for later. "Okay Atlanta is a go; the cop's name is Sherman. If he's an Atlanta native I'm betting he got beat up every day on the playground."

We all laughed. In the South, the Civil War, or the *late unpleasantness between the states,* is not ancient history, it's still a living thing. Folks in the South use General Sherman's name as a curse word and I ain't kidding.

I didn't waste much time getting on the road. Once I settled in for the drive I called Jewels to give her my whereabouts.

"Hey Boss, what's up?" she answered.

"I'm on the road to Atlanta to talk to Connell's friend on the Atlanta PD. I'm hoping he can give a little guidance on this case. Plus, I'd like to have an inside man to bring my proof to when I get it. Hold down the fort until I get back."

"Roger."

"Did you have a good weekend?" I asked.

"We did, we painted the dining room."

"Hmmm sounds like fun," I quipped.

"The shower after was fun," Jewels said.

"TMI!" I laughed and drove on.

It began to rain as I passed through Nashville. Now I know the spring showers bring May flowers and all that rot but it needs to not rain when I'm on the freakin' road. God, I hate to drive in the rain, everyone gets crazy. I hurried when I could but the rain slowed me down considerably and I spent the next three and a half nerve racking hours with the steering wheel clutched firmly in my mitts while my head swiveled watching for idiot drivers. I became worried I was going to be late for my meeting so I hit my Bluetooth.

"Say a command," the computer voice demanded.

I smiled. Talking computers make me feel like I'm an extra on Star Trek. "Call Detective Sherman."

The phone rang and on the fourth ring I got his voice mail. "You've reached Detective James T. Sherman; I'm out solving crime and can't talk to you right now. State your business."

I grinned at the message and then there was a loud beep. "Detective Sherman, this is Tess Maher and I'm running a bit late due to the weather. I'll get there as soon as I can and I hope we can still meet."

I programmed the coffee shop into my GPS and drove on in the rain with the wipers slapping the rain off the windshield, reminding me of a Janice Joplin song.

The place where I was to meet Detective Sherman was close to his zone, the GPS took me straight to it. I spotted him from a half a block away. He was leaning against the building to the right of the front door and he looked like a cop.

"Detective Sherman?" I asked holding out my hand. He straightened up and it turned out I was wrong about the playground activities of Detective Sherman, who was 6 foot 6 and built like a brick shit house. I also guessed he worked out every day since there wasn't one ounce of fat on the man. Not only had he probably never been beaten up but I bet grown-up bad guys didn't even get lippy with him.

"Detective, I'm Tess Maher, Connell's little sister."

He shook my hand as if he didn't want to; he clasped it for a mere instant and didn't apply any pressure.

"Uh huh. Let's order." His voice was gruff and I knew he didn't like me on sight.

"Great, I'm buying." I walked into the coffee shop and he followed.

"That you're Connell's kid sister and I get a free lunch out of this are the only reasons this meeting is happenin'. As I rule I don't socialize with PIs. Don't like, don't trust 'em," he groused.

Yep, he was one of those. Lots of cops don't like private investigators, they think we skirt the law, take matters into our own hands, and that we're self-serving. Well, two out of three ain't bad.

"I don't like black jelly beans, but neither of those things has any bearin' on this case," I said with a shrug. I turned to the barista and recited my order; a fruit salad and coffee. Sherman ordered a roast beef sandwich with Anjou and chips. Damn him. We found a table and settled in.

"So Connell didn't give my any details. Fill me in and I'll decide if I eat lunch with you or carry it back to my desk," he grunted at me.

"I've been hired by a family to look into the death of a man in a rehab center." He just stared at me so I took the cue to continue. "His widow stands to gain a lot of money and the kids from the first marriage get squat."

"Un huh. And why was he in a rehab in the first place?"

"He was dying of cancer; he had several surgeries and was there to recover from them. He also was in such bad shape he needed round the clock nursing care."

"So you got a guy who was dying and he actually died? Stunning. Tell me what the mystery is?" The guy was a laugh a minute.

"His ex-wife and his children believe the widow is capable of murder."

"What ya got is speculation, supposition and shit. What ya don't got is proof." He sat back in his chair as if he were resting his case. "You don't have a case."

"The deceased asked a nurse at the rehab to get in touch with his lawyer, he told her he wanted to change his will, he asked her not to tell his wife. The conversation is noted in his medical records. The nurse confirmed it." I dared him to challenge that.

"Hearsay. Besides, no lawyer is gonna change a will after a person has been put on morphine and I assume your guy was."

I nodded my confirmation.

"Okay, so nothing he would've signed would hold up in court. She had nothing to worry about. There goes your motive."

"The kids say the widow did everything she could to keep them away from him."

Sherman shrugged. "So they say, maybe they're liars and bitter at being cut out of the will, maybe they were brats."

"What if she really did murder him?" I asked.

Before he could shoot me down, our number was called. I went and fetched our food and drinks. It took me two trips and Sherman did not offer to help. I could hardly believe Connell was friends with this guy. I didn't have to like him, I reminded myself, I just needed him to help me. I sat down and before I could doctor my coffee, Sherman started asking questions.

"He was expected to die, right?" I nodded. "Then why kill him? Why just not let him live out his few measly days and let nature take its course?"

I had no answer which wouldn't tip my hand to the fact I was getting my info from dead people. I sure as hell wasn't going to tell him I saw the whole thing played out in my dream. Neither was I going tell him I committed a B&E in his town to get the solid info I had. I kept my mouth shut and just stared at him.

"Furthermore, how do you know he didn't ask her to end the pain? Tell me you're against assisted suicide in such cases. Are you one of them quantity of life bullshitters? Hell, I'd eat my own service revolver before I went out in such a shit manner." He tore off a chuck of sandwich and chewed it as if he was mad.

I took a bite of my fruit salad. It was good, but not as good as the roast beef the detective was chowing down on. I watched him with envy in my heart.

"Okay, say he did ask her to help him die and she did. I got no gripe with that, in fact I have nothing but sympathy for anyone in such a terrible state," I said between bites.

Sherman pointed his delicious looking sandwich at me. "What you say and what I'm hearin' sound like two different things."

I sat and looked at him for a minute before I replied. "Detective Sherman, my grandfather died when I was fifteen. He was a big strong man and so the cancer took a long time to kill him. One day as my grandfather lay in the hospital I overheard the doctor tell my mother he'd live until his heart gave out. He would live in agony and pain. It took five long horrible months for him to die. The hospital was close to my high school so every single day I walked to the hospital and sat with him. I'm the youngest so my sibs were away at school and I think a couple of 'em were married. So I chose that duty. I did my homework and got him ice and water, and watched as he got thinner and weaker and as he forgot who I was or mistook me for my mother or my sisters or my grandmother. As he slipped further and further away I sat by his bed and looked at all the machines pumping things into him and carrying stuff away from him and thought about killing him. I wondered how long it'd take for him to die if I pulled all the wires and tubes out of him. I even decided I could do it and get away with it. I really didn't think I'd go to jail, after all I was only fifteen. Oh, I knew the machines would send the alarm straight out to the nurses if I pulled 'em out. My dilemma was how to block the door until he died. I could never solve the problem; the bed was on wheels, the machines were too, the only chair available wasn't sturdy enough to do the job. I know in retrospect I could've smuggled in a hammer and a wooden wedge and gotten it under the door. But at fifteen I couldn't see beyond what was in the room to use for the job. I could only sit and watch him die. When he finally did, I cried with relief because he was out of his pain and suffering." I paused and stared hard at the detective to let my words sink in. "So I get it. If I thought the widow arrived one night and just couldn't stand to watch him suffer one more second and smothered him with a pillow, I get it. If he asked her to kill him and she did, I get it. But what if he didn't ask. What if he had one more thing he needed to do before he shuffled off his mortal coil? What if he couldn't rest or couldn't leave until he completed one last act on this earth? What if she slipped in there one night and in a premeditated manner took what was left of his life? Just because all one person steals from another is a few lousy, pain ridden days, it's still murder in my book. She took his last moments. She took his free will. He deserves justice."

I took a deep breath since I had rather upset myself. I could feel tears stinging my eyes. My grandfather's death still elicits such strong emotion from me even after so many years. Sherman just sat there, staring at me. Finally he leaned back in his chair, which creaked under his weight.

"I don't like murder either, it pisses me off. Bring me somethin' I can use to indict, somethin' good, somethin' real. Now finish your lunch."

We didn't talk anymore, we just ate. After lunch, standing on the sidewalk, I thanked Sherman for his offer of help and we went our separate ways. Something had shifted during our lunch and I found I felt a little better about him. I hoped the feeling was mutual.

I decided while I was in Atlanta I'd try and see Dr. Jocelyn Gordon, the doctor at the rehab center. She hadn't returned any of our phone calls as far as I knew but I was willing to try again so I hit my Bluetooth.

"Say a command," it intoned at me.

"Call office."

"Hey Boss, what's up?" Jewels answered.

"Jewels, did we ever get communication from Dr. Gordon?"

"No, we did not."

"Nuts. Okay, think I'll take a run at her while I'm in Atlanta, I'd really like to kill two birds with one stone. Gimme her number please."

Jewels rustled around for a moment, and then rattled off Dr. Gordon's number. "Thanks Jewels. Anything going on I should know about?"

"Nope, no barbarians at the gate at present."

I disconnected, took a moment to get into character and then called Doctor Gordon on the Bluetooth.

"Dr. Gordon's office." The woman sounded business-like and busy.

"Hello, this is Tara Johnson with Great Eastern Life; I need a few minutes of Dr. Gordon's time to speak with her about a deceased patient, Jon Kincaid. He was at the Marietta Rehab Center and he passed back in January, she was the attending physician. I need to tie up some loose ends about his case." I crossed my fingers.

"I…who are you with?" She didn't sound convinced.

"Great Eastern Life. I only have a few questions and I won't take up more than ten minutes of her valuable time."

She sighed. "When do you wish to see her?"

"Today, if possible. I'm in Atlanta and I'd love to avoid making another trip down from Nashville. Ten minutes, just ten minutes." I put a pleading note into my voice.

"She has a ten minute hole in her schedule in one hour; I'll pencil you in, but please remember she has to eat lunch," she said firmly.

"It's a deal, you give me ten minutes and I'll make sure she eats. Could you give me that address please?"

She did and I punched the address into the GPS. I realized I was not too far away and found the office park without any trouble. I killed the hour wait Googling Dr. Jocelyn Gordon, a GP.

Close to the appointed time, I took the elevator to the third floor and followed the signs to Dr. Gordon's office. The place was like most doctors' offices everywhere: quiet, muted colors, generic paintings on the wall, a television playing the news with the volume so low you had to strain to hear it, outdated magazines, and plastic plants.

"Hi, I'm Tara Johnson, Great Eastern Life." I smiled and handed the woman behind the counter a business card. "I have a ten minute appointment with the good doctor."

She did not smile, just pulled out the reading glasses which were almost lost in her frizzy auburn hair and stuck them on her little pug nose. She proceeded to eye my card as if it held the secret location of the Holy Grail.

Behind me two elderly patients were having a conversation.

"Oh Lord, she got the sugar? Oh it's a cryin' shame, she on insulin is she?"

Before I heard the answer, the woman holding my card pinned me with a laser stare.

"I'll be timing it. The doctor is through that door, third office on the left." She pointed and I walked.

Jocelyn Gordon was seated behind her desk in her office, looking at a file.

"Dr. Gordon?" I extended my hand. "Tara Johnson, Great Eastern Life. I'd like to thank you for seeing me on such short notice."

Dr. Gordon was an attractive ethnic woman in her mid-thirties. I would've guessed she was Hispanic. She glanced up at me, removing her stylish eye glasses and pinching the bridge of her nose for a moment. She pushed a strand of dark hair away from her heart shaped face and tucked it behind her ear. I couldn't help but notice a large diamond stud. She gave me a tired smile.

"Please have a seat. I'm not sure how I can help you, Ms. Johnson. Jon Kincaid was a very ill man, terminal. He died, that's really all of it."

"Was his death sudden?"

"Sudden?" Her dark brown eyes widened. "He's been dying for two years, so I'd hardly call it sudden."

"What I mean to say is, did his death happen sooner than you expected even if only by a few days?"

She looked at me thoughtfully. "I thought he had more time. There was a new experimental treatment using stem cells I wanted to try and he had agreed to do it only two days before his death. After he and I discussed the new regiment, I discussed it again with his wife."

"How did she react to the idea?" I wanted to know.

"Funny you would ask. She didn't seem to be on board with the idea, even though the new treatment might have prolonged his life and actually given him more quality." She paused and looked off into the distance. "Hmmm, now as I think back on it, her reaction was just plain odd. She tried to talk him out of the idea, telling him it was experimental, it might not work, it might cause him greater pain, and so on. When he refused to agree with her she became belligerent with him. I finally asked her to step out into the hallway and explained she was upsetting her husband."

"How'd that go?" I wondered.

"She blew up, became very angry with me, and called me a goddamned spick. I told her to go home and calm down. We exchanged a few more rounds of harsh words and I threatened to have her escorted out of the building."

"What was her reaction?"

"Her reaction was dramatic; she'd have my job, deport my ass back to where it came from, the standard sort of kind of thing. I didn't bother to tell her I was born in South Georgia." Gordon smiled. "Ms. Kincaid strikes me as a woman who is always confident she'll get her way and others will bend to her will or her money." The doctor stopped talking and looked at me sharply. She added quietly, "I've just spoken out of school, I beg pardon."

"Not to worry, Dr. Gordon, I appreciate your candor. Did you see Ms. Kincaid after you had the confrontation?"

The doctor looked down in thought. "No, not until I called her to give her news about her husband's death. She came to the center to make the arrangements to have his body transported."

"Can you remember anything out of place or odd on the night Jon Kincaid died?"

She cut me a very sharp and penetrating look. "What an odd question for an insurance agent to ask. I will surmise you suspect something isn't kosher about Jon's death." She tilted her head to one side and smiled a tiny smile. "Otherwise you could have sent a form. I'm right, aren't I?"

Crap, I thought she had me.

"I'm just trying to tie up some loose ends. I asked the question out of my own curiosity based on what someone else has said to me." I shrugged as if it wasn't important.

She pinned me with her dark brown eyes. "Since you mention odd, the patient across the hall from Jon asked me about the new nurse he'd seen the night before. He claimed this mystery woman had visited Jon's room and he wanted to know why Jon was getting special privileges. I dismissed his question until now. What do you know that I don't know?"

Doctors are like nuns, they know when you're lying, and I knew I had to be careful with my answer or I'd out myself for real.

"Did you get a good description of the mystery nurse?" Always answer a question with a question when you don't want to answer the question. I swear it works.

"He said she had 'real blond hair, platinum like a movie star, lots of eye make-up like a hooker, and her nurse suit was tight in all the right places.' He added he would love for her to give him a sponge bath. You can see why this stuck with me." She grinned at the memory. "So, what do you know?"

"Can you confirm Kincaid was on morphine?" I asked. I knew the answer but was hoping to divert her.

"HIPAA, I'll need more than a business card to share such information. But you are welcome to draw your own conclusions. Will you tell me what you know?" she asked.

I looked at my watch. "Our ten minutes is up and your very serious front desk Nazi will come in here any second and toss me out on my ear, so I'll take my leave of you. Thank you so much for your time, I know how busy you are and I appreciate you seeing me on such short notice."

I stood up and extended my hand to her. She put a business card in it.

"That has my private number on it. When you get all the loose ends tied up, I'd appreciate a call." She was persistent.

"I promise." I started to take my leave before she could question me further when she stopped me in my tracks.

"The patient in question is still a resident at Marietta Rehab and his name is Kevin Stewart. I think you might want to talk to him."

I grinned and kept walking. The front desk woman cut narrowed eyes at me and the two elderly women were still deep in conversation, something about Bernie's inability to make water. I sped through the reception area and made my escape.

23

Rat in a Cage

I bid Atlanta a fond farewell and hit the I-55 heading north. I promised myself one day I'd actually take time to come to Atlanta and shop, since the shopping is just so good there. I sighed and hit the Bluetooth.

"Say a command," it said.

"Call office."

Jewels answered after several rings, which was odd; she was usually faster.

"Boss, I'm sure glad you called." She sounded breathless.

"What's up?" My Spidey senses were tingling.

"Well, we got an odd package in the mail. It's about the size of a shoebox and addressed to the office so I opened it and found a very dead rat."

"Ewww. What the hell?"

"I called Connell and he came and collected it. He said it might just be a prank in very poor taste. But we both knew better."

"Can you see how it died?"

"Its little throat was cut."

I winced at the sheer grossness. I don't like rats, they're probably my least favorite critter. Still, I hated for any animal to be tortured.

"Anything else?"

"Its mouth was wrapped up in red string, holding it shut."

"Postmark?"

"Chattanooga."

"Hmmm, well if I had to guess I'd say we got an Atlanta rat and the widow is becoming increasing wroth with me and this is a message to keep my mouth shut. And she's seen one too many wise guy movies."

"Cheer up; it could've been a dead fish," Jewels said.

I laughed, hung up, and kept driving. You gotta love black humor. A thought occurred to me and I hit the Bluetooth.

"Say a command," it intoned.

"Call Detective Sherman."

Sherman caught the phone on the second ring. "Sherman."

"Detective, this is Tess Maher. I have some interesting news on the case I'm working."

"I'm all a twitter."

"I had a meeting with the attending doctor and she told me she had offered a stem cell treatment to my guy. She believed it would prolong his life and give him better quality. The widow was against it, vehemently opposed." I held my breath and waited.

"Well, well, well. You might just be on to somethin' here. Keep diggin' and lemme know when you got more." He hung up without saying good-bye, big surprise.

Dinner was almost ready when I came in the door, so I pitched in and helped Mommy set the table. Daddy, YaYa, and Connell wandered in about then.

"Hey Connell, I didn't know you were joining us this evening." I hugged my brother.

"Well, I wanted to see how the meeting with Sherman went. He can be a little tough to take sometimes and I wanted to make sure he didn't ruffle your feathers and cause you to kneecap him." Connell grinned.

I grimaced. "He's a... Well, I don't know how to take him. He certainly has an opinion about PIs, seems to think we're one step below whale shit which is on the bottom of the ocean. But he listened to my story. I think if I can get some proof a murder took place, he'll be of help."

"I want to show you my new hunting rifle after dinner. It's in the car," Connell said.

I nodded enthusiastically; I knew he had something to show me which wasn't a rifle. "Sure, I'd love to see it."

"So would I," Daddy said.

Daddy knew something was up, he could smell it. But he wasn't going to ask questions at the dinner table. Thank God, we'd never hear the end of it, or at least I wouldn't.

After what was, for me, a very small helping of pot roast and large helpings of assorted veggies, Daddy, Connell and I excused ourselves. I'm pretty sure we didn't fool anyone; YaYa looked at us sharply as we slipped out the door, but this was a 'don't tell if they don't ask' situation. This saves a lot of bitching about my profession. No one ever bitched about how dangerous Connell's work was, which pisses me off no end.

I may have stomped to the car a little. "Why is it we have to sneak out here to look at evidence?"

"Because Mommy will shit a squealin' worm if she finds out someone mailed you a dead rat," Connell said with a straight face.

I snorted; I couldn't help it, he was funny. "Yeah, well, no one ever has a hissy fit over what you do,"

Connell laughed. "Cause I'm a big strong man."

I punched him in the arm. Hard.

"Ow, damn it."

Daddy laughed. "Do I have to separate the two of you?"

I laughed too but Connell just rubbed his arm, the big baby. He stopped long enough to open the truck of the squad car and we saw a shoe box. I lifted the lid gingerly and exposed a big dead rat with its mouth tied up just as Jewels had described.

"Ick, disgusting," I said. "It's pretty clear – I'm a rat poking around where I shouldn't be and I need to keep my mouth shut or someone might cut my throat. Very subtle. I guess the phone call wasn't enough and she wanted to reach out and touch me." I shook my head. "Damn rat."

"Phone call?" Daddy asked.

I shrugged. "She called and threatened me, told me to stay out of her business, yada, yada."

"Who tipped her off?" Daddy was thinking like a cop; he knew I was very careful in my investigations.

"That's the million dollar question, isn't it? I mean to find out and you can bet your ass and your hat on it," I promised.

"How dangerous do you consider this woman to be?" asked Daddy.

"Well, she killed her husband in cold blood in a rehab center with cameras, while wearing a nurse's uniform. Allegedly. So she's a real determined woman. There's a boat load of money in the estate and she means to keep all of it. She managed to keep the dead guy's kids away from him so they couldn't influence him about the will. At least according to the way I read my information. Kincaid asked a nurse to call his lawyer, the nurse made the mistake of telling the widow out of concern. There was a row. The widow also had words with the doctor about a new treatment for Kincaid which might have improved his condition. She was against it."

"Sounds like a lovely woman," Daddy quipped.

"She's a real Georgia peach. Her step-children hate her, and the personnel at the rehab did too. No one, so far, has had a nice word to say about the woman."

"So universally hated, money grubbing, heartless, ruthless, hmm … I'd say on a scale of one to ten, she's about twelve and a half," said Connell.

I looked down at the rat. "I'll be careful."

I went to sleep much later, wondering if I needed to talk to the fella at the rehab center who had seen the mysterious nurse the night Kincaid died. I decided I did, otherwise all I had was hearsay. My last coherent thought was wondering if I could conduct the interview by phone and thus avoid another trip to Atlanta.

24

Who'll Stop the Rain'

The next morning I crawled out of bed and pulled on clothes to do my run. As I trotted downstairs I realized it was raining. I dislike running in the rain; I must be part cat.

"Good morning y'all," I said as I entered the kitchen.

Mommy, Daddy, YaYa, and every dog in the house looked up as I spoke. The dogs didn't look as excited as they usually did when I was off to run.

"I think I'll be running alone this morning," I said with a laugh.

The dogs ignored me and went back to breakfast. I poured myself a cup of coffee and set next to Daddy.

"So what are you gonna do today?" he asked me.

"I was thinkin' about another trip to Atlanta to check out a lead, but really, I've made that trip too many times in the last little while and I'm just wore out with it. So, I reckon I'll hang around the office and catch up on paperwork." I sipped my coffee and thanked God for caffeine.

"Where do you think you are on this case?" Mommy asked. I knew she wasn't really interested in my work; she wanted to know when the case would be done since she thought it was dangerous.

"Not really sure, this woman has been very careful. I don't have much more than a gut feelin' she committed murder, which won't hold water," I sighed.

"Don't worry, kid, you'll find some way to bring this chippy down, I got faith in ya." YaYa winked at me.

I grinned. "Thanks, YaYa, but if you could put in a good word with St. Jude for me it might speed things up."

"As good as done," she assured me.

"Alright, I might as well get to it." I finished my coffee and grabbed a rain parka from the hook by the back door. "I'll see y'all in a bit. Any of you worthless animals wanna come?"

The four of them looked at me for a moment and then proceeded to lie down on the kitchen floor and pretend complete indifference.

"Wow. Man's best friend? Not." I took off and tried to maintain a steady pace; I wanted to get the run over with as soon as possible. Today my thoughts were on the dead rat. I couldn't get the picture of it out of my head. I wondered again how the widow knew there was an investigation. Furthermore, how did she know I was involved? I'd been careful, sneaky and stealthy. I had lied and worn disguises, used all the tried and true techniques from the PI handbook and still she'd made me. How? The only conclusion was someone was feeding her information, just as Daddy had suggested. The job was to figure out whom and then, if possible, to use the mole to my advantage. Feeding disinformation to someone is a staple of the game. The situation wasn't really a game, but I still intended to win.

I also spared some time to wonder if she'd caught and killed the rat with her own little hands.

The rain was coming down harder by the time I finished my run. It looked like it had set in for the day. I tossed the parka on a hook and strolled into the kitchen. The cast had changed a bit in my absence. Mommy and the dogs were missing, but Daddy and YaYa were still hanging out.

"You better hurry with breakfast and get the hell outta dodge," YaYa said.

I was brought me up short. "What's the deal?"

"Your mother has paint chips she wants us to look at." Daddy said in a long-suffering tone. "She wants to paint the living room."

"Holy shit!" I grabbed several pieces of bacon and wrapped them in toast, rolled it all into a napkin and poured a cup of coffee. I refused to be caught up in a 'what color shall we paint the living room' nightmare. The last time we had painted a room it took three different colors on the walls before the woman was satisfied. Oh, hell no. I kissed the victims I was leaving behind and ran like a rabbit. I would live to paint another day.

I ate, showered, dressed, and was out the door within fifteen minutes. I didn't even go through the kitchen but ran out the backdoor yelling 'good-bye'. I meant to put as much distance between me and the paint drama as possible. I'm a coward, so sue me.

Once I was safely in the Jeep, I hit the Bluetooth and called Georgia. I had a nasty little suspicion in my head I wanted to confirm.

"Hello."

"Morning, Georgia."

"Tess, how are you today?"

"Finer than frog hair split three ways, thanks for asking, and I hope you are too. Listen Georgia, I want you to hear me out before you say anything, please."

"Well, sure." She sounded rather hesitant.

"As I told you, Jonnie knows about the investigation. I want you to tell every one of your children in no uncertain terms I intend to carry on with the investigation no matter what obstacles get tossed in my path. Tell them I said now it's personal to me and I intend to move heaven and hell to prove Jonnie murdered their father. Will you do that?"

"I'll do it. Will you tell me why?"

I shook my head. "Nope, you just have to trust me. No harm will come to anyone by this, so don't worry. I'm just trying to prove a theory, okay?"

"Okay, I do trust you Tess. I'll do it right now. Will you tell me eventually if your theory is correct?"

"I will and don't worry."

Georgia just laughed at me and hung up. I truly felt grimly determined to follow through on the case no matter what happened. I looked up at the sky and realized the dark grey color of it perfectly matched my mood.

"Hey Boss," Jewels said as I came into the office. She was cheerful, which helped to lighten my heart a bit.

"Good morning to you too. So I saw the dead rat up close and personal last night. Connell brought him to dinner."

"Ick, that had to put you off your feed," she grimaced.

I chuckled. "He had it in his trunk and we took a look at the poor thing after dinner. We sure didn't want Mommy to see it; she would've had a conniption."

Jewels laughed. "Oh Lord, true enough. So what's the next step?"

"Well, I've planted a seed. I suspect one of the Kincaid offspring spilled the beans to the widow, call it gut feelin'. In light of my idea, I called Georgia and asked her to tell her children I refuse to stop this investigation under any circumstances. Now we wait and see what happens next." I felt ridiculously smug.

"So are you going back to Atlanta today?"

"Hell no, I'm so sick of lookin' at the I-55 stretch of highway I might just fall out with the vapors if I have to drive it anytime soon."

"Good, there's plenty of paperwork around here and some things you have to sign off on." She got busy stacking up work for me.

I eyed the growing stack. "Maybe I should've gone to Atlanta after all. Furthermore, I'm not answering my phone if my mother calls. When she calls the office phone, and she will, tell her anything but the truth."

Jewels stopped her activity and put one hand on her hip. "Why are you hidin' from you mama?"

"She wants to paint," I stated.

Ring of Fire

Somewhere a phone was ringing. I pried my eyes open and could see my phone was lit up. But there was a voice too in my ear too; I couldn't seem to understand what he was saying. I reached for the phone.

"TisTis! TisTis, wake up!" An urgent voice cut through my sleep clouded brain.

I rubbed my eyes and saw Chick standing above me. "What the hell, Chick? Hello? Hello?" I said into the phone.

"You have trouble at your office, darling girl. You need to get down there right away," a woman's voice demanded.

Panic shot through me like a lightning bolt. I jumped out of bed, regardless of my naked state and Chick standing there. I found clothes and threw them on.

"What?" I said stupidly.

"There is fire in your building," she said.

"*What?*" My head was spinning.

"That Kincaid woman means to set fire to the place to scare you off." Chick looked worried.

"Tess, you must go to your building, she is still there and perhaps you can stop her. Do you understand?" The woman sounded desperate.

"You need to hurry, girl!" Chick added.

The woman on the phone was Lori from the Neon Candle; I finally recognized her. Chick was talking at the same time Lori was talking. It was like weird stereo.

I strapped on my holster and checked my Beretta for rounds. "Lori, Chick is telling me the same thing and I'm on my way."

"Blessings, child."

If she had more to say I didn't hear it; I hung up as I hurried down the steps while trying to be quiet. One keypad for the alarm is at the kitchen door; I disarmed it, rearmed it and scooted out the door, careful not to make a sound. It was a miracle I managed to get out of the house and in the Jeep without waking anyone, no small feat in my house. I figured the canines were sleeping with Mommy and Daddy and was grateful for it. My heart was pounding in my chest like a jackhammer, the Black Widow better hope I didn't catch her doing damage to my building.

"Shit!" I moaned, trying not to panic. I started the engine and called Connell at the same time.

"Yeah?" he answered. He was fuzzy from sleep. I could see him in my mind's eye; his hair tousled from his pillow and his eyes half closed.

"I have a tip the Kincaid bitch is gonna torch my office. I'm headed there now."

"Jesus Christos! I'll meet you. Be careful."

He hung up and I drove to the office. I saw the flames before I got into town and started to cry. I always cry when I'm mad, which pisses me off even more so I cry harder. Vicious cycle.

"THAT BITCH!" I yelled out loud.

I reached my office to find the building burning like an old Christmas tree. It was late and I was sure no one was inside but everything I'd worked for and built was in there. Connell arrived about fifteen seconds after I did and joined me on the opposite side of the street from the building.

"I called the fire in," he said.

Thank God one of us had enough sense to do make the call. I'd been so mesmerized by the flames I was stupid. The members of the Medicine Springs Volunteer Fire Department arrived seconds behind Connell and set about trying to douse the fire.

Andy Riley, head of the department, came running over to me. "Tess, you okay?"

"Yeah, I'm okay. Can you save anything?"

"We're gonna try, honey."

He turned away and started shouting orders to the other guys. They all scrambled like ants in an overturned anthill. Soon water was pouring into the building.

"Chick?" Connell asked.

"And Lori, she called at the same time Chick showed up. I must be on the spiritual hotline."

I stared at the burning two story office building. It had been built around 1900 and was solid and attractive. I had rented my space when I first got my license and was happy there. A few years later the building was renovated, the work was good, the rent increased but only a little and I was still happy. It was my home away from home, the place where I was in charge and didn't have to answer to anyone.

Last year I found out a multinational farming co-op had bought the building. The same company, it turned out, which was responsible for the murder of Chick Donnelly. I thought of moving after I got the information, but instead received an offer to buy the building. The price was so ridiculously low I knew it was nothing other than a bribe. Regardless, I took the offer, borrowed the money, and bought the building. Life went on. Until the fire.

I watched as my pride and joy went up in smoke.

Connell wrapped his arm around my shoulder. "It's just a building, baby girl. You can repair and replace."

I started to cry again.

"I know. God damn it! I hate crying!" I swiped my sleeve across my face. "I'm gonna kill her."

"I didn't hear that. We better call Mars and Jewels; they'll be pissed if we don't."

I nodded. "I'll call Jewels, you call Mars."

"Boss?" Jewels sounded totally awake when she picked up the phone. How the hell did she do it?

"Jewels, our building has been torched." I couldn't hide the fact I was crying.

"We'll be right there."

She hung up and I cried harder. It sucked. I could hear Connell on the phone with Mars and the roar of the fire. I closed my eyes for a minute and tried to get a grip on my emotions. I tried to think. I shared the building with seven other businesses. I was pretty sure no one kept live animals. I knew everyone had insurance; I prayed it would be sufficient for the damage. I realized I needed to make a call to Jim Leach, my insurance guy. I hated to wake him up; I checked my phone; it was 4:17 am.

"Connell, should I call Jim now?"

I had no idea how to proceed. I'd never been in such a situation before. Connell nodded and went back to his phone conversation, so I called Jim. The phone rang many times and just as I thought it was going to go to voice mail, he answered.

"Hello, this is Jim Leach." His voice was slurry and small wonder.

"Jim, Tess Maher. I'm so, so sorry to wake you, but my building is on fire." There was no soft way to break the news.

"God Lord, Tess! Are you okay? I'll be there as soon as I can. Is the department there?"

"They're here, Jim, and doing the best they can. I'm fine."

"Be safe, I'll see you soon."

I broke the connection just as the sound of glass exploding shattered the night. My breath caught in my throat and I instinctively ducked. Connell was still on the phone and only looked up for a moment, assessed there was no immediate danger, and went back to his conversation.

I walked to the Jeep and sank down on the seat. My legs felt weak, as if they couldn't hold me up for another second. I didn't bother to close the door but sat sideways in the seat watching the fire. After a few minutes Connell came to me.

"Sis," he said and took my hand. "You okay?"

"I will be," I said but the tears sliding down my cheeks made my statement a lie.

"I've called the troops and they're rallying. Daddy decided he'd better wake Mommy and YaYa or they'd have his ass for being left out of the loop."

"Oh great." I laughed a sad little laugh and sniffed. "He's right but boy am I gonna have hell to pay over this."

"Before anyone else gets here, let's get our story straight okay?"

I nodded and rooted around in my glove box for a napkin to wipe my snotty nose.

"I was making a patrol and saw the fire. I called it in and called you. Okay?"

"I don't want you to have to lie."

"It's not much of a lie and it's better than you saying Chick woke you up and told you the building was on fire. When there's arson, the first person we look at is the owner."

I nodded my head in agreement and wiped the tears off my face. "True enough and it's a sure bet they're gonna find arson as the cause."

I leaned against the headrest and ran my hands through my hair. "This might get sticky. What if they find arson and decide I'm a risk and won't insure me again?"

"Honey, that's not your biggest problem. Being accused of arson is a far worse problem than insurance."

"Great. Well, bank records will show me in the black so I didn't do it for the money, the usual reason for arson." As my brain turned back on my tears stopped and I began to calm down. "Look, in case there's an investigation, I think a better story might be I received a dead rat in the mail today and couldn't sleep so I decided to come down to the office to catch up on paperwork and found the place engulfed in fire."

Connell raised an eyebrow at me and I raised my hands in a stop gesture. "If I was investigating this fire for the insurance company, I'd pull phone records. No reason to think the person they hire won't be as smart as me. They'll see I called you first."

Connell nodded his agreement and we settled down to wait for Mars, Jewels and her husband Jess, plus the rest of our family. They turned up in short order and I was awash in questions, sympathy, and hugs. I cried some more.

"I don't know what happened," I said about a million times as more and more people showed up and asked the same question. Truthfully, I had no answers for them. I had suspicions, but no proof.

Jim Leach arrived and hurried over to our little group.

"Evening everyone, or morning I reckon. Tess, thank God you're not hurt," he said as soon as he saw me.

"I'm okay," I said again.

Jim took my hands and held them for a moment.

"Only thing that matters. Everything else can be repaired or replaced," he said kindly.

"He's right," Mommy agreed.

"I'll go talk with Andy and see about the damage, looks like they just about have it under control." Jim squeezed my hand one more time and walked across the street to find Andy.

You know the 'good hands' insurance commercial? Jim is the real deal; I felt better as soon as he arrived. I knew he'd take the best care of me possible, and he'd go to bat for me. I felt a huge weight lift from my chest.

"Connell, on the phone you said the building had been 'torched'," Mars said.

"Don't use that word, and let's not speculate here. We can talk later." Connell looked around at our family and friends, and everyone nodded. I offered a silent little prayer Mommy was occupied with Daddy and didn't hear the exchange.

My brother, Brian, spoke up. "I think I'll go open the restaurant and make coffee, tell the boys."

He nodded his head toward the firemen.

"Good idea," said YaYa. "We'll come help you, and maybe we need to make some eggs and toast. I'm thinking some gravy might be on the menu too."

She took Mommy by the arm and said, "Come on, Maggie."

Mommy looked at me; her face was lined with concern and worry. "Tess, honey?"

"Go on, Mommy, I'm okay, I'll be there directly." I tried to smile but couldn't muster one up.

"You need any more hands?" Dugal asked.

"We got this," Brian answered.

Brian, YaYa, and Mommy moved on down the sidewalk toward the Red Dog. Jim and Andy walked over to me.

"We got it under control," said Andy. "Just trying to put it out now." He looked hard into my tear-stained face. "You took some damage, girl, I won't kid you. Melanie's place took a lot of damage too; the fire went straight up out of your place into hers and then right on up out the roof. Everybody else has smoke damage for the most part, there's some water damage too. We saved what we could."

He looked sad. Firemen always hate fire and seem to take the devastation it causes personally.

"Andy, I know you boys did your best and I appreciate it." I felt tears burning my eyes again. "It's just stuff, nobody got hurt."

"Some of us will stay here and make sure there aren't any hotspots. In the mornin' we'll go in and see if we can decide what might've started it. Probably have to call in a fire inspector in from the city. Don't go in there, you got that?" Andy warned.

I nodded. "I got it, I'll wait 'til daylight. Brian's opened the Red Dog and he's makin' breakfast for y'all so tell the others, please."

Andy smiled. "He don't have to do that, but I'll tell 'em. Tess, I'm mighty sorry, the Good Lord knows I am."

"Me too. Thanks, Andy."

"I'll call you in the morning," Jim said and only then did I realize he was in his plaid housecoat. I smiled and waved.

As the sun was coming up, I took one last look at my smoking building and started walking toward the Red Dog. I wanted to sit down, have coffee, and see if I could get the smell of smoke out of my nostrils. My family and friends followed me and we made a sad and oddly dressed parade. I didn't realize until we got into good light most of the people around me were dressed in night clothes like Jim. Dugal's 'Austin Peay U' tee-shirt was on inside out.

The Red Dog smelled like heaven when we walked in and sat down.

"I'll get you some coffee," Dugal offered.

"I guess she figured the rat wasn't enough so she set the place on fire!" Jewels hissed. She was usually on such an even keel it was stunning to see her pissed off.

"What rat? What? Who?" Mars looked so confused it made me laugh.

"Sorry, sorry. We got a dead rat in the mail, very charming, and we believe the Kincaid widow sent it. It didn't come with a callin' card or anything but I'm positive, just as I'm positive Andy'll find arson as the cause of the fire. Again, I blame the widow. What I can't understand is how she knew I was poking around."

"I know you and I know you've been careful. When you do sneaky, nobody does it better," Patrick said and he began to hum the Wings song.

"Thanks, good idea, take my mind off my troubles with your really bad singing," I quipped.

Patrick tried to look hurt and failed. Funny thing was I did feel better. Sitting there in the warmth of the restaurant with the good smells filling the air among a throng of people I loved was guaranteed to raise morale. Nobody died or was even hurt, and the insurance would cover the cost of rebuilding, I hoped. It was inconvenient as hell was all. But I was damn sure mad.

I received my coffee and shortly after I got a huge plate of food. We all ate and even had seconds. There was not much talk as we refueled ourselves.

I leaned back in my chair, and closed my eyes for a minute. I heard the door open and some of the firemen began to trickle in, they all came over and gave me condolences. I knew every one of them, and had grown up with most of them. They were my neighbors and friends, the kid who sacks groceries at the Piggly Wiggly, our family dentist, Mr. Moss, the undertaker, and of course Sammy and Billy. The beauty of a volunteer fire department is everyone on it lives in your community and cares about you. They all felt my loss; they knew how hard I'd worked to build my business. When any of them said, "I sure am sorry," they meant it.

Sunny Ray, the only firewoman in town, stopped at the table. She is a tiny blonde with an attitude.

"Girl," she said, "Andy thinks it arson. If you need any help whipping some ass, you just let me know. Okay?" She grinned and joined some of the guys at a table.

I was saved from everyone's questions for a moment when Sammy and Billy showed up. They pulled up chairs and sat down at our table. Sammy was having a bad hair day; usually his 'Billy Ray Cyrus mullet' is perfect, but right then it was wet and dirty. He knew his cut was out of style but he didn't give a damn and no one gave him grief about it either. Sammy's six foot three, broad-shouldered and muscular from bench pressing car parts. In short, he's built like a brick shit house.

Billy is a little guy, but he's wiry. I'd bet on him in fight, since I know he'd fight dirty. He reminds me of James Dean; he has good hair, smoldering bedroom eyes, and pouty lips. Damn near every girl in town had designs on him. Even covered in sweat and soot, both Billy and Sammy looked real good to me.

"Thanks for being here, y'all," I said.

"Tess, I'm sure glad you're okay," Sammy said.

"But your place is a hell of a mess and that's a fact," Billy chimed in. Okay, so he's cute, but he has no tact.

"Damn Billy, quit buttin' in. We did what we could; me and Billy spent some extra time moving stuff up and out of the way of the water. You're gonna need a wet-n-dry before you pull up the carpet."

"If you want, I'll do it for ya," Billy offered.

"Thanks Billy, I'll take you up on your offer, but keep up with your hours. The insurance will pay for clean-up," I said.

Billy drew back a bit as if I'd hit him and looked insulted.

"I ain't takin' nothin' from you, I owe you." He ran his hand through his blonde hair and the tousled look made him even sexier.

"You don't owe me anything, everything I've ever done for you was out of friendship, love of Chick, and cause I wanted to," I said.

"Well, this here's the same, 'cause I like ya' and I wanna help." When he grinned the little dimple in the corner of his mouth showed and it was all over.

"Okay," I surrendered.

"Now the business arrangements are done with, there's somethin' else," Sammy said. "Some sum bitch set this fire, girl."

I raised one eyebrow at him. "Yeah, Sunny just said Andy thought it was arson. So, whacha got?"

"The back door of your building's been jimmied. Your office door was burnt pretty good, but I could see the frame was busted, like somebody kicked it in. Place smells like gasoline, and the center of the fire's 'bout six feet from the door. Nothin' there to start a fire unless somebody tossed something there."

I nodded. "I thought as much. Reckon I've pissed somebody off and this is a message."

My mother showed up with a coffee pot just as I spoke.

"What message?" she asked as she set the pot in front of my father. "What are we talking about?" She looked around the table waiting for someone to crack under her gaze and spill their guts. She put her hands on her hips and demanded, "Well?"

"Maggie," Daddy said quietly, "the fire was arson."

"Oh my Lord, my precious Lord!" Mommy sat down hard.

"Keep your voice down," Connell's said in a low voice.

Mommy took a deep breath and got a grip. "Who could've done such a terrible thing?" She practically whispered. The question was directed to the room at large, but then she turned to me. "Are you in danger?"

"Mommy, it's a message. Someone wants to frighten me off an investigation. This was meant to scare me, make me tuck tail and run."

One of my brothers snorted but I wasn't fast enough to see which one.

Mommy locked eyes with me. "Then the culprit does not know my baby girl very well."

I breathed a sigh of relief. "More coffee, please. It's gonna be a long day."

26

We Didn't Start the Fire

The rising sun found me standing in front of my smoke stained and water-logged building. There was crime scene tape across the entrance and a handwritten note on the door.

DO NOT ENTER!
THIS BUILDING UNSAFE!
THIS MAY BE A CRIME SCENE!
By order of Chief Andy Riley
Medicine Springs Volunteer Fire Department

I had arrived to try and salvage whatever was left of my office which wasn't charred or melted or burnt. I'd slept about fifteen minutes and felt like I was coated in soot. Even after a shower I wondered if I'd ever smell anything but ashes again; every time I blew my nose, my snot was black. I'd sent everyone who'd been in nightclothes home to change and maybe grab some sleep. I figured I'd beat the rush and come down alone. It was a wasted trip; I could've slept more. I looked around and mentally took a damage estimate, which was not so easy from the sidewalk. I found I was happy to be alone for a moment, even though I knew it wouldn't last. But for a short length of time I could be alone in my own head and revel in my misery.

I was terribly tempted to enter the building despite the posted sign, just to have a look at the inside and ascertain how bad it really was. I wanted to see where the heart of the fire had been; as long as I had to stand on the sidewalk my brain could continue to make the disaster even worse.

I was saved from any stupidity by the sound of a vehicle pulling up behind me, and turned to see a news van.

"Holy shit," I muttered.

A cute, petite blonde climbed out.

"Ms. Maher?" she querried.

"Guilty as charged," I quipped.

"May I have a few mintues of your time, so we can talk about your fire?" She minced up to me as she asked the question.

I figured I was probably a good idea to get in front of this mess. I nodded.

Her cameraman got out of the van and set up the shot. I was uncomfortably aware I was dressed in wrinkled clothes, with uncombed hair and no makeup. Great.

The reporter and her camera guy quickly got into to position and did their sound check.

"Ms. Maher, can you tell us what caused the fire in your building in the early hours of the morning?" She thrust the mic in my face.

"I only know that the building isn't a total loss. I have no more information than that, I haven't talked to the fire chief yet this morning." I tried not to visibly take deep breaths in front of the camera.

"We understand the cause of the blaze may be arson, do you have any comment on that?" Again, the mic was stuck in my face.

"No, as I said, I don't know about the cause." I willed her to go away.

"Was anyone hurt in the blaze?" she asked.

"No, it was the middle of the night, thank God." I gave a brave smile.

I reckon she figured I was going to keep saying the same thing. I wasn't crying or acting crazy so I wasn't good press. She narrowed her eyes at me in irritation.

"Well, we will be keeping up with this unfolding story here in Medicine Springs for you. This is Martha Rainer, live with Channel 9." She made a throat cutting motion to her cameraman.

"Thanks, Ms. Maher. We are going to go find the fire chief, maybe he has some information for us." She removed her mic.

"So that was live? Not to show later?" I asked.

"It was just on the Live Morning Show. I am sorry about your building. Do you know where I can find the fire chief?" She looked around as if she expected him to be standing behind her.

"Probably at the fire hall." I pointed in the right direction.

The reporter and the cameraman mounted their van and drove away. I breathed a sigh of relief. I turned and looked at my poor building, but I didn't move any closer. Instead, I pulled a note pad and pen from my bag and wrote my own sign:

I AM AT TILLY'S WE CAN'T GO IN THE BUILDING AM HAVING COFFEE

Luckily, I had a piece of Big Red gum in my bag, which I chewed and used to stick the note to the door right below Andy's note. Gum is handy for so many things. Oh, sure, I could've called or texted, but it was too damn early. There are people who think just because they're up at the ass crack of dawn that everyone else is too. They make phone calls and send texts which wake the rest of us up and it really pisses me off. Considerate? Oh yes, I am.

I slunk down the street to Tilly's, debating in my head whether I really wanted go in or not. If I did, everyone inside would be all over me for the details of the fire. But my family and friends would know where to find me. Finally, the idea of coffee and orange juice won out.

The familiar glass door banded in red invited me in; I pushed it open to find a small crowd in residence. They were mostly retired folks who found Tilly's a great place to socialize; I saw a checkers game in progress and a couple of guys playing cards and drinking coffee. We don't have a Senior Citizens Center in Medicine Springs, we have Tilly's.

Everyone turned to see who had just come in and then every face took on an expression of sympathy when they realized it was me. I was engulfed in a sea of *Tess, I'm so sorry, how'd it happen? Are you alright? How bad is it?* just as I suspected I would be.

I stood stock still and tried to turn my brain on but nothing happened. My mouth opened and closed and I probably looked like an idiot. Tilly came to my rescue, bustling up in her 1950's waitress outfit. She actually has a little lace doily with her name in the middle, pinned over her heart.

"Now y'all, this girl is shocked down to her toenails! Let her be, you'll find out what happened soon enough. For now, let the child eat." Tilly took me by the hand and led me to a booth in the back.

"Thanks Tilly," I whispered.

"Now don't mention it, but ya know this is big news and everyone in here has done been by the building and seen the note from Andy, so they're all chomping at the bit to get the low down." She smiled at me.

"Here's the low down and you can pass it on. It seems some person or persons unknown tossed a fire bomb into my office.

The insurance investigators, the state Fire Marshall and the Tennessee Bomb and Arson folks will all most likely hit town soon." I ticked off the numbers on my fingers. "That'll give 'em a bite to chew on."

"Oh, it'll be like the circus has come to town!" Tilly exclaimed but I knew she was joking with me.

"Maybe I can get to ride on the elephant," I said.

"I'm thinking this buckin' bronco you're ridin' on right now will be quite enough. Ya'nt the Grandpa breakfast?" Tilly pulled out her order pad and yanked a pen out of her ponytail.

Two people could happily eat the Grandpa Breakfast.

"I reckon the Junior Special will do me," I answered. It came with two less pancakes and no grits.

Tilly took off to place the order. She stopped on her way to the kitchen and imparted some of my information to the card players. She pointed in my direction as she did. I knew she was warning them to leave me be and I was grateful.

In a flash, Tilly brought coffee and extra cream; I smiled my thanks at her and set about making my coffee perfect. I like two spoonful's of sugar and I like it blonde. But you have to be careful not to add too much cream or the coffee won't be hot enough. It's a balancing act. I concentrated on the java and tried not to worry about what I should do next. I figured someone would show up momentarily and give me directions.

I was right. Before Tilly had my breakfast on the table, a stranger walked in the front door and approached the counter. He leaned in and had a few words with Tilly. I studied him; he was about 40, had a little spare tire and some grey in his short hair. He was wearing khakis and a long sleeve pin-striped shirt. He looked average, but I knew he was a PI because he pinged my radar. I waited patiently for Tilly to point me out to him. She nodded her head in my direction. She didn't smile at the man as she did it; she'd already decided she didn't like him. I smiled a little.

The stranger walked over to the table and flashed a badge at me. "Hi, my name is Tim Smithson and I'm a Bomb and Arson Specialist with Grand Republic Insurance Co."

It felt odd to be on the receiving end of the 'hi my name is' routine.

"Have a seat, Tim." I gestured to the bench opposite me. "Coffee?"

"Sure."

I held my cup aloft for Tilly to see and then pointed at my breakfast companion. Tilly nodded and headed in our direction with the pot and an extra cup in hand. She poured for Tim and discreetly went away. She knew I'd tell her everything later.

"So, Tim, what do we do now?" I sipped my coffee.

Tim stirred sugar into his. "Well, I have a dog in the van and I'll take him in and see what he turns up. Ever been through anything like this before, Ms. Maher?"

I shook my head. "Nope, this is all new territory for me, but I've investigated several fires so I know the drill, pardon the pun."

Tim smiled at me and tiny crinkles appeared at the corners of his chocolate brown eyes.

"You got a theory?" He wanted to play it friendly, sort of a colleague to colleague. Fine, I'd play.

"I do. Some asshat jimmied my back door, kicked in my office door, and tossed a Molotov cocktail in the place."

"And why would someone do such a thing?" He seemed genuinely interested and concerned. I knew better; he was looking at body language and sizing me up. "I'll be the first to admit I've made enemies in my line of work. Not everybody loves PIs, as I'm sure you know."

He eyed me, trying to figure out if I was the guilty party or not. "Alright, what else?"

"The back door has scratches around the lock and the office reeks of gasoline. Your dog'll tell you that, although I doubt he'll notice the door. Before you say anything, no, I have not been inside, this is info I got from some of our volunteer fire fighters," I said.

"Hmm, pretty observant for volunteers, wouldn't you say?" he asked casually.

I didn't like what he was implying but I told myself he was only doing his job. "I'd say they're guys with good noses and good eyes, several of whom have retired from fire departments in larger cities. I figure the smell gave away the fact it was arson and someone had the idea of looking for the entry point." I refused to be nervous, I'd run this line of questioning myself too many times.

Tilly brought my breakfast.

"You orderin'?" she said to Tim.

"No ma'am, just the coffee please," he answered.

Tilly nodded, turned on her heel and walked away. Nope, she did not like my breakfast companion.

"Okay, so the dog goes in and then you make your report back to the insurance company. The state Bomb and Arson guys will be here soon to add their two cents worth and maybe the state Fire Marshall too. I don't reckon I need to get antsy about getting in there for salvage, am I right?" I started eating, not willing to let my eggs to get cold. The flavor practically exploded on my tongue. I repressed the urge to sigh out loud.

Tim shook his head at me. "Yeah, this is gonna take a while." He dropped a business card and two bucks on the table and left me to my meal.

Long after Tim had left and my breakfast was consumed, I sat and stared at the empty plate. I was so tired and so pissed. My phone rang and jerked me out of my reverie.

"Tess Maher," I answered.

"I heard you had a hot time last night," said a husky, almost sultry, female voice.

I looked at the screen; the number was blocked.

"I'm sorry, who's this?" I asked.

"I warned you to stay away from me. Are you brain damaged in some way?" Her tone became sharp. "You must be because you failed to listen, as I feared you would, so I felt I needed to reinforce my warning. Do you have it now? Stay the hell away from me!"

"Oh, I recognize your voice now; you're the crazy Widow Kincaid! You should have it embossed on a business card, black with raised gold lettering. I know a guy." I wanted to reach through the phone and strangle the bitch. "You set my building on fire, you could've killed someone – oh wait, you already have."

"You are a very bad girl and now you've been punished. If you fail to go away, I will employ stronger measures." Her voice was silky and soft.

"How'd you know?" I had no hope she'd tell me who the leak was but I had to try.

She laughed and it sounded like crystal tinkling; it was creepy as hell. "Oh, now everyone must have their little secrets. And what you don't know will hurt you." She was enjoying herself.

"Are you kidding? Holy shit, you nut job, you sound like the villain in a cheesy movie. So listen up, crazy legs, proof is very thin in this case but now I'll go to the ends of the earth to bring you down. It. Is. On."

"Then you shall suffer." She pronounced it like the bad guy in a B movie and hung up.

I was still staring at the phone in disbelief when Mars slid into the booth opposite me. She was already armed with a cup of coffee.

"What's up?" she asked.

"Lady Macbeth just called to claim credit for the fire and threatened me with worse if I don't leave her alone," I said, rolling my eyes.

"Wow, how weird and bad movie-ish, but then I guess folks who murder people and set shit on fire are nightmares by virtue of their actions. What else did she say?"

"In what may be the most bizarre conversation of my life, she declared I hadn't heeded her warning and now I would suffer, place exclamation points at the appropriate places. You should've heard her voice, it went from soft and seductive to cruel and snappish all in the same conversation. She really sounds like a psycho nut bar with delusions of grandeur on the side! Wanna take bets she has a big white Persian?"

Mars didn't laugh at my lame joke. "Call your brother."

"He'll be here soon enough."

My phone rang again and I looked at the caller ID. It was Derek. I took a deep breath and answered. "Hey, good looking."

"Hey, just saw you on the news. You didn't think to call me? I'm a fireman you know." His voice was light but I knew he was upset.

"I'm really sorry. I've been overwhelmed, first with the fire, the firemen, the reporter, and just now the fire investigator." I was talking fast.

"Darlin', I just want you to know I'm here for you, okay? I'm not looking for excuses or explanations. Do you need me?" He was so sincere.

"I don't want you to change your routine for me. From this point on I'll be grilled by the Fire Marshal, the investigation and probably more reporters. There isn't anything you can do for me." I regretted that statement as soon as it was out of my mouth.

He didn't speak for a few seconds. "Sure. Well, let me know."

"Derek, if you want to come down here and hold my hand and comfort me, I won't say no." That sounded pathetic.

"Let me know when. I'll call you later, okay?" He didn't sound mad. Hurt, maybe, but not mad.

"Okay, later." I broke the connection and laid my head down on the table. Damn it, damn, damn and damn. I screwed the pooch and hurt his feelings. Damn. Wisely, Mars didn't say a word, just left me to wallow.

My self-pity party was interrupted by Jim Leach.

Jim Leach arrived before my brother. He was armed with a file folder in his hand; probably a copy of my policy. Good thing, too, since mine was no doubt burnt to a crisp. He waved to us and scored a cup of coffee off Tilly.

"Morning Tess, morning Mars. Thought we might wanna give this policy a look see," he said, waving the folder in the air. "Andy called and he says somebody broke in the back door of the building and threw a fire bomb into your place after they kicked in the door."

"I got the same information from Billy and Sammy. This really affects when I get the money needed to fix the place since it's a criminal investigation now," I said.

"There has to be an investigation into the fire which proves to the satisfaction of the insurers you didn't set it yourself." Jim chuckled but he didn't sound amused, he sounded kind of embarrassed.

I nodded. "I figure Connell is out of the loop for the investigation, so the state Fire Marshall'll send somebody down. The Tennessee Bomb and Arson folks may come down too. The insurance bomb and arson guy is already in town."

"He's in your building, him and his very large dog. I can't push this forward even thought I want to, you understand. 'Course I did tell the investigator I was positive you were innocent of any wrong doing." Jim tried to look comforting but to me he just looked worried.

"Not a problem, Jim, I know things have to be done by the book. I've been on the other side of this a few times myself, so I know how it works. Thanks for everything." I smiled at him.

"Good, I'll keep you posted and don't you worry. Now let's take a look at the policy. First, from what Andy tells me, your place is a mess and you have a total loss in the front of the office. So, here's what your policy will cover, and I quote, 'office furniture, office machines, computers, telephones and other equipment used in the daily tasks of running the business.' You have a $500.00 deductible."

"But first I have to be cleared of the crime before I can get a check, right?" I asked.

Jim cleared his throat; he sure didn't like to talk about the investigation. I guess he was worried I'd be mad at him. "Right, right. But don't you worry. What you need to work on is the inventory of everything you lost; computers, phones, furniture, and so on. I reckon that'll take a few days."

"Well, Jewels and I will put our heads together and see if we can't figure it out," I said sadly. The list was something I didn't look forward to compiling. I felt a little sick.

Jim patted me on the hand. "Cheer up, girl, we'll have you back to making a living before you can say, 'Bob's your uncle' and that's a fact."

He grinned and so did I.

"Jim, can I order a tarp for the roof? From what I understand we have a big hole. A tarp would protect us from the rain." The idea bothered me, the rain falling unchecked into my already ruined building. Illogical, I know.

"Sure, and get someone to put it up. You just can't go inside. Save the receipt for the tarp and the labor." Jim patted my hand again. "This is gonna come out okay."

"I know it will, but it sure sucks in the meantime," I said sadly.

Jim left us and met Connell coming in the front door. They stood and conferred for a minute or so.

Tilly brought the coffee pot for warm-ups.

"Mars, you need some breakfast?" she asked.

"Fruit and yogurt please, Tilly," Mars answered and Tilly headed for the kitchen.

"Good thing I posted a note as to my whereabouts," I said as Connell reached the table.

He grinned. "Yep, but I'm the law and I would've tracked you down. Morning Mars." He grinned even wider at her. "So, what's up? You look grim."

"Well, I've just received a completely psycho phone call from the Kincaid woman, or as I like to call her, Lady Macbeth. She insinuated she set the fire to further warn me off the case since the rat wasn't a big enough deterrent. She threatened more dire consequences if I didn't go away." I sighed. "She really is crazy as a shit house rat."

"Let's see if we can trace it back to a number that belongs to the bitch," Connell growled and walked outside with his phone in his hand. He intended to twist some arms and get the call logs to my phone.

Tilly brought Mars' breakfast to the table and looked at me. "So, was that fella from the state or the insurance?" she demanded. "Cuz I gotta say I didn't like him."

I had to grin. "The insurance; he's a bomb and arson guy with a dog. I bet there's an audience on the sidewalk right now waiting for him and the dog to come out."

Tilly raised an eyebrow. "Yep, I reckon so, jest like the circus. Maybe I oughta pop some corn."

"Tilly, I need a temporary base of operations. Running things from this booth has its advantages, one of which is food and another is your coffee. But I gotta find a place to set up 'til I can get back in my building. Any ideas?"

"Doris has space in the back of her shop, you oughta call her," Tilly suggested.

"Good idea," said Mars as she polished off her yogurt. "I bet she'll help you out."

Doris Remington, owner of Remington's Antiques, was a neighbor of mine and she liked me. Of course, given the circumstances she might not want to rent the place to me. I pulled out my phone and dialed.

"Remington Antiques," a cheery voice answered.

"Hey Doris, it's Tess."

"Oh, Tess honey, how awful! I'm just devastated for you! If there's anythin' I can do to help, please tell me?" Doris has a deep Southern drawl; it practically drips magnolias and moonlight.

"Doris, I need temporary space to run my business. I know it's a lot to ask considering my building got torched and the arsonist has not been apprehended, but whatdaya think?"

Doris was silent for a moment and I was afraid she was going to say no but then she drew a breath and proceeded to blast my ears off.

"Why do you even think you need to ask? I'm insulted, absolutely insulted, and mortified you would think I could fail to help you or be afraid to help you or somethin' silly. Do you think I'm a coward? Or I'm a fair-weather friend? Or I'm not a good Christian? Oh my God! Tessely Anne Marie Maher, you get yourself down here right this minute, I'll have James clean out the back room! And don't you dare argue with me neither!"

As if I could get a word in edge ways. "Yes ma'am, no ma'am," was all I could manage. I finally ended the onesided conversation by saying, "I am on my way over, tell James I said thank you, bye now, see you soon, and thank you."

Whew! She was like a bull dog with a ham hock once she got something in her head. I decided to give her an hour to get the space ready.

27

Strange New Place

After two more cups of coffee, Mars and I headed to my new locale. Amazingly, it was ready for me. James must have worked at warp speed. There was even a desk with a potted plant on it, a good luck bamboo. Very nice. Our new office space was surrounded with boxes, barrels, crates, and pieces of furniture in various states of repair. It was all pushed up against the walls and covered in sheets so the place was neat and tidy, but still it was odd and a little claustrophobic.

Mars perched on a corner of the desk and surveyed the place. "Well, it's cozy."

I snorted. It was a bit cozy, but I was grateful for a place to call home even if it was in the back of an antique shop.

Within minutes of our arrival we were engulfed by family members who wanted to argue about hiring help for the clean-up. There ensued a round robin where my mother kept insisting there were plenty of hands to do the job. Then I explained the entire building had to be cleaned and painted; the insurance would pay for it and they could help out but not do all the work. We did a back and forth about a dozen times while I just kept saying no and finally everyone shut up. Well, everyone except Mommy.

"You can't tell me no, I'm your mother," Mommy said and was completely serious.

"Mommy, this is business, my business, and I am going to hire help." I looked her dead in the eye and did not blink.

She scrunched up her nose at me and shook her head, but wisely did not say another word. I may have won the round, but definitely not the war. I looked at Mars, who had been silent, and we both smiled.

After putting my family straight and throwing them out, I called a cleaning company. The owner promised to come over and give me an estimate as soon as the authorities cleared the building. Then I called Jewels and gave her our new address.

"Well as much fun as this has been to watch, I have to go and earn some money now." Mars grinned at me.

"You're a bitch, do you know that? I am suffering here and you're deserting me. Fine, go on then, and don't look back."

"I'll call your brother and tell him where you are," Mars offered.

"You just wanna talk to him without me listening. Don't think I don't know he was playing with your knee at breakfast."

She just grinned and wrinkled her perfect nose at me before she leaned over and kissed me.

As soon as Mars was gone I made phone calls to all of my tenants to inform them of our troubles. I called the hardware store and ordered a large tarp. Then I called Billy to make arrangements for him to pick up the tarp and the large ladder from my house so he could put the tarp in place. He assured me he'd get it done. I hung up just as Jewels waltzed in the door.

"Well, this is different," she admitted as she perused the new place. "Sort of shabby chic that went on over the line and hit shabby."

I snickered. "Yep, but it'll do for now. Sure beats working out of the car."

"What's next?" she asked.

"First I need to tell you Lady Macbeth called and bragged how she set the fire to make me go away."

Jewels' eyes grew wide. "Whoa, she really is crazy. So what do we do?"

"You make sure this is right under your hand all the time." I handed her a Glock. She knew how to use it; the business had paid for her training.

Jewels took the gun without hesitation, checked it out, and put it on the desk next to her.

"Take it home with you when you leave here. You need a carry permit. Call and get one set up, okay?"

"Yes ma'am, got one, and now what?"

"Did Rod come by the office and pick up the camera I wanted him to use for the insurance surveillance job?" I asked.

When Jewels nodded, I sagged a bit with relief.

"Thank God, I was a bit worried we'd lost more equipment to the fire," I admitted.

I knew we'd be reimbursed for any loses but getting money from an insurance company can be a long and arduous proposition.

"Call him, give him the low down, and see if he's gotten the cameras in place. If so, the images were downloaded to the office computer. Check on the remote server to see if they downloaded before the fire. I'd hate it if we lost a day. Please?"

"Got it, what else?"

"Go buy new computers, an external hard drive, coffee pot, pens, message books, whatever we need."

"Burner phones?"

"Sure. Hey, see how much one of those fancy coffee makers with the single cups of coffee and tea cost. I think one might be a good thing to have."

"I'll go to Dixon for everything. Do we wanna transfer the office phones to me?"

"Yep, 'cause I'm going to Atlanta again. I see no reason to sit here on my ass. I wanna talk to the fella who claims to have seen a mystery nurse visit Jon Kincaid the night of his death."

"Boss!" she exclaimed. "You got a witness!"

I held up my hand in a "stop" gesture. "I maybe have a witness, let's don't count our chickens. He might not've seen anything, or he might not be deemed a credible witness, or the nurse he saw might have been a little green man scoping out the place for possible invasion. Who knows? I wanna interview him and then we'll see if we have reason to celebrate. Rest assured, I'm gonna to turn over every rock to find the way to bring this bitch down."

We parted company, Jewels to shop, a thing she loves to do, and me to drive yet again to Atlanta, a thing I don't love to do. Truth to tell though I was happy to get away from town for a few hours and away from the sight of my poor building. It looked sad and forlorn and smoke damaged as I drove past it.

As I had foreseen, there was a crowd of folks on the sidewalk craning their necks for a better view of the disaster. Connell was in front, trying to keep people from getting to close. I called him since I didn't want to stop and get drawn into the drama.

"Yeah?" he answered.

"Anything on the phone?" I asked.

"Burner phone," he snapped.

"Bitch, but I'm not surprised. She's cunning. Okay, I'm off to Hotlanta," I said.

"You watch your ass,"

"Yes sir." I cut the connection. I sure as hell didn't need such advice; I knew I'd kicked over a hornet's nest. I meant not to get stung.

The drive to Atlanta was an uneventful trip. Thankfully my PI kit was in the Jeep and in it was a blond wig and green contact lenses; I had a fist full of my real business cards in my purse. I'd use the wig and contacts to make sure no one recognized me from the last visit to the rehab. Sometimes when you fool people they get pissed off and won't talk to you anymore. Go figure. Being just a PI with no real authority to make people talk to me, I needed for all parties to like me. If they at least didn't hate me, I stood a better chance of seeing Mr. Stewart instead of getting tossed out on my ass.

As I drove, I fielded phone calls from Jewels, Jim Leach, my mother three times, and all my sibs including Michelene, my personal cross to bear in life.

"Hi Tess, how are you doing?" Michelene said in her professional voice, calming and fake.

"I'm good, thanks for askin', and you?"

"Do you feel you need to talk about the trauma of the fire?" she asked.

I felt my eyebrows shoot up and get tangled in my hairline. "Really? Are ya' kiddin'? Jesus Christ on a biscuit, Mich, you're killin' me! It was a fire and shitty but it's not like I lost the family dog. Everythin' that burned can be replaced. It's a pain in the ass, not traumatic."

"Are you in denial?" she asked, her voice dripping with sincerity.

I hung up. God Almighty, sometimes my psychologist sister made me crazy and the ironic thought made me laugh out loud. I found my mood had lightened.

I located a Stop-n-Rob market about a mile from the Marietta Rehab Center and used their not very clean bathroom to put on my disguise. The blonde wig worked with my skin tone and the green contacts helped even more to change my appearance. It wasn't a dramatic change, but it was just enough to throw someone off. People have a tendency to remember red hair, but every other woman in America is a blonde. When I was finished I looked very professional and believed my new look would work.

The woman on the front desk of the rehab center was not anyone I'd run into when I'd been there posing as a prospective client. A nice break for me.

"Hi, how are you?" I asked.

The woman looked up and said, "I'm just fine, how can I help ya?"

Her name tag proclaimed her to be 'Bobbie'. I reached across the desk, took her hand and shook it firmly as I said, "Bobbie, my name is Tess Maher from Maher Investigations." I released her hand and placed a business card on the counter. "I'm here lookin' into a possible murder and I'd like to speak to a Mr. Kevin Stewart."

Bobbie stared at me with her mouth open; she seemed to be in shock. In fact, she looked rather like a carp as my Grammy used to say. Some folks have a bad reaction to the idea of murder. Finally, the woman blinked several times.

"I … I need to talk to my boss," she stuttered.

"Great." I smiled. "You go right ahead, I'll be right here."

She stood up and practically ran down the hallway toward the director's door. I could hear her agitated voice as she spoke to her boss but couldn't understand what she was saying except for the word 'murder'. I had made an impression.

The sound of hurried footsteps came to my ears and Bobbie and another woman appeared. The new woman stepped forward and extended her hand to me.

"I'm the director, Ms. Thombs. I understand you wish to interview one of our residents, Mr. Stewart. Could you please step into my office so we can discuss this?"

"Of course," I said and waited for her to lead the way. I sure as hell didn't want her to know I already knew the location of her office.

Ms. Thombs' office was nicely appointed, leather chairs, antique desk and some rather nice copies of old masters on the walls. All in all, the atmosphere was relaxed and comfortable. I'd only seen it in the dark last time.

I appraised the women herself as she sat behind her desk. I put her at a well preserved forty-something. She had light brown hair in an attractive but not trendy style, and she was slim and well-dressed in a tailored suit. She was all business, but not severe, and she came across as easy to relate to – on purpose I was sure.

I sat down and decided to lay my cards on the table as plainly as possible. "Ms. Thombs, I am a private investigator from Nashville and I've been hired by the ex-wife and the children of Jon Kincaid to look into his death."

"Oh my!" she exclaimed, genuinely taken aback. "May I ask you why they would think Mr. Kincaid was a victim of foul play? After all we're talking about a man who had terminal cancer."

She looked perplexed but I knew she was worried about the reputation of the institution. I knew I would be if I was in her expensive leather pumps.

"I really can't give you any details at this time but rest assured if this turns out to be true, no one believes anyone here is to blame in any way, shape or form." I smiled and tried to look sincere.

She smiled back. "Thank you. May I ask why you wish to speak to Mr. Stewart?"

"I think it might be possible he saw something out of place the night Mr. Kincaid died. I understand his room is right across the hall from the room Mr. Kincaid occupied. I'm just trying to cover all my bases here."

She was silent for a moment, assessing the situation and trying to decide how much of a threat I might be to her and to the rehab center. I tried to look non-threatening.

"I'm afraid this one's above my pay grade, I'm going to have to kick it upstairs. You're welcome to wait while I make the call, we have a sitting room. Bobbie will show you where it is and even get you a cup of coffee."

"Oh, coffee would be great. My last cup was at least 100 miles back down the highway." I rose, shook hands again and went to find Bobbie.

"Bobbie, your boss told me you could get me a cup of coffee and show me to the waiting room." I was laying on the charm a bit thick.

"Why sure, I'd be happy to. As a matter of fact, we have coffee in the waitin' room. It's down the hall the third door." She pointed toward the residence wing. She lowered her voice. "Can I ask you a question? Do you really think Mr. Kincaid was murdered?"

"Bobbie, I mean to find out."

I walked down the hall and into the room indicated. I felt pretty sure I wasn't going to get permission to speak with Kevin Stewart, so I'd have to get forgiveness instead, because I was damn sure going to talk to him.

I took out my compact and held it in such a way I could spy on Bobbie without her seeing me. A handy skill I picked up as a small, nosey child. About thirty seconds later the phone rang and Bobbie's attention shifted to the caller. I slipped out of the waiting room and moved down the hall. I knew the room number where Jon Kincaid spent his final days, 155, so I knew it wouldn't be too difficult to find Kevin Stewart. He had to be in 154 or 156. I went to 154 first because the door was open. I poked my head inside and found a woman in the bed.

"Oh, pardon me; I was looking for Kevin Stewart." I smiled at the elderly woman.

"Hmp, you related?" she asked.

"No, ma'am."

"Then take a piece of advice from me and don't stand too close to that old reprobate, he's a squeezer." She frowned.

"Beg pardon?" I was confused.

"He likes to squeeze lady parts, if ya' know what I mean." She stared at me hard.

The light dawned and I chuckled. "Don't worry. I'll stand an arm's length away, just to be sure."

She pointed to her left with her thumb. "Next door and don't say I didn't warn ya."

The door to Kevin Stewart's room was partially open and I knocked as I opened the door. "Mr. Stewart?"

A man was lying propped up in his bed, watching television in a wife-beater and boxers. From my unobstructed view, he was wrinkled, wiry, and about a hundred years old. Stewart put me in mind of a bandy rooster my uncle Hubert Lee had once owned; he too had been tough and wiry.

Stewart looked up at me and smiled. "Yep, that's my name, don't wear it out. Now who might you be, doll face? And I hope you're gonna say you're the new girl they've hired to give sponge baths."

"Does that pick-up line work on your planet?" I asked sweetly.

Stewart began to laugh and it was a big, huge belly laugh, far too big to come from the small man in the bed.

He finally calmed down enough to say, "And you're feisty too." He leered at me. "I like my women feisty."

"I just bet you do." I grinned.

My retort set him off again. He laughed so hard his face turned red and I became seriously worried about his heart giving out on him.

Stewart wiped the tears from his eyes. "What's your deal, McNeil?"

I jumped right in, "Mr. Stewart, my name is Tess Maher and I'm a private investigator. I've been asked to look in to the death of Jon Kincaid; he was your neighbor across the hall."

"Oh yeah, I remember him, had a real bitch for a wife. Poor bastard probably died to get away from her." Stewart rubbed his hand across his bald, freckled head and pinned me with a stare. "So whaduya wanna know?"

"Mr. Stewart, I'd like to record this conversation if you don't mind. I'd be much obliged."

He nodded and I took my digital recorder out of my bag and flipped it on.

"I understand you saw a nurse you'd never seen before the night Kincaid died, and no one has ever seen her again. Is this correct information?"

"Yep."

"Any chance you could be mistaken? Maybe you saw her on a different night, or maybe you dreamed her?"

Kevin Stewart shook his head in denial.

"Maybe I'm old and senile and don't know what the hell I'm talkin' 'bout, you reckon? Or mabbe I'm blind as a bat?" Then he smiled as only a dirty old man can smile. "Chickadee, let me tell ya' somethin', little enough happens in this here shithole that changes the pace, so I remember when something does. Just like I'm gonna remember you. And my eyes are still pretty good, so I know what I saw."

He paused to give me the up and down stare was designed to make me feel as if he was imagining me naked. Yuck.

"Also, I appreciate a great pair of knockers and I'm not likely to forget or mistake a new set. Even when they're a bought and paid for set." He chuckled and his chuckle was dirty too. "Men don't care if they're real or not just so long as they're big, and these was."

He winked. Jeez, what an old reprobate he was, the woman next door had been right! I smiled my very best come-hither smile at him. I needed the info this guy had and if smiling like a ten-dollar hooker would get it for me then I was going to smile.

"Mr. Stewart, would ya be willin' to testify in a court of law you had seen a stranger exitin' Mr. Kincaid's room on the night he died?"

"If it'd get me the hell out of here for a few hours, I'd testify I saw the devil hisself dancin' down the hallway in a god damn mini skirt." He grinned at me.

"Yes sir, thank you sir. Is there anything else you remember about that night which might be pertinent to Mr. Kincaid's death?"

"Well, I think that ass was familiar."

"Pardon?"

"On the nurse, girly, keep up now. I been thinkin' 'bout it, as I have damn little else to ponder on, and that ass was one I'm pretty sure I seen before. I love knockers, but a superior ass does draw my attention." He smiled as if he was remembering the aforementioned superior ass.

"I'm sure, and so can you remember whose ass you were looking at?" I could hardly believe I was having this conversation in real life.

"I reckon the ass in question sure did look a whole lot like the ass on a certain Ms. Kincaid." He winked again.

Bingo, I thought. Then I heard footsteps and voices coming in my direction. "Mr. Stewart, I appreciate your time and candor and, as I think I'm about to get bounced out of here, I'd just like to say goodbye and thanks."

"Any time you wanna come by and give me a sponge bath, sugar lips, I wouldn't say no. You got a fair set of knockers yourself."

"Mr. Stewart, you are a hot mess."

"You have no idea, Chickadee."

He winked again and I grabbed my recorder as I headed for the door. I pulled it open and came face to face with Ms. Thombs and Bobbie. The director's face was twisted like an opossum who'd been eating briars. Bobbie looked like she'd gotten her ass chewed. I felt kinda bad about causing her trouble.

"You want to explain your presence here?" The director's voice had a decided chill in it.

There were just so many good answers to such a question, but I figured I was in enough trouble without pissing the woman off further.

"I was just leaving," I said hastily.

"If I see you again, I'll have you arrested for trespassing, am I clear?" Ms. Thombs snapped.

"Crystal," I said and beat a hasty retreat.

# 28

On the Road Again

I jumped into the Jeep and took off. Man, oh man, I was excited! I had the goods on Lady Macbeth, or at least I had probable cause and a witness who could place her in the rehab center on the fateful night. I could only hope it would be enough to convince the cops look at this thing. I pumped my fist in the air several times as I negotiated the streets of Atlanta. I hit the Bluetooth and called Georgia.

"Hello Tess," she said.

"Georgia, I think we may have somethin' we can use to prove Jon was murdered."

Georgia drew a sharp breath. "Tell me everything."

"There's a man who's in residence at the rehab center, his room is right across the hall from the room Jon occupied. On the night Jon died, this resident saw a strange nurse leavin' Jon's room. He never saw her again and no one else at the center remembers her."

"Maybe he imagined the whole thing," Georgia said.

I shook my head. "I don't think so; this fella seems real certain of what he saw and when. He thinks maybe it was Jonnie Kincaid."

"Wow," Georgia breathed out. "Will it stand up in court? What do we do now?"

"I doubt it would stand up in court if Jonnie has a good lawyer, but it might be enough to get the police to take a look at this thing. I gotta tell you the truth, it's a long shot. Jon was terminal and he died, now we have an old guy on meds who may or may not have seen a woman who looked like Jonnie Kincaid leavin' her husband's room late on the night he died. Look at this as a police detective would and you don't have much but a whole lot of speculation."

"Still, it looks fishy, right?"

"Like a boatload of tuna, but Georgia, DAs and prosecutors only want to take on cases they know they can win."

"It just seems wrong for her to get away with this. I believed Jon when he said Jonnie murdered him, and now it seems to me no one else cares."

"I care, you care, and your kids care, even the ones who deny it. I'm willin' to take this thing as far as I can, but you have to realize we may strike out."

"We might," she agreed. "But at least we can say we tried, right?"

I smiled. "Yep, we can say that. Georgia, one more thing, I've been contacted again by Jonnie. She called me the other day and threatened me. Then she sent me a little present in the mail, a dead rat."

"Oh my god! That horrible woman, I'm so sorry."

"Then my building was fire bombed and I was pretty sure she was responsible. She confirmed my suspicions by calling, not identifyin' herself of course, and taunted me about the fire. She claimed she did it to punish me for not droppin' the case."

There was no sound from Georgia for almost thirty seconds. I even thought maybe she'd hung up.

Finally, she said, "Tess, I think you have to drop this case, it's just too dangerous. If she's crazy enough to set fire to your building, she's crazy enough to hurt you. I'd never forgive myself if anything happened to you."

"Georgia, if she's so desperate to stop me, she must be hidin' something. Don't you wanna find out what?"

"Not at the cost of harm to you. Jon's dead and whether she killed him or not, no further harm can come to him. He's free of her, but you're another matter entirely. I can't let you put yourself at risk."

She sounded so worried I felt bad for even telling her about the rat or the fire. Still, I believed she had a right to the information.

"You did tell your children we were going forward with the investigation no matter what, right?" I was becoming more and more positive one of the kids was our leak.

"I … well yes I did. Oh Tess, you don't think … ?"

"Georgia, I feel sure one of them is the leak, but you mustn't tell them what I suspect. It's possible we can feed Jonnie some false information. You must also keep quiet about a possible witness, I can't stress this strongly enough. As far as the danger to me, I'd tell you not to worry but that'd be a waste of my breath. So instead I'll tell you I'm watchin' my back at all times, I never go anywhere unarmed and I live with the ex-sheriff of the county. We also have four dogs, so I'm pretty sure she can't sneak up on us. She might be nuts, but she's not a professional hitter."

I didn't bother to tell Georgia we'd been snuck up on before, more or less. It hadn't turned out so well for the bad guys.

"Tess, I'm going to lose sleep over this," Georgia said. "I always loathed the damn woman, but now she scares me."

"Frankly, Georgia, she scares me too," I admitted.

"How bad is your building?" she asked.

"Don't know yet, the Fire Marshall and the insurance investigators have to get finished before I can even get in there to access the damage. It's bad, but probably not a total loss. Keep the faith Georgia, I'll be in touch."

I hung up and called Jewels.

"Hey Boss, you should have an incomin' call about now, brace yourself." Sure enough, my phone beeped, right on cue. Jewels said, "Call me after."

I hit the Bluetooth. "Tess Maher."

"Well, I heard you had a little fire, Maher," Special TBI Agent Lyle said in a positively jovial manner.

"Very Special Agent Byle, my favorite TBI agent, always good to hear from you. Did ya finally get a new hairdresser? You sound so chipper." I despised the woman.

"Always chipper when you're out in the middle of Shit Creek. I keep an eye on you just for old time's sake and I know all about your building," she taunted.

"Well now, I've never had a stalker, I'm kinda flattered."

"Maher," Lyle snarled at me. "I made a special call to the state Fire Marshall just for you. He's going to take a real fine-tooth comb to your fire. Oh, and did I say he's a very personal friend of mine?"

"Y'all go to group therapy together? It's so nice you have friends outside of the TBI, I worry about your social skills." I grinned because I was having so much fun. "I sure do appreciate you gettin' me super-duper treatment from the state Fire Marshall, that's just too sweet of you. Why, it's like gettin' sprinkles on top of my ice cream."

"He's going to do everything he can to prove you set the fire yourself, laugh that off." Lyle sounded pissed.

"I think it's lovely you've taken such an interest in me, Agent Byle, bless your heart and I do mean it in the Southern way. As much fun as this renewal of our delightful relationship has been, I have other fish to fry. It's always such a treat to speak with you, but sadly duty calls. Oh, but you know what, since you've been so nice to me let me give you a little fashion tip, spend a little more money on your wardrobe, quit buying your clothes from the Co-op, you dress like a boy. It don't work for ya. Give my best to your BFF, Very Special Agent Void."

I disconnected and laughed at my humor. I was sure I'd pay for it down the line but I didn't care right at the moment. The TBI couldn't stick their noses in my mess since it wasn't drug related or Medicaid fraud, illegal gambling, or half dozen other things, but they could just be a big ol' pain in my ass.

The phone rang and I answered it with a grin on my face. "Maher."

"Hey Boss, I couldn't wait for you to call me back. Did you talk to your biggest fan?" Jewels asked.

"Oh yes I did and it's always good to hear from someone with a badge who hates my guts. She's called the Fire Marshall and asked him to pay careful attention to my fire; she wants to prove I set it. It'll be fun to make her eat her words."

"What if the state Fire Marshall likes her better than you? It's not as if we haven't seen corrupt state officials before."

"Yep," I said.

My mind wandered for a moment to dear old Donna Maples, our former county property commissioner. She'd been accused as an accessory after the fact to Chick's murder. She'd rolled over in a big way on the three remaining bad guys and Aggroco, the large agricultural company which had hired them all. She was currently in my brother's jail waiting out the trials, since he figured she might not survive otherwise.

"Good ol' Donna," I muttered.

"Yep, the bitch. What do you need me to do?"

I sighed. "Will you call Mr. Neuyen, explain about the fire and lost computers and tell him we'll be back up in no time." A thought hit me. "Jewels, do we have a picture of Lady Macbeth?"

"No, Boss, we do not."

"Then one more thing, and do this first call Georgia and see if she has one, please."

"On it, boss."

It took less than a minute for Jewels to get back to me. "She does not, boss, and neither do any of the children. Seems no one liked her enough to have a picture."

"Wow, well, not surprised. I want a picture of her; a faceless adversary is much scarier than one whose face is known. You know?"

Jewels laughed. "Yep, I get it, like the Ringwaiths, they were so terrifying in the Lord of the Rings 'cause they had no faces."

"Gimme her address."

"Boss, you … never mind. I was gonna say be careful, but I know you." Jewels sighed.

"I'll be careful, I brought the tele-photo and I'm wearing a wig. She won't see me and if she does she won't know who I am." I was feeling a little indignant at her doubt of my talents and abilities.

"Oh okay, she'll just think you're some nut job stalking her and call the police. Good thing we just got two checks in the mail today, I'm gonna need bail money," Jewels joked.

I laughed. "Girl, you're getting way too cocky. Address please."

"147 St. Simon's Cove, Acworth, 30101."

"Thank you, I'll be home later under my own steam, thank you very much."

"I hope." She hung up.

"Doubting Tomasina," I said to the empty air as I punched the address into the GPS.

I stopped at the first market I saw to hit the bathroom. I also picked up coffee, power bars, and water. Since I had no idea how long the exercise might take, I decided to stock up.

Ten minutes later I was back in the car. I looked at the little GPS map and then the GPS lady started talking to me. She led me right to the neighborhood. Some neighborhood it was, too, very high end and built surrounding a golf course. It was one of the many rather expensive developments which have grown up around Atlanta in the last twenty or so years.

Keeping to a moderate speed, I cruised past number 147. It was a very elegant large faux Tutor, with a lawn which was manicured within an inch of its life. I looked for a place to park so I could get some good pictures without being seen. I drove one street over and found a spot which allowed me to look through the trees and see the front door of the Kincaid house.

I reached into the back seat and opened my PI bag, extracted my camera and lens and hooked them up. My good camera is a Nikon D5500 and I love it because it never fails me. I'm not a good photographer but the camera makes me look like one for sure. I pulled a pack of Big Red gum out of my glove box, stuck a couple of pieces in my mouth, and settled down to wait. Wait I did. When it got dark, I attached my low light filter to get the night shots.

By nine o'clock my stomach was rumbling and my bladder was sending urgent messages to my brain. I stubbornly sat in the Jeep, determined to wait the woman out.

About ten PM my luck changed, thank God because I'd been ready to call it a night. The front door of the house opened and I trained my binoculars on the door. A slim, well-dressed woman walked out toward the car parked in the driveway. I couldn't determine how tall she was from the distance.

She turned back to speak to a younger woman who was still standing inside the door frame. I was too far away to hear the conversation but it appeared Jonnie Kincaid was making a point about something with her daughter; she was jabbing her finger at the girl. I wasn't positive, but I was fairly sure I had the play-ers right. Jonnie turned back to the car; I traded the binoculars for the camera and snapped merrily away. I got several of the daughter too as she stepped out onto the front porch.

Let me say I was several hundred yards away from the Kincaid house and there was no way in hell Jonnie Kincaid could have seen me. None the less, as she opened her car door, she turned her head in my direction and I could have sworn she looked right at me. It made a chill run down my back. Despite the chill, I got a perfect shot of her, 'cause I'm a pro.

The damn woman dried the spit in my mouth, but because I'm a glutton for punishment, I decided to follow her. I couldn't help myself, it's what I do.

I gave her a head start. I had to, it was late for the neighborhood and no one else was stirring. Besides, there was only one way out, so I felt it was a pretty safe bet she wouldn't lose me. After sixty seconds, I followed. We headed into downtown Atlanta and she kept to the side streets.

Jonnie slowed and turned down Peachtree Rd. NE without using a turn signal. I went on past, figuring I could drive around the block. Wrong. Wrong. Wrong. It took me several minutes to get back to Peachtree Rd. NE. I cursed fervently all the way. When I finally found my way back, Jonnie's car was parked at the curb so I drove on past her. She was being helped from the car by a young valet; I glanced at the façade of the building as I cruised by. It was distinguished by lovely architecture, stone arches, soaring pillars and gargoyles. I believed it was a club, given the valet parking, but not a dance and drink 'til you puke club. No, it was a leather chairs, soft music and waiters wearing white gloves kind of club.

I cruised the block again and circled back to the building. There was no sign of Jonnie, her car, or the valet. I pulled over to the curb, parked and ran up the stairs to the front door. There on the impressive wooden and brass door was a teeny, tiny, brass plate which read, 'The Pineapple Club.' So much for advertising.

I turned back to my car just as the valet came running up.

"My apologies for making you wait, if you'll give me your keys, I take care of you immediately." He smiled and his face lit up. He was young, earnest and cute. I figured him for a college boy. He held out his hand for my keys.

I smiled at him and tried to look embarrassed. "No, I can't stay, I just remembered something important I forgot to do. But thank you and you have a good night."

"Yes ma'am, you do the same. I'll see you next time." He flashed his perfect white teeth at me.

He was flirting and under normal circumstances his attention would have done wonders for my ego. However, it meant he might remember me, not something I wanted. With no way to repair whatever damage I'd done, I jumped in the Jeep and took off. I was delighted I hadn't taken the time to remove the blonde wig or the green contacts; I hoped the disguise might muddy the waters, somewhat. I had no idea what Jonnie was doing in the Pineapple Club or if the knowledge would further my investigation. Out of morbid curiosity, I Googled the club and found it and the motto: *Discretion is our by-word, comfort is our motto.* I bet it was too.

I knew that somehow Jonnie had made me and we were playing goose chase and she was playing with me. I visualized her cooling her heels and laughing at me. I put my head on the steering wheel and banged it several times. Then I drove home.

29

Evil Woman

I arose bright and early the next morning, way too early since I'd driven home from Atlanta, which had once again made me grateful for GPS. Without it I would probably have still been driving around Atlanta as the sun came up.

Curiosity about the pictures I'd snapped of the widow and her daughter pulled me out of bed. I quickly plugged my camera into my laptop and had a look. Most of the shots were very good, clean shots which captured the features of both women. Jonnie Kincaid had aquiline features, and I was being kind. Her face was long, her nose and chin rather pointy, her hair was a sort of strawberry blond but more strawberry than blond. It looked as if her stylist had tried to make the color look natural by weaving light and dark colors into the 'do. It looked kind of tiger striped. If I had her kind of money, I'd sure have a better hair color. I decided her stylist ought to be brought up on charges. Really had to admit the woman had good taste in clothes though, her outfit was stylish and had probably been tailored for her.

The daughter, I was sure I was right since the family resemblance was unmistakable, seemed a shadow of her mother. Anna's features were so similar to Jonnie's, but her hair was dull, dishwater blonde and limp, and she was hunched over as if she feared being hit. Her posture left a bad taste in my mouth. I was coming to dislike Lady Macbeth more and more and I hadn't realized such a thing was possible. She killed helpless men, little furry animals, and torched my building in the course of her getting what she wanted. However, her own daughter, who was a full-grown woman, feared her mama. Jonnie Kincaid was a bad woman and I meant to make sure she paid for her sins.

I saved the photos to my laptop and toddled off to get my run in for the day. I sure didn't feel like doing it on less than four hours sleep, but the day was wasting and I had things to do.

My parents and grandmother were in the kitchen when I finished running.

"Breakfast?" Mommy called out.

"Yes please, give me ten minutes," I answered.

It actually took fifteen but when I returned Mommy was putting my plate on the table. I knew she threw the eggs in the skillet when she heard the shower cut off, but I let her pretend she was a timing wizard.

"Wow Mommy, thanks. I don't know how you do it!"

Mommy smiled and turned back to the stove.

Daddy winked at me. "So, what's new?"

"Oh, lots and lots," I said around mouthfuls of eggs and bacon. Daddy raised one eyebrow. "Well, I may actually have something. I got a tip one of the residents of the rehab center had seen somethin' suspicious the night Jon Kincaid died. So I tooled down to Atlanta and interviewed him."

I paused in my narrative to sip some coffee.

"Well?" YaYa asked impatiently.

"He claims to have seen a nurse leaving Kincaid's room the night he died. This was a nurse he had never seen before and no one else saw her on any night. He further claims he believes her to be Jonnie Kincaid in a wig and nurse uniform."

"What makes him so sure?" Mommy asked as she sat down.

"Well, he claims to be an expert in derrières," I said with a straight face.

There was silence and raised eyebrows all around the table.

I grinned. "Seems every butt he has ever seen is filed away in the memory banks of his filthy little mind."

Everyone laughed.

"He actually said that?" Mommy asked.

"More or less," I admitted.

YaYa laughed. "What an old coot!"

"He is, but I kinda like him." I grinned and Mommy rolled her eyes at me.

"It is enough to open an investigation? He's old, I take it?" Daddy asked. I nodded. "He's infirmed in some way?" Again, I nodded. "Then the thinking might be he's incompetent because he's on medication or senile and imagined the whole thing." Daddy's cop brain had clicked on and was running.

"I asked myself all the same things, but Daddy, he's sharp as a tack. He's also willing to testify in court. I don't know if it's enough, but it is more than I had twenty-four hours ago. It might be enough for the widow to trip over."

Daddy looked thoughtful. "You could be right, so push it in her path and see."

I snagged my laptop from my bag and opened it. "I took pictures of her last night so I could put a face to the name." I pulled the pictures up and set them to a slide show.

"Oh my, she's one ugly woman. She looks like a dog wearing make-up!" YaYa chortled.

"Mama, that's unkind," Mommy admonished YaYa.

"But not untrue," Daddy added.

YaYa snickered again. "Well, she can't help being ugly but she could stay home."

"YaYa, you're terrible," I said but I was laughing.

YaYa just flashed her evil grin at me. I love my granny.

Jewels was already there when I got to work. I saw she had her own desk, which made our space a bit more crowded. I wondered how long this arrangement would have to last.

"Morning Jewels, can you call the Marietta Rehab? I wanna check back with Kevin Stewart and see if he's still willing to talk to the cops about the Kincaid murder."

One of the shop cats wandered in and jumped up on my desk. She began grooming herself. I pushed her out of my way so I could set the laptop up. She ignored me, as cats often do.

"Sure thing." Jewels dialed the number and handed me her phone.

It rang three times while I petted Zsa Zsa, the petite calico who demanded love from me.

"Marietta Rehab, this is Bobbie, how may I direct your call?" Bobbie's voice sounded odd, high and very nasal.

"I'd like to speak to Kevin Stewart please," I said.

There was a sharp intake of breath. "Is this a family member?"

"No, this is Tess Maher of Maher Investigations, I was there yesterday. Is something wrong?"

There was a moment of silence.

"Yes," Bobbie said in a snippy tone of voice but she sounded on the verge of tears as well.

I got a sick feeling in the pit of my stomach.

"I shouldn't tell you this 'cause you're not family, but Mr. Stewart is dead." She whispered the last word.

"Bobbie, I'm so sorry."

"You should be, 'cause I think it's all your fault. You come waltzin' in here and got him all stirred up and excited. His poor old heart just couldn't take it and now he's gone." She began to cry.

She was right. Kevin Stewart was dead because of me, but probably not in the way she thought.

"Bobbie, can you please give me details please?"

"He was fine last night at supper; he was in his room watchin' the WWF on the TV when last check was done at eleven. It's all in the night report." She paused and drew a shaky breath. "But this morning at breakfast call, he was found … dead."

"I am so sorry for your loss, I can see why you're so upset. Mr. Stewart was so full of life and cheerful."

"Oh, he was, he was, and always had a joke or a story. I know he was inappropriate as all get out, but I figure if a man lives to be so old, he can act up sometimes." She sniffed and I could hear tissue rustling.

"Bobbie, did anyone know about my visit with Mr. Stewart yesterday besides you and the director?" I had a nasty suspicion growing in my gut.

"Well sure, I mentioned it to Rose when we changed shifts and Ms. Thombs was still pis … I mean, she was still real upset cause you slipped by her and talked to Mr. Stewart and all. She was stompin' around here, snappin' noses off left and right, mainly mine. So really, I reckon everyone knew about it."

I starred at the ceiling for a moment or two. "Well, I reckon I was the talk of the town."

Bobbie sniffed. "Oh, you were. You know it's funny, but when Gina heard about it she didn't want to stand around and gossip like usual when somethin' juicy happens. And it's odd ya know, 'cause anytime somethin' new happens we all chew it to death. It's not too lively around here, as you can imagine. But Gina just turned on her heel and went down to the nurses' station. Most days I swear I can't figure her out."

"Anyone else react strangely to the gossip?"

"No, not really. Well, Cindy thought it was funny as a crutch, which is not surprisin'. Bet she won't think it so funny when she finds out Mr. Stewart died from a heart attack. Look here, I need to get off this line before Ms. Thombs catches me talkin' to you of all people, then Mr. Stewart won't be the only one 'round here who's dead." Bobby gasped. "Oh my Lord I can't believe I said that."

She hung up. I sat staring at the wall in front of me. Zsa Zsa head butted me for more petting and I scratched her ears while I digested this new turn of events.

"What's up, Boss?" asked Jewels.

"Well, I call shenanigans on this. I went to see Kevin Stewart at the rehab yesterday and today he's dead. Sure as hell ain't no coincidence." I could just feel myself getting madder and madder.

"Boss, you don't look so good, your face is blood red." Jewels sounded alarmed.

"I'm pissed! He was an old guy, just tryin' to live out his last days in relative comfort and I liked him. I mean, he was horribly wrong and politically incorrect, but he knew it and he didn't give a damn. He was funny in a terrible but harmless way and now he's dead. I know the black widow bitch did it, I just know it!" I slammed my hand down on my desk. "God damn it!"

Zsa Zsa jumped down and left the room. I covered my face with my hands.

"Boss?"

"This is all my fault. I had to go marchin' in there like I owned the damn place and announce who I was and what I wanted for all the world to hear. Man, oh man, I was like a rooster crowin' on a dung hill. Shit! I got a man murdered."

"Whatcha gonna do?" Jewels asked.

"Go beat the hell out of something. I gotta get rid of this mad so I can think." I stood up and grabbed my bag and walked out.

I was so angry I was afraid to speak to anyone for fear of biting off their heads. I'd been so cocky and so determined to bring the bitch down I'd slipped up and now an innocent man was dead and I was no closer to getting the goods on her than before. My fear was he'd died in vain.

I stomped out to the Jeep and climbed in, deciding the only safe place for me would be the gym. Maybe I could find someone to spar with and let off some steam.

I wheeled into the parking lot throwing a bit of gravel in the process, of a small gym, called the Ring. It's not fancy; if you want massages and facials and smoothies then you have to go to Dixon.

I grabbed my emergency workout bag and stomped inside. Gill, the owner, was at his desk.

"Gill," I said curtly and kept walking to the changing room. Over my shoulder, I said, "I need someone to spar with."

I spent the next hour and a half getting my ass handed to me by Gill. I decided I was out of shape, but my head was clearer.

I thanked Gill and limped to the Jeep, deep in thought. I knew Jonnie Kincaid had murdered Kevin Stewart, but how? He wasn't hooked up to an IV so that was out. It was no good speculating, I needed some help. I called Detective Sherman of the Atlanta PD.

"You got Sherman." Charming as ever, I thought.

"Hey Detective Sherman, this is Tess Maher. You got a minute for me?"

He sighed heavily, "Only because I don't have enough aggravation in my life. Whacha got?"

I sighed myself. "Well, maybe nothin', but I'd like for you to listen to my story and give me your opinion." He remained silent and I took it as a sign to continue. "I got a tip one of the residents of the Marietta Rehab had seen a mystery nurse on the night Jon Kincaid died. I drove down to see him and indeed he had seen a strange nurse that night."

"And this affects me, how?" he grumbled.

"Well I charged in with guns blazin', so to speak. I announced who I was and who I wanted to speak to and everyone heard me.

It also seems Mr. Stewart and I were the topic of conversation so everyone who came in to work heard the story."

"So what'd this Stewart tell you?"

"Not only had he seen the mystery nurse but despite the very blond hair she was sporting, he was certain she was Jonnie Kincaid." I let the bomb settle on Sherman.

"Hm, so a guy in a nursing home sees someone strange in the middle of the night and identifies her. I'm assumin' he's an old guy, maybe his eyesight ain't so good, maybe he's on meds. This ain't goin' nowhere, you got to try harder."

"He's dead."

"Ahhhh, now you just got interestin'. Maybe you got somethin', kid. Tell it." he growled.

"Like I said, everyone knew why I was there. I managed to get about ten minutes with him, more or less, and now he's dead."

"So whaddaya want?" Sherman asked.

"I just want someone to take a look at him and see if there's any outright cause of death besides a heart attack, you know like a puncture mark or pillow fibers or something." I hated the pleading note in my voice but I couldn't help it.

"Look Tess, this ain't some CSI show. Our ME office has a budget, I don't think I can pull big enough strings to get this ancient, sick dead guy autopsied," Sherman growled.

"Come on, Sherman, give me a little sympathy here, I need some help," I begged.

"If you're looking for sympathy, it's in the dictionary between shit and syphilis." he said dryly.

Funny guy, very funny. He sounded just like my brother Connell. I tried again. "All I'm saying is this is suspicious. I went in there one day and he's dead the next. Can't you get someone to take a look at him, draw his blood, and check for anything out of place? I'm not asking for an autopsy, but just a thorough once over."

He was quiet for a moment and I could practically hear him thinking. This was a guy who was a good cop and good cops hate bad people. I just knew he was going to help me.

Finally he said, "Let me see what I can do, maybe – just maybe – I got a couple of favors I can call in. I'll get back to you. But no promises you got it?"

I pumped my fist a little. "Thanks, and I mean it. If this guy was murdered, I feel guilty, you know."

"Yeah, yeah," Sherman said and hung up.

Someone at Marietta Rehab had called Lady Macbeth and told her about my visit, I'd bet my ass and my hat on it, but who? I had my suspicions.

30

Here I Go Again

I was feeling fairly optimistic by the time I arrived at the office, uh, antique shop. Jewels looked up from her new computer as I walked in the place. I noticed all three of the shop cats had taken up residence with us. They were perched on different pieces of furniture, each watching Jewels rather intently.

"You're looking a bit calmer, where'd ya go?" Jewels looked at me critically.

"Ah, I just let Gill wipe up the gym floor with my ass for an hour or so. Great therapy at half the price. I see you have a fan club." I indicated the felines.

Jewels laughed. "I'm glad to hear it, not the ass whipping but the fact you're feeling less lethal. You were kinda scary. The tuna I had for lunch might explain my popularity. Georgia called while you were out, by the by."

"Hmmm, wonder what's up?" I said as I dialed Georgia's number.

"Hello Tess, I have some…well I guess it's bad news." She sounded so down and sad, not her usual self at all.

"Georgia, what's happened?" I had such a sense of foreboding and got a queasy feeling in the pit of my stomach.

"I know how Jonnie knew you were investigating her and before I go any further, let me say I'm so sorry."

Holy shit, I knew a bombshell was coming. "Just spit it out, Georgia."

"Jillian."

I had leaned toward Jillian as the mole. "But why the hell would she do it? Why would someone consort with the enemy?"

"She's so proud and this whole mess has embarrassed her. Jillian thought the best way to stop the investigation was to tell Jonnie about it. She hoped her step-mother might find a way to get rid of you," Georgia said sadly.

"The enemy of my enemy is my friend, huh? You tell Jillian, Lady Macbeth tried and failed. I'm more determined than ever to bring this bitch down. Jillian didn't help her case, she only made it worse, 'cause now I'm pissed."

Jesus! I was hopping mad even though I had suspected Jillian. What really pissed me off was the hard work I'd done at the gym to calm down was wasted. I could feel my calm slipping away and I got even madder. I took a deep breath to try and steady my nerves but it didn't work. Jillian had thrown me under the bus and because of her I had a dead rat, a mother on the war path, and a burned down office. Not to mention Jewels and I were crammed into a storage room the size of a meat locker in the back of an antique shop! Oh yeah, and Kevin Stewart was freakin' dead! Jillian needed an ass kicking in the worst way.

A thought had been nibbling at the back of my brain all day, so I asked, "Georgia, does Jillian know anyone at the Marietta Rehab where Jon died?"

There was a moment of silence. "I don't think so, none of my children ever visited Jon there. Jonnie had them barred from the place. Why would you ask?"

I debated the wisdom of telling Georgia about the death of Kevin Stewart and decided the information could wait. Georgia was already upset and I didn't want her to think Jillian's stupidity might have caused a man's death, even inadvertently.

"I'm just trying to tie up some loose ends. Look Georgia, don't worry about any of this, Jonnie would've found out sooner or later. She just found out sooner. I know she's guilty and we're gonna nail her, I promise. Don't tell the other kids or Jillian I know. I will tell her myself and not throw you under the bus."

"Tess, you are very kind. I don't want any argument from you, I am going to double your fee. You deserve it."

"Georgia, you can't," I protested.

"Of course I can, I'm rich and I spend my money as I see fit. There'll be a check in the mail this afternoon." She sounded pleased with herself. "It's the least I can do."

I sure couldn't argue about needing the money. I had no new cases at the moment and we had just spent a ton of money re-equipping the office.

"Okay Georgia, no argument but thanks."

"Well it makes me feel better. Please be careful and I'll talk to you soon. Bye now." She hung up.

Jewels looked at me expectantly.

"Georgia is going to double our fee on account of I am doing such a bang-up job proving Jonnie killed her husband." I grinned.

"Well, we need it. I've spent a king's ransom on the office."

"God bless your tiny little mercenary heart," I chuckled.

"Well somebody has to worry about money and payin' the bills around here and that someone is me."

The look in her eye challenged me to deny it. I didn't, of course. She was right.

"Boss, you didn't tell Georgia about Mr. Stewart's murder."

"His mysterious death, you mean. Naw, I didn't think she needed to hear about it."

"Why?"

"Jillian called her step-mother and told her I was investigating Jon's death and Jonnie was my suspect. I guess Lady Macbeth didn't appreciate it. I didn't want Georgia to think Jillian may have led her to kill the poor ol' guy."

"Ya think?"

"Which brings us back to the question, who told Jonnie I'd visited the rehab? It wasn't any of the Kincaid kids, none of them had been near the place. The place has a couple of dozen people who work there and any of them could've been in her pay. Damn! I just can't believe she murdered Kevin!"

"Why do you say 'in the pay of' instead of friends with the widow?" Jewels asked.

"From the notes scribbled in Jon Kincaid's chart, as near as I can tell everyone universally hated the woman. She was rude, crude and socially unacceptable in her treatment of everyone from the techs to the doctors. But someone must've been willin' to take her money. There's just no other way she could know I interviewed Stewart unless she's having me followed."

I stopped and thought for a minute. I was always careful to check my rearview mirror to see if the same car was behind me in traffic. I'd even been a bit more paranoid of late. No, I didn't think I was being followed.

My cell phone rang and I saw it was Mars. "Hey, babe."

"What's up with you?" she asked.

"At this moment? Just tryin' to decide what to do," I answered.

"Me too," she said.

Ominous.

"So you wanna have a bite of lunch? I think I need to go back down to Atlanta but I can wait for a bit."

"What are you doin' in Hotlanta?" Mars asked.

"I need to see if I can find out some info on this case, so I'm gonna snoop around the Marietta Rehab Center."

"You want company for the ride?" She sounded funny.

"You come into some money so you don't have to work?" I teased.

"I've just cleared everything off my schedule for the rest of the day. So?" she queried.

"So let's eat Italian and then take a road trip," I suggested.

"Agreed. Meet you in ten." Mars hung up and left me to wonder what the hell was wrong.

Jewels was answering some e-mails and phone calls which might bring us some income when I left her under the careful supervision of the shop cats. The three block walk to Il Pomodoro Siciliano on the square gave me more time to ponder but not enough for answers. The restaurant is stucco on the outside with vines and flowers everywhere. It looks just like a villa in the hills of Sicily. Inside the villa motif continues with muted yellow walls, grapevines, cozy nooks for seating, soft lighting and violin music playing. Debi Fertitta, the owner, greeted me as I entered.

"Tess!" she exclaimed and hugged me. "I'm so sorry about the fire. What can I do to help you?"

I smiled, gratified for her sincere sympathy. "Feed me."

"Done. What else?" She smiled.

"We're waitin' on the Fire Inspector and the insurance people to figure it all out."

She leaned closer to me and said in a conspiratorial tone of voice, "I heard it was set on purpose."

I nodded. "Jim Leach and Andy Riley think so and I agree with them."

She blew out a breath and shook her head. "It's unspeakable. Do you have any idea who'd do such a thing?"

I smiled. "Oh, I have a good idea."

"I see." She nodded in a knowing way. "Well let me show you to a table. We have a new wine; it's a red but with a sweet, fruity flavor. I think you'll like it. Will anyone be joining you?"

"Mars is coming."

"Oh, good. I haven't seen her in forever. Here you go, this booth will give you some privacy, and you must be tired of everyone asking you about the fire. I'm guilty of it too, my apologies."

I sat down. "None needed, Debi, I know you actually give a damn about me and I am grateful."

Debi leaned over and hugged me. "I'll be right back with the wine." She hurried away.

I love Debi, she is tiny, dark and sultry and sweet as pecan pie. It's hard to believe she has relatives in South Florida who can make a person disappear for a price. Oh well. You can't help who you're related to, right?

"There you are!" Marcella called out.

She looked fabulous as usual. Her cobalt blue tailored suit was flawless, and her black shoes and bag matched exactly. Her long dark hair fell in perfect ringlets down her back. She was beautiful as always, but today there were signs of strain on her face.

"Hey girl, have a seat. Debi is bringing us wine."

"Good, I need it."

Mars looked down in the mouth about something. Since I was a detective I decided to detect.

"What's up, girlfriend?"

"Your brother," she said simply.

"My brother? What's he done? Does he need an ass kicking? I'm in the mood to deliver one."

"Nothing, he has done nothing wrong or bad to me. I'm just so frustrated." She put her face in her hands for a minute. "Sorry, I'm not sure I can articulate this."

My eyes widened in surprise. Mars was the salutatorian of our high school class and her speech was killer. She talked to people for a living, and she couldn't find words? Hmmm, more and more mysterious, I thought as Debi showed up with the wine and two glasses.

"Mars," she said, and kissed her on the cheek. "It's so good to see you. How's your momma and daddy?"

Mars smiled. "They're both dandy, thanks for asking."

"You're going to love this wine, try it and let me know what you think. I'll have Boydra come over and take your orders. Enjoy." She bustled away.

It occurred to me I had never seen the woman when she wasn't in a hurry; probably why she weighed a buck oh five. I poured two glasses of wine, took a sip and said, "Spill it, sister."

Mars took a sip of wine and sighed.

"Connell..." she stopped and tears filled her big green eyes. *Oh shit*, I thought.

"Mars?" I pressed, alarmed.

"I'm in love with your brother," she blurted out.

Boydra arrived with menus and I already knew what I wanted: to order and get rid of her as quickly as possible.

"Hey Boydra, how you doing? Can I get the lasagna, please?"

"You sure 'nuff can. A salad comes with it, what kind of dressing ya'ant?"

Boydra was young, about nineteen, and blonde, pleasingly plump and cute. She was also a good waitress, she always got the orders right and was unfailingly polite. Her name was the result of her father, Boyd, and her mother, Audra. Creative, right? I knew Debi was trying to put some polish on her because she was as rough as a cob.

"House vinaigrette."

"I like ranch myself. It just goes with everythin', ya know?"

She pronounced 'ranch' with a long 'a' making it rhyme with branch. In the South, ranch dressing is one of the food groups, along with coffee and bourbon.

"And how about you, Marcella?"

"Give me the grilled tilapia on the cedar plank and a salad with lemon juice please, Boydra."

"I will but can I jess say you're gonna blow away, girl, 'cause you don't eat enough to keep a baby bird alive. I'm jess saying, hon." Boydra smiled and headed for the kitchen to place our orders.

I had to laugh at our waitress; it seemed our lunch also came with opinions and advice. I turned my attention to the problem at hand.

"Okay and my brother makes you cry, because?" I asked.

"Because it's complicated. One: we have both been down the road of romance before and it ended badly for each of us. Two: he's the sheriff of the county in which we live, he's busy and in the public eye. Three: while it may have escaped your notice, I am black and this is the South. A small town in the South, to be exact." She sighed and drank more wine.

I sat there for a minute, feeling stupid. "Okay I get number one, but if you never take a chance on love then you're gonna grow old with a bunch of cats. Love is dangerous but it's worth it, isn't it?"

"Do not dare talk to me about taking a chance on love, Tessely Anne Marie Maher," Mars snapped at me.

I opened my mouth to speak and shut it again. I sat and stared at her for a few seconds while I got my thoughts in order.

"You might be right when you say that, I might even be the poster child for not taking a chance. I never took the step with Chick out of fear and now he's dead and I'll always wonder if I screwed up my life for good." I stopped talking and took a breath. "If I had it to do over, I'da gone for it."

Don't let me cry, I prayed. I had to make the conversation about Mars and Connell and I couldn't make it about me and my pain.

"Two, he is the sheriff and he must maintain a certain amount of decorum if he wants to get reelected and I know he does. Three, you are worried because you're black and this is the South and so there's prejudice and bigots under every rock, which may affect Connell's career. Do I have it all correct?"

"Well, when you put it in such a way…" She smiled, a tiny upwards curving of her lips.

"I'd have to agree that there are redneck bigots, I bet I can't throw a rock in any direction from the front door of this restaurant and fail to hit one. I guess we all live in our own little bubbles and I don't think in terms of race. I don't think of you as a 'black woman' or an 'African American woman', I just think of you as Marcella."

She started to speak and I held up a hand to stop her. "Maybe I'm wrong but I think most folks live in a bubble and think if they like somethin' or someone everyone else will as well. And vice-versa. So I couldn't imagine anyone holdin' ill will toward you 'cause you're black. But now I realize maybe I'm wrong."

She took another sip of wine. "Look, I do well here in business, my family and I have lived here all our lives, my parents teach school, my sister works at the bank right across the square and she's up for promotion, my brother works at the courthouse as a bailiff and is seriously considering law school. Folks know us and maybe most of them don't think when they see me, 'there goes that uppity Marcella Price, an African American girl who thinks she's as good as a white woman', but some do and you know it."

Such strong emotion washed over me it took my breath. She was right and I did know it, I realized there were stupid people everywhere. I felt a little sick to my stomach.

"You're afraid if you and Connell become a couple he won't get reelected because of small minded assholes," I whispered.

She nodded her head. I hadn't thought of such a thing, in fact the idea had never crossed my mind. I felt like an idiot. People who judge other people by their skin color, religion, country of origin, sexual orientation and whatnot just baffle the hell out of me. I took my rose-colored glasses off and looked at my best friend.

"Wow, I'm so sorry I can't fix this. I don't know what to say, I'm truly at a loss. Holy shit. I love you." My voice sounded shaky.

I shrugged and held my hands out with the palms up in that helpless gesture we all use from time to time.

"I support you in all of your choices even the ones I think are beyond stupid like when you dyed your hair purple. I will fight anyone who hurts you, no matter who they are. I have your back now and forever and my support might not change any of this but you've got me in your corner," I said quietly.

Tears slipped from her beautiful eyes and slid down her perfect cheeks. Her bottom lip quivered. "I love you too. But this is real life. I can't screw up Connell's career, he loves his job. What would he do?"

"Okay, first you're anticipatin' trouble and might be makin' mountains out of molehills. Connell does a great job, he listens to people and makes 'em feel important. He solves things, finds lost stuff, crime is down, he started a youth program, the department even fields a baseball team and he loves his mama. In short, people like him, hell in the last election no one even ran against him. People like you too, Mars, you're a successful real estate saleswoman and you're sweet as pie."

Mars looked at me with real misery in her eyes.

"What if because of me he doesn't get reelected and we have to move somewhere else to get jobs?" she whispered.

I blew out a breath in exasperation at her. "Jesus Christ on a bicycle Marcella Diane Price! What if a meteor falls out of the freakin' sky and crushes you both tonight at supper? Now you remind me of a story Mommy used to read to me when I was a kid, I think it was called *The Three Sillies.* Hell, my girl, you can't live your life on 'what ifs' because if you do you, you'll be paralyzed!"

"Your family likes me, right?" Mars asked.

"They love you. Hell, my mama compares me to you all the time and I lose by the comparison. How about your folks? Will they be okay with you and Connell?"

It seemed such an odd question to ask. Everyone liked Connell, except the people he arrested and the ones he caught causing trouble. Even most of them didn't hold a grudge.

"Oh, I think they'd be fine with him, they're pretty enlightened for the most part. It's not family I worry about, it's everybody else."

"Everybody else can just stick a feather up their ass and be tickled," I said. "So, now what?"

"Now we talk, him and me. He says he doesn't care what people think and anyone who didn't like it could kiss his ass. He is, and I quote, 'not a giver of fucks', end quote."

I laughed; the sentiment sure summed up my lovely brother.

"But I want to make sure he knows what he is getting into," she said.

"Mars, does he love you?"

"He says he does," she admitted.

"Okay, so have the talk one more time to satisfy your conscience and then start making plans for a life together. You both deserve to be happy."

"Thanks. That means a lot you know."

"So when are you gonna have the talk?" I asked.

Boydra arrived with our food before Mars could answer.

"Here y'all go now, enjoy it and if y'all need anything else, you jess gimme a shout." She grinned and hustled away.

"So, when?" I prompted Mars.

"Well he's workin' tonight which is why I offered to go to Atlanta with you."

"And I thought it was 'cause you loved me so good. Well, finish your dinner and let's get on the road," I joked.

We didn't hurry over our meal; when food is exquisite you should take the time to savor it. We applied ourselves to the meal before us, talking between bites.

Boydra showed up to check us and I gave her my card to pay for the meal. Mars looked as if she was about to argue and I shook my head at her. Boydra returned with the ticket, I signed it and resumed eating.

When we finished we had to rave to Debi about the food, the new wine, and how well we thought Boydra was coming along.

"You might suggest if folks ask her for an opinion, she should give it. Otherwise, just take the order," I said.

"What did she say?" Debi asked, rolling her eyes.

"Well she herself prefers ranch dressing, and Mars doesn't eat enough to keep a baby bird alive." I laughed.

"Lord God Almighty!" Debi said. "She's gonna' be the death of me! How many times did she call you 'hon'?"

"Only once," Mars and I answered at the same time.

Debi laughed and walked us to the door. "Ciao girls, te amo." She kissed us on our cheeks and sent us on our way.

"Your car or mine?" Mars asked as we reached the sidewalk.

I knew she wanted to drive her little sports car.

"Fine, yours," I capitulated. Besides, we'd be in Atlanta much sooner if she drove.

Somehow she manages to drive with the needle set on 90 and never gets stopped for speeding. It's puzzling. Plus, truth to tell, I hated driving in Atlanta, with their 29 lanes of traffic all going 95 miles an hour and every driver trying to kill me, so she could have it. We hit the road and made off to Georgia.

"So, explain this trip to Atlanta," Mars said as she adjusted her stylish and expensive sunglasses.

"I've got a theory. I went to see an old guy in the rehab center where Jon Kincaid died. This old guy remarked he'd seen a strange nurse leaving Kincaid's room the night of his death. No one else saw her. It was odd enough to make me take a trip and interview the old guy. I recorded the conversation and the next day the old guy's dead."

Mars whistled low and long. "Hmmm so we're going why?"

"We are going cause someone in the damn rehab center called Lady Macbeth and told her I'd been there snoopin' around and talked to Kevin Stewart."

"The dead guy?"

"The dead guy. I mean to find out who told. There's almost no evidence in this case, so every scrap I dig up that links Jonnie Kincaid to anything is imperative. I want this bitch worse than grits."

We hit Atlanta at the perfect time for shift change at the rehab center. I directed Mars to pull into the lot and park so we faced the door. Then we settled back and waited.

"What we're waitin' for?" Mars asked.

"We're waitin' for my favorite Goth chick to take a much needed smoke break. When she does, I'll be able to catch her alone and no one will see us talkin'."

"So you're pretty sure she isn't your mole."

"I could be wrong, but she doesn't strike me as the type of person who'd sell out to someone she doesn't like."

"Okay, she has moral integrity to go with her tattoos, but how do you know she hates the widow?"

"Oh, 'cause everyone hates her. I'll bet money Lady Macbeth treated Sin like dog shit and Sin cordially hated her for it."

"Sin, as in do bad things, sin?" Mars laughed.

I smiled. "Her given name is Cynthia, here they call her Cindy. Believe me, I have never seen anyone who looks less like a Cindy. She says her friends call her Sin. From the way she pronounced it I know her signature reads S-I-N."

"Of course, and in Edwardian script. Black hair, tattoos, and many piercings too?"

I nodded. "Black hair, lots of eye makeup, the tats and piercings are hidden under her clothing."

"So how long do we sit here?" Mars asked.

"Sin just came on duty. All the residents have to be checked out by Nurse Ratchet, if she's on tonight, and then Sin will take her break. There are a couple of 'ifs' in this, if Sin is workin' the night shift, if she's workin' tonight…"

Mars laughed, "Nurse Ratchet, you're bad."

'You haven't had the pleasure of her company." I leaned my head back on the headrest. "So, Mars, you love my brother. Wow, I'm just so blown away."

"Why?" She was defensive.

"Hmmm, 'cause I thought you had better taste."

She hit me on the arm. Hard.

"Okay, okay. It just seems so funny. I mean, he used to play dirty tricks on us, chase us with spiders, hide in the bushes and scare hell out of us. He called us dumb ol' girls and claimed we had cooties. Now here we are in a parkin' lot in Atlanta talkin' about bridesmaids' dresses."

"Jesus Christ, we are not! I mean, we haven't gotten there yet!" She blew out a breath at me. "We haven't said the 'M' word yet."

"Oh, you will, despite all the misgivings you both have about the institution of marriage, you'll do it. I know you and you want to do things in the conventional manner, and you want the dress. Don't argue, you do. Besides, if you make an honest man of my rotten, half-assed brother it'll make the whole black/white thing more palatable to folks. Not to mention the idea of depriving my mother, your mother, and YaYa out of wedding preparations. Please."

"You know if it comes to it, they'll make all of us crazy, right?" Mars muttered.

"Not me. If you two do this thing, I'm leavin' for the South of France to work in a wine press for a full year. I'll learn how to smash grapes with my feet. You can call me when you get knocked up and not before."

"You suck. But you sure have the feet for the job."

"Why yes I do on both counts, but I'll be sane and the rest of you will be droolin' idiots. Hell, you can all get committed to this place." I pointed across the parking lot at the rehab center.

"I like eggplant." She stated out of the blue.

"Ick, a disgusting vegetable."

"Smartass. The color, not the food. I like the color for my bridesmaids' dresses. It'll look good on everyone."

"Hmpt. Thought you hadn't gotten that far," I teased.

"I'm just sayin', it's a color which will look good on you and on my sister."

The sister in question, Nichole, shared the same good looks with Mars. I pictured her in the eggplant color first and then myself and nodded.

"You're right, we'll look fantastic, especially me. But the dress has to be cute, not hideous. Why are all bridesmaids' dresses always so horrible?"

Sin picked that moment to make her escape from the rehab center. She took the same route I'd seen her use previously. I gave her a thirty second head start.

"Sit tight. If anyone in a uniform comes out of the door, text me."

I casually crossed the parking lot, keeping in the shadow of the building. I turned the corner and spotted the girl; her back was turned to me and she was fumbling with her cigarette pack. I slid up behind her and flicked my lighter just as she put a black cigarette in her mouth.

"Holy fuck!" she exclaimed. The cigarette fell from her lips and I caught it.

"Take it easy. I just wanna talk," I said and handed her back her smoke.

She took it from me and I noticed her hands were shaking. I'd given her a scare, just as I'd planned. I wanted her off balance.

"What the fuck do you want?" she snapped at me. "I know who ya are, ya know, I figured it out. You been here twice, once pretending to be somebody's daughter, and I know damn well you're the detective who came in here to talk to Kevin." She held my wrist while she lit her cigarette. "Man, let me tell you how pissed Ms. Thombs is. If anybody catches me even talkin' to you I'll be outta here on my ass. And I need this shitty job to get through school."

"Nobody saw me, 'cause I'm good at what I do. I even have someone keepin' watch on the front door. I want five minutes of your time."

"What's in it for me?" She blew smoke out of her nose.

"Maybe you'll help me catch the person who murdered Kevin and Jon Kincaid."

She froze with her cigarette halfway to her lips. "What?"

"They were both murdered by the same person," I assured her.

"Well if you got proof of it, why don't you call the cops and get the bastard arrested?" she demanded.

I shook my head. "I just have lots of speculation and suspicion. Which is why I wanted to talk to you."

"Me!" she squeaked. "I don't know nothin'."

She took a long drag from her cigarette. She was lying; I'm good at catching lies. Usually a person will look down and to the left if they're lying. A practiced liar is harder to catch. Sin, despite her name, was not practiced.

"I have it on good authority everyone in the place knew I'd been here and what I wanted. They all knew I'd actually spoken to Kevin even though Ms. Thombs didn't want me to. She was pissed, so very pissed."

"Oh, you have no idea." Sin smiled at the memory.

"I believe somebody who works here promised Ms. Kincaid he or she would report any happenings in this place which might interest her. I further believe the same somebody called Ms.

Kincaid after my last visit here and gave her the info. I wanna know who."

"How would I know?"

"I think you know a lot. People blow you off; underestimate you because of your choices in hair and make-up. They just categorize you as an airheaded, dipshit, troublemaking, dope-smoking, Goth kid. Right?"

She blew a cloud of smoke and shrugged. "I don't give a shit what people think o' me. If I cared, I'd dye my hair blonde and wear pink and go to church three times a week."

The image made me grin. "My point is, I know you see things. I want you to think about who was friendly with Ms. Kincaid, who may have said something odd about her, or acted out of character. Who's turned up with a little extra money in his or her pocket?"

Sin gasped.

"Holy shit!" She drew more nicotine into her lungs. "Holy shit!"

I tried to be patient while she processed the information rushing around her brain like a gerbil on a wheel.

"Oh my fucking God! I don't believe it, this ain't real! I gotta be wrong about it!" She took another puff and I noticed her hand was shaking. "It's Gina."

"Gina, the African American nurse I met the first time I was here?"

"Gina the sanctimonious bitch, holier than thou, fuckin' whore Martin! Yeah, one and the same. She thinks she's better'n anyone else in the world and she got Kevin dead! I'm gonna kill her."

Sin dropped her smoke and ground it out with her toe, then reached down and picked up the butt.

"Fucking bitch!" she snarled and started to walk past me.

I grabbed her arm to stop her. "Sin, calm down, I don't want her to know you know. I need to check phone records first. I need proof."

"But she's a hypocrite! I wanna wring her scrawny neck like a chicken!" she snapped and tried to pull away from me.

"Sin, listen to me, your red-neck is showin'. Calm down. If you lose your cool and jump all over Gina, she might call Ms. Kincaid and tell her about it. Ms. Kincaid might just decide Gina is a liability, just like Kevin was a liability."

Sin stopped struggling and stared at me with wide eyes. She drew a breath to speak and then stopped. She pondered a moment. "You really think it could happen?"

I nodded.

"Whoa, I mean I hate Gina worse than head lice but I sure don't wanna be the cause of her dyin'. That's seriously bad karma, ya know."

"Tell me why you think the spy is Gina."

Sin stood there for a few seconds gathering her thoughts. "First, she kinda kissed Ms. Kincaid ass, ya know, askin' her if she needed anything special, and bringin' her coffee when she made her rounds, that kinda bullshit. When the rest of us were bitchin' about what a bitch Ms. Kincaid was, she never joined in, and everybody joins in on gossip and bitchin', right? When we came on duty and found out you'd been in the place and had talked to Kevin without permission, it was delicious gossip. But Gina da Queena da Bitches just hustled on down the hall to her office as fast as her skinny legs would carry her. I thought it was damn funny, ya know, odd, at the time. But a few days before everything happened, she'd bought a big flat screen and had to come in braggin' about it. After bitchin' about all her bills the week before."

Sin was calming down as she talked, which gave me hope she wouldn't pop Gina in the mouth at the first opportunity. She shook out another cigarette and lit it.

"So," Sin continued, "Gina was on the take from the Kincaid bitch from the get go. Holy shit, I just can't believe it."

My cell phone vibrated in my pocket. "Speakin' of Gina, I think we have company. I'm gonna step behind this bush and you're gonna act as though everything is cool. Got me?"

"Yeah." Sin took another drag on her cigarette and walked slowly back toward the front of the building. I stepped into the shadows. Sin made it to the corner before she came face to face Gina.

"What?" Sin snapped.

"I heard voices," Gina said.

"You're hearin' voices? No one here but me. Maybe you should get a shrink," Sin quipped.

"Get your ass back in the building, we have a crisis," Gina snarled at Sin.

"Your crisis ain't my problem," Sin snapped.

"Put that damn cigarette out right this minute!" Gina demanded.

"Get the fuck outta my way." Sin moved toward the other woman, who gave ground at the last second. Sin blew smoke in her face as she brushed passed her.

"I'll write you up!" Gina threatened the other woman.

"Knock yourself out, bitch. You ain't the boss of me."

Gina gave Sin a few seconds to get ahead of her and then walked around the corner of the building; she looked back toward me just before she did. I froze like a rabbit when a hawk shadow passes overhead. I didn't even breathe. Gina turned and disappeared around the corner of the building.

I texted Mars: *They in building yet?*

Yes, the answer came back to me.

I made my way to the car, being extremely careful to stay in the shadows and I kept an eye on the front door until I was safely in the car.

Mars looked at me. "Wow, I thought she was gonna catch the two of you."

"It was close, but I stepped back into the bushes and she didn't see me. She did hear Sin and me talkin', said she heard voices. Sin blew her off."

"So did you get anything?"

"Yep, Sin thinks the guilty party is Gina, the woman who almost caught us. Gina's the night nurse, whom Sin hates by the way. Seems it's pretty mutual. I had to convince Sin not to confront her. I hope she'll listen to me. I need some time to hack into phone records to prove Gina called or communicated in some way with the widow on the night Kevin Stewart died. Then I need to dig and see if I can find any other connections between Gina and the widow."

"Hey, how do you feel about dinner and grabbin' a hotel room for the night? It's a long drive back. We could get up early," Mars asked.

"Not a bad plan, but I feel like I could make the run between Atlanta and home in my sleep, I've done it so many times lately," I answered.

Mars nodded. "Yeah, so let's don't. I'll call your mama."

31

Night Moves

You know how it is when you wake up in a strange place and wonder for a few seconds where the hell you are? I woke up in the hotel room outside Atlanta and took a few moments to get my bearings. I could hear Mars snoring softly in the other bed. Her snoring had not awakened me – no, what had awakened me was Chick and Kevin Stewart standing by the foot of my bed.

"Hey Chick, I see you've made a new friend," I said rubbing the sleep from my eyes.

Chick grinned at me. "Well yep, I have, and he thinks you're flat out prettier'n a speckled pup."

Kevin leered at me and grinned; if haints could drool, he was, ectoplasmically speaking.

Chick turned to him and frowned. "Enough, you ol' fool, you're staring at the woman I love."

My heart clenched in my chest and my eyes burned.

"So," I said trying to sound casual, "to what do I owe the pleasure?"

I sat up and pulled the covers up to my neck. I sleep naked and the idea of being leered at by Kevin weirded me out. Okay, he was a dead guy, but he was still a perv.

"Well, we thought you needed to know you was right about how Kevin here died." Chick pointed his thumb at Kevin.

"Yep, that Jonnie Kincaid bitch did me in fer sure." Kevin nodded emphatically.

"Okay, could you give me a bit of chapter and verse, Kevin? And by the way I am so sorry."

"Sorry? For what? 'Cause I'm dead? Hell, I ain't felt so good in years, as a matter of fact I don't know if I ever felt this dang good. Don't nothing hurt; I'm as spry as a new colt and happier than a hog in slop. Don't you be sorry, girl."

I had to laugh. "How about if I'm just sorry someone killed you and I'm sorry it's my fault?"

Stewart cocked his head at me. "No, it ain't your fault; it's that Kincaid bitch's fault. She come in ta' my room late and woke me up checkin' my pulse. She was wearin' different hair from the last time, kinda street walker red ya know, a wig I reckon, but it was her all right. So I says to her, 'what can I do for you, Chickadee?' She reaches down and cupped my boys in her hand. I can tell ya, I was so surprised I damn near had a heart attack on the spot. She says, 'oh it's what I can do for you' just as bold as brass, ya know?"

I just nodded, trying not to be embarrassed as hell while Kevin continued.

"She leans over and whispers, 'I hear you had a visitor, a woman detective.' I could only nod, ya understand, I was kinda taken in the moment. Then she squeezed the family jewels hard enough my eyes damn near popped out. She says, 'What did you tell her? Damn nosy detective bitch, what did you tell her?' The crazy woman demanded an answer, she clamped down on me and her voice was mean and cold as a snake. 'You saw me, didn't you, you old bastard? You told her?'

"I nodded at her and she squeezed harder. 'Yes,' I whispered 'cause that was all I could muster. She starts strokin' me more gentle-like and, take me for a fool, I relaxed. Next thing I knew there was a pillow over my face and all her weight on top of me. Lights out. Don't let nobody tell ya sex can't kill ya'."

I couldn't decide if I should be horrified, disgusted, or just laugh out loud. All seemed appropriate after such a story.

"Jesus Christ, the woman is a monster and a serial killer," I whispered. Then I had to correct myself. "Okay, okay, maybe not a serial killer, but a murderer and a monster."

Chick nodded. "You're right, and you need to remember it. She'll try and kill ya, TisTis, if she thinks you got any proof against her."

"Hey, whacha doing?" Mars asked.

I turned my head and saw her sitting up in bed, staring rather wide-eyed at me.

"Talking to Chick and the dead guy from the rehab center," I pointed at our visitors.

Mars looked in the direction I indicated and said, "Hey Chick." Then she looked at me and whispered, "Which dead guy?"

I laughed. "He can hear you. It's Kevin Stewart. I was right and Lady Macbeth did murder him." I left out the gory details because frankly the less I thought about Kevin's genitals the happier I was. Ick.

"Damn, that is one fine woman!" Kevin exclaimed, his eyes practically standing on stems as he stared at Mars.

"You'd do well to remember your libido is what got you dead, Kevin Stewart, and shut up now," I suggested.

"Am I supposed to understand what you just said?" Mars asked.

"Well he let a woman sneak up on him with a pillow," I answered.

Mars nodded her understanding. "Wow, I'm afraid I actually do get it."

"Tell Mars she's looking beautiful as ever," Chick said.

"Chick says you're beautiful," I said.

Mars smiled. "I miss you so much, Chick. Do you know about me and Connell?"

Chick grinned. "Tell her I do and I'm tickled. They better be namin' a youngun' after me is all I gotta say."

"He does and he's pleased and says you better name a kid after him." I choked up a little.

"We will, I promise we will," Mars said, her voice rough with unshed tears.

I took a deep breath. "Anything else we need to know, like what the crazy bitch is gonna do next?"

"Hell, honey, I'm dead, not omnipotent. I can't tell the future, you know." Chick grinned at me. "I can just keep watch on her and warn you, it's the best I can do. I wish it was more."

"I know and I wasn't being critical, just frustrated, you know? She always seems to be one step ahead of me."

"Me too and I'm worried as all get out about ya. She's not right in the head and you've got her riled up somethin' fierce. Just promise me you'll be careful, okay?" Concern was apparent in his eyes.

I raised my right hand in a pledge. "I promise."

"Love you," Chick said.

"Love you," I said and they winked out but not before I got one more leer from Kevin. I turned and looked at Mars. "They're gone."

"You okay?" Mars asked.

"As I'll ever be," I admitted. I sank back into my bed. "I just want to hold him and feel him. Mars, promise me you won't blow it with Connell. Promise me you'll do everything in your power to make the relationship work and you won't run away from it. Promise me."

"Promise," she whispered. "You know, I could almost hear him."

I fell asleep with tears on my cheeks.

32

Proud Mary

I opened my eyes and took a minute to adjust to my surroundings. I yawned, stretched and decided on a plan of action. I reached for my phone to call Sherman and found my roommate staring at me from the next bed.

"Wow, last night was kinda surreal, you know? With Chick and the other guy here in our room, I mean. Wow." Mars shook her head in disbelief.

"Yep, welcome to my world. So I was thinkin' before we head home, I would like to call Detective Sherman and see what he knows."

"Sherman? In Atlanta? You gotta be kiddin' me," Mars laughed and climbed out of bed.

While she was in the bathroom, I called Sherman.

"Sherman," he snarled in to the phone. Yikes, I surmised he was not having a good day.

"Detective Sherman, Tess Maher."

"Whaddaya want, Maher, I'm a very busy man and I'm in a lousy mood." I didn't think he was kidding, man oh man he sounded pissy.

"I'll give you a chance to have breakfast with two beautiful women this morning," I offered in a hopeful manner.

He was silent for a moment. "Hmmm. Okay, that's an attractive offer and I need a break. Same place as before in about half an hour?"

"Sure…" He hung up on me before I could finish speaking. Charming. "Hey Mars, hurry up! We got a breakfast date."

Twenty minutes later, a record by the way, we were out the door and on the way to our breakfast meeting with Sherman.

"Tell me again why we're gonna go see this detective?" Mars asked as she deftly negotiated the streets of Atlanta.

"I just thought while we're here I could see him face to face and find out if he has any more information for me. He doesn't like me, and might blow me off by phone. But it's harder to ignore me in person." I grabbed for balance as Mars wheeled around a corner. "Jesus Christ, Mars, I'd hate to go jail in Atlanta!"

"Oh, calm down, I haven't had a ticket in years and years." She grinned at me.

"The Rolling Hill Sandwich Co. is right down there on the left." I pointed and Mars began the hunt for a parking place. "Hail Mary full of grace, find for us a parking space," I chanted.

Laugh if you will but it always works, and sure enough Mars spotted a perfect place right across from the café and wheeled into the curb. Sherman was waiting for us in front, leaning nonchalantly on the wall. When he laid eyes on Mars, he practically stood to attention. They all do. It's a bitch to walk in her shadow.

"Hey, Maher," Sherman said to me, but he was looking at Mars.

I could either let him stand and drool at her or I could introduce him. I couldn't decide which was worse but before I could act Mars took the decision out of my hands.

"Hello, Detective Sherman," she purred, extending her hand. "I am delighted to meet you, I've heard so much about you. I'm Marcella Price."

She was really laying on the Southern charm. Then she smiled and Sherman practically melted on the pavement.

"Delighted, Ms. Price. Let's get inside and find ourselves a comfortable place to sit."

Suddenly I didn't even recognize the man! He took Mars by the elbow and guided her into the establishment, leaving me to follow in their wake. Good thing I was accustomed to being ignored when I was with Mars or I might have gotten my little baby feelings all hurt.

We placed our orders and found seats, with Sherman still entranced by Mars.

"So Detective Sherman, how thrillin' is it to be a police detective in such a large, dangerous city?" she asked, practically batting her eyelashes.

The man blushed, I swear he did.

"Well," he cleared his throat, "it's not borin', I can assure you. Atlanta's crime rate has dropped in the last few years but that doesn't mean there's nothing to do." He began to warm up to his subject. "We have a lot of issues with gang violence, drug and sex trafficking, the run of the mill domestics that turn deadly, but every now and then we get a truly juicy crime that requires real old-fashioned police work to solve."

The man sounded like the star of a TV cop show. I did a mental eyeroll but kept a straight face.

"So fascinatin', Detective, I'll bet your life is in danger every time you strap on a gun." I could hear the dew dripping off the Spanish moss in Mars' voice. I was tempted to reach under the table and pinch the fire out of her.

"Oh, it's not all bad. Please, my friends call me Jimmy." He actually smiled at her. Unbelievable.

"Jimmy, yes, suits you to a tee. Strong, stable and yet friendly and approachable." Mars smiled again.

We had a freakin' dog named Jimmy when I was a kid and he was friendly and approachable too. He also humped the cat constantly. Thankfully our number was called and I started to get up and get away from the increasingly deep bullshit at the table.

Jimmy put his hand on my arm to hold me in my seat. "Don't move a muscle, I'll fetch our food and be right back."

He practically skipped away.

"Jimmy? Really? Why are you charmin' this man out of his pants, might one ask?" I cocked an eye at my friend.

Mars just smiled and batted her eyes at me. "Well, sister girl, you need this man to help you out and he's not being so very cooperative, or so you've said. I'm simply greasin' the wheels a bit."

"Just be careful you don't grease the wheels so much he accidentally slides into your vagina." I grinned at my own wittiness.

Mars snickered at me but before she could say a word the new, charming Detective Sherman arrived with our food. He made a show of setting our orders in front of us and laying the napkins and plasticware out. He did it all with a flourish and I had to bite my tongue to keep from asking him if he waited tables in his spare time.

"Thanks Sherman, so how are things in your world?" I queried.

"Huh? Oh fine, fine. Marcella, do you need anything to make your breakfast complete?" Sherman asked, ignoring me again; the man was smitten for sure.

"Oh no, thank you. Everything is just wonderful, Jimmy," Mars said while batting her eyes at the detective.

"I sure am glad you invited me to breakfast this morning, the day started out lousy. Now it's become delightful," Sherman said.

My astonishment was complete. Holy God, he used the word delightful! Who knew he even had an understanding of the word?

"Did you grow up here in Atlanta, Jimmy?" Mars asked.

Sherman chuckled. "Oh yeah and before you ask, I was harassed about my unfortunate last name until I went off to college. I was bullied without mercy. Lucky for me I'm a pretty big fella and so I usually held my own."

I jumped into the conversation. "Well, I'm sorry about your unfortunate childhood but so glad we could improve your day. Have we made your day sufficiently good enough you can give me five minutes of your time?"

"Well I reckon so. Never mind, don't ask, I know what you wanna know," Sherman said and looked at Mars expectantly. "We're gonna talk a little shop here now and I hope it doesn't offend or upset you."

"Why heavens no, but thank you for your sensitive nature. I do so appreciate it." Mars smiled at him.

Good God, it had been awhile since my gag reflex had been tested so thoroughly. I tried not to sigh out loud.

"You wanna know what I found out about Kevin Stewart. Well, I called in a favor with the ME, had her make a trip to the funeral home before they did him up. You owe me large, by the by, I had to take her out for a big dinner and that girl can sure as hell put it away. Anyways, she did a once over on your guy. She found petechial hemorrhage in his nose, eyes and throat, plus there was mucus in the back of the poor bastard's throat."

I sat up straighter in my seat.

"Don't get excited, there was no more hemorrhage than if he had just quit breathing on his own. There were some fibers which turned out to be cotton consistent with bedding, but again he was sleeping on cotton sheets. Even with a full autopsy there might not be enough to prove he was smothered but I'm bettin' that how she did it, if she did it. This is a hard thing to detect or to prove, 'cause it looks pretty natural." He held out his hands palms up. "So we got nothin'."

I felt myself sag. Man, I was disappointed. I'd hoped there would be more proof against the widow. The bitch was smart, I had to admit.

"It's okay, Sherman, you did me a favor and I do owe you. Let me pay you for the dinner and I'll still owe ya and you can call it due anytime. Thanks, and I really mean it." I tried, but I couldn't keep the disappointment out of my voice.

"Look Maher, you gave it a shot and that's all you can do. Maybe this broad will slip up somewhere else and you can nail her. They all slip up sooner or later, believe me. She ain't no practiced criminal and she's gonna give you an openin'. I'd bet my badge on it."

"You sound like you give a damn, Sherman," I said.

"Maher, I hate bad guys and I believe in your gut instinct here. This Kincaid, she's a real bad guy and so she needs to be brought down. Just keep your eye on the ball and you'll get her." He seemed so sincere.

"Thanks," I said. "I'll keep you posted."

"Or your brother will. We talk, ya know. Seems you got a trial comin' up soon, you ready for it?" Sherman took a sip of his coffee.

Mars and I both sighed at the same time.

"This is for one of the bad guys whom our DA thinks actually pulled the trigger on Chick," I said. "He thinks it, and Donna Maples is gonna testify to it." Her name made my tongue feel slimy.

"She the county official who was in bed with the hired guns?" Sherman asked.

I nodded and said, "Yep, and she turned state's evidence and she's gonna walk away scot-free. The bad part of me wants to lay in wait for her some dark night and take out the back of her skull with a crowbar."

Mars nodded and patted me on the hand. "But instead we're gonna don our big girl panties and go into the court room so we can watch Donna Maples squirm her way out of prison." She nodded her head once more to emphasize her statement.

"That blows," Sherman commiserated. "But you got the trigger man and the other two. I was given to understand one of the bastards won't go to trial since he suffered some brain damage. Brain damage *you* inflicted on him, I hear." He smiled at me.

"I didn't set out to make the man dumber than he originally was, I was just trying to keep my own self from gettin' dead. I can't help it if he has a thin cranium. Anyway, seems he's in no condition to testify in his own defense and it'd be a waste of the taxpayer's time and money to go on with a trial, blah, blah, blah. Donna has implicated him and so he'll go to a mental institution, I reckon. He's a murderin' bastard and wherever he goes, it'll be too good for him. I don't know where he'll end up and frankly, my dear, I don't give damn." I said, giving a bit of a nod to Clark Gable. After all, I was in Atlanta.

"With a rock. Well, as long as you don't hold no grudge or nothin'. Damn girl, I'd sure hate to have you mad at me." Sherman chuckled.

"You know a lot about Chick's death and the trial, Jimmy," Mars said.

"Like I said, me and Connell, we talk. We been friends for a long time. He helped me through my mother's death and I helped him through his divorce. Chick's death took a toll on him and we've talked about it. He also told me you were the prettiest thing he'd ever laid eyes on and he wasn't lyin'." He smiled. "If he don't do right by ya, let me know and I'll shoot his useless ass."

Mars smiled and dropped her eyes. I could tell she was touched by his words.

"Sherman, you'd have to stand in line," I said.

33

Take the Long Road Home

Mars and I hit the road so we could miss the goat screw which is Nashville rush hour traffic. Mars seemed quiet, even pensive.

"Hey girl, what's up?" I asked.

She shook her head. "Well, I've just been thinking. Connell is telling people about us, that's big."

I grinned. "Why wouldn't he tell people? I know, I know, we had the talk about race and the South and public office and what not."

"What not? It's not a trivial thing; you can't just blow it off. I think Connell might want to run for higher office one of these days. What if our relationship gets in the way?"

Higher office? Whoa, news to me. I felt sad for a moment, or jealous or something, because someone else knew something about my brother I was not privy to, wow!

"Really?" I asked. "Like mayor or something?"

Mars blew out an exasperated breath at me. "Missing the point, girlfriend. Our relationship could hurt his chances for election, yet he's going public with it. That is…amazing and wonderful and brave." She was getting all teary.

"Well, of course it is. You know if you and Connell get married then you'll be my real sister like we pretended when we were kids, remember?"

"Yes," she breathed the answer and I got teary too.

We talked about love and marriage and dresses for the rest of the ride home. It was a very good trip. Mars dropped me at the office and sped away. Connell was about to get a visit, or I didn't know my girl.

Jewels had already left for the day so I looked for messages and found none. No news is good news, or so they say. I hoped they were right, whoever the hell 'they' were.

My head was so full of relationship ideas and questions I could hardly think of anything else. The trip to Atlanta had really started me thinking.

I got home and wandered out to the garage looking for Daddy. The garage stands separately and to the right across the drive from the house. Daddy has a shop set up in there so he can work on guns, his other great love besides my mother. His email is smithyogun@gmail.com.

"Daddy?" I called out.

"In here," he answered.

I wandered in and found him hunched over a workbench with a Smith and Wesson .38 Bodyguard. At least I was pretty sure I was right, but it was hard to tell since it was in pieces. He had his magnifier light turned on and was studying the parts.

"Whacha doing?" I asked as I kissed him on the forehead.

"Well, this is Nate Jounigan's .38 and he wanted me to clean it and check it out for him. Seems it pulls to the left real bad, so

I'm gonna check the sites and the laser, but I reckon it's operator error on his part. How was your day?'"

"Productive. Operator error?"

"Well, Nat's right handed. I think he curls his finger around the trigger a touch and creates the pull. He claims he dropped it and that could screw things up but it's a fixed sight so I have my doubts," Daddy explained as he put the gun back together; I noted how fast he did it. "Let's see if I'm right."

He handed me goggles and ear protection which I put on. He donned his own and fastened the gun in a gun vise where it couldn't move when he fired it. He lined it up with the ballistic box, which was filled with medical grade cotton; don't ask, just know it stops the bullet. He fixed a new target in place, walked back to where I was standing and fired the gun six times. Every shot hit dead center in the target. He looked at me and cocked an eye, reloaded, and fired again with the same results.

"One more time for good measure," he said as he reloaded.

The results were identical.

"So I reckon you're gonna tell 'Big 'Un' he doesn't know how to shoot a gun?" I quipped. Nate Jounigan is a big fella and had been all his life; his daddy had tagged him with the nickname.

Daddy smiled back. "Well, I think I might be a bit more diplomatic."

"Daddy … I need to talk," I said quietly.

He nodded at me while he removed the gun from the vise and returned it to his work bench. He began to dismantle it again in order to clean it.

I cleared my throat. "So most of the time people get married because they love each other, right?" I asked.

"Yep, seems to be right in my experience," he agreed.

"Then how the hell does it go so wrong? Do you know an estimated sixty-five percent of all spouses have affairs? Sixty-five percent! Daddy, that's crazy. Did you know eighty-five percent of my business is for clients who think their spouse is cheatin'?

Furthermore, of the women clients who hire me to check out their husbands, ninety-eight percent of them are justified in their suspicions. Of the men who hire me to check out their wives for cheatin', fifty percent of them are right. Without infidelity I'd have to sell footwear at the Shoe Palace," I finished dejectedly.

"Uh-huh, well at least you'd get a good discount." Daddy chuckled, continuing to tinker with the .38. When I didn't, he said, "What's brought this on, daughter?"

"I just don't understand how you go from loving and adoring a person and wanting to spend the rest of your life with him or her to sneaking around in cheap motels. It boggles the mind." I shook my head.

"Well, yes, it does. I fell in love with your mother the moment I first saw her. I *knew* she was the one. It took me a bit of time to convince her, she had quite a lot of suitors in those days you know. Anyway, I don't know if I understand the need to stray myself. I reckon some folks get bored or maybe their spouse stops payin' attention to them or works too much or they just stop carin'. Maybe they meet someone who lights that spark again and think they have to act on the emotion."

"Daddy, it's absolutely none of my business, but did you ever … stray?" I could hardly believe I was asking my father such a question.

He smiled and put down the gun. "Nope, never. You mother hooked me and then we had kids and parents to take care of and we leaned on each other through every day since. That's not to say I don't appreciate a beautiful woman, but your momma is the only woman for me. Maybe we're just lucky."

"Don't you ever get tired of being with the same woman day after day—bored, ya know?"

Daddy laughed out loud. "Have you met the woman we're talkin' about? Borin' is hardly a word I'd use to describe her. What put all this in your head?"

I reached in the mini-fridge behind Daddy and pulled out a beer. "This murder case, I guess, and I just finished another one where the wife wanted proof her husband was cheatin' but in reality, she was the one cheatin'. She wanted to catch him so she could get a better settlement. Maybe what I do has made me jaded and cynical and caused me to lose faith in the whole love thing." I held the beer aloft. "Want one?"

He shook his head. "I think it's more than that, this conversation sounds personal. Who you been talkin' to?"

He picked the gun up again and looked at the hammer. He turned it back and forth and nodded to himself.

Once a cop, always a cop, I thought. "Mars."

"Oh, Marcella. Well then I'm not surprised you're thinkin' a bit on love and fidelity. There seems to be somethin' going on with Marcella and your brother Connell." He didn't look at me when he said it.

"Can't get nothin' past you, Daddy. Make sure they know I didn't tell, I'd hate for my brother and my best friend to thump me."

Daddy laughed. "Not to worry, I don't intend to say a word until they've got somethin' to say to us. I reckon soon enough there'll be an invitation to a dinner for your mother and me and the Prices."

"You good with this?" I asked.

"I am."

"Mars is all wrapped around the axel over the race thing. She's worried people will take offense, and Connell won't get reelected, and maybe if he has aspirations for higher office he won't be able to win." I blew out a breath. "It's not stupid for her to think that way, but it is stupid that people judge other people because of superficial shit like skin color and religions and whatever else people judge other people over. It pisses me off." I took a big swig of beer hoping to wash away the bitter taste.

"I would never have known," Daddy said sarcastically. "Look honey, people are people and lots of 'em are scared of the unknown, including people with different skin and different religions and different ways of lookin' at things. But Marcella and her family have been here in this town forever and a day. Everybody in the county knows 'em and most like 'em, 'cept for the real hard cases. I'm not sayin' a few eyebrows won't be raised but I think it'll all come out right." He reached over and patted me on the shoulder.

"I sure hope so."

"We got trial tomorrow," Daddy casually dropped the fact into the conversation.

"Yep, we do and it's gonna suck." I took another sip of beer.

"True enough. Well, I reckon we ought to go help your mother and grandmother get dinner on the table." Daddy placed the gun on the workbench.

"Yep," I said. I polished off my beer while Daddy polished the gun.

"Higher office, ya say?" Daddy asked.

He wrapped his arm around my waist and we walked across the driveway together. I felt a little better after our talk, but I still couldn't help but wonder if maybe he and Mommy were just lucky. How do I know if I, or Mars and Connell, would be as fortunate?

We went in and I watched as my father walked across the kitchen and hugged my mother from behind as she stood chopping carrots for the salad. They blended into one being as they leaned into one another, both of them with their eyes closed, the knife frozen in mid-chop. Wow, if that was luck, I wanted some, but I was scared I'd never find it, or maybe I'd missed my chance.

I decided then and there to get a cat. I'd become the Crazy Cat Lady of Medicine Springs. It would just be easier.

34

Dressed for Success

The next morning, I arose, did my morning routine, and picked out something business-like to wear to court. I wanted to look cool and professional when I was anything but. Not being much of clothes horse, my business look outfits are limited but I found one I thought was appropriate; the suit was black and I chose a blood red silk blouse to wear under it. It fit my mood, you know?

I hit the bottom step into the kitchen and was surrounded by canines who all seemed to think they were going somewhere too.

"Sorry, y'all," I said as I reached down to ruffle ears. "No run this morning."

Anyone who thinks dogs don't understand human had only to look at the sad faces of the creatures at my feet.

I walked into the kitchen proper and found a lot of my family. As a matter of fact, *most* of my family was sitting at the table.

"Morning all," I said. "I didn't expect everyone to be here or I would've dressed up."

My sister Moira smiled at me. "Wouldn't be anywhere else, Sis. Want some coffee?"

I considered for a moment; coffee was my drink of choice but my stomach was already churning with anticipation of the day. Caffeine won over nausea and I nodded at Moira. She moved to accommodate me.

"Thanks. So how is everyone?" It was a stupid question but one I had to ask.

Dugan looked at me for a second.

"We're all holdin' up and none of us are lookin' forward to this process. We are all kinda worried about you. This'll be the first time you lay eyes on the guy who tried to kill you." He eyeballed me real good, as if he could discern my emotional state.

"Well, keep in mind this is the first time he's laid eyes on me since *I* tried to kill *him*, so he might be nervous too." As an attempt at humor it fell flat; nobody laughed.

"Don't worry, we're all here for you. It will be fine," Michelene said.

She looked at me earnestly and I could see the worry and concern in her face and hear it in her voice, which was dripping with pity. What annoyed me most was she was playing big sister to my little sister; her arms were clasped behind her indicating confidence and authority. Body language will give you away every time. I thought I'd proven I could stand on my own two feet and didn't need to be soothed or petted. Or maybe I was just overreacting.

"I'm not worried; I'm just not lookin' forward to this is all. I'm concerned the defense will try and hang me out to dry. After all, it was me who gut shot Joe and left him in the woods to die. Not exactly the work of a Sunday school teacher, right?"

Michelene said, "Well, it is completely understandable you should feel this way given it is his lawyer's job to try everything and anything to get the man a lesser sentence. However, you cannot let anything the defense says about you resonate with you or impact your mental state in any way."

I wouldn't have been surprised if she'd reached and patted me on the head.

"Michelin," I said, deliberately mispronouncing her name, "Don't make me talk ugly in front of my grandmother."

YaYa laughed out loud. When we were kids we annoyed my sister by calling her Michelin – as in the big fat tire guy. She hit me with a hairbrush one time when I wouldn't leave off calling her the name while she was talking on the phone to her boyfriend. Of course, I was also making kissing noises and had my arms wrapped around my back as if I was hugging someone.

"You don't have to be hostile with me. I'm on your side; I'm trying to comfort you. Truly, I'm very worried about your state of mind," Michelene said earnestly.

"Mich, shut up 'cause what you are doing is pissin' me off. I'm not mentally unstable and I don't care what the defense team say about me as long as Joe gets life, so don't coddle me. Coddle people who pay you to do it." I doctored my coffee.

"Girls," Mommy warned. "Michelene is only trying to help, Tess."

"She's not, she's only making it worse and she needs to stop now because I'm gonna stop being nice startin' in three … two … one." I kept working on my coffee.

"Now you are acting irrational," said my sister in her very calm head shrinking voice.

"See you all at the court house," I snapped, dumping my coffee into a roadie and headed for the door.

"Tess!" Mommy called but I just kept on walking.

I knew Michelene thought she was helping when in fact she was not. When you ask someone to stop doing something then they should cease doing the offending action, even when the person is a trained professional!

I damn near broke a finger when I snatched the door open and almost dropped my coffee too. I knew I was acting like a child but I just didn't give a rat's ass. I mounted my Jeep and drove into town.

I hadn't gotten far when the phone rang.

"Yes?" I snapped.

"How you doin', sister?" said Mars. "Stupid question?"

"Well I just showed my ass in the kitchen in front of most of my family and damn near broke my finger on the Jeep and almost spilled my coffee trying to make my get-away. But I look awesomely fine this mornin'. How you doin'?"

Mars laughed. "Well, I haven't bitten anyone's nose off yet but the day is still young. Where are you?"

"I'm 'bout halfway to town. Where're you?"

"Tilly's. Wanna meet me?"

"Well, I reckon we've got the time to have more coffee and still drive to Nashville. Save me seat." I broke contact and the speed limit to get to town.

Mars was waiting for me and had more coffee on the table when I sat down. She leaned over and kissed me.

"What set you off?"

"Michelene," I answered.

Tilly came over and hugged me and then Mars. "I know I don't have to ask how you girls are doin' today 'cause I know the answer. But, I'm just sayin', you hold your heads up and don't let nobody get under your skin, y'hear?"

"Yes ma'am," Mars and I answered simultaneously.

"Now what can I get you girls?" Tilly asked as she whipped out her order pad.

"Just coffee Tilly, and thanks," I answered.

"You can't go into the lion's den on coffee, girl, now how 'bout some toast at least and maybe some grits too?" She stared at me 'til I nodded my agreement. "I'll bring some for you too, Mars, and you'll eat." Then she spun on her heel and headed to the kitchen.

"I wonder if Daniel ate a good breakfast before he went into the lion's den," Mars mused.

I shook my head. "Naw, Tilly ain't that old."

We both laughed.

"For real, Michelene was only trying to help. It is what she does after all," Mars said.

"Do not defend her; she is a supercilious, self-aggrandizing, arrogant, self-important bitch. She thinks she knows more and is smarter than everyone else on the planet. She was only worryin' over me 'cause she thinks she's been appointed to save the whole world and, girl, she has a deep need to rescue people because it makes her feel important. Well, I DO NOT NEED A SAVIOR! I just need to get on with this shit!" I drank my coffee.

"Don't mince words now, tell me how you really feel. And you've been reading the dictionary again, very impressive."

I just looked mean at her over the rim of coffee cup.

"You just stormed out of the house, didn't you?" Mars asked – or rather accused.

I wiggled my head back and forth. "Well…yeah I did, which I admit is childish. But honest to god, Mich will not shut up once she gets on the trail. She loves people in crisis. I really had no choice."

Mars rolled her eyes. "So no one knows where you are?"

"I told them I'd see them in court, so yes they think I've gone to the court house, and in a few minutes I *will* go there," I said.

Mars smiled. "Uh-huh, right after you eat your toast."

"And grits." I stuck my tongue out at her.

"Mature, very mature," Mars assured me.

35

Cup of Coffee

Thirty minutes later, fortified with a gallon of coffee, toast, and grits, we jumped into Mar's Thunderbird and headed to Nashville. We didn't talk on the ride, which was fine with me. I needed to think about what was going to happen and Mars was intuitive enough to leave me alone in my own head. I would see Joe, the guy I shot. I would see Donna Maples too. I hated her worse than the three men who had killed my best friend and kidnapped and terrorized me, despite the fact the bitch had never laid a fake acrylic fingernail on me. I dreamed about killing her, and in every dream I killed her in a different way. My subconscious is very creative; warped and twisted, but creative.

We made it to Nashville in record time and parked in the big lot in front of the court house. The Nashville courthouse is a massive building with many steps leading up to it and two huge fountains on either side of the gigantic doors at the entrance.

It's an impressive structure, built in 1936 by Frederick Hirons Emmons Woolwine. I know because I wrote a report on it when I was in seventh grade. The place is enormous, several hundred thousand square feet, with impressive art deco details, and it's intimidating as all get out.

Once inside, we had to go through security. We placed our belongings in a tray and walked through the metal detector. I had left my weapons locked in Mars' trunk, since it might be frowned upon to be packing. Men with guns watched our every move. It was quite different than the courthouse back home. We collected our belongings and asked for directions to the correct courtroom. Again, back home, we only have one courtroom so you always know exactly where to go. But this was the big city — more crime, more courtrooms. Voices were subdued in the wide hallways with their soaring ceilings, and our footsteps echoed on the marble floors. It seemed sanctified, like a church. I reckon that feeling causes folks to act reverently. To me, it felt like a place where common ordinary folks came to get justice, which was sure as hell what I wanted.

Mars reached over and grabbed my hand as we walked down the hallway. I took a deep breath to steady myself; I knew the day might be horrible. I also knew I had to be there; even if I didn't have a piece of paper in my bag demanding my presence, I would still have been present.

We entered the designated courtroom and took a few seconds to get our bearings. My family members had not arrived yet. Mars and I picked a place mid-way in the audience and sat down. I looked at the defendant's bench and there sat Joe McKenzie, the man who murdered Chick and tried to murder me. A cold knot composed of hatred and sorrow formed in my stomach. I wanted to puke. Instead I made myself took a good look at Joe. He looked far different from the last time I'd seen him. He'd lost a lot of weight, a common occurrence when you take a slug in the stomach. It messes up your ability to process food and causes you to be on a liquid diet for months. I thought about how much it sucked for Joe for about five seconds and realized I didn't feel one morsel of guilt. I couldn't see his face but I knew sooner or later during the proceedings, I would.

I had thought Donna Maples, Joe's cohort in crime, would be in the courtroom but I failed to spot her.

Connell slid into the seat next to me. Mars waved at him and smiled. I kissed him on the cheek.

"How you holdin' up kid?" he asked.

"Shitty," I said. "And you?"

"Shitty."

I stretched my neck and let my head hang over the back of the bench for a minute. "God, this sucks. I wanna go to the river and float downstream on a tube and drink beer from a cooler."

Connell smiled. "Sounds good. But you know you'd hate to miss poor ol' Joe telling the world how mean and awful you are and how you shot him in cold blood cause you're crazy as a shit house rat when all he was doin' was takin' a midnight stroll in the woods, carrying a gun."

I narrowed my eyes at him because you cannot hit an officer of the law in a courthouse, even if he is your mean older brother. "Asshat," I said sweetly.

Connell grinned and reached over to pat Mars on the leg. "You are looking particularly well this morning, Marcella." He winked at her and she grinned a big stupid grin back at him.

"Oh, for god's sakes, give it a rest," I snapped, but I didn't really mean it. I kind of liked to watch them flirt.

The rest of the clan arrived en masse; we took up two full rows. Many of my sibs patted me or squeezed my shoulder as they filed in; YaYa kissed the top of my head, and then Connell's. Hard on their heels came Ricky Wynne, the mayor of our town, and his wife Beverly, Donna's sister. I knew they hated to be in the court room, but felt obligated to show support for Donna. Beverly saw me and gave a small wave and a sad little smile. I returned both. I felt sorry for her; she couldn't help being related to a bitch.

"All rise and draw near and those with business for this court shall be heard. The Honorable Judge Marko Fontaine is presiding," the bailiff intoned.

Everyone stood as the judge entered and took his place at the bench. Judge Marko Fontaine looked every inch a hanging judge, solemn and no nonsense. I hoped he'd throw the book at Joe.

At the DA's table, sat a couple of people I didn't know. I recognized the back of Johnny Johnson's head; he was the Simpson County prosecutor. Johnny was a good guy who knew the law backwards and forwards and hated bad guys. I felt sure he'd help get a fair verdict. There was a woman sitting next to him, Dina Shabayek, the Nashville prosecutor. I'd met with her prior to the trial and felt pretty good about her abilities. She stood and addressed the judge, looking so posed and confident and, let's not forget, beautiful. Dina is a dark skinned woman of Egyptian descent who is tall, slim, and gorgeous enough to be in a fashion show. Yet she was in a courtroom in Nashville dealing with murderers. I shook my head at the thought.

There were two men and a woman seated at the defense table. Neither man was the guy we'd dealt with last year during the Aggroco mess. I wondered if he'd been fired.

"Your Honor, if it please the court," Dina began. I closed my eyes for a second and just listened to the sound of her voice as she listed the charges one after the other. "The State will present evidence which will prove beyond reasonable doubt Mr. McKenzie did with intention and premeditation murder Mr. Donnelly in cold blood as part of a larger conspiracy. The State intends to present proof showing Mr. McKenzie conspired with Richard Journey and Martin Greenly to commit all the crimes with which he has been charged. The state has provided notice to defense counsel it is seeking for the death penalty in this case."

There it was! The death penalty! I closed my eyes and took a deep breath. I asked God to grant it. There you go, proof I am a truly horrible person. I prayed for another human being to get the needle. Joe deserved to die, in my opinion. He was a scummy murdering bastard, he murdered Chick, he tried to murder me and I wanted him to fry.

The judge looked at the defense group. One man stood and buttoned his suit. "Your Honor, I believe the proof will show Mr. Joseph McKenzie was nothing but an unfortunate man who fell in with low companions who misled him and now blame him for a crime of which he is innocent."

"Thank you, Mr. Crowne. General, please present your first witness," Judge Fontaine said.

"Your Honor, State calls Donna Maples to the stand," Dina said.

I felt my heart clench up in my chest, suddenly a wave of nausea hit me like a brick. The coffee and toast came back to haunt me with a vengeance! I swallowed in a desperate attempt to keep it all down. Beads of sweat the size of marbles popped out on my forehead and my whole body turned cold as ice. I wanted to put my head between my knees. *Please don't let me vomit*, I prayed.

A woman stood up and walked to the witness stand. I didn't recognize her at first. Donna Maples had always dressed in skin tight clothes to show off her figure; she had big but perfect hair, a touch much in the make-up department, spray tan no matter the season and six inch heels no matter the occasion. Overdone – not streetwalker overdone, just-little-town-in-the-South overdone. In short, she always looked like the former beauty queen and cheerleader she had been.

The woman I saw take the witness stand looked nothing like the Donna I had known. She was dressed demurely in a crème colored suit with a pale pink silk blouse and low heels. She was even wearing pearls. Her hair was about four shades darker than I had ever seen it and not big, and her make-up was barely there and understated. She looked like a damn Sunday school teacher!

Donna sat down in the witness box and one of the court officers asked her to raise her right hand and swear to tell the truth, the whole truth and nothing but the truth, so help her God, blah blah blah. Bullshit!

She spoke much softer than I'd ever heard her speak before and she seemed to lack the old self-confidence. When she quit talking and moving I realized what else about her had changed; she looked older and much thinner. I guess contemplating your sins will have that effect.

I realized my hands were clenched into fists in my lap. I wanted to beat the bitch to death; I could see myself doing it in my imagination. I would just keep hitting her in the face until she quit moving. I hated her like God hates sin, maybe worse. She needed to get the death penalty and instead she was going to get off scot-free. I felt the sharpness of tears forming and closed my eyes. I refused to cry. I intended to sit on the hard, wooden bench and watch the proceedings like a grown up, but, oh, I wanted to howl like a wounded child.

Connell reached over and took my hand. Mars took my other one. It's a good and wonderful thing to be loved and to have backup when you need it. I squeezed their hands tight.

Dina approached Donna. "Ms. Maples, will you describe for the jury your relationship with the defendant, Joseph McKenzie?"

Donna looked innocent as a lamb at shearing. "Well, he worked for a company called Aggroco out of California. Last year the company contacted me about buying some land in Simpson County. He's one of the men who came to look over the property and complete the deal."

"Ms. Maples, when did you realize how violently Joseph McKenzie and his companions had dealt with Charles Donnelly?" Dina asked.

Mr. Crowne jumped to his feet. "Objection, Your Honor, council is leading the witness!"

"Ms. Shabayek, tread lightly," Judge Fontaine warned. "The jury will disregard the last question."

Dina nodded. "Did you have misgivings about your dealings with Joe and his companions?"

Donna shook her head. "Oh no, not at first. I drove them out to the land and they took a good long look at it. I know they went back several times because they called and asked me all kind of questions."

"Can you tell the court what happened on the evening of April 21st of last year?" Dina moved closer to the witness box and waited for Donna to answer.

Donna began to shake as if she were about to cry. "It was the day of the Catfish Festival in Medicine Springs. Joseph McKenzie and Martin Greenly came to my office. Even though it was a Saturday, they'd called and said they needed to meet with me. I agreed, of course. As soon as they came through the door I knew something was wrong."

"Objection, Your Honor! Calls for conjecture from the witness!" Mr. Crowne said.

Fontaine was silent for a moment. "Strike the last sentence from 'as soon as' from Ms. Maples testimony," he instructed the court reporter. He then turned to the jury. "The jury will disregard the last sentence."

Dina didn't turn a hair. She even smiled at Donna. "Please continue with your recollection of the events of the day."

"Well, they seemed mad, you know, and nervous. They looked all over my office like they were lookin' for somethin'. They even checked the closet. Then they told me what they had done to Chick." Donna started to cry.

"By Chick, do you mean Charles Donnelly?" Dina asked softly.

"Yes, Charles Donnelly." Donna nodded, choking on Chick's name. "They shot him because they were scared he knew something about the land being poisoned. Joe bragged about it. He complained about Tessely Maher snooping around; I had told them she was lookin' in ta' Chick's death, I'm ashamed to say. I also told him she wouldn't leave the investigation alone 'cause she's like a dog with a bone once she gets somethin' in her head. That's when Joe said he'd take care of her too just like he had taken care of Chick…"

"Hearsay, Your Honor," Crowne interrupted.

"Your Honor, Ms. Maples was a co-conspirator and the murder was revealed during a meeting between co-conspirators. This information will also be confirmed by Mr. Greenly when he testifies," Dina protested.

The judge was quiet for a moment. "I will allow it on those grounds."

Crowne looked like he had something to say but the judge cut him a cold look.

Dina took advantage of the moment. "Ms. Maples, what else do you recall about the meeting?"

"They talked like idiots and they thought they knew every-thing! They thought they could scare Tess off easily. But I knew better, I knew she wouldn't give up!" The more worked up Donna became, the more she sounded like her old self.

Crowne jumped up. "Irrelevant, Your Honor, move to strike."

Fontaine sighed. "Strike the last statement from Ms. Maples. The jury will disregard. Ms. Maples, you must refrain from telling the court what other people are thinking, you have no way of knowing the thoughts in the heads of others."

"I've known her since she was born; I sure as hell think I know how she was gonna act," Donna snapped at the judge. "If it wasn't for her…"

She didn't finish her sentence, which was a good thing; I was pretty sure she was going to blame me for her predicament. I had a Scooby moment right there in the courtroom: *We would've gotten away with it too except for that dang Tess Maher.*

"Careful, Ms. Maples," Fontaine warned.

"Joseph McKenzie and Martin Greenly threatened Ms. Maher in your presence?" Dina pressed on.

"Yes, Mr. McKenzie said they'd put a stop to her meddlin'." Donna looked down into her lap; she was the perfect picture of fear and loathing. I knew she was acting; she wouldn't have turned a hair if I had ended up stone dead just like Chick.

"You believed Mr. McKenzie when he threatened Ms. Maher?" Dina asked.

"Yes," Donna whispered. She dabbed at her eyes, wiping away her crocodile tears. I hated her more with every passing moment.

"Yet you didn't report Mr. Donnelly's murder to the authorities nor did you report the threat to Ms. Maher. Why not?" The prosecutor leaned on the witness stand railing and looked Donna in the eye.

"I was frightened of those men, they were thugs and murderers. I just knew they'd kill me too." Donna broke into sobs and Dina handed her a small packet of tissues. It was a nice touch and I thought I really might puke.

Again, Crowne bounced up from his chair.

"Your Honor, objection, Your Honor, please! This is a conclusion and supposition as well. Ms. Maples is drawing conclusions about what my client would and would not do and I further object to her calling my client a murderer."

He was prissy as all get out; I didn't like him one little bit.

. "If the shoe fits your client needs to wear it." Donna snapped.

I almost laughed out loud but managed to control myself. I didn't think she was making any friends among the jury. I turned and looked them over: there were eight men and four women. Three were African Americans, one Hispanic and one Asian. No one had sympathy on their face.

"Your Honor…" Crowne started but Fontaine held his hand up to silence him.

"Ms. Maples, do try and control yourself. Please strike 'I knew they would kill me too.' I'm gonna let the rest stand. Your objection is overruled, Mr. Crowne. Continue, Ms. Shabayek." The judge shot a warning look at Crowne, who looked very unhappy.

"When you say 'those men', please name them for the court," Dina urged.

Donna drew a shaky breath. "Martin Greenly, Joseph McKenzie and Richard Journey."

"You've been offered immunity from prosecution if you testify against the defendant, haven't you?" Dina asked.

Donna had the good grace to hang her head in shame. "Yes."

"Ms. Maples, you realize people are going to doubt your testimony because of the immunity issue." Dina was trying to get in front of the immunity thing, hoping to try and soften the idea for the jury. She was also trying to steer Donna away from the 'Bitch' cliff she was about to go over and back to the 'Sunday School Teacher' script the prosecutors had written for her. They couldn't afford for the jury to hate her and ignore her testimony.

"I understand that but … but I'm tellin' the God's truth. It's all true, I swear." Donna's voice was rough with tears.

Dina looked at the prosecutors' table and some sort of a signal passed between them.

"Your Honor, the prosecution reserves the right to redirect if necessary."

The judge nodded. "Mr. Crowne, your witness."

The defense attorney stood up and walked to the middle of the room; he just stood and stared at Donna for a good fifteen seconds. He intended to unnerve her and it worked. She looked even more shaky and uncomfortable.

"Ms. Maples, you received a lot of money from Aggroco, did you not?" he asked.

"I received money." Donna sounded very unsure of herself.

"A lot of money. Enough money to set you up for life. If you testify against my client, you get to walk away, despite the fact you took a bribe and concealed a crime from the authorities. It's the deal you cut. However, in point of fact, you're an accessory before and after in the death of Charles Donnelley. Yet, all charges go away and all you have to do in return is help them send my client to his death. Have I missed anything?"

As Crowne spoke, Donna's eyes got wider and wider until she looked like an owl. His speech had undone all the good his silent stare had created. He had badly miscalculated. She was pissed.

"How dare you talk to me like that? You have no idea what I've been through. I thought I was helpin' to bring jobs and money into my community. But I was tricked, bamboozled, hoodwinked and hornswoggled by bad men from the big city who came to my little town in hopes of hoodooin' the country mice who live there. They came and did murder and terrorized me to the point I was scared to death to go to the sheriff. I couldn't sleep or eat out of fear; all I did was pace the floor. My hair started falling out! You dare to stand there in your expensive suit and try and tell me what I did or how I felt or what I had to endure to survive? I have been sure I was gonna die ever since the terrible day Joe told me what he'd done."

Donna began to cry great, racking sobs. She buried her face in her hands and she shook all over. The judge called a recess to give Donna the opportunity to pull it together. We all stood up as he left the bench.

"The hell with this, I've enjoyed as much of the circus as I can stand and I wanna go home. No one else is gonna get a chance to testify today," I announced. "It's gonna be the damn Donna show."

I picked up my bag and headed for the door, I was just sick to death of the whole damn shooting match. Mars came out behind me.

"You want to go outside and just cool down?" she asked.

"No, I wanna go home!" I insisted.

"Tell you what, I'll go and ask JJ what he thinks. If there's a chance you'll be called then we can go to a coffee shop right up the block and someone can call us and tell us to come back, okay?"

"Fine, I'll wait outside," I said grudgingly.

Mars tuned on her heel and went back toward the courtroom and I left the building. I decided I'd wait for her in front of one of the big fountains. The water was spraying into the air and the sun was creating little rainbows everywhere. It was beautiful and I decided I could stand there all day enjoying it. I had only been there a minute or so when a voice shook me out of my revelry.

"You and I need to talk."

I spun round and there stood Jonnie Kincaid; I had no trouble recognizing her from the pictures I'd taken. I had to admit she was even less attractive in person. She glared at me as if she wanted to kill me on the spot, and she probably did. Man, she was scary as hell, but then crazy people usually are. Her pupils were dilated and her mouth was pulled back in a red lipstick enhanced snarl. Yep, she was one frightening bitch. I didn't say a word since she wanted to talk. I figured I'd let her.

"You're poking your fucking nose in where it does not belong. I've warned you several times now and yet you persist in ignoring me. I do not like to be ignored. So let me say this in very small words you can understand, since you are so damn stupid: If you don't keep out of my business and quit poking around in the death of my dear departed husband, you are going to wind up every bit as dead as he is." She stared at me. "You got it?"

"For real? You're gonna stand on the steps of the courthouse and threaten to murder me? Holy shit cakes, woman! You've watched the Godfather one too many times." I really couldn't believe it.

Her eyes got all squinty and she hissed at me, "Try me, bitch, I'll fucking bury you." Her eyes narrowed into near non-existent slits and she stared at me for a few seconds. Then she just walked away.

Mars arrived just in time to see the back side of the woman.

"Who was that?" she asked.

"Lady Macbeth, and she just delivered a death threat in person, in broad daylight on the steps of the freakin' courthouse!" I took a deep breath. "I'm hungry."

"You're nuts, the bitch knew you were here and waited to get you alone so she could tell you she was going to kill you! She's stalking you! Good God Almighty! She's frightening as hell." Mars was shook.

"Turnabout's fair play, I've been stalking her. But she just upped the ante, now I gotta get the proof to put her away. Can we please go eat?" I begged.

Mars rolled her eyes and threw her hands in the air in exasperation. But she led the way and we rolled on down the street in search of sustenance. We didn't have to search far; we slid into a comfortable looking coffee shop. I ordered coffee and a ham and cheese sandwich and Mars ordered fruit salad, of course.

"So, what did JJ think? Will I testify today?" I asked.

Mars shook her head. "He's really not sure, so he doesn't want you to get too far away. Okay?"

I stared at the ceiling. "Shit! I want to go home and never have to look at Donna 'the bitch from hell' Maples as long as I live."

"I know, baby, I know. With any luck, her testimony will be all it takes to put this asshole away and we can all move on." Mars was trying to placate me.

"Yep, move on to the next trial with the next asshole, at least I guess we'll be spared a trial with Rick. Hmmp, I feel weird about it, ya know? Like I should feel some remorse over his brain damage, and I don't."

"He did try to kill you," Mars reminded me.

"Yep, he did." I blew out a breath but before I could say anything else they called out our order. "I'll get our food."

36

One Way or Another

After lunch, we found out I didn't have to testify, so I went home. All the way to the car, I had my 'crazy bitch' radar on high. I was willing to bet my last mint-flavored condom Lady Macbeth knew exactly where I was, since she was stalking me. She must have hired a pro, because try as I might, I could never make anyone. I was a bit bothered by my failure. A couple of times I thought maybe someone was tailing me, but he or she was sure as hell good. Finally, I decided I really didn't give a damn who might be following me. Mars and I took the long road home, figuring if there really was a tail on me, we might as well make the bastard earn his money.

The trial went into day two but no one called me to testify. I used the time away from the courtroom to be a very bad girl – or a very good one, depending on your point of view. My first order of business was to call my new best friend, Sin, and ask her to give me Gina's cell phone number. She was only too delighted to help me out, *such* a sweet girl. Yes, that was sarcasm; she was annoyed I had called her and told me so in mostly four letter words. She's an inventive kid. Finally, she relented and gave me the number.

Then I looked up Gina's social security number; I needed it since almost everyone from the cell phones companies to the electric company uses Socials as identification. They are much easier to get than you might think, too. Scary, but true.

It was quick work to find out which phone carrier Gina used, and to pull up her account using her social. I love my job. I played around for several hours before I finally hit on her password; I knew most of her interests and her momma's name from the background check I'd run. Her password was a combination of her first name, the year she was born, and the word football. Easy peasy.

The widow's phone numbers were in Jon's medical records, so I pulled up Gina's phone records and started looking. It took less than fifteen minutes to find what I needed: twenty-two phone calls between Gina and Jonnie during Jon's stay at the rebab center. There were six phone calls the day I was in the nursing home to see Kevin and then nothing since. I reckoned Gina saw the writing on the wall and pulled in her horns. If she was smart, she was hiding under a rock somewhere in Asia Minor.

It was still no smoking gun but it proved my theory; someone in the nursing home was keeping Lady Macbeth informed. It was now time to find out where Jonnie has procured the potassium. The source would help me nail her. I called Sin back.

"Yeah?"

"Sin, it's Tess."

There was silence for a few seconds and rustlings sounds. Sin whispered, "Shit, girl! I'm at work! Whattaya want now?"

"I need to know what drugs went missing the night Jon died and who was on duty the nights Jon and Kevin died."

"Are you fuckin' kiddin' me? How'm I supposed to find out?" she whispered fiercely.

"Who's in charge of the drug supply there?" I tried to sound calming in hopes of soothing her.

Sin sighed. "The charge nurse has the key to the drug cabinet. I mean, we don't have a lot of drugs here, and what we do have is mostly administered by IV or needle. That shit's counted like it was gold, I tell ya, and if something went missin' heads would roll."

"What if the missing drugs wasn't a pain killer or a sleeping aid, nothing of street value? Then would it be gossip?" I asked.

"Well, probably not, and the nurses try and cover their own asses, ya know what I mean. If it was the real deal, they'd have to report it or risk losing their license. But if it was constipation meds, no one would care much." Sin raised her voice, "Don't get your panties in a wad; I'll be there in a minute." I knew she wasn't talking to me.

I needed to get my info fast before she hung up on me. "Sin, I need to get access to the computer in Gina's office, or whichever one keeps the drug records."

"Are you crazy? You gotta death wish or what? What are you gonna do walk in and ask her politely? Shhhhhhit." She was whining.

"Find out when Gina's gonna be off duty and when Lillian Perkins is gonna be on. I only need a few minutes on the computer; I just have to see what, if anything, went missing." I crossed my fingers.

"Jesus Christ, you're gonna get me fired sure as God made gophers. Was I Hitler in my last life and you're my fuckin' karma?" She paused to draw a ragged breath. "Okay, lemme look at the schedule. I'll call you back." She hung up.

I felt fairly satisfied Sin would come through for me. The next big hurtle would be Lillian; she was terrified of Lady Macbeth and with good reason. The bitch was crazy and she'd murdered two people. My only dilemma was, did I call Lillian and talk her into my plan to trap Jonnie or did I wait and surprise her? After a few seconds of deliberation, I decided surprise would be the way to go.

My phone rang. It was Sin.

"Tell me something good," I said.

"Lillian is on tonight at seven. The computer with the inventory is in the closet with the drugs and she'll have the key. Dude, I do not like this! I'm freakin' out, I can hear my own heart beatin'! That can't be good."

"If we want to stop the murders, then we have to take the risks to do it. I'll zip in and out quick like a freakin' bunny; no one will ever know I was there. Turn your head and you won't know either." I tried to sound as if I was in control and really knew what I was doing.

Sin huffed out a breath. "Fine, just fine. You gonna call Lillian and tell her you're comin'?"

"Nope, I think I'll surprise her."

Sin just hung up. I couldn't blame her, she had every right to be mad and scared. There was no way I could promise everything would be fine and there would be rainbows and unicorn farts, but I meant to try to make it all work out.

I had a couple of pieces of business before I could leave for Atlanta. The images from Rod's cameras needed to be reviewed.

"Jewels, will you please review all the pictures from the cameras? Will you also call Johnny Johnson, just to double check and be sure I'm not scheduled to appear in court today? If you do that, I can hit the road to Atlanta again."

"Sure, Boss." Jewels said.

I listened to Jewels make the call while I checked my go bag. I threw some extra ammo in the bag as well.

"Boss, you're good," Jewels assured me.

I left Jewels to hold down the fort while I made another monotonous trip to Atlanta. I was sure getting tired of looking at the same stretch of highway.

37

Bat Outta Hell

Four and a half hours later after an uneventful trip and fueled with caffeine from two pit stops, I pulled into the Marietta Rehab Center. It was 6:45, just in time for shift change. I sipped my coffee and twenty minutes later I saw Gina exit the building.

She seemed nervous, looking over her shoulder as she crossed the pavement. Probably worried Lady Macbeth was going to fly around the corner and run her down, can't say as I blamed her. She reached her car and left the parking lot without encountering her doom. I waited another fifteen minutes to give Lillian time to get settled in her office. Since she was going to hate seeing me, she should at least be physically comfortable.

I walked in the front door and Sin looked up from her book. She didn't acknowledge me, but cut her eyes to her left, indicating the location of Lillian. I kept walking and found the nurse in her office at her computer.

"Good evening, Lillian," I said.

She was startled; her eyes went wide and she backed away from me by scooting her chair across the floor. She looked over my shoulder as if she expected to see Jonnie or the devil bringing up the rear.

"What in the name of God are you doing here?" she gasped.

"I need your help," I said simply.

"I don't want anythin' to do with you. I told you everythin' I know, now please leave. Just please go!" She was terrified.

"Lillian, you know two people have been murdered. You know Jonnie Kincaid is the murderer. You must suspect she's tyin' up her loose ends. You've come to the same conclusion I have, you believe someone in this facility has been passing Jonnie information about the comings and goings here. You're right. Now let me assure you, the mole is in danger too. Jonnie won't hesitate to commit murder again if she believes she needs to protect herself and the money."

I gave Lillian a moment to digest what I'd said. I knew in my heart of hearts she was a decent person and couldn't allow anyone else to die if she could help it.

She held her hands up in front of her in a placating gesture – or to push me away. "No, no, no. I don't know anything at all. Please go away."

I didn't say a word. I just stood there and stared at her. I was pretty sure I could out last her.

Finally, she hung her head in defeat.

"What do you want me to do?" she whispered.

"I need to look at the drug inventory for the night Jon died. I also want to see who was on duty the nights he and Kevin were murdered. I won't involve you; I'm only going to use the information as leverage to get a confession out of Jonnie Kincaid. I swear."

"I won't have to testify? I do and that bitch doesn't kill me, I'll still lose my job." Tears swam in Lillian's eyes.

"Promise. I'll ask Sin to keep lookout for us too, so I can get in and out without anyone knowing I was here." I crossed my fingers.

"Sin? She knows too? Oh my God, this is a nightmare." Lillian buried her face in her hands.

I waited, despite the fact I wanted to shake her 'til her teeth rattled; we needed to hurry before we got caught flatfooted. People had died, and more people might die if we were caught. I tried to maintain my calm and not push too hard. I felt sure she'd give in and help me, eventually. She was in the profession of saving lives. Keeping people from being murdered had to qualify. It was so quiet in the room I could practically hear her thinking. After a few minutes, she looked at me. The woman was shaking like a leaf in a gale.

"Okay, I'm just so scared," she said.

I nodded and dialed Sin, who caught it on the first ring.

"Sin, watch our backs," I said.

"Yeah." Her reply was very terse.

I nodded to Lillian. "Where do we start?"

"The drug inventory first. I have the key and the work schedule records are on the director's computer and her office is locked."

The drug closet was next door, literally. Its name didn't do it justice; it was more than a closet, it was the size of a small office, with no windows and floor to ceiling shelves. The shelves were full of little white baskets full of drugs and each shelf was labeled with the contents. Makes for a quick pick, no fumbling around looking for the correct medicine. There was a refrigerator humming in one corner with an inventory sheet taped to the door.

The computer was at a small desk at the back of the room. There was also a printer, I was delighted to see. We could print off the information without leaving the room. Lillian shut the door behind us and locked it. She turned on the computer and began to scroll backwards until we got to the night of Jon's death.

Lillian drew in a sharp breath. "Shit!"

I looked over her shoulder and saw the notation: *100 mEq Potassium unaccounted for, probably just a miscount.* It was signed by Gina.

Lillian looked over her shoulder at me and her shock was palpable.

"Gina helped her, oh my God! She knew, she…" Lillian started to cry silently, big, fat tears slipped from her eyes and rolled down her cheeks.

"Look Lillian, I'd bet Gina never knew or even suspected what the crazy bitch was up to. Gina may be an unpleasant woman but my gut says she's not a murderer. I'd bet Jonnie tricked her away from this room so she could steal the Potassium. I feel sure I'm right about this, really I do." I patted the woman on her shoulder. "Can you make me two copies of this please?"

Lillian nodded and hit a button, machine sounds happened and two copies of the document popped out. I folded them and slipped them into my pocket.

"Were you on duty the night Kevin died?" I asked.

"No, I remember coming in and finding out about his death. I can promise you Gina was here," she said bitterly.

"I still need a copy of the schedule, every piece of evidence I can gather will help me nail Jonnie Kincaid with murder and put her away. We're done here, can you erase your search?"

Lillian nodded. "I…the director's office, it's locked anyway."

"Yep, got it covered," I said.

We left the room and Lillian locked the door behind us. We approached the director's office where I picked the lock in nothing flat.

"How in the world did you learn how to do that?" Lillian seemed amazed by my skill.

I shut the door behind us and locked it. "YouTube. Can you get into this computer and bring up the schedule?"

"Yes, the password is…well I have the password." She stared at me.

"I don't need the password, Lillian, I just need the info to stop a murderer," I said and dutifully turned my back while she typed in the password.

"I…I know, it's why I'm helpin' you. Please don't think less of me 'cause I'm scared of her and afraid of losin' my job. I also think what we're doin' is illegal as all get out. You can turn around now."

The schedule popped up on the screen and we looked for the dates we needed.

"Don't worry, no one will know you helped me except Sin and she ain't tellin'," I assured her.

"If what I've done tonight gets Jonnie Kincaid life in prison, then I'd do it a thousand times over. She's evil, I mean like Satan evil. I'm sorry if you think I'm a coward, but she terrifies the living hell right out of me." Lillian wiped a tear away but she sounded fierce.

"She's bloodcurdling and that's a fact, but if she goes jail then we have ended her reign of terror. Try not to worry; I'll let you know what happens."

I squeezed her shoulder and she hit print.

"Can I two copies please?"

Lillian nodded. Five minutes later I made my exit, waving at Sin on the way out. She pretended not to see me.

As soon as I got into the Jeep, I called Detective Sherman and hoped he'd hear me out.

"Sherman," he said brusquely.

"Tess Maher."

"Whaddayawant, Maher? I haven't had dinner yet."

"I could buy you dinner?" I offered.

"Nope, I gotta a real date tonight so make it fast."

"One of the drugs which mimics heart attack is Potassium Chloride. There are 100 eMq, enough to kill a man, missing from the drug closet at Marietta Rehab. Those 100 mEq went missing on the night Jon Kincaid died. Jonnie Kincaid received more than twenty phone calls from one of the nurses at the center, the last call being the night Kevin Stewart died. The nurse in question was on duty the night both men died." I stopped and drew breath.

"You got documentation on all this?" Sherman asked.

"Yep, copies of the drug inventory, copies of the phone calls, copies of the duty schedule. You want 'em?"

"God damn it, I'm trying to have dinner, but yeah I want 'em," he growled.

"I could meet you?" I offered.

"Nikolai's Roof. You know it?"

"I have GPS, see you soon."

I punched the name in and began my adventure on the streets of Atlanta, a town I was getting pretty good at navigating. My adventure lasted twenty-five minutes, the address was practically downtown. The place looked nice, kind of classy, not the sort of joint I pictured Sherman grabbing a burger.

I'm here, I texted.

I know, came the answer.

I looked around for the detective and spotted him walking my way. I got out of the car to meet him.

"Thanks Sherman, this means a lot to me." I handed him the paperwork.

"I ain't doin' this as a favor to you, Maher, I'm doin' this on the off chance you're right and this Kincaid woman is a killer. If, and that's a big if, she's done murder, then I want her."

"Is your date good looking?" I teased.

"Best looking woman in the Northern hemisphere; this is our anniversary." He was studying the papers.

I studied his downturned face. It was funny, I hadn't even entertained the idea of him being a married guy. Guess I figured he was married to his job.

"Is she gonna be pissed you left the table to meet me?"

"Nope. After all these years, she understands the job. Besides, she's at the table enjoying a Mai-Tai. Mind if I keep these?" He waved the papers at me.

"Nope, those are extra copies. Can I ask what you intend to do?"

"Well I intend to have a steak, rare, with a loaded potato, several drinks, very satisfying sex, and an excellent night's sleep. In the morning I'll look at your evidence in good light and let you know then. Okay with you?"

"Very okay with me, thanks again."

I got in my car and pointed it toward home; I had a little nugget of hope in my heart that finally I'd nail Jonnie Kincaid. I smiled to myself as the miles zipped past me.

I'd made it nearly all the way home when my cell rang and startled me. I hit the Bluetooth and said, "Maher."

"Sherman. It's morning and I looked at what you got."

I grinned. "I hope your evening was all you hoped it would be, Detective."

I decided his wife really was understanding, since he had gotten out of bed in the middle of the night to call me.

"And more. Here's what I see: this info along with the two deaths and the tape of Kevin Stewart should give me enough to bring this tootsie in and sweat her a little. I'll talk to my boss first thing when I get into the precinct, but I'm fairly sure she'll let me run with this. Can you get me a copy of that interview?"

I blew out a sigh of relief. "I'll send it as soon as I get home. Sherman, you have no idea what this means to me."

"Don't get all mushy on me, Maher, I'm just a guy doing his job."

"Sure. Anyway, I know she's guilty and I want her to pay. She's evil and crafty and she's made it damn personal now. Did I tell you she threatened to kill me if I didn't stop snooping?"

"For real? Wow. Surprising that someone finds you annoying enough to wanna kill," he said.

"On the steps of the courthouse in Nashville, no less."

"Hmmm, ain't that a kick in the ass. She's got brass balls for damn sure," Sherman laughed.

"Glad you can laugh about it. One more thing, this nurse, Gina Martin, I really think she might be in danger – actually, I'm pretty damn sure she is. Anything you can do about it?" I asked.

"Well, I can't put her in protective custody until this goes somewhere, but I can suggest she take a vacation."

"I guess it'll have to do." I was worried; I didn't like Gina but she sure as hell didn't deserve to end up dead.

"You almost home?" Sherman asked.

"Almost, about forty-five minutes out."

"Keep it between the ditches, Maher, and tell your no 'count brother I said he sucks." Sherman laughed at his own humor.

"Will do." I disconnected and laughed out loud.

I'd worked hard on this case, lost my office, been threatened several times by various people and finally, finally I had a little light at the end of the tunnel.

As if on cue, Chick materialized in the seat next to me. I barely flinched, but my heart clenched at the sight of him and all the regret rose up in me.

"TisTis, you gotta take the next right at Dry Creek Road. Somebody's waiting on ya' 'bout three quarters of a mile down this road right at that big curve."

Just as Highway 100 cross from Davidson County into Hickman County, there's a big sweeping curve and an even bigger drop off to one side. There had been more than one fatality in there. But Chick was right and I could simply go around and outfox whoever was waiting on me.

"Damn!" I took the next right and drove like a bat outta hell toward home. I didn't think my ambusher would follow me since I was sure my death, if he meant to kill me, was supposed to look like an accident. Despite such a comforting thought, I turned off my headlights and drove in the dark. I knew the road like the back of my own hand and there was just enough moonlight to be able to navigate. "Thanks, Chick."

He smiled. "You know I got your back. Always did, always will. You should be fine, he won't know you played an end run on him for a bit and by then you'll be home. He's a hired gun."

"Yep, she only personally kills old or sick men who are defenseless. I gave a bunch of info to Connell's friend, Sherman, a detective in Atlanta. We might be seeing the end of this mess. Hey, how'd you know?" I wondered.

"She made a phone call; I told ya we was watching. As far as an end to this? I sure hope so. She's one crazy, pissed off woman." He sounded worried.

For one instant, I had a crazy idea of my own. I thought about slipping around the guy waiting for me so I could surprise him, or at least get a tag number. "Chick?"

"It's a rental, and you need to keep driving," he answered.

"So you *can* read minds," I stated.

"Only yours, darlin'. Only yours."

38

Hanging Judge

On the fifth day of Joe's trial I got an early phone call from Johnny Johnson.

"Morning, girl. You awake?" his familiar voice said.

"Well I am now, JJ, what's up?" I asked as I yawned and sat up, but I knew.

"I think we're gonna need you in court today, we've finished with all the other witnesses. You ready?"

I chuckled. "Hell no, but I reckon I'll get ready. How much hurry do I need to put on this?"

"We'll resume at ten, I'd like you outside the court room about 9:30 so we can go over any last minute details. Don't dally too much, okay?"

"Okay JJ, see you then. Bye."

"See you soon. Bye, bye." We both hung up and I flopped back down on my pillow. I had heard the main defense attorney,

Crowne, had done many variations of a dog and pony show so far to help his client get off. He had most probably failed. Donna's star quality performance, my brother Connell's testimony, the e-mails retrieved from Donna's computer which were read into evidence, Marty's compelling and convincing chronicle of the events, and Joe's fingerprints on the alleged guns were enough for the murder and conspiracy charges. My testimony would put one more nail in Joe's coffin.

I rolled over and started making phone calls to rally the troops. I called Mars, Connell, Mommy, and Jewels, secure in the knowledge I could depend on them to put the word out. I decided a shower was next on my list.

Mommy, Daddy and YaYa were waiting when I hit the kitchen.

"You ready for this?" Daddy asked.

I nodded. "Yes. No. Probably. Y'all coming?"

"Right behind you, kid," YaYa said.

Mommy handed me coffee. "You can do this. We're behind you. I know how strong you are. Go in there and bury this bastard."

She did not insist I eat breakfast, which proved the gravity of the situation.

I kissed them all and made the drive to Nashville. I was as nervous as a long-tailed cat in a room full of rocking chairs. JJ had warned me the defense would do everything possible to discredit my testimony. I tried not to think about what they might say, just tried to keep my head clear. My phone rang about 3000 times but I didn't want to talk to anyone.

JJ and Dina were waiting for me outside the courtroom. They both looked cool and collected. I felt sure I looked like a train wreck.

"Hey y'all," I greeted them.

JJ hugged me. "How you doing, kid?"

"As well as can be expected under the circumstances." I grinned at Dina.

"The defense will try and trip you up, discredit you and might even fall back on the idea you were somehow guilty in this mess. Don't let them make you mad, just stick to the facts. Try to get the jury's sympathy, okay? Keep your cool." She squeezed my hand and I could feel her strength.

"I'll do my best. I know how important my testimony is to the case," I said.

JJ and Dina escorted me into the courtroom. They took their seats at the prosecutor's table and I sat behind them. I prayed for strength and clarity to remember all the facts about one of the worst days of my life.

As the room filled up around me, I became distracted. All my family and many of my friends showed up in court, convinced this would be the last day of the trial and there would be a sentencing. Before the judge took the bench, the courtroom was packed. I smiled, waved and nodded to people as they caught my eye. It seemed everyone in Medicine Springs wanted to be present to see justice done. Mommy must have been busy on the phone to rally so many people.

I was pretty sure Joe wouldn't get the death penalty, almost no one does these days, and more's the pity. Not to get up on my soap box over the issue, but in the case of irrefutable DNA and forensic proof, some bastards need to get dead. Of course, we only had a lot of circumstantial, but still. Joe really needed to die.

Mars and Connell sat down on either side of me and I felt better having them there. Too soon, I heard my name called and it was time. I walked up to the witness stand and took an oath to tell the truth. I looked out on the gallery and saw my family and friends looking back at me.

Dina stood up. "Ms. Maher, I would like for you to tell the court of the events of Sunday, April 22nd of last year."

"I accompanied my family to the races in Medicine Springs after church. I went to the ladies after the main race was finished..." I began.

"Alone?" she asked.

"Yes, alone. The day had been very emotional and I needed a moment to collect myself."

"Please tell the court what transpired next," Dina prompted.

"Someone entered the restroom and I saw in the mirror that a man was behind me. I started to tell him he was in the wrong bathroom but he knocked me unconscious before I could."

"Ms. Maher, did you leave willingly with the man?" Dina asked.

"No, as I said, he surprised me in the ladies' room and hit me in the head."

"Please tell the court the name of the man who assaulted you," she said.

"Joseph 'Joe' McKenzie," I answered.

"Will you point him out for the court, please?"

I pointed to the defense table. "He is sitting at the defense table, next to Mr. Crowne."

"Thank you. Let the record reflect the witness has identified the defendant, Joseph McKenzie. Ms. Maher, will you continue with the events of the day?"

I described every moment from waking up in a basement bound hand and foot, to hitting Rick in the head with a rock. My hands started shaking and I took a deep breath to get a grip on my emotions. I didn't feel guilty exactly, but it was a horrible experience and I wanted to be finished with my testimony.

Dina was all sympathy. "Can you continue?"

I nodded my head.

"Please tell the court what happened next," Dina said kindly.

"I left McKenzie and Journey in the woods, made it to the road, and a farmer picked me up. I don't remember anything else until I woke up in the hospital." I shuddered.

"Your Honor, the state would submit the certified medical records of Ms. Maher. This details her injuries. If it please the court, I would like to read the list of injuries."

The judge nodded and Dina read, "The victim sustained a concussion, a gunshot wound to the head over her ear which required seventeen stitches, a broken jaw which required the jaw to be wired, 6 broken ribs, and numerous cuts and contusions."

Dina walked the list over to the court officer and turned to me. "Do you find this list to be an accurate description of the injuries you sustained, Ms. Maher?"

"Yes," I agreed. My stomach turned a bit.

"Your Honor, State would like to submit pictures taken after the kidnapping into evidence, and have them marked as the next collective exhibit." She walked over to me and handed me the pictures.

There I was in brilliant Technicolor and I thought I would vomit.

"Ms. Maher, are you alright? Can you continue?" Dina asked.

I clenched my jaw and nodded.

"Do you recognize these photos which have just been handed to you?" Dina asked.

I nodded again. "Yes."

"Can you tell us when this first set of pictures were taken?"

"They were taken the first day I was in the hospital."

"And when were these taken?"

I was awake in the next set, and the bruises were darker. "I think these were taken the next day. We took pictures every day for about a week," I said quietly.

"I would ask that I be permitted to publish these photos to the jury, Your Honor. The jury should be warned the pictures are disturbing."

The judge nodded. I stole a glance at the jury and saw many of them were wide eyed and a few looked a bit sick from what they were seeing. *Good*, I thought.

"Ms. Maher, the defendant and his co-conspirators suffered injuries at your hands. The defense would have us believe you were the aggressor. Truthfully, you did a lot of damage to the defendant and his co-conspirators, one of whom will probably never fully recover. Can you explain to this court the level of violence you employed?"

"All I can tell you is I was determined to live. I did everything I could to make sure of my survival. I just didn't want to die," I answered.

"Your Honor, I have no further questions for the witness." Dina sat down.

Crowne stood up. He buttoned his jacket and approached the witness stand.

"Ms. Maher, you claim my client kidnapped you in broad daylight from a public place. How was that possible?"

"I…" I started to answer but he cut me off.

"Did you fight him?"

"No, I…"

Dina stood up. "Objection, Your Honor. If the defense counsel would please allow Ms. Maher to complete her answer without interruption."

Crowne continued, "Did you call for help?"

"Uh…"

"How is it no one noticed you being taken away?" He demanded.

"Objection. Speculation. Ms. Maher can't testify as to what others noticed or didn't and why," Dina said.

I kept my mouth shut; I knew he was attempting to rattle my cage. When I stared at him, he seemed a bit disconcerted. He was hoping I would lose my shit.

"This seems a rather fantastical circumstance," Crowne stated.

"Your Honor, this is badgering," Dina spoke up.

The judge frowned at the defense attorney. "Mr. Crowne, you are on thin ice."

"By all means, Your Honor. Ms. Maher, please answer the questions." Crowne practically sneered at me.

"I was taken by surprise from behind. The defendant hit me in the head. I have no idea how he got me out of the building. I do know everyone else was watching the races. There was no one to see my kidnapping." My poker face was in place.

"No one, in broad daylight, saw anything. Is it possible because you left willingly?" Crowne leaned forward.

"No," I answered.

He clearly expected me to have a longer answer, but I knew I needed to keep my answers short and sweet and not give him any ammunition to use against me. I'd been well prepared by JJ and Dina.

"It's your word against his. There are no witnesses, as you have already stated. This does cast doubt on your testimony. The court might wonder, the jury might wonder, and indeed I wonder if you really were the victim here."

"Objection. Is there a question here? Defense counsel is testifying." Dina sounded a bit snappish.

"Sustained." The judge sounded snappish, too.

"I was kidnapped by the defendant, Joseph McKenzie." I wanted to say more, but wisely clamped my mouth shut on the rest.

"You shot the defendant. You severely wounded the other two men. How did you manage so much damage if you were the victim? It certainly sounds as if you were in control of the situation from the start."

"Yes, I shot him, and wounded the other two," I admitted.

Crowne smiled a wolfish smile at me as if he had me where he wanted me. "Why don't you tell the court what really happened, and please remember you are under oath. We believe there is much more to this then you have told. There is speculation in some law enforcement circles that you and the defendants were involved and you had a falling out?"

"No," I said.

"Perhaps you decided to cut your losses and simply murder the defendant?" Crowne seemed very proud of his idea.

"No," I said again.

"Objection, Your Honor!" Dina spoke out. "This is defense counsel's pure speculation: the defense has no proof of any connection between the defendant and Ms. Maher. This is not even a fishing expedition; it is the spinning of fantasy. We move to strike."

Judge Fontaine cast a steely glaze at the defense attorney. "Mr. Crowne, we do not deal in rumor in my court room. Strike the question and the jury will disregard."

"Yes, Your Honor. Ms. Maher, perhaps you believed, mistakenly, this man had a hand in Charles Donnelly's death and you sought revenge." Crowne moved closer to me. "Ms. Maher, you are under oath and I am sure you know perjury is punishable by imprisonment. You don't wish to risk jail, I am sure. You wouldn't fare very well in prison." He smiled at me.

Dina stood up. "Your Honor, the defense is badgering the witness."

"Mr. Crowne, this is your second warning," Fontaine stated.

"Your Honor, I am simply trying to get to the truth. Ms. Maher, would you have the court believe you managed to escape captivity, seriously wound three men whom you claim were trying to kill you, and come out relatively unscathed?"

I counted to three before I spoke. "Yes."

Relatively unscathed, who the hell was he kidding?

"Isn't it true you were the aggressor? You stalked and attacked these men who were unaware of your presence?" he snapped.

"No. No. No. I was trying to save my life." I answered.

Dina stood up. "Your Honor, is there a point to this line of questioning, a term I use loosely in this case? Is the defense attorney going somewhere?"

From the look on his face, Judge Fontaine was clearly irritated. "Mr. Crowne, the witness has answered and the court is getting weary of this line of questions. Are you done?"

"I submit to the court the lists of injuries done to Mr. McKenzie by this witness and I ask to read the list in to evidence."

The judge nodded.

"Joseph McKenzie suffered a gunshot wound to the abdomen for which he underwent six surgeries to repair the damage to his internal organs. He coded, meaning he died, seven times. The gunshot wound was delivered, by her own admission, by Tess Maher." He looked at the jury as he spoke.

"I was fighting for my life," I stated.

Crowne leaned toward me. "The truth, Ms. Maher, tell the court the truth. What really happened?"

"I was fighting for my life," I repeated.

"The truth, Ms. Maher, is you intended murder." He voice was raised.

"I was fighting for my life."

Crowne slammed his fist on the bar in front of me. "TELL THE TRUTH!"

"Your Honor!" Dina said angrily.

"Mr. Crowne, you have been warned. You are badgering the witness and I will not put up with any more of it." Fontaine did not look happy.

"I was fighting for my life," I said it calmly and locked eyes with Crowne. I was determined not to let the bastard get to me.

Crowne looked at the jury again, then he walked back to the defense table and had a discussion with his co-council. After a moment or two he turned to the judge.

"The defense is finished with this witness, Your Honor." He must have known the jury wasn't buying what he was selling.

"General, redirect?" The judge instructed.

Dina stood up. "No, Your Honor, the State rests its case-in-chief."

"Ms. Maher, you are excused."

I wasted no time getting out of the witness box. I felt like I had been drug through a knothole backwards. I took my seat with my family and got winks and nods from them all.

"Does the defense have any witnesses to present to the court?" Fontaine asked.

I expected Crowne to call Joe to the stand, but to my surprise he didn't. Probably a wise move, I was sure Joe would only dig his grave deeper with his winning personality.

"The defense rests, Your Honor," Crowne said.

"Is the State ready to proceed with closing argument at this time?" Judge Fontaine asked.

"We are, Your Honor," Dina answered.

"Are you prepared to give your closing arguments, Mr. Crowne?" the judge asked.

"The defense is ready, Your Honor," Crowne answered.

"Ladies and gentlemen of the jury, this concludes the proof presented at this trial. Because the State has the burden of proof in this case, you will hear from the State twice. The State will argue first, and the defense will be permitted to respond after the State's first close. After defense counsel makes his closing argument, the State will be offered a chance to make rebuttal-closing argument," the judge instructed.

Dian stood and addressed the jury. "Ladies and gentlemen of the jury. Overwhelming evidence of the guilt of Mr. McKenzie has been presented today. The defense would have you believe Mr. McKenzie is a poor lost soul who had fallen in with bad companions who led him astray. I offer to you the facts: Mr. McKenzie has been in and out of trouble on his own for most of his life. Mr. McKenzie is no Boy Scout. The state believes him to be the man in charge of the operation for procuring land in Medicine Springs, TN. We base this on information given in testimony. As such he made the plans, gave the other men orders and made sure they were followed. From Donna Maples, you have heard how he acted a bully and how he frightened and intimated her, and how he bragged about the murder of Charles Donnelly. Tess Maher testified, under oath, that she was kidnapped and held hostage by the defendant, who attempted to murder her." She continued to read off a list of evidence against Joe. "This man is a dangerous menace to society. If justice is to be served, you must find him guilty. You must. You can do no less and still live with yourselves. You can do no less if you desire to make the world a better place. You can do no less if the peace and safety of places like Medicine Springs are to be preserved. You must find Joseph McKenzie guilty on all counts. You have been presented with the facts. Please do your duty."

Dina took a moment to look each juror in the eye before she resumed her seat.

Crowne stood up, buttoned his jacket, and moved to stand in front of the jury. He pointed to Joe.

"My client grew up in a broken home with an alcoholic, abusive father, and lived in abject poverty. He got in a few scrapes in his youth, by his own admission, but what man among us hasn't? He even spent some time in juvenile detention. Then he turned his life around, determined to get on the right path. He was hired by Aggroco, one of the largest producers of fruit and vegetables in the world. They took a chance on him. In fact, he has been chosen as employee of the year for three years in a row. Since his employment with Aggroco he has been an upstanding citizen who attends church regularly, contributes to charities, pays his taxes, is a good neighbor, and a great employee. He has not had so much as a parking ticket. In short, this man you see before you has done everything humanly possible to change his life and become a decent, contributing member of society. How then did he come to be in this court room fighting for his freedom and possibly his life?" Crowne paused for effect and I tried not to puke.

Crowne was laying on the charm, and he was leading man handsome, so the members of the jury were hanging on every word. Several of them were nodding in agreement.

"Joseph McKenzie found himself in a precarious position. He was sent by his employers to Medicine Springs to do a job. The job was to procure land for his company, which would in turn bring employment and revenue to the town. But Joe's companions were in a hurry, willing to cut corners and take chances. Sadly, people died. One of the people who died was an employee of Aggroco, James Todd. We may never know the truth surrounding his death, but we do know he was shot by one of the witnesses who gave testimony here, Tessely Maher. How do we trust her when there is so much we do not know about her involvement? Did she have a hand in Mr. Donnelly death? Was she really kidnapped? Is she really a victim? Again, we may never know. So much finger pointing obscures the truth. You've heard testimony from Donna Maples, who swore under oath that Mr. McKenzie admitted to the commission of the murder of Charles Donnelly. Let me remind you, Ms. Maples broke the law by accepting over a million dollars from Aggroco and she has been given immunity from prosecution. So how do we trust her word? I don't believe we can. The question remains: who killed Charles Donnelly? I say the prosecution has failed to show proof Joseph McKenzie actually did the deed, or even put him at the scene of the murder."

I could feel my temper rising. My face felt hot and I had to physically restrain myself from jumping up and screaming. I was sitting between Mars and Connell and each of them reached over and took my hands. I calmed down, but only a little.

Crowne continued, "Oh yes, the prosecution has shown you all manner of what they claim is evidence: guns, maps, emails, autopsy reports, pictures, medical records. An endless parade of what they claim is proof my client is a murderer. But I will tell you they have not shown you unequivocal proof. Which, ladies and gentlemen of the jury, is what you must have to find my client guilty of any of the crimes with which he is charged. You must demand iron-clad, undeniable, incontrovertible proof. You do not have it. Therefore, you must acquit Mr. McKenzie. Take a good look at Mr. McKenzie. You see a good, decent, god-fearing, law-abiding man who found himself in an untenable situation which spiraled out from beyond his control. He is a young man; if you send him to prison, given the dangerous conditions, bad food and bad medical care he will endure, he may not live to be an old man. This will be on your conscience."

Crowne returned to his seat with a sad look on his face.

Dina stood up and walked to the jury. "Joseph McKenzie has been in and out of trouble for much of his life. He is a man many people fear because he would do whatever it took to get what he wanted. Charles Donnelly, James Todd, and Tessely Maher stood in his way. You have seen the guns, read the ballistics reports, heard testimony from one of his co-conspirators, Donna Maples, and from one of the victims, Tess Maher, and many, many others. His fingerprints are on the murder weapon and on the gun which killed James Todd. True, Mr. Todd was shot by Tess Maher when he, McKenzie, Journey, and Martin came to her house in the dead of night to murder her in her bed. But her shot was not the one which ultimately killed Todd. His life was ended by a shot to the back of the head, delivered from a .357. Mr. McKenzie's fingerprints are on the gun. The prosecution believes Charles Donnelly was a victim of circumstance, a man who was in the wrong place at the wrong time. James Todd was a victim of being a loose end. Tess Maher was a person whom McKenzie believed knew too much. Mr. Crowne would have you believe Mr. McKenzie is a victim of circumstance, a man who was not in control of the events which took place in Medicine Springs, yet the evidence and the testimony will tell you otherwise. This is a man who let nothing stand in his way, a man who is ruthless. He is guilty on all counts. I implore you to find him guilty. Do your duty and take a dangerous criminal off the streets before he kills again." She paused for effect. "One more thing: we have no idea how old Mr. McKenzie will be when he dies in prison. But we do know how old Charles Donnelly was when he died by McKenzie's hand – he was twenty-eight years old."

Dina resumed her seat.

Tears were rolling down my cheeks and I feared I would start sobbing. My chest hurt, my heart reminding me once again how broken it was. I looked at the jury and saw several of them were staring at me. I wondered what they were thinking.

Judge Fontaine addressed the jury. "You have heard testimony, seen the evidence, and now you must do your duty. Bailiff, please see them to the jury room."

The jury stood and the bailiff escorted them from the courtroom.

"We are at recess until the jury returns with a verdict," Fontaine said. Then he stood up and retired to his chambers.

"All rise," the bailiff commanded.

"What do you think?" I whispered.

"I think we have a good shot at life," Connell whispered back.

I refused to go down the street to eat or get coffee. I wanted to sit in the courthouse and wait for the jury to find him guilty as charged.

They deliberated for a mere two hours. We were called back into the courtroom and I entered with a black hope in my heart.

Judge Fontaine looked down at Joe from the bench with an expression as grim as the grave. The courtroom was so silent you could have heard the proverbial pen drop.

"Will the foreman please read the verdict?" he asked.

The foreman stood and read from a paper in her hand. "In the death of Charles Donnelly, we find the defendant guilty of aggravated murder in the first degree. In the death of James Todd, we find the defendant guilty of murder in the first degree. In the kidnapping of Tess Maher, we find the defendant guilty. In the assault to commit murder of Tess Maher, we find the defendant guilty. In the bribery of a public official of the state of Tennessee, we find the defendant guilty. In conspiracy to commit murder, we find the defendant guilty."

She resumed her seat.

"Joseph McKenzie, a jury of your peers has found you guilty of all charges which were brought against you. Under state law it falls to me to pass sentence on you. Mr. McKenzie, you can never truly pay for the life of the innocent man which you took, but you'll pay a terrible price none the less. I hereby sentence you to life in prison without the possibility of parole."

Fontaine smacked the bench with his gavel. "Members of the jury, I thank you for fulfilling your civic duty in this matter. Deputy, please take custody of Mr. McKenzie. This court is dismissed."

I was so relieved I almost cried. It didn't change anything, Chick was still dead, and my life was forever altered, as were the lives of everyone who loved him. But Joe McKenzie would never see another day without bars between him and the sun. It was a victory and it had to be enough.

The deputy took hold of Joe's arm and slapped the cuffs on him, turning him sideways and as he did Joe's eyes locked on mine. The look was cold and deadly. I was glad he was restrained, because if looks could kill I'd have been a grease spot. I made myself smile at him.

Crowne jumped to his feet. "We will appeal this unjust verdict!"

Fontaine never said another word, he simply stood up and pinned Crowne with a steely look.

"All rise," the bailiff intoned.

Everyone did and the judge left the bench. I saw Crowne was in a frantic conversation with his client and the other attorneys, probably assuring him he'd get the verdict overturned. *Fat chance*, I thought.

"I say this calls for a celebration dinner at the house later!" Mommy declared.

Everyone agreed. It would be nice to wash the taste of the trial from our mouths.

"Okay, it's been great fun, but I have to go back to work, not like I've been slacking over the last week, but I'll see you all later," I said.

YaYa pulled me close. "This is good, kid. Be thankful."

I sighed and closed my eyes.

"I am YaYa, I am. But I'd be more thankful if Joe got the death penalty. He doesn't deserve to live," I said loud enough for everyone in the courtroom to hear. Several people turned in my direction.

"You're right, he don't, but let me tell you somethin': you don't never teach a man a lesson by killin' him and Joe has some lessons to learn, I'm thinkin'." YaYa nodded her head at me emphasis.

I smiled at her. "You just might be right."

"Always am," she declared. "So you hurry up and do what you gotta do and then come home. I'm gonna make a special treat for this celebration: white rose pudding."

I raised an eyebrow. She usually only made rose pudding once a year at Christmas. It really is made with roses and tastes like heaven on a spoon.

"Okay, I will hurry."

I hugged and kissed my family, but it took a while to actually get out of the courtroom. I was hugged, patted, and congratulated by most of the folks from home who had shown up. Sammy Jensen was there and he wrapped me in bear hug.

"How you doing girl?" he asked.

"I'll do. Where's Billy?"

"Aw, you can't get him to come to the big city, there's too many cops here for his likin'. 'Cides which it's probably best he don't never lay eyes on McKenzie."

I considered his wisdom and nodded. "Probably right. By the way, we're havin' a 'thank god Joe's goin' to prison' party at the house later, you're invited."

Sammy smiled at me. "Aw, I reckon I can see my way clear for that."

He kissed me on the cheek.

I eventually made my exit. I turned my phone on as I left the court house and it immediately rang. I thumbed it on.

"Hello."

"You must think you're very clever." The voice was cold as a glacier but I recognized it.

I stopped dead in my tracks and surveyed my surroundings.

"Good morning, Jonnie," I said cheerfully. "Where are you?"

"Bitch! You think you've proven something, you have less than nothing. Coincidence and happenstance cobbled together to make a bullshit pie. Your detective friend fancies himself as something brilliant but he's just another underpaid asshole," she snarled.

"Not like the overpaid asshole you tried to sic on me? I saw how well he did his job." I couldn't help twisting the knife a bit.

"Don't break your arm patting yourself on the back. I don't know how you knew and it doesn't matter. The gloves are off. I'm coming for you." Her voice was low and cold.

If she had been wearing gloves so far, I couldn't wait to see what happened next. Still, I couldn't rest poking the bear.

"God, you sound like a bad movie script. You sure you don't wanna tell me you master plan for world dominance before you fail to kill me?" I said. What can I say? I am a smart ass.

"Let's see who laughs last." The line went dead.

I sighed and called Sherman, since I was pretty sure he was the catalyst for the crazy phone call.

He answered, "Sherman."

"Tess. What the hell happened?" I demanded.

Sherman laughed. "Well, good morning to you too, Sunshine, I hope you're havin' a pleasant day. So, I got the green light from my boss, called Jonnie Kincaid and invited her down here to the precinct. She was reluctant and suspicious but I convinced her it was in her best interest to get in front of the info I had."

"And then?" I was impatient and he was dragging the story out.

"Then she waltzed in her like she owned the damn joint, Miss High and Mighty. I can see why you don't like her. I showed her some of what I had, told her what I suspected, and asked if she had anything to say to me. Turned out she had a lot to say to me, mostly 'bout my parents never havin' been married, how she had the mayor on speed dial, she'd have my job, and something about what a dumb, redneck cracker I was. Can't remember the exact wordin', cocksucker may have been in it, but none of it was flatterin'." He chuckled.

"Wow. Well, she just called me, insinuated she had someone try and ambush me the other night on my way home from Atlanta, and now she was coming for me in person," I said. It was a little white lie but I felt no guilt.

"Well, well, well, ain't she just the cat's meow? Alright, she's got a tail on ya but I bet you know how to lose him."

"Yeah, I think I'd better start practicing my cloak and dagger, mad ninja drivin' skills."

"Yep. After I had my conversation with Kincaid, I called the nursin' home and got your friend Nurse Gina's number. Had to pull rank on 'em to get it. Anyhoo, I gave her the lowdown on what we suspected. Told her she needed to go see her sister for a few days and if she didn't have a sister, she needed to get one. She kinda freaked out and started spewin' information at me so fast it was hard to take notes. She's scared of two things: getting dead and going to jail. But I think she'll be a good witness if we can manage to keep her alive." He was grinning, I could tell. "She promised to call me every day."

I laughed with relief. "This is all good, Sherman."

"Don't go counting your chickens, Maher, this broad is gonna be a tough nut to crack. At the end of the day we only got circumstantial at best; a good lawyer'll chew us up and shit us out." The grin had disappeared from his voice.

"Yep, and she can afford a good one. Okay, thanks again, Sherman. Keep in touch," I said.

"Maher, you got good instincts, not like I'd expect any less from you given your DNA. You watch your cute ass; this ain't over by a long shot." Sherman hung up.

He was right – not just about my ass, even though it was cute, but about the case. I could almost feel crosshairs being trained on me. I wanted more coffin nails for the bitch and decided it was time to call Georgia and the Kincaid offspring and bring them into the loop. I wanted confirmation that Jillian told the Lady Macbeth about the investigation. If I could get it, I might be able to tie the bitch to my office fire and add another log to her funeral pyre. It was worth a shot.

I jumped in the Jeep as my family caught up to me.

"Hey gang," I greeted them.

My father cocked an eye at me and leaned on my door.

"What do you know?" he asked. Damn he was good; he could read me like a book. "Somethin's happened from the time you walked out of the courthouse 'til just now. What?"

I just looked at him for a few seconds. I could see Mommy and YaYa were all ears and had to decide how much to tell them. Too much and they'd have coronaries on the spot. Too little and they'd be all over me like ducks on a June bug.

"I have collaborating evidence which links Jonnie Kincaid to the murder of her husband and Kevin Stewart. I gave copies of said evidence to Detective Sherman of the Atlanta PD, since the murders happened in his city. He called in the widow and had conversation with her. He claims she'll be a tough nut to crack and I agree. Therefore, I'm gonna call the Kincaid children and the ex-wife for a pow-wow. One of the Kincaid children tipped off Lady Macbeth about the investigation and I want her to admit it while I record her. That is all I know."

By the time I'd finished my narrative several more members of the clan had gathered around the Jeep. No one spoke for several seconds as they digested my info.

"You figure to get the kid to admit this and use it against the widow?" Daddy asked.

"How will that help?" Mommy asked.

"It may help to prove Jonnie knew I was investigating her, makes her a suspect for the arson to my office and it just makes her look guiltier. I need every scrap of evidence I can get on her, this case is too thin."

I remembered the taunting phone call from Jonnie when she said the same thing. She was right, we had very little.

"I wanna bury her in circumstantial evidence and hope it will be enough to indict and get a conviction," I answered.

"Whaddaya think the odds are, kid?" YaYa asked.

"Not great. We have to spook her, trip her up, surprise her so badly she makes a mistake," I blew out a breath; when I heard myself say it out loud it seemed even thinner.

Do you ever get a feeling of doom? Like something bad is just over the horizon, just out of sight but coming your way like a freight train? I had one and tried not to show it to my family. I must have done a lousy job, because YaYa reached over and patted my arm.

"Chin up, Toots, you'll rule the day yet. Have a little faith." She grinned at me.

I nodded, she was right. "I know this woman committed two murders, burned my building, and tortures little animals. She's a bad person and I know we'll nail her. I have faith." I blew kisses. "See ya tonight."

I punched up the office as I drove away and Jewels answered on the first ring.

"Hey Boss. How did it go?" she asked.

"Joe got life, he made mean eyes at me, his lawyer promised to appeal, blah blah blah."

"Okay, that's about what you thought would happen, right?" she asked.

"Right but it's still a letdown. I got work for you. Please call Georgia Kincaid and all her children, I want a pow-wow to bring 'em into the loop. Let 'em know what I know so far."

"Un-huh and what are you really after?" she asked.

I laughed. "You know me too well. What I really want is to get Jillian to admit, on the record, she informed Lady Macbeth of the investigation. I just need everything I can get to make that bitch look bad."

"Right, I'll start making calls. You on your way back in?"

"Yep, see you soon." I broke contact and headed for home, careful to keep a watchful eye out for whoever was tailing me.

39

Smoke on the Water

"Boss," Jewels said as I walked in the office, "the Kincaids will be at their country house this weekend, apparently getting it ready for the summer, and they'd be delighted if you'd join them."

I laughed. "I'll bet they aren't all delighted."

"But wait, there's more. According to the state bomb and arson investigator, the insurance investigator, the state Fire Marshall, and Jim Leach, you're cleared of any involvement in the burning of your building!"

I closed my eyes and took a deep breath, it was such good news. I'd been a little worried.

"Details?" I asked.

"Your financials, for a start. They're good, so there's no money motive. The force it took to kick the door in was more than you could deliver; they said it had to have been a very large man. I guess no one has seen you kick box. Next, no one has any record of you buying extra gasoline in the county and your car is too hard to miss. It was decided someone would have spotted you. You make enemies in your line of work, so they'll be looking for someone with revenge as a motive. I gave everyone who wanted it the info on all the cases you've been working. You're in the clear." She smiled.

"Wow, thank you, God, thank you. I admit I was a little bit worried about my fans in the TBI. So this means we can get started on construction?" I breathed a huge sigh of relief.

"Yep, I've already made calls to get the bids started." Jewels was beaming.

I hugged her. "Thanks, Jewels, for sticking with me through this and being the friend you are. Thank you."

I suddenly had tears running down my face. Jewels did too. "I love you and I'm proud of the work we do and I get to work here with you. You're welcome."

I threw my head back and yelled, "Wooo-hoooo!" as I swung Jewels around the room in silly dance, but oh God I was so happy! My antics woke up the cat, who looked at me disdainfully, jumped down off my desk, and sauntered away. I laughed some more.

"Can we get in the building?" I asked.

"Yep, we are free to enter as we please." Jewels grinned at me.

"Call all the other tenants and give them the green light, then call my mother and tell her. I'm positive that'll be the only phone call you have to make to family, she'll inform the troops." I grabbed my keys from my bag.

"Where are you goin' now?" Jewels demanded.

"I'm getting my workout clothes and changing and going to the office. I can't wait to get in there," I answered.

I was as good as my word; I changed in a flash and then headed to the building. I thought I was prepared for what I would find. I was wrong. As I crossed the threshold into the hallway, the stench hit me in the face. It was horrible and made my stomach roll. I walked toward my office and realized what a mess the wood floors were; the water had damaged them severely. I really hated that, the floors were original to the building.

I climbed through what was left of my door and froze in my tracks. The door was laying several feet inside the room and was burned to a crisp. The walls were toast; most of the furniture in the front room was black and twisted. The pictures on the walls were ruined and my license, which had been hanging above Jewel's desk, would never be the same. The computer was a melted grey lump. The external hard drive was in even worse shape. Good thing we had a backup in the cloud. There were just so many things in the room I couldn't recognize. I should know what everything was given the locations, but I couldn't wrap my brain around what I was seeing. It was just all burned and melted. I felt a lump form in my throat.

There was a hole burned in the ceiling. I looked up and could see Melanie's bookkeeping service – or what was left of it. She might have suffered a total loss from what I observed, everything just looked black. Beyond her space I could see sunlight through a blue tarp.

Suddenly the light was blocked out by a person peering down at me: she was small and spare of frame, and her long brown curly hair was trying to escape from the tie-dye bandana she was wearing around her head.

"Hey, Mel. You got here fast," I said.

"Hey Tess, I've got friends in the department so I got the word and came down. I'm sure sorry about this mess." She wrinkled her nose at me.

"Me too, fortunately everyone has insurance. I hope you didn't lose anything irreplaceable. I just feel terrible."

"Why? You didn't start the fire. I lost my fish, but ya know, they were fish, honey." She chuckled ruefully. "All my files are backed up on a remote and I was tired of my office furniture anyway. How 'bout you?"

"Same. Mel, since it is officially arson…"

"Hmp, anybody you know?" Mel interrupted me.

"Most likely, so if you feel like you need to move out cause this building…"

"You can stop right there. How long have we known each other, girly girl? Since you were in knickers and trailing after your brothers, that's how long. You've been a friend to me and I won't jump ship just 'cause the water's gotten a little choppy. Don't think you can get rid of me so easy. I reckon the rest of your tenants'll feel the same."

I smiled. Despite her speech, which made her sound ancient, Mel was only a few years older than me. "Thanks Mel, that means a lot."

"I'm glad we got a tarp for the windows and the roof, which did us some good, I'm thinkin'."

I smiled at her. "Billy climbed up there and attached it."

"I'll thank him for it when I see 'em. The boy's turned out alright. Keep calm and carry on, then," she said and disappeared as abruptly as she had appeared. I blessed her.

I went into my private office. The fire had caused very little damage there. It mostly looked smoked up; the walls were grey and the blinds coated with soot. I hoped to write them off as a total loss, they looked just horrible. The carpet was a mess from the water, too.

"Wow! This place smells like somebody pissed on a campfire!" Brian yelled from the other room.

I poked my head out. "You have such a way with words, brother."

He grinned at me for a moment and then grew serious. "So how bad?"

"Mel's office is a total loss, mine's about half. Everybody else probably only has smoke damage, thank God! I'll know more when the other tenants get here and get a good look. Jewels is calling them all. The roof'll have to be repaired and I'm gonna try and make the insurance cough up the money to have the entire thing replaced."

"Oh my God, the stench in this place is awful!" my mother exclaimed as she entered through the burned door frame. "And why are you two in here without masks on, are you insane?" She didn't wait for an answer. "It can't be healthy. Here, put these on," she demanded as she pulled masks from the bag she had draped over her arm.

Her bag held more surprises; she produced rubber gloves, work gloves, aprons, goggles, and heavy-duty trash bags.

"Let's get busy," she ordered. She must have had it ready just waiting for the all clear call. She was something.

"I need to order a dumpster." I hadn't thought of it earlier.

"Fine, make phone calls, your brother and I will start filling trash bags," Mommy said.

My brother rolled his eyes at me but did as our mother bid him. I escaped to the hallway to make my calls. Sometimes, my mother was a force of nature.

Mars and Darlene came in the front door and I waved to them.

"I'm making phone calls; Mommy and Brian are already inside." I explained.

"Oh goody, she'll work us down to our socks," Mars said and Darlene giggled.

I called Jewels. "Hey babe, could you call and find us a dumpster? Then would you call Georgia and tell her I will be happy to join her and her family on Saturday morning? I should be sick of the smell of this place by then."

"Oh Boss, how bad is it really?" She sounded worried.

"It's every bit as bad as you might imagine. After you make the phone calls, come down and have a look for yourself," I offered.

"Roger." Jewels hung up.

I headed back inside the office to find a beehive of activity. Trash bags were being filled by folks so suited up they looked like they worked in a toxic waste dump. Fire is weird; it can burn an entire room and you might still find one unburned treasure to salvage. We didn't find much in the way of salvage in the front office though, just burned and melted slag. What a mess it was to deal with and the longer we worked, the less it seemed we accomplished.

I was shoving something I didn't recognize into a trash bag when a voice at my back said, "Well this is certainly one hell of a mess."

I turned around and found Eddie Murdock standing in my door way – rather, he was filling what had been my door way. Eddie is big and fat and obnoxious, and he fancies himself a real ladies' man. Ugh. He's the son of the guy who owns the local paper, the Noon Day Times or, as some wags like to call it, the 'No Duh Times'. This is due to the fact by the time the Noon Day runs a story, everyone in the county already knows all the details. Keep in mind it's a daily paper, not a weekly.

"People keep saying that," I sighed as I pulled off my surgical mask. "What can I do for you?"

He smiled what I was sure he thought was a sexy and alluring smile. I've seen sexier sick cats.

"Well, you haven't been returning my phone calls and I thought you might like to make a statement in person about your little fire here." He cocked his head to one side like a large bird.

"Well, it seems I've had a rather large fire, the cause of which has yet to be determined. No one was harmed, except some fish. Mel's place is a total loss and mine is about a fifty percent loss. Most of the other offices have received only smoke and water damage. Everyone had insurance. Plus, you've already run an article about my fire which was not so nice. That's it, end of statement." I stared at him hard.

"Word on the street is arson," he said it in a knowing voice.

I snorted, I couldn't help it.

"Word on the street?" I echoed. "What street, Eddie? Main Street? Or is it Mimosa Avenue? This ain't the big city, pal, there's no network of snitches for you to go to, just people gossiping in the Piggly Wiggly."

I became aware all activity in the office had stopped and everyone was giving their undivided attention to our exchange. I was being snippy and a bitch but I decided I wasn't going to tell him jack shit. Let him work for the information.

Eddie drew himself up to his full 6 feet 2 inch height. It didn't help and he still looked like the Pillsbury Dough boy, just not as cute.

"Look Tess, I'm just trying to do my job you don't have to be snippy about it," he whined.

"Eddie, you could do your job a lot more efficiently if you weren't such a dick. You could come in here and say something sympathetic to me about the fire, which would set me up to be nice in return. But you come struttin' in here and talk smack to me about what a mess I got, actin' like you know somethin' you don't know. I've had many, many long days with about no hours of sleep, lots of anxiety, too much caffeine, and a fair amount of pissed off to top the mix. Go write somethin' and leave me to my misery."

I turned back to the trash bag I'd been filling and ignored Eddie. After about ten seconds of him staring holes in my back, I heard him turn and lumber away.

No one said a word to me; they all quietly returned to their work.

The dumpster arrived and we filled it with stuff which had once been useful. When you look at a good portion of your life and it's nothing but burned pieces of paper and melted plastic, it reminds you how fleeting life is, how transitory, and how precious too.

After, I wasn't sure how many hours passed, Mommy addressed the crowd.

"We are having dinner at the house this evening. All of you are invited, so bring an appetite. It's time to stop now, we don't want to work ourselves into the ground, so finish what you're doing and let's go home."

We dutifully finished our tasks at hand and as we started out of the building, I yelled at the ceiling, "Hey Mel, you coming to the house?"

"Sure enough, I'll be there," the answer floated down to me.

I checked my phone for the time and was amazed when it read 4:07. I could have sworn we had been working for many more hours. I took one more look at my charred building, then I climbed into the jeep and drove home.

Many people came to the house, and most of them brought something to add to the meal. It is the South after all, and we rarely turn up empty handed. We talked and laughed and ate and drank. It was a surreal night, like the events after a funeral. I felt like I was moving through a dream. I can't tell you who was there or what food was consumed. It all tasted like ashes, even my YaYa's world famous rose pudding. I spent a lot of the night trying not to cry.

Nine to Five

I slept late the next morning, or rather afternoon. I was exhausted and sore to boot. After I woke I lay in my bed and pondered the events of the past few weeks. A crazy woman had, sent me a dead rat as a present, set my building on fire, hired a thug to run me off the road, all designed to scare me off a case. My mind was officially boggled; how did I proceed in light of such information?

Since I was no longer working undercover, I could stop being circumspect. Maybe I could push the bitch into revealing herself in front of witnesses, or even confessing. I was pretty sure she was too smart to out herself, but it was nice to think about.

I decided lying in bed daydreaming would not push the matter forward. I needed to shake the trees and rattle the bushes or bite something. I got up determined to get my run completed, grab a fast breakfast, and then tackle the problem head-on.

When I got downstairs the kitchen was empty, which was odd. I poked my head into the dining room and called, "Mommy? Daddy? YaYa?"

The only response was the pitter patter of doggie feet coming my way. The herd of four rounded the corner into the kitchen and looked at me expectantly as if they wanted food or something.

"What's up, gang? Where are all the other humans? Has the rapture happened? Did the mothership finally arrive?"

With every question I asked, the dogs wagged their tails harder and panted at me in excitement, pink tongues lolling from their mouths.

"You want breakfast?" I asked.

They exploded all around me, dancing and barking, the silly things.

"Okay, come on."

I got food and bowls from the pantry and filled them. Everyone set to work eating the kibble. When I was little I tried a bit of kibble myself because the dogs ate the stuff as if it was ambrosia. It's not, so save yourself the trouble. I scored yogurt and a grapefruit from the fridge; there was coffee in the pot and it was still warm. It dawned on me my folks were at my building and had let me sleep in. So sweet but completely unnecessary. One of the downsides to living at home at my age is, sometimes, they forget you're not still a child.

I put breakfast aside to do my run. The dogs actually left their kibble to keep me company. It was nice to be outside and it helped to blow the ash out of my nostrils and the cobwebs out of my brain. By the time I'd finished my run, I'd also finished creating my plan of action.

I grabbed my phone and called Jewels as I cut up grapefruit.

"Hey Boss, what's up?" She sounded chipper. "And how are you holding up?"

"Well, I'm better than I was yesterday and not as good as I'll be tomorrow. Gimme the address for the lake house, please."

"It's up around Kentucky Lake. Number fourteen Jonathan Point Rd. in Benton Kentucky. I have confirmed all the Kincaids are there and waiting on you."

"That's a decent drive, about two hours I think." I was silent for a minute, remembering the last road trip I'd taken and how I managed to avoid getting run off a bad stretch of road. I had to wonder if someone would try to waylay me again on my way to the lake.

"Boss?" Jewels asked.

"Huh? Oh, it's nothing, just zoned out. Okay, I'll GPS it. Will you call Georgia and tell her I'm on my way? Give her an ETA. Hold down the fort."

"Will do." She broke the connection.

I finished my breakfast and grabbed a quick shower. I had really slept in, by the time I got to Georgia's lake house it would be late afternoon. I broke some speed limits on the trip, with my GPS lady giving me directions all the way.

Kentucky Lake is massive. It's the largest artificial lake by surface in the United States and despite its name it also crosses the state line into Tennessee. It's a recreational mecca for every kind of water sport and activity and the land of the vacation home. I had no trouble finding Jonathan Point Road in Benton, Kentucky, it ran alongside Jonathan Creek. The homes were breathtaking, and, if I knew anything about real estate, expensive.

I found the house with the large number 14 on the mailbox; it was a lovely log house with a circular driveway. Very cool. I pulled in past the SUV, Volvo wagon, and two sports cars in the drive and parked. I paused for a moment to admire the house and the view as the sun dipped low in the sky. My moment was interrupted by the phone.

"Hello?"

"Maher, Sherman. We may have a problem."

"Great, just what I wanna hear. What kind of a problem?" I got a sudden pain in the pit of stomach.

"Our suspect has dropped off the radar. It looks suspicious, so much so warrants have been issued. Innocent people don't usually bug out, ya know. I talked to the daughter and she says she doesn't have a clue. I'm inclined to believe her." He sounded grumpy.

"Where does this put us?" I asked. Warning bells were going off in my head so loudly I was surprised Sherman failed to hear them.

"I think she's pulling a Houdini. If she's smart then she's on a plane to South America right now," Sherman said.

"Okay, but all the same, I think I'll watch my back real careful like. She's nuts and pissed off, a rather dangerous combination," I said grimly.

"Uh-huh, that'd be my advice. Keep your gun hand free and unencumbered." Sherman hung up.

"Great," I muttered as I climbed out of the Jeep.

I walked up the front steps and rang the bell. A dog barked from somewhere inside and Georgia answered the door. She seemed pleased to see me.

"Welcome Tess, I'm so glad you're here. You must have good news for us, I hope." She smiled.

Georgia ushered me in the door. The place was beautiful, but not over the top, and rustic, but not Davy Crockett rustic. She or her decorator had exceptionally good taste.

"Please come in and have a seat, I've made coffee," she offered.

The floor plan was open and I could see most of the downstairs from the front door: a living room, dining room, both large, doors to the right, and beyond the dining room there was a staircase to the left. All of the Kincaid offspring were seated in the living room. I nodded and smiled at all of them and took a seat in a chair where I could see their faces.

Georgia had a coffee carafe, little chocolate confections, cream, sugar, plates, cups, and spoons laid out on the coffee table. "Help yourselves."

"Oh, these look delicious," I said as I took two chocolate treats. Two is the perfect number. Take one and everyone knows you're only taking it because you feel obliged, take three and you're a pig. My momma taught me to have good company manners and sometimes I actually use them.

"I hope you like them," Georgia said.

It was quiet as we all doctored our coffee and the Kincaid offspring helped themselves to the snacks. I studied them as they did.

A little dog came trotting into the living room, a Pug. He sat down next to Georgia and looked at her with anticipation.

"No Pugsley, you do not get people food and you know it," she said, glancing down at the dog.

Pugsley – man, how funny – looked sad but undaunted. He turned his little head toward me, trying his best to look fetching. I ignored him. He circled the room and tried to get goodies from the Kincaid offspring, with no luck. Finally Pugsley crawled under the coffee table, laid down, and sighed heavily.

I cleared my throat and set down my coffee. "So where is Coco Chanel?"

"Oh, she's crated in our room; she and Pugsley simply do not get along. When we spend several days down here, I bring her and try to convince them to get along." Sarah was so earnest.

Sandra took a bite of her chocolate delight and said, "When we're down here for several days, I try and convince Coco Chanel to jump in the lake."

I had to smile just a little at her before I started. "Let's get straight to it. The Atlanta PD seems to believe we have a case, so they brought Jonnie in for questioning. Since then she's disappeared. Her daughter, Anna, says she has no idea where her mother might be and that's most likely true according the cops. I agree and think Anna's in the dark about this entire business.

In my opinion, Jonnie Kincaid is unbalanced; I'd advise all of you to be careful until she's found."

Five sets of nearly identical grey eyes focused on me. It was a little bit disconcerting.

"You really think she's a threat to us? I mean, she's hell on wheels when she's murdering a helpless, almost dead man, but I find myself being strangely unafraid," Sandra snapped.

She glared at me as if she dared me to argue with her. I had to burst her bubble.

"You're probably right, Sandra, but she's in big trouble and there's a lot of money at stake. I get the feeling she's rather attached to the money. Since we've started the investigation into your father's death and the police have questioned her, she's desperate. I've had a couple of run-ins with her and I believed her when she threatened to kill me. Crazy people do crazy things 'cause they're crazy and there's no way to anticipate which way they're gonna jump. Don't underestimate her." I matched her stare.

"Hell of a PI you are if you're afraid of her, she weighs a buck-o-five with rocks in her pockets." Jillian shook her head in disgust.

"Girls! Tess has worked hard to get to the truth and she did it for you, for all of us. The least you can do is be grateful and polite," Georgia admonished her daughters.

"Tess is a professional; she did it for the paycheck," Jillian snapped back.

Before anyone could answer, Sarah spoke up, "I think we're all just a little tense. I know I for one will be glad when this mess is behind us, and I'm sorry you had so much trouble because of us, Tess."

"The mess may eventually be behind us someday, maybe even someday soon, but the ramifications will never go away. It's the gift that keeps on giving. Whether we get money or the bitch gets caught or not, we are forever scarred by this horseshit!" Jillian practically spat at me.

"Jilly, calm down, it isn't Tess's fault. She's our friend! Because of her we stand a chance of getting justice for Daddy." Sarah was practically in tears.

"Fuck Daddy," Sandra snapped.

I decided to remain calm and professional.

"Look, we got the Atlanta DA to open an investigation, and now warrants have been issued. This was based on the testimony of a nurse at the facility who is convinced your father wanted to change his will. The doctor on call really expected him to last a few more days and was surprised he died as suddenly as he did. Add this to the fact the doctor had suggested a new stem cell treatment which might have prolonged your father's life and Jonnie fought against. It's all circumstantial and unless we can get a confession out of Jonnie, the murder charges'll be dropped for lack of evidence, probably. Even if we get to court, the testimony of the nurse and the doctor might make a jury sympatric, but won't be enough to get a conviction. But we have some traction."

"So this is all circumstantial, and we might not even get her into court. What's the best we can hope for?" Miles asked.

"Fortunately, there's more: 10cc of Potassium went missing from the rehab the night your father died," I offered.

Everyone looked at me with question marks in their eyes, except for Miles. He took over with the explanation.

"Potassium overdose can mimic a heart attack. No one would be surprised to find large amounts in the blood, since potassium levels rise after death."

"I have the records from the rehab and it shows the drug went missin' the night of your father's death. There's even more: according to phone records, one of the nurses was in contact with Jonnie on a regular basis. I believe she was feeding Jonnie info about the comings and goings at the rehab. This nurse is scared out of her wits of Jonnie, by the way, and rightfully so. According to the Atlanta detective, this nurse will most likely testify against Jonnie. So we have conspiracy to commit murder, we add it to the mix, and we got a stew going." I looked around to see if everyone got it.

No one said anything for a moment and then Georgia broke the rather uncomfortable silence. "Tess, you have more to tell us, don't you?"

I nodded. "Jillian, I know you've been in contact with your step-mother."

The other siblings gasped in shock and maybe outrage. I didn't give anyone the chance to speak.

"Jillian, I understand why you thought you had to do it, but a terrible thing has occurred because of your communication. You told Jonnie I was investigating your father's death in the hope she'd threaten me and scare me off. By the way, she tried – she sent me a dead rat, burned my office building down, and hired an assassin. So when I advise caution in dealing with her, I have good reason."

There were more gasps in the room and even Pugsley crawled out from under the coffee table and seemed to pay attention.

"She murdered another resident who saw her the night of your father's death. She knew I had talked with him because you told her," I said quietly.

Jillian's eyes grew wider and wider until I thought they would pop out of her head.

"No, it can't be true! You're wrong!" she cried.

Jillian turned to her mother first, then she looked all around the room at her siblings, who were staring at her in disbelief.

"I told her about the investigation because she's powerful and connected; I thought she'd make you stop. I didn't want anyone to find out Father had been murdered, the stigma is just too horrible to bear." There was a pleading tone in her voice.

"You talked to that whore? After she blocked us from seeing Dad before he died? How the hell could you?" Sandra snarled.

"Try and understand, Sandy, I did it to protect us," Jillian said.

"Oh my God, Jilly, you did it to protect you and your fucking lifestyle. What would people think if they knew your father was involved in something as sordid as murder? Who gives a damn! Honest to God, what the hell is wrong with you?" Sandra said.

Sarah just looked at her sister with pity. "Oh, Jilly."

"Jillian, I need for you to make a statement saying you gave Jonnie the information about the investigation. It will add more weight to the case," I said. "It's slim but we need everything we can get. Please."

Jillian was sobbing. "I didn't mean for anyone to get hurt, I just wanted you to go away."

"Jillian, will you do it?" Georgia asked gently.

Jillian cried harder and we all waited on her to regain her composure. Finally, she nodded her head. I breathed a sigh of relief. All her siblings were still staring at her like she was a traitor and I reckoned in their eyes she was. No one spoke for several moments. We just sat and listened to Jillian sniffle and hick-up.

Finally, Georgia said, "Tess, I have some pictures to show you of my family in happier times. They're in the bonus room downstairs, will you join me?"

"I'd be glad to." I stood up and drained my coffee. "The cookies were wonderful, thank you." It seemed so lame but if Georgia wanted to lighten the mood I was willing to help her.

"I'm so glad you liked them, I buy them from a local bakery called the Confection Shoppe. Come on, it's this way. Y'all want to join us?" She looked at her offspring.

"Mom, this needs to be discussed," Miles said.

"Come on, please," Georgia urged. I figured her trip down memory lane was an attempt to get everyone in a better mood. I hope it worked. You could cut the tension in the room with a cleaver.

Reluctantly they all put down plates and cups and stood up. They were an unhappy bunch, I can tell you. I felt sure they wanted to have it out with Jillian without their mother's presence, but Georgia intended to diffuse the situation with memories of happier times.

"It's this way," Georgia said. She led us across the living room where she opened a door, revealing steps. When I got to the bottom of the stairs, I saw we were actually in a basement. It had been completely refinished and made into a cozy room complete with a fireplace. It certainly didn't look like our basement at home, which has concrete floors, concrete block walls, and exposed ductwork.

Georgia went over to a bookcase and removed a couple of photo albums. "I keep saying I want to scrapbook all these, maybe I will now."

Her children laughed, all of them except Jillian who looked decidedly unhappy and uncomfortable.

"I mean it!" Georgia declared.

"We know you do, but you can't be still long enough for such a project," Sarah said with a smile.

"It would detract from your golf game," Sandra said.

"We could make it a family project," Georgia suggested.

All her children groaned. I had to laugh; it sounded like my family, where someone is always proposing a project much to everyone else's dismay.

"Let's sit here and take a look at our young selves," Georgia said and indicated a sofa.

She patted the place next to her and I sat down. Sarah sat next me and Jillian sat on the other side of her mother. Miles and Sandra leaned over the back of the couch. Georgia opened the album and held it on her lap so everyone could see. The first pictures were of a young Georgia and a handsome young man whom I presumed to be Jon. There were more pictures of the couple with a single child, then the twins. There was a happy family portrait with all six of them smiling for the camera. Given all the events which had happened, it made me sad.

"Ugh," said Miles, "Look at those braces, I looked like I was getting signals from outer space! I think I went by 'Metal Mouth' for about two years."

Georgia laughed, "You were about fifteen then and everyone knows the brains of all fifteen-year-olds are controlled from outer space."

Everyone laughed, because everyone had been fifteen and knew it was a true statement. I noticed Jillian's mood had not lightened, small wonder.

Georgia turned the pages and we looked at birthdays, anniversaries, graduations and a wedding. Georgia retrieved another album and opened it. The pictures changed; Jon was no longer in them.

Georgia turned a page and I caught a glimpse of her and the four children just as the lights went out. We were underground and it was so pitch dark for a moment I felt the air was gone too. Then I got a grip.

"What the hell?" I muttered.

Everyone began to ask the same question, but quietly, as if they were all afraid to make noise. I felt in my gut Jonnie was behind the blackout and we were in some sort of deep shit, so I unholstered my gun.

"Everyone just sit quiet for a minute and let me see if I can find out what's happening," I said.

I struggled to get my keyring out of my pocket and fumbled with the flashlight for a moment as I headed up the steps. Just as I got to the top step, the door slammed in my face. Cold beads of sweat broke out all over my body. What the hell is it with me and basements? I swore to god if I got out of there I would never as long as I lived set foot in a basement again. I heard someone coming up the steps behind me.

"What is it?" Miles asked.

"Don't know," I admitted. I put my shoulder to the door and gave a push; it didn't budge. "Hey Miles, we're in some trouble here and I need a little help to get this door open. Maybe the two of us can force it."

I heard Miles come up the stairs and then he stood next to me on the top step. There was barely enough room for the two of us to stand together. I holstered my gun and turned sideways so we could fit. Miles moved closer to me so we were face to face and practically touching.

"On three, hit it with your shoulder," I said.

"Okay." He sounded nervous, which was only fair because I sure as hell was too.

"One, two … three." We hit the door hard and pushed for all we were worth. Nothing.

"What the hell?" he asked.

"What's going on?" Georgia called from the bottom of the stairs.

I could picture Georgia with the girls all gathered around her, scared expressions on their faces.

"I don't know. Don't make a sound, and let me listen for a second," I said.

I put my ear to the door and I heard someone moving around and a strange sound, like liquid sloshing or being poured. Pugsley growled and then yipped as if he'd been hit.

"Holy shit," I whispered because I could smell it then: gasoline. The instant I recognized the odor I heard a soft whooping sound and I smelled smoke.

I grabbed Miles by the sleeve.

"She's set the house on fire," I told him. "There has to be a way out, let's think. Panic will get us dead."

I groped for my cell phone; to my disappointment there was no signal in the god damned basement, of course. I handed the flashlight to Miles and kept the cell phone to light my way.

I looked him in the face and he looked scared as hell, but to his credit he was not panicking. "Is there another way out of here? Windows, crawlspace, sub-basement, anything?"

"No, it's a basement dug out of the hill with only one way in or out." Miles was starting to sweat.

"Come on," I said and pulled Miles back down the steps.

We had to hurry; the faint whiff of smoke was evident even down at the bottom of the stairs.

"The house is on fire, the door is locked, and we have to break it down," I said calmly, or at least at least I thought I sounded calm.

Everyone began shouting at once. The smell of smoke was getting stronger and I could envision the floors above us merrily burning.

"Everyone be quiet a moment and let's think!" Georgia commanded. "We need something to break down the door."

There was tension in her voice but also a determination not to give way to fear. I thanked God for her.

"Tell me there's a bathroom with a shower down here," I begged.

"Why, yes, there is." Georgia sounded puzzled.

"Great! Okay, everyone who can fit in the shower, climb in right now. If we can breach the door and there is an inferno up there, which I'm pretty positive there is, wet clothes and wet hair will help us not burn immediately. So in we go, get real good and soaked."

The three girls groped toward the shower as Miles lit the way for them. After a moment, I heard the sound of the water running. I also heard a scuffling sound behind me and I turned my light toward the noise. Georgia was pulling books off the bookshelf.

"What the hell are you doin', Georgia?" I demanded.

Georgia never even looked up. "Putting these albums in a roll-along, I will not leave them behind."

Great! I rolled my eyes. Instead of admonishing her, I ran back up the steps, gabbed the railings and kicked the door with both feet. It didn't give an inch. *What the hell has she wedged it with?* I wondered.

"It's Jonnie, isn't it?" Miles said from behind me and I jumped about three feet straight up.

"Wow! Don't sneak up on me again or I might die of a heart attack before I can burn to death."

"What are we gonna do?" Miles asked.

"Well yeah, I was just standing here asking myself the very same question. We have to bust this door down and make a run for it, and we better hurry. What do we have down here we can use?"

Miles was silent for a few moments. "No tools, all's in the garage." He chuckled. "We just have my great-great-great granddaddy's civil war sword."

If I remembered correctly, those where big and heavy and with any luck there might still be an edge on the thing.

"Miles, we need to bust the door up or chop it down, so go get the sword!" I demanded.

He took off. I was sweating from the heat beyond the door and from fear. My stomach was starting to knot up and my knees were feeling shaky. Before I could catalogue the rest of my symptoms, Miles came back.

"Okay Miles, you're stronger than me, so I want you to give the door an experimental whack right in the middle of the panel where the wood is thinnest."

I pointed my cell phone light at the spot where I wanted him to strike. He handed me the flashlight and raised the sword over his head.

"Let me get out of your way." I stepped down behind him.

Miles hit the door for all he was worth and chips of wood flew back and hit me in the face.

"Stop!" I commanded and stepped up next to him to look at the damage.

"Wow!" Miles exclaimed. "I took a good chuck out of the door!"

"We have to time this just right. We gotta be ready to run when we bust through, so let's go get wet." I explained. I handed Miles the flashlight.

"Georgia, whatever you're doing needs to be finished now, we gotta go. Come to the shower with me!" I urged.

I hurried back down the steps and snagged Georgia by the arm. The girls were emerging as I entered the tiny bathroom.

"Go stand at the foot of the stairs!" I commanded.

I handed my cell phone to one of the twins and Georgia and I dashed into the bathroom. Under the shower we went and stood in the spray while it soaked us to the bone. I had to work very hard not to puke, I was so scared.

Seconds later, we were done.

"Miles!" I yelled.

He appeared, gave me the flashlight and, while he jumped into the shower, I threw all the towels I could locate in with him.

"Bring those when you come out," I told him.

Miles was fast and within 60 seconds were ready to make a break for freedom.

"Everyone, stay down here until I call you and then move like you mean it. We've gotta be fast and try to keep physical contact with each other so no one gets left behind. We need to keep low to the ground where there's less smoke so we're not overcome. Everyone clear?"

I heard murmurs of assent from the women. Miles distributed the wet towels amongst everyone, and then he and I went back up the steps. I held the flashlight so he could see how to wield the sword. He hit the door. *WHACK! WHACK! WHACK!* The smell of smoke grew stronger every time he struck the door. Then the sound he had been making with the sword changed; he'd broken through the wood! The smoke poured through the hole like a cloud.

"Cover your heads and mouths with the towels." I shouted down the stairs and almost choked myself.

I pulled my wet shirt over my mouth and wrapped a towel around Miles as he continued to chop away with the Civil War heirloom like a man possessed. His great great great granddaddy was cheering us on as the hole kept getting bigger – I'm being literal, I saw him through the smoke.

Then I saw Chick standing on the other side of the door.

"Girl, you gotta hurry!" he said.

"We are!" I snapped.

The smoke was getting denser and denser. "Miles! Stop!" I reached out and grabbed a piece of the jagged wood and pulled a great piece out of the door, making the hole bigger. I turned and shone the light on the women.

"Come on!" I demanded.

My words came out muffled, so I motioned them with the flashlight. Miles was pulling more pieces of wood from the door and the hole was big enough to escape through by the time the Kincaid women joined us as the top of the steps. My eyes were streaming tears from the smoke and I thought I was going to pass out any second. My determination to live was the only thing which kept me from screaming and running in panic. I clenched my left hand into a fist and dug my nails into my palm to help myself calm down. I stuck my flashlight into my mouth so I could use both hands when Miles and I lifted Jillian through the hole.

Once she was through, I jerked the flashlight from my mouth.

"Start crawlin' to the door, we're right behind you!" I shouted and was rewarded by a coughing fit.

"The whole place is on fire!" Jillian screamed from the other side of the door. "There's something wedged under the door. I can't budge it!"

"Keep movin'!" I demanded.

Next Miles and I got Sandra through the hole.

"Pugsley! I found Pugsley!" Sandra cried.

I had forgotten the damn dog. Crap! We shoved Sarah through the hole and then it was Georgia's turn. She was still clutching the handle of a fucking suitcase.

"Please!" she begged.

Miles and I handed the damn thing through.

"Look out for the suitcase!" I yelled and someone took it from my hands. I had discovered drawing breath through my wet shirt before I yelled worked moderately well.

Miles and I lifted Georgia through the hole and I could hear all of them coughing on the other side.

"Go, go, go!" I shouted.

"You next," I said to Miles.

He looked terrified, face illuminated by the light of the flames. Still, he shook his head.

"It'll be easier for me to lift you up and then you can help me get out. You trying to lift me will be too difficult," he said.

He was right and I couldn't argue with his logic. Miles pitched the sword through the hole, hilt first. I gave him the flashlight, which he put in his mouth then he made a cup of his hands to boost me up. I went through the hole like a shot, and willing hands caught me as I fell.

I could hear the roar of the flames; it was like nothing I'd ever heard in my life and I hoped I lived long enough to recount it to someone. I took a second to look around me and believed I had died and gone to hell! The walls, the floors, and even the ceiling were all on fire, the furniture was burning. Everywhere I looked everything was a wall of living fire. I almost fainted from the sight of the house engulfed in flame.

"I am not dying like this," I mumbled.

I reached back for Miles as he wiggled through the hole. When I turned to move away from the door, all the Kincaid women were on the floor. They had waited for us.

Jillian handed Miles the sword and Sandra handed me the cell phone. She was clutching Pugsley to her chest.

"We couldn't leave you," she said.

"Let's go," I shouted. "Wait! Where's Sarah?"

"Oh Jesus! She's gone after Coco Channel!" Jillian sounded hysterical.

Miles and I locked eyes for a second.

"Get 'em out of here, Miles. I'll get Sarah. Don't stop for anything. You gotta break through the door and then the oxygen will make the fire burn higher. Don't stop."

For a second I thought he was going to argue.

"I got this," Miles said, and started crawling toward the door with the sword extended out in front of him like he was charging the entire Yankee army. Then they were all moving on their hands and knees toward the door. A rafter or something fell down behind me and I jumped a foot. I turned my back on the four people dragging a dog, a suitcase and Civil War sword in the direction of escape. I tucked my cell phone into my bra and made my way to the stairs. I found my goal in seconds and crawled toward the second floor. Sarah was crouched on the landing with the dog carrier.

"I couldn't, I couldn't leave her to burn. I'm sorry," she sobbed.

"It's okay, Sarah, you gotta pull it together or we're all gonna burn." I grabbed her hand and turned to retrace my steps. In the few seconds I'd been on the landing, the stairs were on fire.

"Jesus," I muttered under my breath.

Sarah's eyes were huge and filled terror.

"I can't." She jerked her hand from mine and shirked back.

"Sarah, you have to do this," I said urgently. "If you don't, Coco will die."

Sarah sobbed and held the carrier closer to her, her breath was ragged and rapid. I still had the towel over my head and quickly yanked it off and threw it over the carrier.

"Come on Sarah, we have to save Coco, she's depending you!" I was pleading.

Sarah drew a shaky breath and nodded her head. I adjusted the towel around her head and pulled my t-shirt over my nose.

"Let's go, we need to run." I said. I gently took the carrier from Sarah.

We clasped hands and ran down the steps like our asses were on fire. The flames were all around us and my skin felt hot. It was like running through a tunnel of fire. When we reached the bottom step I tripped and we went down in a tangle of arms and legs and dog. It took precious seconds to sort ourselves out as the roar of the fire grew louder. By some miracle were got to our knees and began to move again, I pushed Sarah in front of me. We were moving fast and didn't stop or falter as the house began to fall down around us. I promise you can crawl pretty damn fast when you're scared to death of death.

Flames were in front of us and all around. I began to think weren't gonna make it.

"Hurry, hurry," I whispered, not wasn't sure if I was asking God or Sarah.

She stopped moving. "I'm not sure which way to go. I can't see!"

Chick was standing in front of us and motioning us to hurry, waving his hands like a third base couch. Behind him I saw what I thought was the front door; it was on fire and it looked like the doorway to hell.

I pointed to the door.

"We gotta run through it! We can't stop!" I yelled.

"Come on, come on, come on!" Chick was shouting.

"Move!" I screamed.

We leveled ourselves to our feet and ran for all we were worth. I was right behind Sarah and suddenly she disappeared. I realized she had made it through the door and I sprinted.

I burst through the wall of flame, rolled across the front porch and tumbled down the stairs. I lost the dog carrier in my landing, but could hear Coco Chanel whining nearby. I lay there panting for a few seconds, trying to get my bearings; I might even have passed out for a nanosecond. It was so insane I really can't be sure. A quick inventory assured me I wasn't burned or broken. Surprisingly, I seemed to actually be okay. Everyone else was lying in the grass too, thank God, even Pugsley, who appeared to be alive as well.

"We need to move further from the house," I croaked. My throat felt as if I had swallowed razor blades.

I scrabbled for the dog carrier and found it. We crawled on our bellies because we had no strength for anything else and as we crawled we were hacking and coughing and crying and laughing, happy to be alive. Holy God, air never tasted so damn sweet! I fell on my face and just lay there breathing. I believed I would live to see my mother again.

After an eternity, I rolled over.

"Cell phone," I croaked and fished it out of my bra. The phone was wet and I wondered if it would work as I punched 911 into the keypad. It rang and I decided I was in love with cell phones almost as much as I was in love with air. On the third ring, a woman answered.

"What is the nature of your emergency?"

I almost cried. "The house at 14 Jonathan Point Road is engulfed in flames, it's a case of arson and an accelerant has been used. There are six humans and two dogs who have escaped. We all appear to be unharmed but an ambulance would be a good idea."

"I am dispatching immediately," she assured me, "I'll stay on the line with you until they arrive. Can you tell me your name?"

"I am Tess Maher and I'm alive." I was laughing and crying and breathing.

"They're on the way," the nice lady at the emergency services said in a calm voice. "Can you move further away from the house?"

"I'm alive!" I repeated.

"Yes ma'am, just remain calm, you're doing good and help will be there soon. Can you move further from the house?" she repeated.

"We have. Thank you, bless you."

Everyone was lying on the grass around me and we were all breathing as if we had run a four-minute mile. It may not have been a mile but by God it felt like the longest distance I'd ever run in my life. I just lay there and breathed in sweet blessed oxygen.

"Thank you, God, thank you," I kept saying over and over while tears ran down my face. "Thank you, Chick."

"Sorry I wasn't here sooner." He sounded apologetic as he sat down beside me. Pugsley walked over and began to examine Chick. If I'd had the strength, I would have laughed.

"S'okay," I muttered. "We're out and safe, thank you."

The 911 operator kept asking me if we were okay, if anyone was injured, and reassuring me I was doing well and the EMTs would be there shortly, not to try and go back into the house and probably more I can't remember. I tried to coherently answer her. Her voice was a lifeline to sanity and I clung to it.

I wondered vaguely how long it might take for the emergency folks to arrive when a horrible thought hit me: Derek might be on the truck. I would die if he saw me in my bedraggled state. Reality set in and I started laughing at my own fuzzy brain; we were in a different state. I choked and coughed for what seemed like hours. Finally, I climbed up to my knees and heard Georgia behind me talking.

"We have to stop her, she's going to get away, she's running, goddamn it we have to stop her!" She was talking to her kids.

"Mom, we need to move the cars away from the house." Miles was thinking again.

"You got my keys," I reminded him.

Miles staggered away from our pathetic group. Jillian was holding Pugsley, Sarah was holding Coco, and Sandra was holding Sarah. Georgia was talking again but the sounds of the flames behind me were getting louder and louder and suddenly I couldn't hear Georgia anymore.

A black veil descended over my eyes, but it wasn't from unconsciousness. I felt as if I was lifted up and transported. Was I dying? Everything around me disappeared and I found myself riding in the backseat of a car with Jonnie Kincaid, who was driving like a fiend and laughing like a maniac.

"I whipped all your asses! I win! I win! I get all the fucking marbles!" She yelled as she beat on the steering wheel. She started to sing. "Leaving on a jet plane, don't know when I'll be back again."

She laughed louder as if it was all a hilarious joke. It was creepy as hell. She was so happy because she thought we were all dead and she'd won and she got all the money and she'd beaten us and the charges against her too. I got pissed off.

The view out the windows showed nothing but darkness. Even with her headlights on, the road was still dark. It was twisty and Jonnie was driving too damned fast. I wondered for a moment if I was dead and in hell. I started to tell her to slow down, but realized she couldn't hear me. In that instant, I knew I was experiencing a vision of Jonnie. I was seeing something from the living world. I don't know how I knew, but I did. I just watched and tried not to be terrified, which didn't work at all as panic was rising up in me.

By the glow of the instrument panel, Jonnie's face looked so eerie and strange. The lights emphasized the planes and angles of her face, making her look like something out of hell. She really was nuts, I decided. Most insane people don't look insane, but man oh man she was wearing crazy like a suit.

Right in front of me, a man materialized next to Jonnie. It was Jon! He stared at her for a full minute as she drove and laughed, oblivious to him. Jonnie turned the wheel to take a particularly sharp curve.

Jon called her name, "Jonnie!"

She whipped her head around to the passenger seat and saw him too. I knew by the way her eyes widened with fear and she couldn't look away.

"No! No! No! You're dead! I made sure of it!" she screamed in terror.

"Boo," he said quietly.

Jonnie missed the curve. Her tires rolled over the shoulder; she fought with the wheel like a wildcat, but it wasn't enough. She couldn't right it, couldn't regain control, and the car plunged over the embankment with the headlights illuminating her way down. The car began to flip slowly as it tumbled down the hill, rolling over and over. There was no human sound, no cries for help, only the sound of metal being tortured by rocks and trees as the car made its descent.

I had a moment of disorientation when I realized I was no longer in the backseat and was startled to be standing in the middle of the road looking down the embankment. To my right, Jon was staring down at the car.

Chick was on my left. "I got ya, girl."

Jon continued to stare as the car finally came to a stop, upside down against a huge tree. The noise ceased, smoke and steam pouring from the crushed vehicle. The last spinning tire stopped and was still. Jon turned to look me in the eye and everything went black.

I came back to myself flat on my face in the front yard of Georgia's house with everyone asking me questions at once. The fire was still roaring like a ravenous monster.

"Are you okay?"

"What happened?"

"Did you faint?"

"Can you breathe?"

"Are you hurt?"

There were more questions than I could answer; my head was spinning like a dervish. I rolled over ever so slowly, sat up, and wrapped my arms around my knees then I put my head down for several seconds and just breathed. What a weird experience on top of almost burning to death.

"I'm okay," I mumbled to my knees.

I raised my head up because I wanted to make sure Georgia understood what I said next. "But I don't think we have to worry about going after Jonnie, she won't be getting on a plane tonight or ever."

Georgia moved into my line of vision, she was still on her knees and she stared hard into my face.

"What happened? What did you see?" she demanded.

I had never had a vision before; I felt like I'd been rode hard and put away wet. I paused to get my thoughts in order before I tried to explain it.

"Georgia, I saw Jonnie driving in a car with me in the backseat. Suddenly Jon was next to her and he … well, he frightened her and she lost control of the car. She went down an embankment. He looked at me afterwards and I realized he did it to save you because he knew she would never stop trying to kill you and his children. He did it because he loved you all. I know it's true, I saw it in his face and somehow he conveyed the thought to me." I drew a deep breath, which hurt like hell.

"Do you know where?" Miles asked. I vaguely wondered where he had moved my car.

I shook my head and was immediately sorry. "I'm not sure; it was kinda hard to know in the dark. Jonnie missed a big sweeping curve and went down an embankment." The irony was not lost on me.

I guessed the police would find her, but how the hell did I explain how I knew? Maybe I should just shut the hell up and let someone stumble over the body.

It was as if Georgia read my mind. "I think we should tell the police she left and we believe she was heading to Nashville to catch a plane. Someone else will notice the skid marks and find her body." She pinned me with a look to make sure I understood.

I nodded my agreement and the others all did as well. We would keep our mouths shut so no one would think me crazy.

I started laughing again and heard sirens in the distance; help was on the way.

The last thing I saw before I lost consciousness was Chick.

41

She Works Hard for the Money

I awoke and floated toward consciousness only to find my mother leaning over me yelling, "YOU HAVE TO FIND ANOTHER LINE OF WORK! YOU WERE ONLY ALMOST BURNED ALIVE BY A CRAZY WOMAN! YOU ARE GOING TO BE THE DEATH OF ME YET!"

I smiled and gratefully fell back into blissful unconsciousness.

The End

Author Tish Owen

Tish Owen, is a woman of abundance. She was born and raised in Nashville, TN where she resides with her husband Patrick, a Teddy Roosevelt rat terrier, two insane cats who actually run the show, and an African Gray parrot who is much smarter than most humans.

Tish is a mother, grandmother, wife, author, brewer, sailor, animal lover, business owner, coordinator of Pagan Unity Festival, Goddess and the Moon Retreats and Spirit Fest Metaphysical Market Place. She owned Goddess and the Moon from 1991 through 2016. She is current in office space, where she reads Tarot, makes candles and other magical items based on her book, *Spell It Correctly.* She runs Goddesses and the Moon Press, is an editor for Goddess and the Moon Metaphysical Journal, and is one of the hosts for Maiden, Mother

& Crone podcast. Tish has appeared on A&E's Cursed, been a guest on many radio programs including Art Bell's Midnight in the Desert, and has been the subject of numerous magazine and newspaper articles.

Her first book, *Chasing the Rainbow* is a how to on the nuts and bolts of facilitating festivals of all kinds. Her second book, *Spell it Correctly* is an in depth handbook on spells and magic. Her third book, *A Death on Sunday* is a murder mystery with a paranormal twist, of course. *A Death In The Family* is the second in the series.

Writing in her unique "Southern Folk" style, Tish blends together her arsenal of knowledge of psychic phenomena, the occult and her love of Southern culture.

Website: tishowen.com
Facebook: Tish-Owen-Writes and A Death on Sunday
Publisher: Goddess and the Moon Press
Contact: heytish@gmail.com and goddessandmoon@gmail.com

www.ingramcontent.com/pod-product-compliance
Lightning Source LLC
Chambersburg PA
CBHW070756120726
47910CB00001B/185